Little Pig, Little Pig

Neale Cooper

To Christie-
Best Wishes
Neale Cooper.

Little Pig, Little Pig

Neale Cooper

To my Wife Sharon, and my Girls Emma and Evie
Whose love and support has been with me
throughout.

Acknowledgements
To Andrew Fuller – abf design, a lifelong friend and
superb Designer whose patience, ideas and
enthusiasm helped shape the cover design for this
book

To Ernie Almond of BBC Three Counties Radio who
provided me the opportunity to discuss my work to a
million people across the airwaves.

Prologue

Mary Foster craves a life away from the rat race that is modern day society. Together with her husband Daniel they give up their life in the city and move their family to rural North Yorkshire. However, their peaceful idyll is not all it seems as a series of mysterious events surrounding their daughter soon turns their world upside down.

For Mary it's a reminder from her past!
With cruel irony, the paranormal experiences she had as a child are now returning to confront her. The past she thought she had buried had now returned to haunt her! Only this time the stakes are high, this time the lives of her family are put at risk!

Before long Mary is in a race against time to save the people she loves.
It's a battle that will take her to the very edge, a battle she cannot fight alone, a battle she knows she cannot afford to lose! Together, with the help of an enigmatic Parapsychologist they embark upon a crusade to rid Mary's daughter of the deadly demon – the Lycan that now possesses her.
A nightmarish scenario unwittingly created through the innocence of a simple child's fairy tale.

Chapter 1

Looking down from her bedroom window across the grey, rugged canvas of the Yorkshire moors, Mary Foster breathed a long, slow sigh of satisfaction. It had just passed early dawn, a time of day Mary liked to share with no one.

She was satisfied, because she and her family had come so far from life in London, where the daily ingredients of being a working parent had served up its fair share of stress.

Staring out across her front garden, enclosed within a stone wall, Mary admired the giant, mature horse chestnut tree standing regally beyond the garden's entrance. As autumn set in, the leaves had become tinged with a golden hue. She turned to look over her shoulder at her husband, Daniel, still asleep on his side, in the bed. She recalled long days, now distant, long hard days where her husband, a dedicated IT Consultant in the city would more often seem like a stranger, hardly ever at home. When he was there, he was often distracted and hardly seemed to notice her and the children.

Mary recalled how she would battle through the morning madness with other commuters, attempting to get her own children to school and nursery before going on to her part-time temping job in the city. Now, though, that was all behind them. This was their home, their rural patch of North Yorkshire, bought and paid for out of the success of Daniel's career in the city, but also out of the capital made from their London home, the Victorian suburban terraced house. Courtesy, she thought, of an inflated property market.

The day had started grey. Mary stared down toward the village nestled at the bottom of the valley. It seemed distant, shrouded in the early morning mist, each building appearing as a pale gradation of its natural dark-grey, stone brickwork. Her eyes drifted off to the peaks beyond. For Mary, it felt like the first day of the rest of her life, a life she wanted to rebuild, start afresh—a joyous, peaceful time, shared with those she loved—but not at that moment. It had just passed early dawn, a time of day Mary shared with no one.

* * *

Breakfast each morning in the Foster household tended to be a disorganised affair; at least that's how it would seem to Mary, unless she made an early start. Daniel would sleep in and rely on his wife to stir him from his slumber. Eleanor would wake early and cross the wide wood-panel floored hall from her bedroom to Mary and Daniel's room. Dishevelled, ruddy cheeked, her blonde curly hair tossed over her head, she would drag Toby, her favourite bear, with her.

That morning was no exception. The new Foster home sat imposingly on the hill above the small village of Ravenside below. With a south-facing frontage, the double-fronted house stood alone in isolation. With large windows on either side of the centrally-placed front door and three large impressive windows above it, the early morning sun would break through the upstairs east bedrooms with fanfare. Mary and Daniel occupied these rooms, which were situated at the front, while the rooms at the back of the house belonged to Eleanor and David. The house was said to be over two hundred years old and steeped in history, a fact that appealed to Mary when the family were looking to resettle in the north. From the front door ran a long, meandering slate path, the colour of the slate, a dark grey, the same colour as the imposing tiled roof. The path ran down to the stone wall and the small front gate. A name plaque hung from the front of the gate: "The Hungry Harshes." The house was so named after a feature of the local North Yorkshire landscape, created some two hundred years earlier, when extensive mining of the landscape for lead ore was a significant industry in the area. Open cast working on the hillsides by mining teams, searching for lead veins, would often result in deep scarring or clefts known as the hungry harshes.

It was also said that the house had been owned by previous landowners who themselves had a significant stake in the lead-ore mining industry of the area. The valley had once bristled with families eking out a living, the men from mining in the hills at the top of the valley, the women from small-scale, arable farming of the land, set deep within the valley basin. The house itself had borne that very imposing look of authority, sitting high on the valley hill, looking down on the village below.

* * *

"David, time to get up!" Mary cried at the foot of the stairs. It was seven a.m. on a Tuesday morning. David was their oldest child, eleven now, and recently enrolled at nearby Avonswick comprehensive school.

"Coming!" was the reply, not from David's room, but Eleanor's. She had jumped out of bed upon hearing the call; her footsteps resounded through the ceiling, as she ran to her bedroom door.

"Mum, I've got a wet nappy!" Eleanor cried, as she opened her bedroom door. Eleanor had just turned five and was about to start full-time school, but she was not able to stay dry through the night. Mary, in nightie, dressing gown, and slippers trudged up the stairs "Oh, Ellie, you know how to take it off!"

"But, Mum, I can't," Eleanor said.

Mary got to the top of the landing and, with a sigh, walked the few steps to Eleanor's room. She stopped at David's bedroom door and, giving it two sharp taps, she opened it and leaned in. "David, come on, time to get up!" The bedclothes stirred, as she closed the door behind her.

After ensuring the little girl was dry, the two started to make their way down for breakfast. "Dan, you'll be late!" Mary said, stopping and calling to her husband.

"Ok! Ok! I'm moving. I'm moving!" he said from their room.

Downstairs in the kitchen, Mary had made coffee; she could never start the day without a cup of coffee. Various breakfast cereals were laid out on the pine kitchen table, standing centrally in the room, bowls and spoons all at the ready. David walked in, sat down, and poured some Corn Flakes, while Mary helped Eleanor to a bowl of Rice Krispies; pouring the milk was Eleanor's favourite part. "David, your football kit is washed and by the backdoor; be sure to keep your boots in the bag I've provided," Mary said. The immersion heater started to run; Daniel was in the shower. "Mum, can I have Billy and Luke home tonight?" David asked, looking up at Mary and breaking off from drinking a cup of milk.

"Sure, but muddy boots and kit at the door! I do not want mud trodden through the house!"

"Sure, Mum." David replied before continuing to finish his milk. After tilting his head back to finish the final gulp, David put his cup on the table, got up, and hurried out of the kitchen to get his schoolbag. "The cup goes in the dishwasher!" Mary shouted after him. "Not on the table." While Mary cleared the used breakfast crockery away, Eleanor sat down to colour at the table.

Shortly afterwards, Daniel walked in, showered and scrubbed, dressed in a clean white shirt and grey trousers, the cuffs of his shirt fastened by a pair of gold cufflinks, a wedding anniversary gift from Mary. He approached Mary from behind, as she loaded the dishwasher and kissed her firmly on her cheek. "Morning, Ma." Ma was Daniel's affectionate name for Mary. He wandered round to the other side of the table, where Eleanor sat, not noticing her father; she was fully engrossed in colouring. "Morning, Ellie, and how is my Ellie this morning?"

"I'm ok, Dad," Ellie said, too busy to look up.

Daniel and Mary had been married now for twelve years, David, their eldest child born a year after they married. At thirty-four, Daniel had no particularly distinct features; he was slim at five-feet, eleven-inches, and wanting to keep fit, he had recently started running across some popular peaks around Ravensdale. His small angular head with high cheekbones, his rather pointed and well-structured roman nose, supporting a pair of wire-framed glasses, gave him the impression of being an intellectual.

While he might not have particularly looked distinct, his career to date had been relatively distinguished, or at least successful enough for them to make enough money to relocate, start afresh, and reset their energies on building a new life, run at a slower pace. He had started well, joining a large banking corporation from university. Providing systems support, he'd worked his way up to the appropriate board level. This wasn't without his stresses, as both he and Mary were looking for change. They decided to explore other options. Twelve years in banking terms was good; he'd made enough money and built enough confidence to pursue his dream of starting his own business. Daniel had kicked this off in earnest, while the family were still based in London. He'd gone into partnership with a colleague he'd known from another city banking institution; the two had met some years previously and, when life and work in the city had begun to discourage them, they often got together and talked of making a start on their own. That had become reality, and the two were once again travelling into London on business, offering clients consultancy and services in the information technology sector.

That morning, Daniel was off for a mid-morning meeting in Manchester with some potential new clients.

Daniel sat down at the table, just as Mary turned to hand him a fresh cup of coffee. "Thanks, Ma. Did you see if the papers had come this morning?"

"Yes, and no they haven't," Mary said, her voice lifting, as if implying impatience.

"Oh, is David gone?" Daniel asked, looking around suddenly.

"He's here somewhere," Mary said.

"Ma, I'm not going to be back until about six-thirty tonight. If we agree in principle on the details of the contract, today, then it may be nearer eight-thirty."

Mary's eyebrows rose in response.

"Well, there are some rather nice bars in the city centre; this deal would deserve a celebration," Daniel said sheepishly.

Mary was all too aware of how Daniel liked to "celebrate," from years of working in the city which was awash with wine bars, pubs, and restaurants.

"Just don't be back too late! I'm going to visit Ellie's new school, today…" she said, making a reference to Ravendale primary school nestled in the village below. "And I've got Karen coming from the interior designers. I want to look at fabrics for the sitting room. I'd like to talk to you about this…are you going to want dinner?"

"What are you going to do?" Daniel asked.

"Pork chops," Mary said.

Daniel cringed. Pork chops were not his favourite. "Er, well, no, I'll get something, Ma."

At that point, there came a loud rattling of the letterbox. Mary walked the route from the kitchen door at the back of the house, into the hall, and down past the main stairway to the large front door, and picked the morning newspapers up off the mat.

As she turned to walk back to the kitchen, she heard a sound and turned to hear the creaking of the hinges and the clattering of the gate at the bottom of the path. *Probably just the paperboy,* she thought.

* * *

The remaining time spent at breakfast that morning was a quiet affair. Dan read the papers while eating toast; Ellie continued to colour, not once lifting her head from the intensity of colouring in the book she was working on. The silence was punctuated only by David clattering the kitchen door open with his schoolbag and kit bag strewn across his shoulder.

Neale Cooper

"David, do be careful!" responded an irritated Dan looking up from his paper.

"Sorry, Dad, I'm ready when you are," David replied. That morning, father would drop his son off to school in the nearby town of Avonswick. This wasn't always the case; most mornings David would take the short walk into the village to wait with other children for the school bus to collect them and take them on to school, but the bus driver had a habit of being on time and had little tolerance of waiting too long for late stragglers.

Today David was going to be a late straggler; he felt it best to cadge a lift off his father, since he would be passing the direction of the school, anyway.

Dan folded his paper and got up from the table. Going to the kitchen drawer, he opened it and felt for his car keys; tossing them up in his hand he moved around to Eleanor, still engrossed in her colouring. Daniel bent over her and planted a kiss on her head.

"See you later, Ellie. Have a good day. Daddy loves you."

"Bye, Dad," Eleanor said, distractedly at the table. Her knees were now tucked up under her on the chair; she didn't once look up or break her rhythm in colouring; the felt pen in her hand just continued to etch back and forth.

Dan moved to the side door of the house. Adjacent to the kitchen was a small utility room, where all hats, coats, and shoes were kept. Dan slipped on his shoes and dutifully side-stepped back toward his wife. Sidling up to her, he kissed her on the cheek.

"Have a good day, Ma. Wish me luck!"

"Good luck, and don't come home too late, and don't drink too much—you're driving!"

"David, don't forget to hand your homework in."

"I won't, Mum," David said.

With that, Daniel and David set off, leaving the door ajar. Mary looked at the kitchen table; Daniel's empty mug and plate still sat on it. "The cup and plate go in the dishwasher, not on the table," she yelled uselessly after them through the open door.

Pushing the door shut, Mary turned and walked to the edge of the table, leaning across to pick up the empty cup and plate. She looked inquisitively down at Eleanor; the child was now colouring feverishly, turning one page after the other, the care and attention to detail that had been there at the beginning had now gone. Edges that had been dutifully coloured around were now carelessly etched over.

"Hey, Ellie! Why don't you go upstairs and have a wash, darling!" Mary instructed. There was no reply, not even a physical reaction from the little girl. She continued etching feverishly over the colouring book. This time, Mary responded in a stronger tone.

"Ellie! Come on, it's time to get ready. We need to go out this morning."

Again, the little girl did not look up, but she stopped colouring, turned the pen around in her hand and replaced the lid. Without looking at her mother, Eleanor set the colouring book down on the table and shut it. She then climbed down from the chair and shuffled out of the kitchen, down the hall, and started to ascend the stairs to the bathroom.

Just for a moment, something had made the hairs on the back of Mary's neck stand up. The kitchen now fell silent. Mary was left standing alone; she dared to move her fingers to the book on the table. Since Eleanor had left the room, Mary had not taken her eyes off the book. Tentatively, she opened the cover of the book, then the next page, and the next page. What she saw froze her inside; each picture in the book had been etched over randomly, almost aggressively in one colour—black! There was no rhyme or reason for this, Mary thought. Ellie was good at colouring. She used her imagination well; she used a variation of bright colours, but this…this had been done without thought, without care…and yet, somehow, it seemed deliberate. Mary slowly sat down on the chair that had been occupied by her daughter. As she did so, she flicked the pages of the colouring book with a greater intensity. All the remaining pictures had been etched the same, almost blotted out in deep dark black!

Mary slowly closed the book, for the first time in a long, long time her worst fears had returned to her.

Chapter 2

To the best of her knowledge and her memory, Mary Foster had been, throughout most of her short life, a restless spirit. Her Father, a draughtsman had worked hard all his life in the civil aviation industry. As a result, the family had a modest but comfortable existence living just to the west of London in Staines, convenient for the commuting distance to the nearby London airports of Heathrow and Gatwick. Mary's mother had worked for a while as a bank clerk; the family never lacked direction on the best and most profitable ways of investing their money. As a result, the family were able to afford a modestly sized house in one of the up and coming areas of the town.

The family possessed no particular leanings to any religious faith and would lead a fairly ordinary lifestyle. While life itself was reasonably good for the family, for Mary, an only child, it was not enough. Mary alone sensed that she had always possessed ability, an insight that others just didn't seem to have.

Always feeling different, a little vulnerable and out of step at school, Mary had made a break from family life as soon as she could. Never very academic, she embarked on some secretarial courses as a teenager and sought to bury her sense of restlessness by taking a number of agency temping roles with city businesses, amongst the hustle and bustle of London, at the same time, sharing the rent on a flat in Islington with two other girls of similar persuasion.

It was while working in an office pool in a bank on one assignment when she met Daniel. Now, a year older than her husband, at thirty-five, her restless spirit and failure to settle had dogged them both, again. Married and with David and Eleanor, they had worked hard to seek an ideal, different direction, one that offered them greater solitude and…Mary thought, peace of mind.

Now, tall and slim at five-feet, eight-inches, her tumbling and teased shoulder-length auburn curly hair began to betray signs of age, with flecks of grey beginning to shine through the softly uncoiled corkscrew curls. Her hazel eyes and the mind that lay behind them remained sharp, however, and just as it seemed to Mary that she had escaped her past and the feeling of eternal restlessness that haunted her, her anxiety had begun to return.

For the remainder of that morning, Mary could not get out of her mind what she had seen Ellie do with her colouring book at the breakfast table. Like a recurring, nagging doubt, it tossed restlessly back and forth in her head. She could not bring herself to revisit the kitchen table where the book still lay. She tried to reassure herself she was over imagining things, but she couldn't completely dispel her fears.

Later that morning, Mary and Eleanor took a walk into the village; the early morning grey skies had lifted slightly and some autumnal rays of light from the sun broke through the clouds, spattering light onto the surrounding hills, nice enough to walk the short distance rather than take the car.

From the house to the village was a fifteen-minute walk along a quiet road. The narrow road twisted and turned down into the valley; it was framed on either side by a stone wall. There were no footpaths as such, but the wall on either side had not been built any higher than three feet, overall. Walking was treacherous, but traffic was light, if not absent, and pedestrians could at least see and be seen by vehicles.

Apart from the earlier incident, Mary's thoughts had been occupied with Eleanor's new school. The plan was for Mary to visit the school that morning and meet the teachers, and then Eleanor would start two days later. Ravensdale primary school stood on the edge of the village. The village itself was not too small, but intimate, it contained a number of small shops consisting mainly of a newsagent's and small post office; an imposing church sat central in the village, and the Bucks public house sat across the village square from the stores; an old coaching inn, the pub, provided a scenic attraction and social gathering centre for the village.

The schoolhouse, like the pub and many of the other buildings in the small village were more than two hundred years old and built from local materials—York stone.

Entrance to the school was via a walk across a large concreted playground and through a wooden double door, into the main entrance hall. After a brief wait, Mrs Forbes the headmistress of Ravensdale primary school met Mary and Eleanor. Of medium height, she was a slightly dumpy woman, with shoulder-length brunette hair; she was immaculately dressed and had a prim and snappy approach.

"Good morning, Mrs Foster, hope you are well?" she asked briskly, while jutting her right hand toward Mary. "And this is…?"

"Eleanor!" Mary interjected.

"Eleanor, and how are you?" Forbes asked.

"Ellie, say hello, dear. Mrs Forbes has asked you a question." Mary encouraged the little girl to reply but Eleanor was shy and beginning to inch behind her mother's coat.

"I'm all right" Eleanor finally replied.

"So, Eleanor is starting with us Thursday, right?" Mrs Forbes asked, looking to Mary for a response.

"Yes indeed."

"Does Eleanor have any special requirements or needs the school should be made aware of?"

"No, she has no requirements," Mary said, looking down at her daughter.

"Good, does Eleanor have any difficulty in making friends at all? You know…mixing with other children? Does she like to join in activities?"

"Well, actually, she is a little quiet, but she does have a few friends, and they play together quite well."

The three of them then proceeded to walk around the school, Mary and Eleanor led by Mrs Forbes.

"We encourage the children to develop good interactive and social skills, sharing experiences with other children; you know the sort of thing," Mrs Forbes said, speaking over her shoulder to Mary who was trailing behind her.

"Ah! Miss Strand."

The threesome stopped at the doorway to a classroom at the end of a long passageway.

"Miss Strand, this is Mrs Foster and her daughter Eleanor. Eleanor will be joining us for the remainder of the autumn term."

The three women continued to chat for a while longer, Miss Strand, a tall, sandy-haired young teacher with an intense stare had previously taught special needs children; her senses were acutely tuned to deviance or abnormalities in a child's behaviour. She smiled at Eleanor.

"So, Eleanor, what do you like doing best?"

"I like to draw and paint," Eleanor replied. The young teacher took the little girl by the hand and led her around the classroom.

"Well, Eleanor, I think you are going to fit in quite well here," Miss Strand said.

The gathering soon broke up, and Mary and her daughter left the school for the village shops and then walked up the hill to home. Mary was satisfied; the school seemed clean and tidy, the teachers nice; she sensed intensity in Miss Strand that had made her a little uncomfortable, but she shrugged it off.

* * *

The afternoon was quiet. Mary had taken one call from Daniel; he had called, excited over the morning's meeting.

"Mary, it looks like good news. I think we're close to closing the contract! I'm going to stick around in Manchester for a while with John." John was Daniel's Partner in their business. "We're going to grab a bite, so I'll be home late," Daniel blurted out, the excitement in his voice barely disguised over the phone.

"OK, Dear. Remember, don't drink too much. You're driving," Mary's said.

* * *

Mary made a cup of coffee and sat down. The house was silent. Eleanor had gone to play in the garden. Watching Eleanor playing through the kitchen window, Mary could see the similarities between them. The way Eleanor could just play on her own, the way she seemed contented, playing in her own company, talking to herself, creating characters, creating stories. None of this was any different than the way many children played. But Mary dared to fear the worst. What if…just what if Eleanor's world of play seemed dangerously close to her own dark experiences? God forbid, what if Eleanor had inherited the gift? No, not a gift, a curse! She reflected once again on the episode that morning with the colouring book. Mary glanced again into the garden.

The way Eleanor moved and talked, she seemed to be fixated in a self-contained cocoon! Mary's thoughts were racing; until now, Eleanor had not demonstrated any unusual abilities. She had been a perfectly normal child up until this point.

Mary broke her gaze from the little girl and, for a moment, she felt an icy chill; she rubbed her left shoulder with her right hand and pulled out a chair from the kitchen table. Sitting down, she clasped both hands together and recovered her thoughts.

Daniel was her second marriage. They had been together for nine years and, in all that time, Mary had not revealed to him the secret of her past.

Mary had understood that she was special from a young age. Everyone else knew Mary was special. Her gifts, as a young girl, playing in the garden of her parents' home had manifested themselves in a similar way to that which she now saw in Eleanor.

Mary glanced down at the table. The colouring book was still sitting there just as she had left it that morning; she hadn't dared to touch it again, but she felt compelled to take another look. Setting aside her coffee, she tentatively pulled the book toward her and flicked open the pages. What presented itself to her was the same as it had when she had flicked through the pages of the book earlier that morning.

At that moment, she felt a chill again; the air seemed still. Outside, the only sound that she could hear was an increasingly agitated sound of a group of crows; this made Mary look up and peer out of the window. She couldn't see Ellie! She looked from left to right across the garden, and now, the squawking of the crows was growing increasingly louder; the response between the squawking seemed quicker, more intense.

Mary got up from the table and walked to the kitchen window. She put her face closer to the glass, but still she could not see Ellie. The garden was mainly lawn, leading from a patio. To the back and sides of the garden was a dense thicket of shrubs and trees. Was Ellie in there?

Then Mary looked down onto the stone patio floor. Wasn't that Ellie's doll?

Standing by the edge of the sink and leaning over to look out of the window, now, for the first time Mary felt a sense of panic. *Those damn crows*, she thought, *what are they squawking about?* The rasping, squawking of the birds had now grown to a fever pitch.

Then, in not more than a second's instance, Mary saw it. She saw it but could do nothing about it! A large black crow flew out of nowhere toward her. Mary had no time to move, as the crow, now swooping at full speed, crashed through the kitchen window where she had been standing, shattering glass everywhere. Mary screamed, closed her eyes and, for a fraction of a second was able to turn her head away.

The large black mass of feathers hit the edge of the kitchen sink and dropped like a stone onto the kitchen floor. By now, Mary had dropped the cup of coffee; it crashed to the kitchen floor, smashing to pieces.

As it fell, Mary instinctively closed her eyes and stepped back, tripped, and fell backwards onto the floor. She hit her head on the table leg and, for a moment, complete chaos reigned. Then everything fell silent!

Mary pulled herself up with her arms. Sitting up now on the kitchen floor, she could feel her heart pounding. She rubbed the back of her head; she had taken a nasty knock during the fall, and then she panicked. She felt something running into her eyes. Mary wiped her forehead and then looked at her hand; her forehead was bleeding. Then she wiped her left cheek with the back of her hand; turning it over, she noticed more blood. Particles of shattered glass had hit her in the face, and she had suffered minor cuts to her forehead, cheek, and lip.

Shock began to set in. Still sitting on the floor, she began to breathe heavier and heavier, letting out great gasps of breath. Beginning to shake, she summoned the courage to glance across the kitchen floor; not three feet from her was the black, feathered mass of the large crow, completely still and motionless. It was dead; the shock on impact had killed it instantly.

Shattered glass lay everywhere, intermingled with broken china.

Mary pulled herself to her feet, but as she did, broken glass that had landed on her when she fell clattered to the floor. She could hear glass break under her feet. It was silent, now; there was not a sound inside or outside of the house. *Strange*, she thought. The crows that had reached a crescendo of noise had now gone!

Summoning her senses, she remembered Eleanor, and once again, the panic she felt only seconds earlier returned.

With her heart now racing, she looked up through the shattered glass window, and there, framed through the broken pane, she could see Eleanor standing perfectly still, her legs and feet together, her arms down by her side. The little girl looked pale, but she stared at Mary with an intensity that sent Mary cold. What the little girl said next froze her mother.

"It's all right, Mummy, it's all right. It's only an accident, everything is going to be all right!"

Mary's eyelids flickered, the room began to spin, and, in Mary's world, everything suddenly went dark.

Chapter 3

"Dan, Dan! Can you hear me?"

The voice faded in and out over the phone, but the sense of urgency had been clearly communicated. Daniel was standing in the middle of Princes Street in Manchester. His meeting wrapped up, and with the account in the bag, he had enjoyed a light lunch with his new Customers. Now, stepping out on the street to make his way back to the car, the call on his mobile phone had waylaid him.

A heady cocktail of excitement and adrenalin at winning the account, plus a couple of glasses of fine burgundy over lunch, had made him fumble for the phone when it rang.

"Hold, hold on!" Daniel replied, struggling to get the phone to his ear, while adjusting his briefcase.

"Dan, it's me!" came the voice over the phone. "It's me, Wendy!"

"Hold on, I can't hear you; let me move away from the road."

Dan moved into an adjacent shop doorway where the sound of the traffic died away.

"Hello, who is it? Mary…? Mary, brilliant news; we've won the account!"

"Dan, it's not Mary. It's me, Wendy, your neighbour."

Wendy Cheney, together with her husband Derek, lived across the street from Daniel and Mary. Their house, a small bungalow, sat up on the hillside slightly above the Hungry Harshes and, being a bungalow, it appeared considerably more modern compared to that of the Hungry Harshes.

The Cheneys' children had now grown up and moved on. Both in their early sixties themselves, the Cheneys had settled into peaceful retirement in Ravensdale.

Wendy Cheney, who had been home alone that afternoon, had been in the garden taking washing in off the clothesline, when she heard the commotion from across the road. First, she heard the sound of the crows, then the breaking glass. She had tentatively approached the Hungry Harshes to investigate, only to find Eleanor, the little girl, standing there frozen and shivering. She'd then seen the broken glass from the kitchen window and had looked in; to her horror, she discovered Mary lying on the floor, her face covered in blood.

"Wendy, what's up?" Daniel said, surprised by the call. This was the first time his neighbour had ever phoned him, and he wondered how she could have got his mobile number.

"Daniel, there's been an accident!"

Dan's heart froze. "What accident? What do you mean? What's happened? Where's Mary?"

"Dan, it's ok; it's ok. She's fine now."

"She's fine—*now*! What's happened?" Daniel said, agitated.

"Well, it wasn't so much of an accident as an incident...you see—"

"Wendy, what the hell is going on?" Daniel cut in before his neighbour on the other end of the line had time to finish.

"Dan, I found Mary this afternoon. She had passed out on the floor of your kitchen...it, it looks like a freak accident. Apparently, a bird, a crow flew into the window, breaking the glass. Mary was standing at the kitchen window at the time, and the bird and the broken glass hit her. She suffered some minor cuts to her face, but she's all right now; she's upstairs in bed. Doctor Ventham is with her."

There was silence. Daniel could not believe what he was hearing, his emotions now jumbled; in disbelief, he let out an incredulous laugh.

"What about the kids? Where are the kids?" Daniel squawked feverishly.

"The kids are fine. We rang the school, and David's got the bus home. Apparently, he was going to have some friends over this afternoon, but we've put them off. I had to turn away the interior designer, as well. They were a bit upset, but too bad." Wendy said.

"What about Eleanor? Where is she?" Dan asked.

"Eleanor's here with me, poor mite. I think she must have seen the whole thing. I think it shook her up a bit, but she's not said anything."

"OK, OK. I'm coming straight home," Daniel replied. The heady excitement of the day's business now lost, Daniel was anxious, scared, and wanting to get home to his family. On the journey home in the car, he had tried to make sense over what he had just heard.

He hoped it was what Wendy had said it was, a freak accident, and not a bad omen, both for their new home and their new life together. He did not know, either, what sight would greet him as he returned home that night.

Every red light, every stretch of traffic seemed to check his progress back to Ravensdale and home and irritated him and raised his level of anxiety.

* * *

Back at the Hungry Harshes, Mary lay half propped up in her bed. The autumn nights were drawing in, now, and the curtains had been drawn with just the bedroom lamps providing the necessary light for the room.

Doctor Ventham, Ravensdale's resident GP had just taken Mary's pulse for the second time. A tall, thin man, dressed in a tweed jacket, he had served as a general practitioner of medicine in the community for sixteen years.

"All right, Mrs Foster, I can tell you that your pulse is normal, no problems there," the Doctor said.

"However, you'll need to keep the dressing on for a few days." As he said this, the doctor looked up at Mary's face and indicated to the applied and clean dressing on Mary's cuts on her forehead, just above her left eye and her lower-left cheek.

The wounds Mary had suffered were fortunately not too deep to require stitching, but they had been deep enough to incur sufficient blood loss which, in turn, had caused her to panic.

Her lip was swollen from the cuts incurred from shards of flying glass. Probably of more concern to both Mary and the doctor was the throbbing pain in her head, caused by the fall and the strike to the head. There were no outward signs of concussion but, nonetheless, Doctor Ventham had thought it sensible for Mary to be resting in bed.

"I suggest you ring the surgery and make an appointment to come and see me, say Thursday?"

"Ok, Doctor, do you think I could get up?" Mary asked.

"If you feel well enough, then you should. When is your husband home? Do you have someone who can look after your children in the meantime?" the doctor asked, his shoulders hunching over his frame, as he continued to put his dressing, stethoscope, and other medical items back into his bag, which was resting at the foot of Mary's bed.

At that point, Wendy Cheney entered the room, picking up the threads of the doctor's questions.

"Don't worry. I've managed to speak to Mary's husband; he's making his way home. I'll stay over here with the children, make sure they've had something to eat," Wendy interjected.

"Oh, Wendy, I'm so grateful to you." Mary said.

"Not at all, you've had a nasty turn; it's a shock, and besides, we have to keep an eye on you with that bump on your head."

"Oh, dear!" Mary sighed. "I just feel very silly. I've put everyone to so much trouble and…and poor, poor Daniel. I've spoilt his celebration!"

"Don't be silly!" Wendy responded. "I'll make you a nice cup of tea. Just lie there and relax!"

Pushing her arms down in the bed in order to sit up a little more, Mary drew breath through her teeth and shut her eyes, as her head throbbed raising it off the pillow.

"You see, you're not able to get up now, anyway!" Wendy observed.

Doctor Ventham gave a faint smile. "Ok, I must be off…oh! Mrs Foster, do you have any aspirin or ibuprofen in the house? I suggest you take them as you need them…take the sting out of that head."

With that, Doctor Ventham picked up his bag and walked toward the door.

"I'll let you out, Doctor," Wendy said.

With that, both exited the room, leaving Mary alone.

Mary's eyes settled on the curtains to the bedroom window, opposite the foot of the bed. A bedroom window was open, and a gentle breeze caressed the curtains, where they were pulled together in the middle of the window. Mary was aware of the bedroom door, left marginally ajar, when Wendy and the doctor had left the room, inching slowly open.

"Who's that! Who's there?" Mary asked. With that, the door inched open a little farther, and Eleanor crept in, her face full of apprehension, as to how her mother would greet her. For a moment that seemed like an age, Eleanor stood in the doorway, her eyes fixed on Mary.

"Ellie, Sweetheart, come here," Mary said, patting the duvet. With that, the little girl walked briskly to the bed and climbed up. Mother and daughter hugged, then Eleanor sat back.

"Are you ok, Sweetheart?" Mary enquired of the little girl. Eleanor didn't reply but, instead, looked down at her hands and nodded her head.

"Are you badly hurt, Mummy?" Eleanor asked.

"I have a very bad headache, Darling. That's why Mummy has to stay in bed."

The little girl looked back down at her hands. Mary could contain herself no longer; she felt the question she needed to ask Eleanor welling up inside her.

"Eleanor, Darling, I need to know one thing."

Mary cupped her hands around the child's face and elevated it to face her own, as she spoke. "What did you mean when you said it was going to be all right?"

"I don't know, Mummy. What do you mean? What do you mean?"

"Well, after the bird had hit the window, you said to me that everything was going to be all right, do you remember? Mummy must have looked terrible with all that blood on her face!" Mary said, trying to tease a response out of the small girl.

Eleanor once again drew her face away from Mary's and looked down at her hands, as she fumbled with a piece of sewn lace on her tee-shirt. Upon seeing this reaction from her daughter, Mary's heart sank.

She knew something was wrong. She knew something troubled Eleanor.

"Izzy told me," the little girl replied.

"Who's Izzy," Mary asked.

"My friend...she talks to me sometimes, and we play together. Today we played dollies!" Ellie exclaimed with triumphant enthusiasm, looking up at her mother.

"Ellie, what do you mean Izzy told you...what did she say?"

Marys' imagination began to run riot; she knew that little girls who held conversations with imaginary friends were not uncommon, but the similarities with her own past experiences, and particularly those in her own childhood had shaken her.

"Ellie, look at me, Darling..." the girls eyes looked up to meet her mothers. "What exactly did Izzy say to you?."

"Oh, Izzy knows. She knew about the big black bird hitting the window; she knew what was going to happen...I knew, too!" Eleanor's reply was pure throwaway...

"And that's when she said to you that, despite what happened, everything was going to be all right?" asked Mary.

"Yes, everything was all right. You are all right, aren't you, Mummy?" Eleanor asked.

"Now, Eleanor, you have to tell me honestly. Does Izzy ever say anything bad to you, you know, not very nice?" Mary asked, bracing herself for the reply.

"Oh no, Mummy, she's never not nice. She can make things happen…" the little girl giggled. "We can make things happen together…like the bird, today."

* * *

Dan had returned home sometime after five in the evening. Walking with haste around to the back door, he noticed the broken windowpane. Wendy had been sitting in the lounge and, upon hearing the back door open, she got up to see who it was.

"Wendy! How's Mary?" Dan asked, looking a little tense and settling his briefcase on the kitchen table.

"She's fine, she's fine," Wendy replied, trying to placate him. "She's upstairs now with Eleanor, in bed; the doctor has been to see her, and he recommends she gets some rest and goes back to see him in a couple of days."

"Where's David?" Daniel asked after his son.

"He's in the lounge, with me. Now that I've cooked them both a meal, they'll be all right tonight," Wendy said.

Daniel sighed. He had driven all the way home and hastened up the garden path, wondering what scene would greet him.

"You go up and see her…I've swept up all the broken glass I can—"

But Dan had already sidestepped his neighbour and was making his way up the stairs to the bedroom.

As he entered the bedroom, he saw Mary propped up in bed with Eleanor curled up at her side. Mary was stroking the little girl's hair. The door creaked slightly, as Dan eased it gently open, and both Mary and Eleanor looked up.

"Daddy! Daddy!" Eleanor jumped off the bed and ran into her father's arms. Dan had stooped to pick her up and cuddle her, and as he did, his eyes flashed back to meet Mary's, as she lay in bed.

"Ellie, Darling, could you do Mummy a favour and go downstairs for a while? Mummy and Daddy need to talk." Mary said.

With that, Dan set the little girl down. Ellie turned to look over her shoulder at her mother and gave a compliant, if somewhat reluctant, nod and slipped out of the room.

"Dan, can you close the door after you?" Mary asked ominously.

Dan dutifully obliged, then walked around to the far side of the bed and sat down on the edge. Surveying her facial wounds and dressings, he chuckled to himself.

"You certainly know how to have a good time when I'm not around," he joked.

Mary took Dan's hand across the bed and rubbed his thumb.

"I hear congratulations are in order? Well done, Darling; another good day's work," Mary said, with reference to the newly acquired business deal.

Dan smirked, looked down at Mary's hand, and then looked up. He could see something in Mary's eyes, but it wasn't happiness.

"How are you?" he asked her.

"Oh, I've had better days," she remarked, trying to avoid the conversation.

"What happened here?" Dan asked, looking straight into Mary's eyes. Mary threw her head back onto the pillow.

"Oh, Dan, everything was going fine. I took Ellie to see her new school, and we spoke to the teachers —"

"Then what!" Dan interrupted. "Mary, look at me."

"Then, then we just came home. Ellie was playing in the garden. I made her put that warm coat on, the one your mother got for her…"

"Then what, Mary, what happened?"

"It was just some stupid bird. It…it flew into the window….it was a total shock!"

"What about Ellie? Was she hurt? Did she see it? Come on, Mary, your face is telling me that this was more than just some freakish accident!" Dan could sense Mary withdrawing. In all the years they had been married, he had never seen Mary act quite like this.

Mary had begun to prop herself up and lean forward toward Daniel, and as she did, she pulled the covers of the duvet up closer to her chest, as if to form a barrier between herself and her husband. Mary breathed a deep sigh and, for the first time in their marriage, she prepared to reveal to her husband her secrets from her past, secrets she was afraid to reveal to him, in case he thought she was mad, a past she thought that might be returning to her, uninvited.

"Dan…" There was silence.

"Dan, there's something we need to talk about, something about me that you are not aware of."

Daniel's eyes locked on his wife, his jaw dropped, and his heart started to pound.

"As a young girl, I had certain skills, certain abilities…" Mary began.

"What skills, what abilities? Mary what are you talking about?" Daniel asked impatiently.

"I'm talking about abilities…abilities to see things, make things happen," Mary replied. Her discomfort was evident to Dan.

"Darling, I don't follow you. What are you saying? That you're psychic or something?" Daniel's voice rose with disbelief; he laughed, again, but noticed that the response from Mary did not mirror his. She seemed tense, nervous.

"Yes, basically that's it. I have some sort of psychic ability…or had, Dan. I've not been troubled by it in more than fifteen years."

There was silence. What he'd just heard from Mary had left him speechless.

"It all started when I was young. I couldn't have been more than five or six, the age Ellie is now. I remember when Nana died." Nana was Mary's affectionate name for her grandmother.

"I felt this awful loss, this emptiness. I missed Nana so much, I think Mum and Dad had expected her to die; she had been ill for some while with cancer, but of course, you don't understand that when you're young. All I remember was Nana being there one day and the next, Mum telling me that Nana would no longer be with us…she'd gone. I remember Mum crying a lot for a while, afterwards, and thinking if Nana had gone to heaven, then she must be looking down and watching us, but I remember being unhappy. I couldn't see her, touch her, or even talk to her. Afterwards, I prayed and prayed that she would come back."

Mary paused.

"So what then?" Daniel asked.

"Well, then, of course, things settled back down, or so I thought, but then I started to have dreams about Nana, dreams where Nana had come back to us. I remember dreaming about going upstairs to my bedroom and closing the door, shutting Mum and Dad out, and just being in the room on my own with Nana."

Mary reached for a glass of water sitting on the bedside table. She took a sip, composed herself, and put the glass back down.

Daniel didn't say a word.

" I…I recall these dreams. They seemed very real to me, very vivid; it was like I was talking to Nana, having a conversation, almost. Anyway, I think I must have woken one night—"

Just then, a gust of wind blew through the window and, catching the drawn curtains, caused them to billow forward, making both Mary and Daniel turn to look. The house now seemed to fall silent. Even though the two children were downstairs with Wendy Cheney, Daniel felt a chill; he felt as if there were just he and Mary, alone together, in the house.

Mary continued, all the time staring down at the duvet covering her, searching her mind to recollect the past.

Neale Cooper

"Yes…yes I remember now. I awoke one night after a dream. I wasn't sure if I was awake or still dreaming. I remember a dim light coming from the corner of my room. I used to have a trunk, you know, like an ottoman I kept all my toys in. Anyway, there was this dim, pale light, almost a glow. I lay there for a while, with my head on the pillow, and the light remained. I thought I must be dreaming, so I sat up and peered through the darkness of the room to where the light was. I could see an outline of a person. I thought it was Mum. I remember asking, 'Mum, what are you doing here?' I rubbed my eyes, but she didn't answer."

"What did you do?" Daniel asked, with an incredulous look on his face.

"I didn't feel scared. I felt I knew this person and that she wasn't going to hurt me. This person was sitting on my toy trunk and, after a while of just sitting there looking at me, it got up and started to move toward me, but it didn't look like it was walking; it seemed to glide toward the foot of the bed. As it got closer, I could tell it was a woman, but not a young woman, an old woman, it was…it was Nana!"

Mary stumbled over the last few words and took another sip of water, all the time apprehensive about what Daniel might say.

"I could clearly see it was Nana, but she wasn't smiling; she wasn't making any expression. Her face and features seemed stone cold. As she drew closer, the light or aura around her—whatever it is you want to call it—seemed to diminish and, just as she reached the foot of my bed, she disappeared. I lay there for a while; I wasn't frightened, but I must have gone back to sleep. Anyway, I didn't tell Mum or Dad. I must have just thought it was a dream."

Daniel thought for a while before responding. "So what did you do? What happened after that?"

"I kept thinking about it for a while afterwards," Mary continued. "Then, one day, Mum was searching through some of Nana's old stuff. You know, she wasn't sure if she was going to keep it or throw it out when she found some old handwritten letters from Nana. I think Nana had written them and was going to give them to Mum but she never did. I remember Mum sitting down with us all, my sister and I included, and reading these letters. It was like Nana was trying to speak to us from beyond the grave. It was harrowing. Mum had tears streaming down her face, as she read them."

"What was in the letters?" Daniel asked.

"It was like she was offering Mum guidance on how to raise us, always love and support us girls in whatever we did. Be patient with us, even when our will and desire to do something contradicted her own views; show tolerance and she would be rewarded. I guess they were things Nana wanted to say but never found the time to sit down with Mum and talk about. Oh, Mum, took it as a sign that Nana knew she was going to die and that she wanted to prepare the way, so to speak."

"And? So, what next?" Daniel was now intrigued.

"Well, the letters and the reading of the letters kind of triggered something in me; it was shortly after this that I started having these intense dreams of

Nana, and pretty soon, I began to experience more visions. It would always start with a light, radiating from the corner of the bedroom, always the same spot! This image of Nana would move toward me then disappear. I began to lose sleep. I wasn't eating, and Mum began to notice. She noticed me withdrawing into myself. I would just sit on my own and do things; you know, reading, drawing without ever noticing what was going on around me. What I was doing made no sense. I would read but not remember anything I had read; I would draw and it would just be the incomprehensible scrawl of some three-year-old. In the end, I had to tell her about Nana and the visions."

"What did she say?" Daniel asked.

"What could she say? I don't think she believed me, but Dan, I didn't make it up. It was real to me, happening only to me! Mum started sleeping with me in my bedroom, I longed for her to see what I had seen. I wasn't afraid. Why should she be?"

"Did she see it? Your Mum, did she see this vision?"

"Once, maybe once, I think she saw it, but the visions diminished after that and, pretty soon, Nan stopped visiting altogether. Dan, it was what was going on in my head at the time that scared me. Seeing Nana again should have been joyous, but it wasn't, it wasn't comforting at all. I felt her with me all of the time, and it affected everything I did. As I said, I couldn't draw or write properly. I suppose I seemed to regress to Mum and Dad and the Teachers, but it was like Nana was transmitting her thoughts or her very presence through me, just through me! It didn't stop there, either." For the first time in a long while, Mary felt she had to get this out in the open. It so happened that, for the first time in their marriage, Daniel was to be the recipient of Mary's outpouring.

To him, it seem like an unburdening, an outpouring of pent-up grief inside Mary.

For Mary, the barriers were down and she meant to continue.

"Other things began to happen; small things went missing at home. I'm sure Mum and Dad blamed me. We also had a small dog, a Yorkshire terrier we called Baxter. I used to play with Baxter in our garden at home; he was a good-natured dog, but after I started getting these experiences with Nana, he would shy away from me or growl and bark and go frantic; it was almost like he sensed something was there, something he didn't like or understand. You know the way they say animals can sense things."

"So, Mary, what happened?" Daniel interjected again.

"I...I began to feel isolated, distant from everyone, Mum and Dad, friends at school, the worse it got, the unhappier I became, and the problems seemed to get worse. No one could get through to me."

To Daniel, the realisation of what he was hearing began to dawn on him. Up until now in his life, what he heard had been borne of fiction...ghosts? Spirits? Whatever you wanted to call them, surely Mary must have received a stronger bump on the head when she fell than he thought; his thoughts turned to calling the Doctor to make a return visit.

"Listen, Mary, I…do you know what you're saying? I'm finding this a little difficult to take in, thought. Are you saying that, as a child, you were possessed?"

Mary let out a large sigh. "Yes, in a word Yes!

A further awkward silence ensued, then Mary continued. "I experienced something called, what was it…psycho…psychokinesis or something like that? I witnessed apparitions; it couldn't be explained exactly how I did it, but that included moving physical objects moving or making them disappear."

Mary stopped suddenly, seeing the doubt in Dan's face.

"Dan, I know you find this hard to believe, but all I have said is true. I'm sorry, my love, I haven't told you after all of these years…it just wasn't something I felt confident I could share with you or anyone!"

Mary slumped back on her pillow, her sense of relief for disclosing her past with Daniel was visible, but it was tempered by a fear of how Daniel would react.

Indeed, for Daniel himself was not sure quite how to react; he wasn't sure whether to laugh or be off hand, dismissing what Mary had just unburdened to him, or whether to go into a rage. He and Mary had been married for twelve years, twelve long, happy years; they'd had had their ups and downs, but this…this revelation felt like his life had been turned on its head. He thought he knew everything about the woman he loved. Mary's family too had never let onto him about her past.

He cast his eyes away from Mary and got up off of the bed. Walking toward the window, he rubbed his forehead with his hand. Whatever else he might be, he was a reasonable, accepting, and worldly man. Business had gone well today, but his wife lay in bed with cuts and bruises, and his concern turned to the safety of his children. He turned to face Mary.

"Why have you never said anything to me before? What did you think I would say?" Daniel asked.

"Dan, I don't know. I feared that it was some sort of curse, that if I told you…Dan, we were so happy, we are still happy. I love you, I love the kids, and I love our life. Had I told you way back at the start of our relationship, I guess I was afraid that you would leave me, we'd be finished, over. Besides, I've had no recurrences now for years. I only had them as a child." Mary feared that Daniel would explode; he seldom did, but he could be moody, and this was the sort of news that could propel him into a bad mood. Instead, much to Mary's relief and surprise, his response was a mix of pragmatism and support. The implication of what Mary was trying to tell him had begun to dawn on him.

"Mary, I can't quite take this all in. It sounds incredible, your telling me you had these abilities as a child, and now you think our daughter may have them as well. What makes you think that?" Daniel stuttered, concerned and frustrated that perhaps he not only didn't know his wife, too well, but his daughter, either.

Mary, now assured that Daniel was following her on this spoke with some confidence.

"I believe…I cannot say for sure, but I believe that what happened here today might have been initiated in some way by Eleanor."

Daniel shook his head in disbelief and paced back toward the window.

"Dan, I believe Ellie has, to a greater or lesser degree, I don't know, I can't say for sure, the same psychokinetic abilities that I once had when I was her age; they are now manifesting themselves in her. The things she's doing, the way she talks, the way she draws, it's like she's not with us," Mary said.

"When did you start seeing all this!" Dan snapped, slightly irritated and turning back to Mary.

"Well, it's been evident today."

"Ok, so let's not get too carried away by this and overreact," Dan cut in. "I've set the account up now with Mullers. I'll speak to John in the morning and work the next few days from home, give you time to rest and recover."

Daniel had an overwhelming feeling of sympathy for his wife. Seeing her lying there outweighed his anger and irritation. He returned to the bed, bent over, and hugged Mary. In turn, she wrapped her arms around him.

"Dan, I am so sorry," Mary said. "I truly believed that this was something from my past, long ago before we met, something I could deal with that would never come between us."

As the couple parted from the embrace, the bedroom door gingerly creaked open once more, causing both to turn their heads and look. Eleanor stood in the doorway. Framed by the darkness in the hall, she looked first at Dan and then Mary. The day's events had upset the little girl, and she now sought comfort.

"Daddy, I want you to read to me. Will you read to me?"

Unbeknownst to both Mary and Daniel, events were now beginning to move with a much more rapid turn of pace.

Chapter 4

For the next few days, things returned to normal in the Foster household. Daniel was as good as his word and stayed at home, working from a room at the back of house that he had converted into a study. When he wasn't encamped in the small room with the door shut firmly, between him and the rest of the world, he would ably assist Mary, who had, by now gingerly got back on her feet and felt she needed to maintain some organisation in the household. *Sore head or no sore head*, she thought, *there are children to shepherd, to feed and to clean.* While Daniel promised great things, feeding the children, clearing up after them and generally demonstrating patience and tolerance were not his strong points. So, more often than not, he was tasked with taking and collecting the children to and from school. This gave him an excuse, Mary thought, at least to get out of that stuffy room. Often, when he was on the school run, she would venture into his male-occupied sanctuary and open the windows to let fresh air in. Daniel never opened them. Preoccupied with work, he had not yet learned to fully appreciate their new life and their new surroundings. Something he didn't have when he worked in the city was an office window that looked out over tranquil, peaceful, rolling countryside.

Eleanor, too, had now started school and, while for Mary the onset of this single event had now offered back some space and freedom in her life, she nonetheless felt a tinge of sadness at having seeing her baby pass from infant to toddler, and now into a new phase. She hoped that it wouldn't take too long for the little girl to settle in.

Indeed, since the events of a few days previous, Mary and Dan had had little discussion about what had happened; they had purposely played down the incident with the crow and hadn't reflected on it with the children. Mary, too, still felt nervous and edgy about Daniel's response and attitude to her past revelations. Had she tricked him? Deceived him? It had occurred to Mary that this was possibly what Daniel might be thinking to himself. She felt guilt, too, that she had associated the episodes from her past so strongly with her daughter's behaviour. Had she judged the situation too harshly? Had she been too quick to label poor Eleanor?

Over the next few nights, following the incident, Mary slept fitfully. The pain in her head gradually eased and, with the house now empty and quiet during the day, save for Daniel in the study, she would sit in the lounge and watch some daytime television or simply just nod off. Wendy Cheney too had called over to check up on Mary's condition. She loved home baking, so she had brought over a huge homemade steak and kidney pie for the family. How all very nice, Mary reflected, nice area, nice neighbours.

Mary also took the time to call her Mother. To Mary, it was more of a reassuring call; she wanted to hear her mother's voice, connect with her…but to Mary, even up to the point that she was making the telephone call, she found she couldn't talk to her or tell her the full facts about what had happened.

"Oh hello, Mum! Everything ok?"

"Everything's fine, Dear; how are the children?" her mother said.

"Yes, they're fine, and you know, Mum, Eleanor's started school now, too….ye, yes! Only this week, a nice little school in the centre of the village."

Mary was all too painfully aware that, during her own childhood, when she suffered her own disturbing experiences, the stress on the family had been great. Her mother in particular had found the whole experience distressing, so soon after the death of her own mother. It had brought the now sixty-two year old Alice close to a breakdown. Mary tried to sound upbeat. Daniel's doing well, Mum; he's just closed a new account, yeah…in Manchester the other day. It'll mean Daniel travelling to Manchester more often…n, no, Mum, he's working here at home this week."

* * *

Over the years, Alice Parsons, Mary's maiden name had been Parsons, had become highly attuned to her daughter's emotions. Following the death of her mother and the subsequent apparitions that Mary had seen, she was particularly attune to any signs of distress in her daughter. She could sense the faltering unease in Mary's voice. Something was wrong, something had happened, but Alice knew her daughter well enough to know that Mary would withdraw from having that discussion now.

"So, why is he working from home this week? He should be out there, shouldn't he? Knocking on doors!" Alice's response was not uncommon of that of an ageing mother, overprotective of her daughter and grandchildren. She had long ago accepted Daniel into her family, their outlook however was completely different. Alice was both strong and enterprising, very much like Daniel, but she was pragmatic, sensible and, above all, stoic in her approach and beliefs. Daniel, she saw had achieved a good deal, but she never could understand the nature of his business and indeed the manner in which he conducted it.

Alice had never let Mary know her true feelings and concerns; it wasn't, as she saw it, appropriate and, besides, she didn't wish to ostracise her daughter.

Alice was however aware of her daughter's periods of fragile confidence and had worried about the move to Yorkshire and how this significant upheaval would affect the family. Being so far away, she felt a little isolated. Having sensed the unease in Mary's voice, she had made a play for it.

"Mum, Daniel doesn't have to be on the road all the time! He doesn't do cold calling," Mary patiently attempted to explain.

There was a silence, then Alice replied, "is everything all right, Mary?"

"Everything's fine, Mum, honestly. We're just getting settled in; the house is lovely, the area's lovely, the neighbours are lovely…" Mary paused. "You must come up sometime and visit."

Alice seized on this opening. " Ok, I've got a WI meeting later this week, but I can come up next week. Would that be all right?"

Mary was taken aback. "Erh? Yeah…er…shouldn't be a problem."

"Ok, I'll make some arrangements. I can catch a train from London up to Leeds; it'll take about two and a half hours, I think. I think that's near to where you are, isn't it?" Alice asked.

"Erh, yeah, I think you're right. I can come down to Leeds, Mum, and pick you up!" Mary, still taken aback, replied.

"And, Darling," Alice continued, "please don't go to too much trouble. Right, I'm looking forward to it now, looking forward to seeing the children!"

"Ok, Mum. Well, let's talk later this week around arrangements. I'll call you Saturday…take care…all our love, Mum!"

With that, the receiver on the end of the line went dead. Alice had promptly hung up.

In some ways, Mary felt relieved. She missed her mother; the events of the past few days had jolted her confidence, and she felt then that her mother was a long, long way away.

* * *

Little Pig, Little Pig

Later that evening after supper, Mary brought a bottle of red wine and two glasses into the large lounge. It was dark outside, the curtains were drawn, and a combination of strategically placed table lamps and the crackling of the open fire lit the room. Daniel was bent over the hearth, adding some additional wood to stoke the flames. By this time of the evening — eight-thirty — Eleanor was asleep in bed and David would normally be playing or reading in his room.

Daniel could sense Mary entering the large room and pulled himself back up to the sofa where he sat watching the flickering orange flames of the fire.

Mary walked behind him and put a wine glass on the table standing beside him, filled the glass with a generous amount of red wine, and sat down in one of the armchairs at the end of the sofa, nearest Daniel.

She took a large gulp of wine then looked down into the glass.

"How are you?" she asked Daniel tentatively "You didn't say a lot over dinner."

Daniel didn't turn his attention away from the fire. "How do you think I am?" he asked, his reply cold and hard.

"I don't know," Mary said. "You've been quiet these past couple of days."

Mary looked up at Daniel and pulled her legs up and tucked them under her on the chair, gripping her ankles with her left hand.

The ambience in the room was relaxing, but the air was tense, and Mary sensed that Daniel was still a little shaken from their discussion two days earlier.

"Dan, listen, I never meant to not tell you about what happened in my past. There was always so much more that was positive; we've shared so many good times!"

Dan broke his gaze from the crackling fire and looked across into Mary's eyes. Worry etched onto his face. He swallowed hard.

"…and I'm not going to let go of those good times Mary, I'll never let go of them. I just wish you felt you could have told me long ago. It would have been alright, we are strong together!"

Daniel reached out his hand to Mary who placed her hand in his, Daniel's show of support reassured Mary.

"I spoke to Mum today, she wants to come up and visit, see the new house. I said she could come up next week."

Daniel didn't reply but instead tilted his head back and took a large swig of wine. Mary sighed, "It would be good to have Mum here; she's not seen the house and she would love to see the children…I want her here!"

"That's fine darling" Daniel replied sitting forward on the sofa and staring intently through his wine glass into the crackling fire beyond.

The light from the fire gave the wine a rich red glow. He continued the conversation, but on a more conciliatory tack.

"I just wish you would have said something to me all those years ago. You've never given any hint to me that these problems were troubling you!"

Mary sensed that this was an opportunity handed to her by her husband to take the tension out of the discussion. She put her wine glass down on the lamp table and climbed off of the chair, kneeling down next to Daniel. She gripped his arm and turned her head to look sympathetically into his face. The red glow from the fire flickered and lit up both their faces.

"Dan," Mary continued in an apologetic tone, "I never meant to deceive you or hide things from you. I'm sorry if you think I have. I'm sorry. I should have shared this with you a long, long time ago."

Dan turned his head to look down at Mary's; the heat and glow from the fire had brought a tinge of colour to their cheeks.

"Maybe I was wrong about Ellie," Mary continued. "Maybe I just overreacted; it's just that what I saw, or what I thought I saw, took me all the way back!"

Mary pulled her gaze away from Daniel's and looked down into the fire. His gaze, in turn, was now fixed on her.

"God, I love our children. I wouldn't want anyone or anything to hurt them."

Daniel lifted his right arm and began rubbing the back of Mary's neck. Her shoulder-length auburn hair broke and parted along the back of his hand. Mary continued to stare into the fire.

"This is a great new start for us, Dan; this is where I most want to be right now, with you and the kids here. I don't want to risk losing that."

Daniel's anger and irritation had evaporated. He slumped back on the sofa but continued to rub Mary's neck.

"So what happened in the end?" Daniel asked.

"How did you come to terms with it…this apparition that was appearing?"

Mary thought about Daniel's question. She hadn't really wanted to go into the full detail, covering this particular part of her life, but she realised that, with the tension gone, it would probably be best to confide in Daniel.

"Well, for a while after I continued to see Nana, the dreams began to get worse. They began turning to truly awful nightmares. I would see Nana at the end of the bed; she looked in pain and then the screaming started!"

"Screaming, what screaming?" Dan asked.

"I'd seen Nana a few times before her death, and just weeks before her death, Mum insisted that we still visit her in the hospice. Oh, it was an awful place. They say it's the place to go to find final peace, but I remember it was truly awful. Everyone looked as if they were dead already." Mary averted her eyes from the fire and looked straight down onto the rug in front of the hearth.

"Go on," Daniel said.

"I remember Nana was very poor, then; she was in a lot of pain and not fully aware of us being there or even who we were. She would scream and wave her arms around; once, she struck me and knocked me over. Another time, I remember her grabbing Mum's arm, while Mum tried to brush Nana's hair from her forehead." Mary paused at this point, looked up at Daniel, and continued.

"She dug her nails into Mum's arm and she wouldn't let go. There was this sort of look on her face. I thought it was evil, terrible, and it scared me, but in fact it wasn't an evil expression at all; it was an expression of fear. Of course, when you're young, you interpret these things differently. Anyway, she gripped Mum's arm so tightly that it started to turn blue! Mum panicked, from what I remember, and Sophie and I started to scream, and some of the nurses rushed over. Nana's nails were so long that they dug deep into Mum's arm, and I remember seeing blood running out of Mum's wrist and arm. They got her off, but Mum had to have bandaging for the cuts. You could imagine that, for two young girls, it was terrifying. It was just awful, seeing Nana like that."

By now, the flames from the fire were burning strongly.

"Anyway, I continued to have these dreams, where I woke and saw Nana, but as I say, they began to get more vivid. She would be screaming in pain, and I couldn't help her!"

Outside, the wind was beginning to pick up and whip around the large, exposed house. It blew down the chimney and agitated the flames from the fire and blew the curtains out from the front window. Both Daniel and Mary looked up. The window was shut!

Mary took another sip of her wine and steadied herself for the next part.

Daniel, sensing this, took a large swig of wine from his glass, as well.

"Then, one night, things began to get a little too real! I remember, because the room was so cold, freezing, I could see my breath, when I woke, but I remember lifting my left arm and wiping my forehead, and there were beads of sweat on it! It was dark, but I had a small light on in the far corner. I felt there was someone there. I felt trapped, I couldn't move. In some way, I was pinned to the bed; I felt I couldn't sit up, couldn't lift my body, and my legs were rigid. I couldn't move them at all, like they were paralysed!"

The flames of the fire flickered and danced more aggressively, now. Mary stared straight into the flames, her words tumbling out.

"I remember, I think I started calling out 'Help me! Help me!' But nobody came, then I felt this sharp pain in my right arm; it felt like pins and needles, at first, tingling, but then it got more painful, like a stabbing pain. I could feel the blood pumping in my right arm, and that's when something made me decide to look to my right!"

Mary stopped abruptly. She took a brief gasp for breath. Daniel was, by now, a captive audience.

"What happened? Mary, what happened?" he cried. The wind outside was getting stronger, and it was driving down the chimney of the old house. The flames were now roaring and crackling, and small pieces of burning wood were spat from the fire onto the hearth, toward Mary.

"I slowly turned my head. I could barely move it. Fear gripped me, and my heart was beating so hard, I began to grasp for breath! What I saw terrified me. It has stayed with me all my life!" By now, Mary had started to weep. She brought her hand up to wipe her eyes.

"What did you see?" Daniel said, leaning forward on the sofa. Mary took a deep breath but continued to stare into the fire.

"It was Nana. She was lying there right next to me. Her hollow, sunken eyes were looking straight at me, her face contorted in pain, just as I remembered it shortly before she died. It was her! Her nails gripped into my arm; she wouldn't let go! Both of us lay there. She was a ghostly, rotting, stinking corpse with these hollow, dark eyes, gripping me and not letting me go. I felt such pain!!" By now, Mary was crying, the emotion and distress breaking through in her voice.

"Did she say anything?" Daniel asked.

"Nothing! Her mouth was open, but it was twisted in pain!"

"What did you do?" Daniel asked, again. "How did you get away from her?"

"I just screamed, as loud as I could. I closed my eyes and screamed. I seemed to scream forever." Mary paused, for just a moment, then started again, needing to finish.

"The door burst open and Dad came in. He switched the light on, and Mum followed him into the room. They must have said something like, 'what's wrong, what's up?' I don't know. I can't remember, but I was still gripped to the bed and couldn't move. I looked around again to my right and Nana was gone! I remember gasping for breath and saying to Mum and Dad, 'It's my arm, it's my arm; please help me, please help me!'

"Only then did Dad pull back the covers of the bed. My right arm, just above the wrist and up to the elbow was bleeding; it had deep gouge marks in it!"

Mary held her right arm up, and pulled back the sleeve of her sweater, as if to show Daniel where the marks appeared.

"Right here! This is where they were!"

"How many marks were there?" Daniel asked.

"Five!" Mary replied. "Five, one for every finger and thumb on Nana's left hand!"

"What happened? Did your parents believe you?" Daniel asked.

"Not at first," Mary replied. "They were convinced that I had tried to harm myself in some way, but I was too young, the age that Ellie is now. I wasn't aware of myself! I didn't think like that!"

"When did they think differently?" Daniel continued to press.

"Well, Mum knew I was having these dreams of Nana, and I had explained to her how real they were. When I got the gouges on my right arm, she quickly put two and two together. She recalled the experience with Nana when we visited her in the Hospice.

"She and Dad were open minded. They agreed to get me some help, after the usual round of normal Doctors, you know GP's. They took me to see this parapsychologist, someone who had an understanding about strange phenomena and events that took place in a 'parallel world,' so to speak, someone that had been recommended to them."

"Who was it you saw? Professor Quatermass?"Daniel said, trying to make light of what Mary was telling him, if only to break the heavy atmosphere that had descended in the room. Indeed, it felt as if it was running throughout the entire house!

Mary, however, was still tense as she spoke. "No, it was this team; I think they were husband and wife. I don't know, can't remember, but they visited us at the house. They were a bit of a weird couple that took it all very seriously. They wandered around the house with this equipment, checking wavelengths or whatever, trying to find certain readings. Anyway, they seemed to know there stuff. I remember they set up cameras and placed them in my bedroom. I'd never been on the telly before, and I remember asking, 'Am I going to be on telly?' They'd sit downstairs sometimes throughout the night, while we were all asleep upstairs.

"Then one night they caught it on camera. I was so relieved. You couldn't see it as Nana, but they explained that there was some...I don't know…either some electro-magnetic presence or spirit body in the bedroom with me. It didn't look like a physical human body but like a white light or blob of light that flashed briefly in the dimly lit room."

Mary paused, leaned back, and picked up her empty glass. Holding it up in front of Daniel, she signalled for him to refill it. He promptly responded.

"I was in the local papers you know," Mary continued, glancing up at Dan, but her expression changed, as she turned her head away to look back into the flames of the fire. "This abnormal, odd girl who could conjure up ghosts, spirits, and demons, that's how I was seen. I had a terrible time at school, during those early years, hardly any friends; nobody wanted to talk to me or play with me. That's why I'm worried about Ellie. She doesn't make friends easily, Dan."

"Mary, Ellie's only just started a new school. It's early days; let's see what happens." Daniel paused to take a gulp of wine. "Anyway, you haven't finished the story…what happened to your grandmother's spirit?"

"They exorcised it—or me! They hypnotised me to create some sort of waking dream. Yes, I can remember it now; they hypnotised me to bring Nana's spirit back and, somehow, they tapped into me, my subconscious or whatever it is, to speak to me while Nana was there, telling me it was all a dream."

Dan leaned forward again. "Go on."

"It was an intense time. I remember the atmosphere in the house was just awful, but after they hypnotised me, the visions went away, and they didn't come again. Nana was gone!"

Just as Mary finished, the door to the sitting room creaked tentatively open. Both Daniel and Mary looked over. "Who's there?" Mary asked in a slightly edgy manner.

The door at the far end of the sitting room behind the sofa was dimly lit, since it was farthest from the fire, but they could make out the small frame of Eleanor, as she shuffled into the room.

"Ellie, what's up?" Mary asked.

"Mummy, I can't sleep," Eleanor replied. "I don't like it in my room. It's too dark!" Mary signalled for Eleanor to come in and she duly obliged. She came up to Mary and snuggled up to her. Mary affectionately rubbed the little girl's forehead. "Daddy, will you read me a story?" Eleanor asked.

"Of course Sweetheart, What would you like me to read to you?" Dan asked, pulling Eleanor up onto his lap.

"Could you read me the story of the three little pigs?" Eleanor asked.

Daniel was a little taken aback. "Ellie, I've read *The Three Little Pigs,* to you for the past few nights…and in the day, too! Why don't we read something else?"

"But daddy, I like the three little pigs! Can we have it, please?" Eleanor said with some determination and not about to change her mind.

"Why that one? What's so special about the three little pigs?" Dan asked.

"I just like it. Please, Daddy, please!" Eleanor pleaded with him.

Daniel relented. The three of them sat looking into the fire. Eleanor snuggled into her father's lap, and Daniel began…"Once upon a time, there lived three little pigs, and one day, the pigs decided that they would build homes for themselves. The first little pig went off to collect straw. When he had enough straw he brought it back to the others—'A straw house isn't very strong,' said the other pigs. 'Mine will be,' said the little pig, and he built his house out of straw. The second little pig went off to collect sticks. When he had enough sticks, he brought them back to the third little pig—'A stick house isn't very strong,' said the little pig. 'Mine will be,' said the other little pig, who had collected the sticks, and he continued to build his house out of sticks." Daniel continued to tell the story, about the third little pig that had built his house of bricks and the big bad wolf, who blew all but the brick house down. By then, Eleanor was asleep. Daniel tenderly but slowly lifted himself off of the sofa, carrying the young girl in his arms. He signalled to Mary that he'd carry her up to bed. As he left the room, Mary sat on the carpet and stared into the orangey red flames. As she did, a tear welled in her eye and rolled down her cheek.

Chapter 5

The moon seemed to shine more brightly that evening, more so than any other night in recent memory. The gusts of wind that had picked up earlier had passed and, although only a gentle breeze remained, rising and falling across the rugged night-time landscape, for October there was a chill in the air; winter was on its way. The wind had blown away the clouds, leaving a clear sky, draped over the moor.

In the valley below, the village of Ravenside was nestled in darkness. The only light that was apparent was that reflected from the cold slate roofs of the buildings from the unusually large and brimming moon.

Sitting up on the hillside, the Hungry Harshes sat bathed in moonlight. Inside the house everything was still. Mary and Daniel had acknowledged what an incredibly beautiful evening it had turned out to be and had gone to bed with their curtains pulled only partially together. This allowed the moonlight to break into their bedroom, casting a shimmering light across the bedroom walls and onto their bed. Their open bedroom window allowed for the faint breeze to now and then catch the curtains. Both the children were asleep; only a nightlight shone from beneath Eleanor's bedroom door. The only audible sound came from the grandfather clock in the entrance hall downstairs, the heavy ticking occasionally punctuated by the eloquent chime every hour.

The gentle, evening breeze that had soothed the night, suddenly picked up, and a huge gust swirled into Mary and Daniel's room, billowing the bedroom curtains and making them flap like a flag on a pole. Daniel was lying on his side on the right-hand side of the bed, facing away from Mary, who was lying on her back, arms out over the sheets. As the large gust blow in, it disturbed Mary, and she turned in her sleep onto her left side. As she settled into this new position, something subconsciously inside her kicked on. Her eyes flickered open and stared ahead of her. She knew something was wrong, but she didn't know what. She had been stirred awake, and her heart was pounding; she was afraid! She lay there for a moment, and then she opened her eyes to glance at the bedside clock. The digital red numbers, big and bold read 3:17. She felt something, but she didn't know what. She felt something or someone was in the room with her, besides Daniel. Her heart pounding and feeling breathless, she raised her head slightly to look toward the window, but she could see nothing, only the curtains settling back into position by the window. Fear gripped her and pinned her to the bed. She managed to pull herself up very slightly and looked over her shoulder to see Dan. He hadn't moved. He was still sound asleep and with his back to her. She looked beyond Daniel to the far bedroom wall, expecting to see something. The wall led to the bedroom door that led out onto the upstairs landing. All she could see was the wall, bathed in the shimmering moonlight and the shadow from the twisted branches of the horse chestnut tree at the front of the house silhouetted onto it.

Something creaked! *What was that?* she wondered. Was it her imagination? Did she hear the floorboards creak? Her breathing suddenly paused, and she took a hard gulp; her mouth was dry. She looked over her shoulder again toward the door. It was slightly ajar, as she had left it before she'd gone to bed that night, but there was no hall light on, so what little she could strain to see in the hall beyond the door was pitch black.

There it was again! The floorboard creaked again, and then again. This wasn't her imagination; this wasn't a bad dream. There was someone out there. It wasn't just the house creaking, either. This creaking had a pattern, like footsteps. It had purpose.

For a while, Mary turned back and put her head down on the pillow and pretended and prayed that this was just her active imagination, but there was another movement of the floorboards. Someone or something was coming up the stairs! Was it one of the children? Mary glanced back at the clock on her bedside; it read 3.21; four minutes had passed, but it felt far longer to Mary. She wanted to call out, but she didn't want to disturb Daniel if this was just her foolish imagination. On the other hand, she longed for Daniel to wake up. The floorboards creaked again. The sound was getting closer…someone was climbing the stairs! Mary's breathing became more intense, and she called out, "Who's there?" There was no reply, so she called again, "Who's there?" Still no reply, but the house fell silent, and the creaking of the floorboards stopped.

"David! Eleanor! Is that you?" Mary wanted to shout this out, but fear and a dry mouth resulted in her half whispering the question. There was no reply. Mary lay there, her back to the bedroom door, her calling out had not disturbed Daniel. For what seemed a long, agonising period, she heard nothing except the gusts of wind from outside. She looked up again at the bedside clock: 3.23.

Suddenly, the sound of the creaking floorboards started again. It was slow, but someone was walking now, just outside the bedroom door. Her heart pounding Mary called out again, this time louder. "Who's there? David, Eleanor this isn't funny!" Still there was no reply. Daniel still hadn't stirred. Mary's heart was pounding so loudly, she felt sure that Daniel must be able to hear it, but he remained asleep, he was lying right next to her, but it felt so far away. Mary didn't dare turn over, fearing what she thought she would see. Again, the floorboards creaked, but this time, the proximity to the bedroom was close, right outside the door. Someone was standing right outside of Mary's bedroom door.

The creaking stopped, but what replaced it terrified her even more and sent shivers down her back and shoulders, for outside the bedroom door came the sound of breathing, almost snorting. It was certainly not the breathing of a child! The breathing had a rhythmic pattern, but it sounded deep and laboured, like that of a fully-grown man who had smoked heavily all his life. It sounded exaggerated! Then the breathing stopped, and there came a new sound, sniffing, like a dog, but magnified five fold! And then the most alarming sound of all resonated from beyond the door. Whoever it was, whatever it was stopped sniffing and a low-level deep growl like that of an animal replaced it. Whoever or whatever it was, stood outside their bedroom door, looking in at them, staring down at both Mary and Daniel. Mary's mind was racing, she was shaking almost uncontrollably in bed, and she felt sure that both she and Dan were about to be attacked, possibly murdered! Finally, not able to contain herself any longer, she used her fear to confront the intruder. From the bottom of her stomach she began to groan, and as she did so, she slowly sat up in bed, and the groan began to rise in varying levels of pitch to a scream.

As Mary screamed, she could here shuffling outside the bedroom door and hastened movement. Whoever was suddenly panicked and began to move. Mary could hear the footsteps now turn and run from the door. It sounded as if they were retreating back down the stairs. The sound of the footfalls were now heavy and cumbersome! With the scream, Daniel jumped up and shot out of bed; he leapt across to the light switch and flicked it on, to find Mary standing in the middle of the bedroom looking toward the bedroom door. The shock of being suddenly awakened led him to scream back at Mary.

"Mary, what the hell is wrong!?"

"There's somebody in the house!" Mary wailed, standing rigid. Just as her voice tailed off, they both heard the shattering of glass from downstairs.

"Who the hell is that?" Mary could now sense the fear in Daniel's voice, his response panicky. He whipped open the bedroom door, and light from the bedroom spilled out into the hall. For the first time, Mary's fears were confirmed; someone had been standing at the door; there were wet, muddy footprints leading from the edge of the stairs to the door. In all the commotion, David had awakened up and run out of his room from the other end of the hall.

"David, stay there!" Daniel cried.

"Dad, what's up?" the boy asked. Daniel refused to answer. Instead, while he tried to assess the situation, he pointed a finger at his young son. "Just stay there!" From the landing, Daniel moved to the balcony and peered over. He could hear the back door to the kitchen being forced and more shattering glass. He switched on the landing lights, but when he peered down the stairs to the hall below, it was still in full darkness. He turned and switched the adjacent light on for the downstairs hall and shouted down the stairs.

"Who's there? Who the hell is down there?" There was no reply, but he felt a cold draft circulating from downstairs moving upstairs to where he was standing.

"I'm coming down! You better not be around when I get down there!" Daniel began to tentatively descend the stairs; they were covered in muddy footprints.

As he crept down each stair, it creaked loudly.

"David, come here!" Mary cried, summoning the boy to her. David promptly obliged and moved to his mother's side. She grabbed him and pulled him close.

As Daniel reached the landing level on the stairs, he stooped and peaked under, looking down the large hall of the house toward the rooms at the back. The door to the kitchen was wide open. In front of it, smashed and in pieces on the floor, lay a vase, which had been standing on a side table. The table itself was also knocked on its side on the hall floor. The house was eerily still, and all Daniel could hear was the faint gushing of the wind outside. He assumed that the intruder had come in or out of the house by the backdoor to the kitchen, and as the wind whipped up, he could feel the cold gusts sweeping up the hall, blowing through the door to the kitchen, which creaked back and forth. Daniel looked back up at Mary. "I think he's gone," he whispered.

"Just be careful, Daniel!" Mary said, pulling David closer.

Daniel looked back down the stairs through the hall and continued his descent. He noticed that the front door had remained untouched; there was no sign of forced entry there. As he reached the bottom of the stairs, he turned and surveyed the scene. Apart from the turned over table and broken vase, he could see a trail of mud leading down the hall to the open kitchen door. He glanced up at the wall. Along the wall, running all the way down to the kitchen door were what could only be described as scratch marks or nail marks. He checked either side of him, there were doors on either side of him; one led to the sitting room and the other to the dining room. Daniel moved tentatively toward the door for the dining room. It was shut and there were no muddy footprints leading to it. Plucking up courage, he grasped the handle of the door and swung it open. As he did, he stepped back from the doorway and peered in, bracing himself, as if expecting some physical assault. The room was in darkness, but the curtains were not drawn, allowing moonlight to light up the room. He reached in and switched on the light. The room was empty; there was no one in there. Daniel then moved tentatively across the hall to the sitting room door. It was ajar by about six inches. He couldn't remember whether he had closed it earlier that evening as he went up to bed. He pushed open he door, which creaked a little, and he pushed it open farther and stood back. The room was in total darkness; the curtains were drawn, and he peered into the darkness but could see nothing. Daniel drew a deep breath, his heart racing, as he felt for the light switch and flicked it on. The room was empty. Not wishing to linger in the room any longer than he had to, he made directly for the hearth and picked up an ornamental brass poker. He looked back down the hall, and saw Mary and David descending the stairs. Daniel signalled to them to stay put. He then drew a deep breath and began creeping down the hall toward the kitchen door, poker in hand; he felt the cool, icy wind all around him. He reached the kitchen door and peered in. The light was switched off. Whoever had entered had not bothered to switch the light on.

Just as he stepped into the kitchen, a shadow flashed passed him, which he caught out of the corner of his eye.

"Who's there?!" Daniel called, his voice as deep and aggressive as he could make it. He raised his right arm wielding the poker, but there was no reply. The shadow had come from outside the window, or so he thought. He couldn't be sure, but he turned to look toward the kitchen door that led into the garden. The door had been forced. The glass in the door had been smashed, and shards of splintered wood protruded at all angles from the door around the location of the lock. Daniel stopped, frozen! He squinted through the gloom to try and see out beyond the door into the garden. He strained to hear any movement from outside, but the thumping of his heart drowned out all sound.

"Mary, Mary!" Daniel had scoured every last inch of the kitchen, and apart from the obvious entry damage, all he could see was the trail of muddy footprints that led across the floor to the hall. He lowered the poker gripped in his right hand.

"Mary, it's all clear. Whoever was here has gone!" he shouted up to his wife, still standing on the stairs.

Mary ran down the remaining stairs and straight to the phone in the hall situated on a small table by the side of the main front door. She picked up the receiver and dialled 999. "Yes, this is an emergency!

I'd like the police!" Daniel stepped back into the hallway.

"Yes, Police? I'd like to report a break in. Somebody is breaking into our house! No, no, they're not here now; we think they have gone! No, no nobody's hurt, thank God!"

Daniel interjected and started talking to Mary, as she gripped the phone nervously with both hands "It was a *forced* entry; the door's damaged; there's some broken glass." Mary nodded and continued to speak into the phone "Yes, yes, it was a forced entry. There's damage to our kitchen. Please get here! Yes ,of course, it's the Hungry Harshes, off Meadow Lane in Ravensdale. Yes, we're the house that sits up on the hill. Please get here quickly! No, nobody is hurt; we're all ok!"

As Mary said this, she realised that she hadn't seen Eleanor. She turned in horror to Daniel standing by her side. "Dan, I forgot Eleanor!" She put the phone down and ran upstairs past David and up to Eleanor's room. She flung the door open and peered across the room in the far corner where Eleanor's bed was. She could see Eleanor lying in bed, with her eyes shut, but something was wrong! Eleanor hadn't awakened during the furore and remained in a very deep sleep. Mary moved closer to her and noticed that, even in her sleep, Eleanor was disturbed. Her face was a ghostly white, and she was sweating and convulsing!

"Daniel! Daniel! Oh my god, Daniel, please come!"

Hearing Mary's call, Daniel ran up the stairs and got into Eleanor's room just as Mary had put her arm behind the girl's neck and started attempting to wake her. The child's night-light wasn't sufficient to see what was going on, so he flicked the main switch. Rushing to Mary's side, he joined her in patting the little girl's cheek. "I'll go and get a cold flannel!" Daniel said and sprinted off to the bathroom.

"Please, Eleanor, please wake up!" Mary cradled Eleanor as her shoulders jerked forward, throwing her head into Mary's arms. All Mary could do was to hold her tight, and, as she did so, the Eleanor began to settle down, her arms went limp, and her breathing appeared to return to normal. Her eyelids flickered, just as Daniel returned. He crouched down and mopped the child's forehead and cheek. Her eyes flickered open, and she stared up into her mother's face.

"Thank God, thank God!" Mary sighed. She laid Eleanor back onto the bed, her head on the pillow.

"Mummy, what happened? What's the matter?" Eleanor asked.

"I don't know, my love. You were having a bad dream," Mary replied, attempting to soothe her daughter.

"I was scared, Mummy! I'm really scared! it was chasing me. I ran as fast as I could, but it was chasing me. I couldn't get away!"

Mary closed her eyes and swallowed hard; she had a sense of what was coming, but she had to ask it, anyway. "What was chasing you darling? What was it?"

"It was the big bad Wolf! He was trying to catch me!"

Mary and Daniel both looked at each other, then Mary looked down at Eleanor. She brushed Eleanor's hair off her forehead and was about to reply, but Eleanor, sensing the look between her parents said, "What, what is it? Did the big bad Wolf chase you and Daddy, too?"

"No darling, no," Mary replied. "You're safe now."

Outside, the wind died away, the moon continued to shine ever more brightly in the sky, and only a few broken clouds remained, revealing a now clear, night sky. In the distance, the siren from a mobilised police car warbled in the night, the vehicle getting closer and closer to the Hungry Harshes.

At the back of the garden, where the lawn rolled up to the boundary fence and the woodland beyond, the creature lay, watching from behind the safety of the trees. From the position it occupied, it had maintained a view of everything. It had escaped to the trees before Daniel had a chance to reach the back door and switch the lights on. It was able to observe Daniel standing in the broken-down doorway. Strong and powerful, it could have taken its prey easily enough, but it sought only to stalk it from the safety of the trees and the surrounding woodland. It had also observed the activity upstairs, the bedroom light of the little girl's room flicking on. With the sirens getting closer, the creature pricked up its ears and diverted its attention from the house. Its long, black, shaggy hair and coat were wet and sleek from the evening dampness, both in the air and on the beast, but the moisture failed to trouble it. Its hands were claws with razor-like nails, covered in thick black hair. It growled beneath its breath, an eerie inhuman noise, not that of any man. Watching the events unfolding around the house, it scent-marked its territory by urinating against a mature beech tree standing by the fenced-off boundary. The resulting steam rose up and dispersed around the creature's body.

As the police car pulled up the lane to the house, the creature pushed its massive shoulders down, to allow it to heave its large, sleek, but muscular frame up onto its hind legs. Its eyes were red and bloodshot, its gait wide, as it placed one huge claw on the trunk of the beech tree. The creature again growled under its breath, as it saw two Police Officers stepping out of the vehicle. As it growled, the creature bared its teeth in an angry, frustrated snarl. It had been thwarted; on this occasion, it had been prevented from doing what it had set out to achieve. As the creature watched the two men enter the house, it pricked up its ears once more, dropped down onto its forelegs, and headed of into the night. It would be back.

Chapter 6

The first Police to arrive that evening at the Hungry
Harshes were greeted by a terrified Foster Family.
Two Officers on evening patrol from nearby Skipton
had been the first to receive the call from the station. It
was procedure that, if there were any late-night
incidents reported at any of the local villages around
the Skipton area, and there were no local village
police presence, then the first call would go to Skipton
Police station. The two officers took statements,
looked around the house, observed the muddy
footprints, broken door, and scratches on the wall,
asked if anything had been taken, took notes, and
drank tea! They reassured Dan and Mary that it was
unlikely that whoever it was would be back again that
night. They said it was all right to shut the back door;
they agreed that what they observed was odd,
peculiar for an opportunist Burglar to leave such
scratches on the walls, and that, as a result of this and
other certain anomalies, would file a report with a
recommendation that a crime scene be set up and, at
the very least, a follow up visit to the Foster home by

a more senior officer would be necessary, which would probably occur in the morning.

With that, they briefly perused the outside area around the Hungry Harshes, shining flashlights up the rear garden and, beyond, into the dense thicket and trees to the rear of the garden. Satisfied that they had taken all they needed to take for the evening, they bid Dan and Mary farewell, leaving the Fosters to endure a fitful night of worry and anxiety.

* * *

The next morning began with bright, clear skies. Dan and Mary were up early; the pair had hardly slept a wink during the remainder of the night and both looked drawn as a result. Daniel had opted to sleep downstairs on the family's sofa; unfortunately, his mind had raced all night with the evening's activity. Mary had taken Eleanor into their bed and, while Eleanor slept well, Mary had not slept a wink, spending the entire night watching over her daughter and listening for her breathing, watching any sudden movements in the girl. Shocked by what they had found when the couple had entered the little girl's room that night, they both agreed that they would rise early, not wait for the Police, and get Eleanor to a Doctor.

As a result of a combination of shock and tiredness, there was little said at breakfast that morning. The couple decided to keep David off from school for the day. They all dutifully sat around the kitchen table eating breakfast in virtual silence. No one in the family wanted to discuss what they had experienced the night before. Mary rang the local

Surgery the moment she knew it was open and booked an emergency, morning appointment with Doctor Ventham.

A call from an officer at the Skipton Constabulary informed them that, as a matter of procedure, an officer would call at the house that morning, around ten a.m. and asked if someone would be at home and available to meet the officer. This provided the family enough time to get Eleanor to the Surgery.

The journey down the hill from the family home into town could have been a brisk walk on such a fine, autumnal morning, but both Dan and Mary agreed that this would be no stroll into town. Wendy had called round to see how the family, and especially Mary, was doing, following the crow incident some days earlier. She was met with an ashen-faced family, solemnly, but purposefully making their way to the car. Once Mary had provided a brief update to a gobsmacked and disbelieving Wendy, the family pulled off the drive with a screech, leaving Wendy to watch over the house.

* * *

Once in the surgery, the family quickly moved through the waiting area to see Doctor Ventham. His small office was unusually crowded, as the entire Foster family occupied the room. The doctor looked at Mary, who still wore a Band Aid-style sticking plaster to her forehead. Believing that this consultation was for her, he initially paid scant attention to Daniel and the two children.

"So, Mary, how are you?" the doctor asked. As he did so, he focused his eyes away from the screen of his PC to Mary who, by now, was sitting forward on a chair with Eleanor on her lap. The doctor looked down at Mary's arms around the little girl's waist and was not remiss in detecting a faint trembling in the mother. The doctor thought this odd; he then looked up at Daniel, who was standing by the small room's door biting his nails. David stood behind him, half leaning against the wall and half disappearing behind the screening curtain that surrounded the bed.

"No, Doctor, you misunderstand!" Mary said.

"It's not me; it's my daughter. It's Eleanor…you see…" Mary's voice trailed off, and she looked down at her hands, as she unravelled a tissue she kept up the sleeve of her cardigan. She began to weep gently and blew her nose. Daniel, seeing his wife was upset, picked up the conversation.

"You see, Doctor, we had a break in at the house last night. We're all a bit tired this morning…" Daniel's voice too began to trail off.

"Oh, I'm sorry to hear that," the doctor said sympathetically. "Was anyone hurt?"

Daniel's concentration kicked back in.

"No, no but, as a matter of coincidence, we found our daughter in bed unconscious; we couldn't wake her!"

"That's right, Doctor!" Mary interjected. "She was convulsing, if you like, still asleep but shaking. it took a while to wake her. It frightened us!"

The Doctor looked at both parents, taking in what they had to say. When they had finished, he got up from his chair. "Can your daughter hop up on the bed, please?" he asked. Mary released her hands, and

Eleanor, who now seemed more composed, if not a little pale, walked across the surgery floor and hopped up onto the bed.

"That's it, just sit there," the Doctor said in an authoritative manner. "Now, what's your name?" he asked Eleanor.

"Eleanor," the little girl replied.

"Eleanor, that's a nice name. How old are you?" the doctor asked, as he placed his hands under the child's chin and felt all around her jaw.

This forced Eleanor to look up at him. "I'm five!" she declared.

"Five! And are you at school, yet?" the doctor asked, reaching into his pocket for a small hand torch, which he shined first in Eleanor's right eye and then her left eye, forcing the girl to blink and pull her head away.

"That's all right. Hold your head still and look at me," the doctor said. "Can you just roll your sleeve up for me please, Eleanor?" he then asked, pointing to her right arm. Eleanor looked across at her mother for confirmation, slipped off her coat, and rolled up her sleeve. Doctor Ventham pulled out a blood pressure kit and strapped it around the girl's small arm. Eleanor looked quizzically, as he began to pump.

Eleanor could feel the band tightening. "It hurts a bit now!" she exclaimed.

The doctor ignored her and kept pumping, then finally stopped. Reading the dial, he released the pump, and the subsequent pressure of the band was released. Taking a pen from his jacket pocket, he turned without looking at either Mary or Daniel and started writing at his desk.

"All right, you can roll your sleeve down now," he instructed Eleanor, without once looking back at her. Mary and Daniel exchanged glances, while the doctor continued to write on his pad. Doctor Ventham then stopped, suddenly, and swung his chair around to face Mary.

"Has Eleanor ever had any fits or seizures previously to last night?" he asked, looking at Mary.

"No, Eleanor has never suffered from anything like that!" Mary said.

"Has she suffered any accidents or recent injuries, either at home or school?" he asked.

"No, none that I can think of," Mary replied, again, this time looking across at Eleanor, who was now swinging her legs over the bed. "Eleanor, sweetheart, have you had any accidents recently, where you've hurt yourself and not told Mummy?"

"No, Mummy," Eleanor said.

"That's ok. Her blood pressure is fine," Doctor Ventham broke in, "and I cannot see anything adversely wrong with Eleanor. If you like I could write to Leeds General and recommend that they make an appointment for a neuro scan for Eleanor, just as a precaution." the doctor threw the question, first at Mary, and then looked across to Daniel.

"How quickly?" Mary replied, sensing that pressing the need for urgency with the doctor was what was needed.

"Let me get a letter off to them today. You should hear from the hospital no later than the middle of next week. Please let me know if you have no letter with an appointment by then," the doctor said.

With that, the consultation ended, and the family left the surgery for home. As they left, Mary sensed in her heart that what Eleanor had experienced the night before was neither physical nor anatomical, but altogether something completely different. Something an ordinary North Yorkshire GP could not easily diagnose.

* * *

By the time the family returned to the Hungry Harshes, they were greeted by a midnight-blue Vauxhall Omega, parked on the drive to the side of the house. Inside, the solitary figure of a man sat at the steering wheel. He looked up into his head mirror, saw the car approach from behind, up the narrow drive, and began to open the door to climb out.

Daniel pulled up a few feet short of the visitor's bumper, watching him all the way. The man pulled up his handbrake and climbed out of the car, then moved toward Daniel.

"Good Morning. A fine morning, isn't it? Would you agree?" the man said, extending the question to both Daniel and Mary.

"That depends upon the evening you had before!" Daniel replied, in a slightly icy manner. The man managed a half grin and extended his right hand toward Daniel.

"Oh, forgive me, my name is Harry Toms, Detective Inspector Harry Toms from North Yorkshire Constabulary." With that, Daniel timidly extended his right arm to shake the stranger's hand.

As he did so, DI Toms pulled out a wallet with his left hand to reveal a police identification card. Toms continued to hold the card on view, first for Daniel then for Mary. The officer reached across the Fosters' car bonnet to extend his greeting to Mary by shaking her hand.

"I'm Daniel Foster," Daniel introduced himself and looked across at Mary, opening his hand in her direction. "This is my wife, Mary, and our two children, David and Eleanor. Shall we go in?" Daniel directed Toms toward the broken rear door that led into the kitchen.

"Nice place you've got here, Mr Foster, very nice!" Stopping at the rear door, Toms noticed the broken frame and the broken pane of glass in the door.

"Oh! I assume this is where the intruder came in?" Toms turned and asked quizzically of Daniel, while indicating the door.

"Yes, this is where we believe it came in."

"It?" Toms came to an abrupt halt and turned to look at Daniel in surprise. He was quick to pick up on what he thought was a discrepancy.

"It, he, she! We don't know!" Daniel replied wearily.

"Of course, Sir," Toms replied.

Detective Inspector Harry Toms had been a loyal and established servant of the North Yorkshire Police service for some twenty-three years. As an eighteen-year-old Toms joined the force as a Bobby on the beat, who would regularly be posted to patrol the Headingley area, a district of the city of Leeds. Now, at forty-one, his career and service had been steady, if not spectacular. He'd been promoted to Sergeant at thirty-two and worked eight years behind a desk in Headingley before opting to go plain clothes and becoming Detective Inspector. Tall and athletically built at six-foot-one, he liked to keep in shape by either running or rowing. He had been married but was now divorced by some ten years. He had one son, an eighteen-year-old who lived with his mother and was about to enrol in a university course. Toms himself had not remarried but chose to live in a flat just outside of Headingley. He had a companion, a woman of forty-three, who worked as a librarian in Leeds city centre, but she had her own flat near his.

* * *

Toms' piercing blue eyes surveyed the damage to the door and the trail left in the kitchen, as both he and the family slowly entered the house. Mary broke off from the group and moved to the sink, picking up the kettle.

"Anyone want Tea?" Mary asked. "I know I do!"

"Yes, please, Mrs Foster, white, two sugars. Thank you," Toms replied, as his eyes scoured the room. David moved past the group and out into the hall to the Living Room, where he embarked upon playing his Playstation. Eleanor decided to stay in the kitchen and pulled out a chair from the kitchen table and sat down. Resting her chin in both hands, elbows on the table, she continued to observe Toms, as he squinted and strained to observe minute detail pertaining to the break-in of the kitchen. Daniel, Mary, and Eleanor watched as Toms moved into the hall from the kitchen.

"Am I right to assume the intruder made his way from the kitchen to the hall?" Toms asked, with his back to the family, in a mild but identifiable Yorkshire accent.

"Yes, we believe so. I...I guess the muddy footprints suggest that must be the case, just look at the trail," Daniel replied, pointing to the floor. As he entered the hall, the Detective Inspector stopped in his tracks. He dutifully peered down at the floor. "Bye, what the hell happened here?" Toms asked in amazement, looking down the hall at the scratch marks on the wall. He observed the turned-over table and vase, left as requested by the officer who called the previous evening. He also observed the muddy trail of footprints running down the hall to the foot of the stairs. *Strange,* he thought. If these were the footprints of the intruder, and he assumed they were, they were not as clearly defined as many he had seen—not as defined as those of a normal man's, for example. There were no obvious boot tracks!

"You'll have to refrain from washing the floor, Mrs Foster, until we can get a good copy of a footprint!" Toms shouted down the hall, back to Mary still in the kitchen, now stirring the pot of tea.

Daniel watched as Toms slowly walked to the foot of the stairs, turned, and looked up.

"It says in your statement that you heard the intruder, as he came up the stairs." Toms was looking to qualify this point.

"Yes, that's right," Mary said, as she squeezed past Daniel, carrying a mug of tea down to Toms.

Toms accepted the mug of tea. "Thank you kindly…er, now, let me just ask again, but to the best of your knowledge, and from what you can see, nothing has been taken, at least nothing of any value?" Toms asked.

"Nothing at all," Daniel replied. Toms took a sip of tea and then looked at Mary. "Now, did anyone see the intruder?"

"No, no," Mary said.

Daniel noticed that his wife had begun to shake. He moved over to her and placed a reassuring arm around her shoulder.

"All we heard was his breathing!" Mary said.

"His *breathing*?" Toms asked, seizing on this point.

"Yes," Mary continued. "I heard him…it…get to the top of the stairs; he was standing at our door!"

"Was the door open or closed?" Toms asked.

"Open, slightly ajar. I leave it with a two- or three-inch crack…so I can hear the children," Mary replied.

"And which door would this be?" Toms asked, as he began to slowly climb the stairs, all the while looking up at the array of bedroom and bathroom doors set out on the landing.

"That one, there!" Mary replied. She had followed Toms up the first three steps and pointed to the door at the top of the stairs. Toms reached the top of the stairs, turned, and looked from the floor down the landing, following the trail of mud all the way. He then looked back down the stairs at the trail of mud on each step.

"Mrs Foster, may I ask, do you have anything of great value upstairs?"

"Yes!" Mary replied.

"Do you mind me asking what that might be?" Toms asked.

"Our children!"

Toms, surprised by the answer, looked sharply down the stairs at Mary. "I understand your concern, Mrs Foster; I meant *other* valuables, such as jewellery? Paintings? Furniture? Money?"

"I know what you meant!" Mary replied sharply. "But we don't really have anything of great value upstairs." Toms began to slowly descend the stairs. Mary could see his mind turning over as he did so.

"Apologies, Mr Foster, but you can see where I'm coming from. What type of intruder breaks into a house, when everyone is upstairs asleep, but takes nothing from downstairs where, I assume, most of the valuable items are to be found? Instead, under risk of detection, the intruder makes his way upstairs where, as you say, nothing of any great value can be found — except your children! He or she then makes good his or her escape, upon being interrupted without taking a single thing!" Both Mary and Daniel looked at each other, neither saying a word to the other. Toms by now had stopped three steps up from the bottom of the stairs, his eyes darting between Daniel and Mary looking for some response.

"Mr and Mrs Foster," Toms continued. "Can you tell me if you know of anyone who would want to harm you or your children?"

"No, no one whatsoever!" Daniel said.

"You have your own business; do you not, Mr Foster?"

"Yes I do. I'm a freelance Systems Consultant."

"And you have no business competitors…let's say, people who would have a grudge resulting from some unsavoury encounter in the past?" Toms asked.

"None that I can think of," Daniel replied.

"Look, when can we begin to put our house back in order?" Mary asked, fearing that the exchange was getting off the subject.

Toms sighed. "Ok, here's what I would like to do; get a forensic bod over here today, basically just dust for some fingerprints, try and get an impression or recreation of a footprint, and maybe take a few pictures around the house, say here, the hall and stairs, the kitchen, and upstairs. You can confirm that the intruder appears to have not entered any other room?"

"It would seem so," Daniel said.

"Better to be thorough. We'll check all the rooms downstairs. Oh! I assume you have insurance for any broken items?" Toms asked, descending the remaining stairs and walking past Daniel and Mary, down the hall, to the kitchen door. Turning to face both Mary and Daniel, Toms looked again at the long deep scratches along the wall.

"Once our forensic guys have been and gone, you can clean up…I'd like to get some pictures of this, though," Toms said, pointing at the scratches. As he moved back into the kitchen, Toms noticed Eleanor still sitting at the kitchen table, with her hands under her chin, looking back at him. He smiled at the little girl to which she responded in kind.

"Do you have any idea who else may have done this?" Daniel asked. "I mean, if this is someone outside of anyone we could think of, are there any likely suspects?"

Toms turned and sighed. "There's always the known criminal element, Mr Foster, people we are aware of who could be active, but it would be unusual for them to come to a community as small and remote as this to commit such a crime." Toms then reached into his jacket pocket and pulled out a small white card; printed on it was his name and contact details. "Before I forget, here is a card with my phone number. If you can think of anything else you might wish to tell me or remember about last night, then please give us a call or at least leave a message." Toms handed the card to Daniel.

"If there's nothing else, I'll thank you, Mr Foster, for the tea and be on my way." Toms turned to walk out of the kitchen door, but he stopped abruptly and turned to Daniel. "Oh, Sir, one last thing. Could you please reverse your car so I can get out?"

* * *

That afternoon, a solitary forensic examiner drove the long journey up to the house from Leeds Constabulary to complete the initial police investigation and analysis. Both Daniel and Mary kicked around the house like a couple of spare brides at a wedding, not knowing what to do, while the examiner endeavoured to take worthwhile photographs of presumed footprints on the floor, dusted for prints along door frames and on certain furniture, and took pictures of many of the rooms in the house, everywhere the intruder had been suspected of visiting. Work complete, he packed up his bag and his camera and headed off, leaving Daniel and Mary the task of tidying and cleaning up after the break in. Mary reflected on the past few days' events. She looked at her family. David was David, a young boy not unduly affected by what had happened. Daniel seemed both perplexed and winded, like he was punch drunk, on the ropes! Mary's confession about her past in the light of the broken window and the bird some days earlier, together with the break in, seemed to have knocked the stuffing out of him. Eleanor, well Eleanor on the surface appeared fine, a little pale, maybe, but otherwise her normal self; she'd play on her own and retreat into her own world as children of her age often did. Mary had decided that she would watch Eleanor closely; after all, this was what Doctor Ventham had advised. Watching her daughter was natural for her, anyway, part of her motherly instinct. More now, than over the previous week or more, did Mary feel that she would like her mother to be with her. She had decided that she would call her first thing in the morning and fix a date over the next week or so for her mother to come and stay at the house. Everything she felt had been suddenly turned on its head. Life had been good when they had first moved in, so much optimism for the future. Now, both Mary and Daniel could not make sense of what was happening. They needed some stability in the home; Mary's mother would help provide that, she thought.

Gingerly, Daniel bent over and lifted up the hall table that had been knocked over during the break in. With care, he picked up the broken vase and all its broken pieces, placed them in a bag, and carried it to the dustbin. Mary had solemnly, but with purpose, filled a bucket with hot soapy water, got a mop, and had begun to mop the floor of all the mud. A carpenter had called around upon Daniel's request to fix the broken kitchen door. The cosmetic appearance to the house, following the break in, was returning to normal. For the family, this would take a little longer. As Mary completed the mopping of the floor, she hoped that, now, maybe just for a while, the family could get a bit of a break, no more hiccups, no more nightmares rocking their world. It was now 4.15 p.m. in the afternoon. David was in his room, Eleanor was watching television in the living room, and Daniel had returned to his study. The phone rang, which gave Mary a start. *What now, who is this?* she wondered. She approached the ringing phone in the hall with a sense of foreboding, stopped, then picked up the receiver.

"Hello?" Mary said hesitantly.

"Hello, is Mrs Foster there, please?" came the voice down the line.

"This is she," Mary replied.

"Mrs Foster, good afternoon. I hope I'm not troubling you," came the voice.

Mary thought for a moment and caught her breath; a faint smile almost broke across her face. *How,* she wondered, *could this stranger possibly add any more trouble to my day than I already have*?

"Who's calling?" Mary asked.

"It's Mrs Forbes, here, from the school."

"Mrs Forbes, what's up? Is something wrong?" Mary's reaction naturally was to think negative thoughts.

"Well, we may have a problem with Eleanor." Mary's heart sank. "What sort of problem? If it's about today, I did explain when I—"

"No it's not about today. I know Eleanor hasn't been with us for very long, but it would be simpler if you came in for a chat, just briefly, nothing too serious, but something the school has noticed," Mrs Forbes said.

"What, what is it?" Mary asked, fearing that what she was going to be told in some way related to the recent problems at home with Eleanor.

"It's simpler if you come in. When would suit you?" Mrs Forbes asked.

"All right, let me come down tomorrow morning. Ten-thirty ok?"

"See you then, and thank you again, Mrs Foster." The caller hung up, leaving Mary alone on the other end of the phone.

Alone and tired she replaced the receiver and sighed. She had no idea what this meeting at the school could be about, but she thought there and then that her life had changed and, from one thing to another, it would never be the same again!

Chapter 7

If Mary had secured precious little sleep the previous evening, the night of the break in, then she certainly did not get much more the following evening. Once again, Daniel slept in the spare room, while Mary slept with Eleanor in her bed. Lying next to the little girl on her side, Mary watched Eleanor's every movement and listened for every breath. Another reason for keeping her awake was the fear that the intruder might return that evening.

Mary had a strong sense that this was no opportunist break in. This had specific purpose, specific motive to harm the family. She kept this fear from Daniel. She was also aware that she did not over-elaborate her feelings of fear to Detective Inspector Toms, for she had no cast-iron evidence about who the possible perpetrator might be and for what reason they would want to harm her family.

Something else she had kept from Daniel, as well, was the phone call from the school that afternoon. She had no idea why she had been summoned so abruptly and, besides, she did not confront Eleanor with an intention to understand the nature of the problem.

Best left alone, there had been quite enough going on for one day, and Eleanor, Mary felt, had gone through quite enough!

* * *

The next morning, the family attempted to adopt an air of normality. Daniel ran David back to school then returned home to work from his study. Mary decided that Eleanor should have another day at home, in order to watch her. Again, Eleanor seemed on the face of it to be the picture of health, but Mary was not taking any chances. While Daniel was out taking David to school, Mary decided to give her mother a call. Alice sounded surprised to hear from her daughter so soon after last talking with her.

"Hello, Dear, not making sure that I have made arrangements for next week are you?" Alice asked, slightly tongue in cheek.

"Ah! Well! Yes, Mum, yes. Just seeing if everything is still on?" Alice could hear the trembling in her daughter's voice; she sounded tired, she thought.

"What's a matter, dear? Is everything all right?"

Mary couldn't hold her emotions in check any longer; her eyes welled up, and her voice broke, as she started to cry.

"Oh, Mum! It's been terrible, just terrible!" Mary sobbed.

"What's the matter, dear?" Alice enquired, her voice taking on a soothing tone.

"It's just been a nightmare here these past couple of days. I don't know what is happening. Mary went through everything with her mother, everything that had beset the family in the past day or so, since they'd last spoken, including the break in, Eleanor's convulsions, and the call from the school.

"Mary dear, try and stay calm. Now, no one was hurt, were they? How's Eleanor now?"

"I'm watching her. I'm scared, Mum. I can't let her out of my sight. I just don't know what will happen next."

Alice knew where this was going to go, so she decided she had better offer the suggestion before being asked. "Mary, would you prefer if I came up sooner?" she asked tentatively.

"That would be good, Mum!" Mary replied. "Could you come up at the weekend?"

"I'll see what I can do, but I think that should be all right."

Having influenced her mother's decision to visit earlier, Mary felt a little more soothed. She prepared herself for the school visit and Mrs Forbes.

* * *

The day had begun completely differently from the previous one. Instead of fine autumn sunshine, the clouds had rolled in overnight off of a stiff, north-westerly wind and left the morning grey and certainly cooler. With an aggressive breeze to deal with, Mary arrived at Ravensdale Primary School for her ten-thirty appointment. Parking her car in the school car park, adjacent to the main building, she climbed out to notice the children from the school coming out for a morning break; it was playtime. As she began walking up to the school entrance, she chanced to look up beyond the children in the concreted play area to the windows that looked out onto the schoolyard. What caught her attention was the sight of Mrs Forbes standing at her office window, staring straight back down at her. The two women made eye contact, but Mrs Forbes did not offer a smile. Mary did not respond with a smile, either. As she walked into the school's reception, she noticed the window with its access to the school's administration office. She bent down and looked in.

"Good Morning. It's Mrs Foster here to see Mrs Forbes."

"Ah, Mrs Foster; yes, please take a seat. I'll let Mrs Forbes know you are here," said the rather prim but elegant lady, sitting behind a desk but facing the office window. Mary took a seat on an unusually low chair in the reception. The school was buzzing. As she waited, she noticed many children coming and going through the main reception. Many of them looked to be about the same age as Eleanor. Mary wondered if any of these children were in Eleanor's class. Indeed, was Eleanor making friends with any of them? Mary didn't know. She looked around the entrance; she was nervous, anxious about what she was about to hear, but she tried to take her mind off her anxiety by studying the walls of the school entrance. Ahead of her was a huge collage of leaves and sticks, stuck to a piece of card on the wall. The picture read "Colours of Autumn" and was designed to show how the children had discovered and brought together the many different types of leaves from the local trees. Everything that had been gathered by the children had been stuck together in the shape of one large tree and included the reds of Acers, Copper Beeches, and Cherries to the ambers and golds of Acers, Horse Chestnuts, and Maples to the greens of the Ash and browns of the Oak. Mary had decided that, while she waited, it would be a good idea to test her knowledge and try to identify as many different varieties of tree as possible. She got to about eight before, out of the corner of her eye, she saw Mrs Forbes approaching her.

"Mrs Foster, we meet again! Thank you very much for coming in to see me this morning. Hope you're ok? Are you?" Mrs Forbes was her normal exuberant self. She shook Mary's hand and led her down a narrow corridor to the headmistress' office. Standing at the entrance to the door, a good five or six paces ahead of Mary, she stopped, turned, and indicated for Mary to enter. Mary duly walked in, followed by Mrs Forbes.

"Please sit down," Mrs Forbes said.

"Mr Forbes, I think you ought to know that I have kept Eleanor off school again today," Mary said, initiating the conversation. We had a bit of an incident at home the other evening, a scare, and we found Eleanor in bed, unconscious, convulsing and, for a while, we found it difficult to bring her round!"

Mrs Forbes listened intently, as she moved to sit down on a chair across from where Mary had positioned herself.

"Good gracious! Is it serious?" the headmistress asked, concerned that one of her pupils should suffer such a misfortune.

Mary sighed. "We don't know yet; we're hoping to get an appointment at a nearby clinic, possibly for a scan to determine if Eleanor has developed anything serious."

"Has anything like this happened to Eleanor before?" Forbes asked.

"No, not at all," Mary replied wearily.

"Oh, you poor thing, you must be worried out of your life." Forbes said, attempting to be of some comfort. Mary's initial salvo had thrown her from the purpose of the meeting, but she resolved to come round to the issue at hand.

"Please keep me informed of how Eleanor is," she said. "It is because of Eleanor that I have asked you here this morning."

Mary stiffened. "I suspected it would be, what's happened?"

"Well, it's not so much a case of what has happened," Forbes continued, "but more a case of what we have noticed in Eleanor in the short time she has been with us."

Mary looked perplexed.

"You see, this came to my attention from Mrs Shand, Eleanor's Teacher. I've asked her to join us. She should be with us any minute." As she said it, Mrs Forbes got up from the chair and moved to a filing cabinet across the small office. She picked up and carried back to the chair a large folder which read 'Eleanor Foster.' Just as she sat back down, there was a short rap on the door, and Mrs Shand walked in.

Little Pig, Little Pig

"Ah, Mrs Shand, please take a seat." The three women sat around a small, circular table. Forbes placed the large folder in the centre of the table.

"Ok, the reason why we wanted to talk to you," Mrs Forbes began, "was with regard some slightly unusual things we've been seeing from Eleanor."

Again, Mary felt her heart start to race.

"I realise that Eleanor has only been with us a day or two," Mrs Forbes continued, "so please realise we are by no means judging her this early."

"What exactly is it that my daughter has done?" Mary broke in.

"Well, Mrs Shand noticed that Eleanor likes to go off on her own during break time. She doesn't tend to stay with any of the other children."

"Is that so unusual?" Mary asked. "She has only just joined the school; naturally, I would expect that it would take a bit of time for her to make friends."

Mrs Shand, who had been sitting listening, dutifully broke in. "If I can just say, yes you're right, it is still very early, but I would have expected Eleanor to begin mixing with some of the other children in my class. Please remember, the school term is not that old, and a lot of the children are new to the school and new to each other..."

"But?" Mary interrupted, slightly impatiently.

"But I have observed that, while other children have formed bonds, Eleanor has also been offered the opportunity to make some friends with other girls in the class. She hasn't warmed to it." Mr Shand's voice trailed off, her body language coupled with her expression, to Mary, seemed timid, almost apologetic.

"But let's be realistic, here, this is only early days!" Mary retorted. "I know my daughter. She is an easy-going, friendly girl."

"Oh no, that isn't what I was trying to imply," Mrs Shand said. Conscious of the fact that she might be stepping on Mary's sensitivities, she backtracked slightly from her position. She's a well mannered, quiet girl, who does what you ask in class. It's just that, on the occasions I've noticed her in the playground, most of the children play within close proximity to each other. Eleanor tends to disappear off to the perimeter of the playground on her own. It's my belief that she is a somewhat sensitive and introverted child who creates imaginary stories for herself."

Mary listened but grew steadily more impatient. "So, what you are telling me is that she is a little bit of a loner. Don't most kids, at some time or another, retreat within themselves and make up stories and imaginary friends?"

"We didn't say imaginary friends, Mrs Foster," Mrs Forbes interrupted. Mrs Forbes gave a knowing look across to Mrs Shand and continued. "I think perhaps we should let you have a look at something else we've noticed in Eleanor's early work." With that, Forbes lifted the folder from the table. "This is Eleanor's, Mrs Foster. It's her folder for keeping artwork and drawings." Forbes pulled out a number of pieces of paper, somewhere between A4 and A3 size. She laid them back down on the coffee table and presented them, facing what she believed was the right way to Mary. "All the classes in year one have

artwork and drawing sessions; it's designed to
develop the children's hand-eye coordination and
develop their flare for creativity. Mrs Shand brought
this to my attention, after she observed Eleanor's
work, during an art hour earlier this week. I wouldn't
say that it's too alarming, and I do not wish to make
too much of a point of it, but we thought you might
wish to have a look at Eleanor's work."

Mary looked down at the pictures and, again, as it
had done a few days earlier, when she had seen
Eleanor drawing at the kitchen table at home, fear
began to grip her. As Mrs Forbes gently spaced the
pictures out on the table, it was clear that they
showed consistency, but they were no product of an
artistic young mind. Instead, the pictures were nearly
all identical to Eleanor's earlier work. Many of them
were just coloured in a black scrawl. There was no
definition, no clear image of anything that Mary could
identify; from many of them, they were just a black
scribble, and yet they appeared aggressive and
threatening!

"We looked at these, Mrs Shand and myself, and
we tried to make out what this creature is." Mary cast
her eyes to two pictures from Eleanor's file, which
Mrs Forbes had saved to the last. They showed what
appeared to be Eleanor's interpretation of some sort of
animal. Mary took the pictures in her hand and
looked closer. The drawings did appear to depict
some sort of animal, but not an animal Mary
recognised. It looked, she thought, like some sort of
wild beast, maybe a dog or a bear, she couldn't tell.
Eleanor had coloured the animal in black, with wild

red eyes and sharp teeth. Something else Mary thought odd, the beast as it appeared seemed to walk upright on its hind legs. The two teachers gave Mary a little time to absorb and perhaps comment on the pictures. When Mary failed to comment Mrs Forbes pitched in. "You see, we found this a little unusual. Mrs Shand had set a theme for the children; this was to create an image or drawing relating to something they knew or could connect with at home. Many of the children, when faced with such a task, will tend to draw images of their houses, their parents, grandparents, or maybe pets! We thought maybe Eleanor has a pet dog. Does she have a pet dog at home?" Forbes asked.

Mary failed to answer; she was both mesmerised and perplexed by what Eleanor had created, but she had little doubt that they were the work of her daughter.

"Mrs Foster? Mrs Foster? Mary!" The two teachers had for the moment temporarily lost Mary.

"What? sorry? I didn't hear what you said." Mary said, coming out of her trance.

Forbes repeated the question "Do you have a dog at home?"

"No, we don't," Mary replied, "and I don't know where this comes from."

"Oh, we thought perhaps this may have been a pet," said a slightly surprised Mrs Shand. Both teachers by now could see that the presentation of her daughter's drawings had unsettled Mary.

"Anyway, we thought it worth you having a look at what Eleanor had done. We don't think there is any major cause for concern, but we will keep an eye on it," Mrs Forbes said.

Mary looked up from the pictures and swallowed hard. She did not want to break down in front of the teachers, and she was keen to make an exit.

"Would you mind if I temporarily borrowed these?" Mary asked, nodding toward Eleanor's drawings on the coffee table.

The two teachers looked at each other; then Mrs Shand said, "No not at all. It's Eleanor's artwork." Mary and Mrs Shand then collectively gathered up the pictures and placed them back in the folder. Mary, trapped in her own thoughts was still preoccupied.

"How is Eleanor?" Mrs Shand asked.

"Sorry?" Mary replied, once again having not given the teacher her full attention.

"How's Eleanor? Is she likely to be back early next week?" Mrs Forbes looked across to Mrs Shand and signalled for her not to push the point at that stage.

"Oh, um yes, should be back next week," Mary said, distractedly, too preoccupied. "Is that all?" she asked the teachers, looking from one to the other.

"Yes, I think that's all for today" Forbes replied and, with that, she rose, signalling the end of the meeting. "Are you sure you are all right Mrs Foster?" Forbes asked.

"Yes, I'm fine." Mary lied through her teeth.

But Mrs Forbes sensed that there was some disquiet. "If there is anything the school can help with, please do not hesitate to let us know."

Mary collected herself, "No, I will do that. Thank you, once again, Mrs Forbes, and to you, Mrs Shand, for bringing this to my attention."

The office door opened, and Mary left the reception and the school main building back to the car park at a rapid pace. She just wanted to get out of there, just wanted to get home and confront Eleanor with the drawings.

* * *

Back at the Hungry Harshes, Daniel had taken a break from work to make himself a cup of coffee in the kitchen. As he stirred the coffee, Mary walked in via the newly fitted door, carrying the school folder.

"Where's Eleanor?" she asked.

"Oh, hello Dear. Where have you been? In to town?" Daniel asked, still not aware that Mary had tended an appointment at the school.

"No, I've been to Eleanor's school. Where is she?" Mary asked, again impatiently.

"I think she's in the living room watching the television."

Mary hunted around the kitchen for the drawings that Eleanor had made at home a few days previously.

She picked up the pad and laid it on the table.

"What have you got there?" Daniel asked, but Mary didn't answer.

"I've just made some coffee do you want some?" Again Mary did not reply.

"Or tea?" Daniel realised that he was not connecting with his wife and decided to return to the study. "Ok, ok. I'll get out of the way!" he conceded.

Little Pig, Little Pig

Mary opened the pad and, next to it, spilled the contents of Eleanor's folder and all her pictures onto the table and began setting them out next to each other. The pattern was just how Mary had suspected it would be. The drawings in the pad were the same. Scribbled through aggressively to form a thick black mass, exactly the same as the pictures Eleanor had done at school. What did it mean? Mary decided she needed to find out.

"Eleanor!" Mary called. "Eleanor are you there? Could you come into the kitchen please?" she asked.

There was no reply. Mary walked down the hall into the living room where she found Eleanor sitting in front of the television.

"Eleanor, I'd like to show you something, please. Would you come with me into the kitchen?" Mary asked.

"But, Mummy, I'm watching the Tweenies!" the little girl exclaimed.

"Watch it later. You can come with me for the moment, please!" Mary said impatiently. With that Eleanor jumped up and reluctantly followed Mary into the kitchen.

"What is it, Mummy?" Eleanor asked.

"Can you come over here, please, Eleanor!" Mary asked. She was edgy by now, her nerves frail but, nonetheless, she wished to remain composed in front of her daughter and didn't want to show any of her anxiety. Eleanor shuffled to the table where Mary stood and looked down at her pictures.

"Where did you get these from, Mummy?" she asked.

"From school, this morning," Mary replied. "I got a call from your teacher, asking me to go in and see them." With that, Eleanor looked up at her mother with the look of fear that a child exhibits when she believes she has done something wrong and has been found out.

"They were concerned by your drawings, Eleanor. I've pulled out the drawing book you were colouring in a few days ago. Here, do you remember this?" Mary pointed across to the book lying on the table. Eleanor looked but said nothing. Mary pulled out a chair from the table and sat down. Looking into Eleanor's face, she could see that Eleanor was scared.

"Sweetheart, you have not done anything wrong," she said, trying to comfort her. "But can you explain to me what these drawings mean?" Mary asked, nodding to the pictures on the table.

There seemed an eternal silence while Eleanor thought of something to say. "They're what I see," Eleanor explained.

"What do you mean?" Mary asked.

"Well, they said at school to draw a picture of something from home, something you've done or seen, so I just drew this." Eleanor started toying with the edge of some of the drawings.

"Eleanor look at me!" Mary said patiently, turning the girl's head toward her.

"What do you mean when you say this is what you see? I can't see anything here, this is just black!"

"That's what I see!" Eleanor exclaimed again.

"How do you see it? How?" Mary asked. By now, she was beginning to get a little exasperated.

"In my dreams, Mummy, there in my dreams!"
Mary sat back in her chair.

"It's there when I'm in my room; the whole room begins to go dark! After a while, there's just this blackness!" Eleanor tried to explain it the best she could.

"So, you are having dreams where you are in a room and it is just getting dark!"

"Yes," Eleanor replied.

"And eventually it goes so dark it just gets completely black?"

"Yes."

"Then tell me, sweetheart, about this?" Mary pulled out Eleanor's picture of the animal. Eleanor looked at it but gave no response.

"What is this, sweetheart? A dog? A bear?" Mary asked

"No, Mummy, it's a wolf!" Eleanor said. With that, Mary could see some distress in Eleanor; she began to fidget more, avoid eye contact, and started very quietly to weep. Mary pulled her closer.

"Darling, it's ok!" she exclaimed as Eleanor began wiping her eyes.

"What does this wolf do?" Mary asked tentatively and beginning to tremble.

"Well, when it gets dark, Mummy, I can't see anything! But I hear him breathing, but I can't see him."

"Go on."

"Well, the wolf bangs on my door. He bangs on it so hard that I sit up. He wants to come into my room,

I think! I think he must want to eat me!" With that, Eleanor started sobbing.

Mary hugged her. "It's ok, dear, it's ok," she reassured the child. "Tell me one last thing, Eleanor, how often have you been having these dreams?"

"I don't know, Mummy, maybe one or two times?" Mary wiped the little girl's eyes.

"Mummy, can I go and watch the telly now?" Eleanor asked.

"Yes, Dear."

Mary sat for a while and thought. Pawing over the pictures again, she tried to make sense of what Eleanor had told her. Was this just a child with a vivid imagination? What had made her see this darkness and the wolf? Was Eleanor indeed experiencing the same vivid dreams that she herself once had as a child when her own grandmother died? Mary felt the hairs on the back of her neck stand up and a shiver travel down her spine. She gathered the pictures up and put them away in the folder. Eleanor mentioned breathing, hearing the beast breathing at her door in the dream. Mary too had heard breathing, an unearthly, eerie noise, not at all like human breathing on the night of the break in. It had also come from her bedroom door! Mary pushed the thought out of her mind.

That afternoon, Mary wrestled with whether or not she should say something to Daniel. She decided she would tell him about the visit to the school and show him Eleanor's drawings, but only after dinner, only after they had cleared up after the evening meal and the kids were off their hands.

For the second night running, following the break in, the evening was a rather subdued family mealtime. The kids hardly spoke. Eleanor picked at her food and ate very little, barely looking up from the table. Mary was concerned; Eleanor wasn't outwardly ill—at least she had no symptoms of illness—and so, Mary thought it probably had more to do with the anxiety about the confrontation and discussion on the drawings. Daniel barely seemed to notice his family chewing over the lamb chops Mary had grilled. He too seemed engrossed in thought. With this un-enforced silence, dinner was slow and largely uneaten. Both David and Eleanor left the table to go to their bedrooms. That left Mary and Daniel to clear up. Mary decided it was time to talk to Daniel about her concerns for Eleanor. She started the conversation tentatively while Daniel stacked the dishwater.

"How's work been today?"

Daniel, surprised, looked up. "It's good. We've started to chase the DEC account. Do you remember I told you about DEC, the company in Leeds that has global offices in Chicago and Melbourne?"

"Oh er, yes, I think I remember." Mary replied, trying to sound interested.

"Well, they want to host web, application, and a database suite on windows 2003 servers out of the US."

"Daniel! Have you been busy all day?" Mary cut in. Server definitions and hosting locations were not a hot topic of hers. It made Daniel stop in his tracks.

"Most of the day, Darling, not all day...." As he said it, Mary noticed that he became further distracted, his eyes became fixed on the new door leading from the kitchen outside, and his voice trailed off. "Where that carpenter's fitted that door he's bloody well left a gap at the top, look!" Daniel exclaimed.

"Dan, have you had much time to sit down and talk with Eleanor?" Mary tried in vain to keep the conversation on her track but it was no use.

"I've got half a mind to bloody call him back! That door will let in a draft along the gap!" Daniel said. By now, he had walked over to the door and was running his fingers along the gap left by the errant carpenter between the door and the frame.

"Dan, I went to the school today to see Eleanor's teachers—"

At that moment, the telephone rang in the hall, and Daniel moved out of the kitchen to answer it. Frustrated, Mary turned and filled the sink with hot water. Taking the dishes from the vegetable steamer, she picked up a washing up brush in her right hand and began the circular motion of cleaning the dishes in the hot soapy water. As she did so, she kept turning the questions over and over in her head. *The wolf, what is this wolf? Where did it come from? These dreams that Eleanor described, the utter darkness and this beast, they seem more like nightmares.* What, she wondered, had triggered such vivid images, so vivid that Eleanor could recount them on paper?

Mary heard Daniel in the distance on the phone.

"Ok thanks, then, see you soon." Mary heard Daniel put the phone down and come back down the hall into the kitchen.

"Who was that?" She looked over her shoulder from her position at the sink to see Daniel walk back in. He seemed to Mary to just stand in the doorway. He didn't answer her. She sensed something was wrong and turned to face him.

"Who was that on the phone?" she asked again. Daniel stood there he looked confused. He started shaking his head in disbelief.

"It was Detective Inspector Toms." Daniel replied.

"Well, what did he want?" Mary asked.

"The Forensics have returned analysis on the footprints. Apparently, they were able to identify in several instances the foot of an animal, like a dog, a very large dog!"

Mary's stomach turned. She dropped the brush into the sink, when she heard Daniel's words.

"They say it's like nothing they have ever seen before!"

Mary pulled out a dining chair from the table and slumped down.

"There's one other thing...apparently they have matched some hair samples they found here and believed to be those belonging to the intruder."

"And...?" Mary asked, feeling a deep dread grip her.

"They've successfully managed to match them to an animal. They say the animal hair could only have come from that of a large dog!"

Chapter 8

Thankfully, for the Foster family, the next few nights had passed uneventfully. Something akin to normal family life had returned, and Mary certainly had kept herself busy. On Saturday, she had spent some time in Daniel's study scouring the Internet. She searched for evidence of published paranormal activity. She was conscious that, till now, there had been no medical diagnosis made of Eleanor's condition. She had, after all, only taken her to see the local GP; Mary still had a sense that whatever Eleanor was suffering from, it was not a medical condition. As a child, the events of her Grandmother's death and the experiences she suffered at the time as a girl had left an indelible mark on her own life, but she could not recall how she had been diagnosed and by whom. What kind of specialist had seen her? Mary hoped that her mother's arrival at the house that weekend would mean that the two women could spend some time together, and Mary could get answers to some of these questions. A lot of what she stumbled upon she thought seemed plain weird and whacko. They were just the indulgences of some sick minds. There were some weird people out there, she thought. Mary used established global search engines to improve her search for information. She looked up links under a search titled "Parapsychologists." One site in particular intrigued her. It was set up by an organisation known as the Accredited Parapsychology Foundation. Based in the UK and the US, the site boasted of some six thousand members. It listed paranormal definitions, regional events, and intriguingly, a list of potential contacts. Reference was given to names, alumni of the parapsychology world, including doctors, professors, and exponents of the profession. Mary searched the site, but she could not find contact details for any of the distinguished names listed. One name seemed to crop up regularly and appeared to be relatively local to Ravensdale—at least Mary thought this person was based in Yorkshire. Doctor Martin Hannay was listed as a current exponent of parapsychological study and research at the University of Leeds, where he occasionally lectured. There was no direct telephone number for Doctor Hannay, but there were contact details for the University of Leeds. Mary decided that, for now, she would just note them.

Mary decided that she would leave it at that; besides, she had other things more immediate she needed to prepare for. Her mother Alice had cleared her diary of events for the next week in order to make space for her visit. She was due to arrive that afternoon.

Mary and Eleanor drove the fourteen miles from Ravensdale to Leeds to meet her. The greeting at the station was warm. Mary embraced her mother, hugging her warmly. Eleanor buzzed excitedly around her grandmother; they had not seen Alice for some while; this was the first time since the move from London. There was a lot to catch up on.

Alice's arrival resulted in a noticeably increased absence from Daniel. Always prickly when his mother-in-law was around, he would withdraw for long periods to his study where he would just concentrate on work, scour the Internet or watch television. This didn't unduly bother Alice, since her concern was for the welfare of her daughter's state of mind and the security of her grandchildren, following the break in. That Sunday afternoon, during a quiet period for both women, Daniel had taken both the children off to get bathed. Alice and Mary were able to take themselves off. It was a fine, clear, autumnal afternoon and unseasonably warm. The two women left the house and trudged to the top of the garden. They settled on a bench at the back of the garden and sat for a moment, looking back toward the house and admiring the views of the moors beyond. Above them, crows circled in the treetops, their deep, harsh shrill of a cry echoing across the valley.

"It certainly is lovely and peaceful here," Alice remarked, as the breeze gently lapped the fine skin of her face.

"We love it, Mum; it's like a dream come true, or at least it was." Mary's voice sounded sad and reflective. Alice looked at her daughter and could see that the events of the previous week had left Mary looking tired and drawn.

"Is the house fixed up now, dear?" she asked.

"Fixed up?" Mary asked.

"Since the break in, have you had all the repairs done that needed to be done? Is the house safe, now?" Alice asked.

"Yes, Mum, we've had a new door and frame put into the kitchen." Mary nodded toward the house. Alice nodded approvingly.

"And what do the police say?" she asked.

Mary snorted in a dismissive manner. "What do the police say? What do the police say! The police don't know who it was; they have no idea!"

Alice gasped, a little surprised by Mary's outburst,

"No, actually, Mum, the police do have an idea who or what it may have been!" Mary said, trying to calm down.

"What it *may* be?" Alice repeated.

"Yes, what it may be!" Mary stopped herself from going further and averted her eyes from her mother's direction. She thought carefully about what she wanted to say to her mother before proceeding.

"Mum, do you remember when Nana died?"

"Yes?" Alice replied, her face revealing a bit of confusion at the turn in the subject.

"Do you remember the dreams I had, the dreams about Nana being with me in my room?" Mary knew that this conversation and where she wanted to take it would be uncomfortable for her Mother, but she needed to persist, nonetheless.

Alice stiffened. "Yes, I remember, dear. It was a long time ago, now, but yes I do remember. It is not a period I care to remember much about. Poor Nana was in such pain."

"I know, I know, Mum. I was there, too, and I seemed to live through it much more vividly!" Mary replied, reeling her mother back in, who was busy trying to backpedal from the subject.

"Do you remember? I experienced some sort of supernatural or paranormal behaviour during that time. Something I have not experienced since!" Mary exclaimed. Alice sat patiently and listened. This was, after all what she had come all this way to hear, as much as she prayed and wished it were not so.

"Well, Mum, I believe that Eleanor is now exhibiting the very same behaviours and mannerisms that I had when I was her age and Nana died. I believe that Eleanor has somehow inherited the same goddamned awful abilities that I had. I believe that she, too, is beginning to have dreams—no not dreams—nightmares, vivid nightmares and that, somehow, through these nightmares, I sense that we are all in some sort of danger!"

Alice sat for a moment and absorbed all that Mary had just told her. "Mary, be honest with me," she started. "Have you ever had any experiences since you were a little girl?"

Mary sighed and looked down at her shoes. "No, Mum, I haven't. I have only ever had just that one period in my life, but I'm scared. I'm afraid that what is happening, now, is a repeat of what happened then!"

"Have you talked to Daniel about this?" Alice asked.

"Yes, Mum, I have," Mary said, her eyes still fixed on her shoes.

"What did he say?" Alice asked, again tentatively.

"He thinks I'm mad, but he did take notice. I think it shook him a bit." Mary looked up at her mother.

Alice again thought for a while before responding. She looked down the garden toward the house; the sky momentarily turned dark, as a passing cloud crossed the watery afternoon sun. The shadow of the cloud was visible to both women, as it rolled across the moors and, just for a moment, an icy-cold breeze wrapped itself around them.

"Mary, have you thought about taking Eleanor to a specialist?" Alice asked.

"I've taken her to our doctor; he's checked her over, but he's referred us to Leeds for a scan."

"I don't mean a medical doctor Mary," Alice replied. "I mean a specialist in psychological behaviour."

Mary was a little taken aback by her mother's question. Momentarily, they both looked down at the house again; this time, Eleanor's bedroom window was open. The little girl had finished her bath and had spotted the two women up the garden. Mary and Alice could see her waving to them. Alice, with a broad smile, waved back to the tiny figure in the window.

"If Eleanor has truly inherited those traits from you, then I suggest, my dear, that you find someone who is better positioned to help you, her, and the family." Alice seemed to underline the point to her daughter in a firm but supportive manner. She had come to know by now from what Mary had told her about Eleanor's dreams, the drawings, and convulsions that this sounded like more than just growing pains in a young child. It sounded like something altogether more serious, something she had seen once before and had never hoped to experience again.

Mary, for her part, had seized upon the opportunity to question her mother about a very sensitive subject from the two women's past. She'd got Alice on the side, and Alice had recognised the symptoms that her daughter was describing. Regrettable though it was, her family needed help, and Alice, having been in this position once before, felt the need to provide all the help she could.

"Mum, can you remember when I had the dreams of Nana. What did you do at the time?" Mary asked tentatively.

"Like you've done, dear, we took you to a doctor, the local GP; at first, we were terrified, not knowing what it was that was wrong with you. As parents, when your child is sick, you fear it could be all sorts of different things, and you always fear the worst!" Raking back over this was painful for Alice but she knew she had to do it.

"It became obvious that the medics could find nothing wrong with you. They even suggested sedating you for a while, but I would have none of it. They thought that, by giving you sedatives at night, you would sleep much more deeply and, therefore, not dream. That was their theory, but we never put it to the test."

A brisk breeze was now beginning to blow with a greater purpose across the moors. Beyond the back of the garden and the trees beyond, the pale autumn sun was beginning to fade, and lights from the house began to shine with a greater intensity. The two women would soon have to move back into the house but, before they did, Mary continued to press, not wishing to lose the grasp of the conversation. She was beginning to get the answers she needed from her mother. Answers to questions she had waited her lifetime to hear.

"Mum, it's important that I understand what you did to help me, when I was Eleanor's age. Who did you take me to see, and can you remember what they said I had?" The questions were coming thick and fast.

"At the time, the GP referred you to a clinical psychologist. They believed that, in some way, the death of Nana had been too traumatic for you, that, as a child, you took the experience of her death and the pain and drew it in. They felt that some form of counselling would help."

"And did it?" Mary broke in. "I don't remember that it did a lot of good?"

"That's right, dear; it didn't do a lot of good. After a while, the psychologist, in turn, referred you to a…what was the word?" Alice racked her brain for the word she was looking for.

"A *Para*-psychologist?" Mary obliged.

"Yes, that's right, dear, a parapsychologist!" Alice exclaimed. "You sound as if you've have been looking into this a little, already. Have you?"

"A little, but I've taken it no further," Mary said.

Alice looked her daughter straight in the eye. "You should!" she exclaimed.

"What did the parapsychologist do?" Mary asked, sensing that she was getting to the part of the conversation that would be of most interest to her. "I thought they hypnotised me."

"They did. Don't you remember them coming to the house and setting up those silly cameras? They thought they could trap whatever spirit or presence we had. I admit, I was a little sceptical, but the leading guy who came, he was a doctor or something; he did manage to hypnotise you. I think he thought he could exorcise the spirit. I admit it seemed to work."

"His name, can you remember his name?" Mary asked.

"Dear, that was thirty years ago, and he was, at the time, I should think, a man in his fifties. He might not even be alive today." Alice replied, looking up at the sky, as another icy breeze reminded her that evening was drawing in. "I think it's time we went in, Dear. "It's getting a little chilly."

The two women, much to Mary's reluctance, ended the conversation and returned to the house. Mary knew that she could not press her mother again that evening, at least not until the children had been put to bed.

* * *

With the start of a new week, Mary decided that, with no further adverse signs of behaviour in Eleanor, the little girl would return to school, but not before she had warned the school and asked them to keep a close eye on her.

For Daniel, work meant returning to the road. Because his mother-in-law was staying with the family, he forfeited the right to work from home, choosing instead to be anywhere but home. The house again was quiet. With the study free, Mary decided to show her mother some of the leads she had identified in the world of parapsychology. The telephone that morning was buzzing; first, Mary received a call from the local police constabulary enquiring after the family's welfare and if there had been any further disturbances. Then she received a call from Dr Ventham, who had rung to check the progress of both his patients, Mary and Eleanor.

Later that afternoon, Mary received an unexpected visit from the Police. Detective Inspector Toms had decided he would call by unannounced. Mary was not fully clear as to what his motives were for calling, but she nonetheless let him in and the three people, Mary, Alice, and Inspector Toms sat in the kitchen. Mary and Alice sensed that Toms seemed uncomfortable, embarrassed. Mary made some tea, while Alice sat across the kitchen table from him. Clasping her hands together and resting them on the table, she leaned forward and stared at Toms, who smiled, said nothing, and then did everything he could to avoid eye contact with Alice. Feeling some unease, Toms was pressed into making small talk with the elderly lady sitting across from him.

"So, Mrs Parsons, you've come to stay with the family for a while?" he asked politely.

"Yes, that's right!" Alice replied abruptly.

"Ah, good, come to offer moral support?" Toms asked, flashing a wry smile.

"That and more!" Alice replied. There were long silences during the conversation.

"Tea's nearly ready!" Mary exclaimed, trying to fill the awkward gaps between her mother and the inspector.

"So, Inspector—"

"*Detective* Inspector, Mrs Parsons!" Toms reminded her firmly, but patiently.

"Detective Inspector, are you any closer to knowing who broke into my daughter's house?"

"No, Mrs Parsons, I can't say we are. That's really why I've popped round, Mrs Foster," he said, redirecting his attention to Mary, "really just to see how you are, wondering if there is anything else you can tell me?" Toms was fishing for more leads; it was evident to the two women that, at this stage, the police had very little to go on.

"Awful long way to come just to see how my daughter is!" Alice exclaimed. She remained firmly on the front foot. Mary again decided to break in.

"Tell me, again, Mr Toms, what were the results from the forensic work the police carried out?"

By now, Toms was sipping his tea from the mug Mary had passed to him. He put the mug on the table and sighed. "I'll be honest, Mrs Foster, it showed us very little we can understand. On another level, of course, it showed us some evidence we are struggling to understand."

"You mean the dog hair!" Mary cut to the chase.

"Amongst other things," Toms replied. "Oh, I'm not saying that the work carried out by forensics was poor, not at all. You see, in actual fact it was very good, but —"

"But what?" Alice interrupted.

"We could not find any trace of a human presence — none at all!"

The two women gave each other a knowing glance. Toms' eyes darted between the two. He was quick to pick this up but didn't press the point.

"There were no fingerprints; the footprints left in the garden, in the kitchen, and across the hall did not show any evidence to that of a man's boot or shoe. All we could find were prints that seemed to belong to a very large animal, like a large dog." Toms looked directly at Mary. "And you tell me you don't keep a large dog, Mrs Foster!" he exclaimed.

"Mr Toms, we don't keep any dog!" Mary replied.

"The dog hair, as you say," Toms continued, "was matched against a number of large animals, based upon the size of the prints we found. It compared to no native dog found in this country. Our forensics lab was intrigued. They decided to do a wider search. Their words were, 'these hairs are indeed unusual, of a coarse, long, and very dark nature.' The hairs would appear to be similar to those of a wolf, Mrs Foster." There was silence, before Toms continued. "But, of course, we do not have wild wolves roaming the countryside; that must be absurd, so we are at a loss!" Silence reigned, again.

"Mrs Foster, do you know of anyone around these parts who keeps large dogs, people you may know, people who may know you or your husband's business?"

"No," Mary replied, without elaboration.

"Would you mind if I take a walk around your back garden?" Toms asked, nodding outdoors.

"Not at all." Mary stood up and opened the back door leading onto the garden. Toms got up and moved to the door. When he got to the door, he stopped and observed the carpenter's work, looking up at the top of the frame then down one side.

"He's done a good job here!" With that, he moved slowly into the garden, paying close attention to every detail. At every patch of lawn he walked near or past, he stared down intently, looking for some small clue. The two women watched him from the window, as he methodically walked up the garden, where the perimeter fencing backed on to the tress and the wood beyond. The fencing at the bottom of the garden was little more than wire that stood about three feet or so high. Toms stopped and looked out beyond the trees into the woods. They seemed cold and unwelcoming. Beyond the initial breach of trees it was still dark; the leaves were only just turning and few had fallen. Toms looked down at the fencing. As the wind blew, rustling the leaves on the trees, he noticed something fluttering on the fence. He moved closer and saw that it appeared to be a clump of black fur or hair that had been caught at the very top of the wire fencing. He pulled out a small plastic bag and gingerly pulled the hair out of the fence. Could it be the same hair found in the Fosters home? It certainly looked as if it possessed the same qualities. Intrigued, and with the hair and plastic bag safely stored back in his pocket, he found a piece of the fence, where a break had occurred, trodden down, almost completely flat to the ground, Toms stepped over it beyond the boundary into the woods. He crouched down, looking for more hair but found none. He moved amongst the dense patches of scrub and trees, looking for further evidence of an animal having been present. Heavy rain a few days before had left the ground still wet, and behind a thicket, he found a small bare area, which opened into a copse.

"You've been here!" he muttered to himself. Looking down, he could see prints in the wet earth. Looking up, he noticed what appeared to be white spittle or saliva on the leaves of some of the scrub. He took out another plastic bag from his overcoat and, with the end of a pen, wiped the spittle into the bag. How odd, he thought, that the spittle was found on leaves at chest height to him. If a dog or wolf had made this, then this was going to be a large animal. He assumed that this was where the animal had stood or crouched before entering the house; the prints pointed toward the house. Again, Toms looked up and around him. The wood seemed eerily quiet; only the faint rustling of leaves broke the silence, together with the sound of a crow in the treetops. Satisfied that he had found where the animal had been, he retreated back into the garden and walked back down to the house. Diligently wiping his feet on the mat before entering the kitchen, he was greeted again by Mary and Alice.

"Mrs Foster, thank you once again for the tea. I shall be on my way!" he exclaimed, walking past both women and heading for the front door.

"Did you find anything?" Mary asked.

"Maybe something!" Toms replied, turning as he did so.

"Oh! One thing, Mrs Foster, don't let the children venture into the woods beyond the garden, not just for the moment, anyway!"

Mary looked baffled.

"I'll see myself out." With that, Toms closed the door behind him. Toms walked down the drive to his car, turned the key in the lock, opened the door, and got in. From where the car was parked, he could see the Cheney's cottage and one or two other cottages leading up the road. He sat for a moment and wound down his window. Just for a moment, the air was still. He leaned his head slightly out of the window; surely, if anyone in the neighbourhood had a dog, he would hear it, he thought. He pulled his head back into the car and removed the clear plastic bag containing the clump of hair from his pocket. Holding it up to the light, he looked at it and then gazed beyond at the Hungry Harshes. There was certainly more to this case than met the eye. This was, he thought, no straightforward breaking and entering, and a sixth sense, honed by years in the force, told him that Mary knew more than she was letting on. She wasn't telling him everything. Toms placed the bag back into his jacket pocket, set the keys in the car's ignition, and turned it on. The engine roared, as he placed his foot on the clutch. Putting the gears in reverse, he slowly pulled the car off of the Fosters' drive and sped away down the narrow lane. He would be back again.

* * *

The wind that had blown most of the day across the north moors, down into Ravensdale, had now eased off to little more than a teasing breeze that rustled the treetops, as the evening drew in. Light clouds had replaced clear skies, and they, in turn, were backlit by the moon. Daniel had made a point since the break in of going around the house earlier in the evening, particularly now, as the evenings were getting darker earlier. He would make sure that all external doors and windows were properly locked and secured.

"Dad! Daddy!" came the call from Eleanor's room upstairs. "Daddy, I'm ready!" Daniel knew that his next task would be putting his daughter to bed with a story. Eleanor had kissed her mother and grandmother goodnight and had gone to her room. Daniel, not wishing to spend any more time with his wife's mother than he had to, knew that reading bedtime stories was preferable, even though he was tired.

"Ok, Eleanor!" he called up. "What's it going to be tonight?" he asked.

"The three little pigs, Daddy. Read me the three little pigs!" Eleanor replied. She had come out of her room to stand on the landing, overlooking the stairs. She jumped excitedly when she saw her father climbing the stairs. Downstairs in the drawing room, Mary sat with her mother watching the television.

Eleanor going to bed had prompted Mary to reach for the remote control and switch the set off.

"There's nothing on, as usual!" Mary exclaimed, getting up from the sofa.

"Would you like a drink, Mum?" Mary asked.

"Yes, please, Dear, my usual," Alice replied. Mary knew that her mother's usual was a glass of red wine. Alice loved red wine; she was a staunch supporter of old world reds, having developed and nurtured this affinity during her work with the Women's Institute. She was an enthusiastic taster at many buffet cheese and wine evenings. Mary disappeared into the kitchen and returned shortly with two glasses and an open bottle.

"Old world, Dear?" Alice asked.

"Of course, Mum, nothing else. French *fleuris*." Mary poured out a healthy measure into both glasses and returned to the sofa, where her mother was seated at one end. Reaching for the glass Alice took it to her nose, as if to simulate smelling the bouquet, and then she took a light sip.

"Very nice," she said. She looked down. Her expression changed, as she started to change the subject.

"Mary, you know I'll support you and help you in whatever you decide to do with Eleanor," she said, running her index finger along the rim of the glass.

Mary felt reassured. She had longed to hear those words from her mother but had not dared ask directly for her help. This was something Alice had to come to terms with in her own mind. Mary longed for her to put the episodes from the past behind her and, once again, help her in what she believed was going to be a devastating and painful experience for the family.

"I know, Mum, and thanks!" Mary took her mother's hand. Alice looked up and smiled.

"We will get through this. If this is something like the past, then we will get through this, together, as a family! And we will be stronger for it!" Mary felt moved. She wiped a tear from her eye.

"You know…" Alice said, then paused. "You know that policeman who came today is suspicious!"

Mary chuckled. "Mum, that's what policemen are; that's their job! To be suspicious of everyone and everything!"

Alice didn't share in Mary's humour. "I think he knows you're not telling him the whole story," she replied.

"Maybe he does," Mary said. "Maybe he's a smart policeman, and he can tell us how to deal with this problem."

"I think maybe we should have a second look at that list of names you have," Alice said. "The ones who deal in paranormal activity." Alice took another, rather larger gulp of wine from her glass.

"Ok, then!" Mary replied. "Let's make some time tomorrow. I'll try to call the University of Leeds and talk to that Doctor Hannay. We can start with him." Mary now felt buoyed by her mother's positive attitude. For the first time since the break in, she did not feel alone and isolated. For the first time, she felt she had the support of someone who knew, along with her, the terrible task they could be facing.

Little Pig, Little Pig

Alice finished her glass of wine in three quick gulps. She gave a brief yawn. "Oh dear! The revelations of the past few days have caught up with me!" she exclaimed, putting her wineglass on the table. "Dear, would you mind terribly if I went up for a bath and then to bed? I'd like to turn in early."

"No problem, Mum," Mary replied. Before she pulled herself off the sofa, Alice patted her daughter's wrist. "Listen, Dear, don't worry. We've gone through worse before. We'll speak to your Doctor Hannay in the morning, see what he recommends." With that, the two women exchanged a brief hug, before Alice got up, bent over her daughter, and kissed her on the head.

"Goodnight, Dear," she said and walked across the room. She stopped before she got to the door and turned to face Mary.

"Oh, do you think I could have another glass of that wine to take up with me, please, Dear?" she asked.

Mary got to her feet and poured her mother another glass of wine. As she handed it to her, she leaned forward and gave her mother one final peck on the cheek.

"Thanks again, Mum, and goodnight." Mary watched as her mother turned and walked out of the room. She moved to sit back on the sofa in front of the raging fire Daniel had started in the grate. As she sat there on her own, she felt at peace. She was not to know that the peace was to be short lived; the feeling of optimism she had would be gone by the morning, for this would be a tumultuous night, the most terrifying and awful night that she and her family had ever experienced, a night that would change the lives of both Mary and her family forever. Mary did not know it, but seeing her mother leave that room was to be the last time she would ever see her alive.

Chapter 9

The stars twinkled in the night sky. The clouds had cleared and the temperature had dropped. It had dropped sufficiently for a light frost to take hold. From the woods at the back of the garden, came the plaintive sound of a night owl. Amongst the foliage near the border of the Fosters' garden, the beast crouched, lying in wait. His thick black coat was soaked from the moisture in the night air. Its eyes, blood red, and with the intensity of the devil, stared down at the house. Its breathing was heavy and laboured. Its nostrils snorted hot air into the night. It growled and hissed beneath its breath, as it gripped the bark of a nearby tree to pull itself up onto its hind legs to get a better view. Everything was ready; this was going to be the night, it would not be deterred again. This time, the attack would be decisive. *Little Pig, Little Pig, let me in!*

When it was sure that it could not be seen it lithely leaped over the boundary fence and reverted to moving on all four legs, cautiously tracking down the garden toward the house. Its long dark ears were pinned back on its head like darts. At the back door to the house, the mighty beast stopped. This was the way it had previously entered the house. It prowled back and forth on all fours, its great black claws clicking on the flagstones on the garden patio, as it moved. It snarled and growled at the frustration of not being able to enter the house. It stared up at the house, its eyes stared with a burning intensity at it focused on Eleanor's bedroom window. It knew exactly where the little girl was, but it could not get to her; it had to find a way of getting to her. It raged at the house, as it stood beneath Eleanor's window on its hind legs, front paws resting against the wall. Saliva dripped from its mouth and nostrils. It would not give up, not this time.

In her bedroom, Eleanor lay asleep in her bed; her body was resting, but her mind was active. At first, she began twisting and turning beneath the bedclothes, but the covers of her bed restrained her. Although her eyes were shut, her face winced in pain, and she began tossing her head from side to side; her breathing became laboured. Her stomach pumped up and down and she began to perspire and, almost instantaneously, she began to convulse! At the rear wall of the house, a spotlight hung beneath Eleanor's window, which the movement of the creature outside had triggered, and the light that flashed on lit up the whole of the back patio and most of the lawn to the back of the garden. The spotlight was so powerful it lit up Eleanor's room, beaming light onto her bedroom walls. A hideous, menacing shadow of the creature flashed across the walls at times, creating a silhouette of the beast that seemed to stand over the writhing girl. Eleanor's mind and subconscious were now fully activated, and the dark fog, which she had repeatedly seen and drawn, had now descended; the beast had now returned. It was the creation from her subconscious. In her head, she heard the words *"Little Pig, Little Pig let me in!"* as a command. Over and over again the words tumbled and repeated themselves to her. *"Little Pig, Little Pig let me in!"* Outside, the beast prowled, waiting for her; inside Eleanor's head it now had full control, commanding her subconscious, controlling her mind. Still asleep, Eleanor threw back the covers and swung her legs out. The girl's breathing had become steadier, and she became more composed. She had lost her battle to control her mind; in her dream, the creature was winning!

For a while, she sat up in bed. Then, still asleep, her eyelids only partly open, she pulled herself to her feet and walked slowly toward her bedroom door. Just as she reached for the handle of the door, the image of the beast that had loomed large on her bedroom wall stopped. She was coming!

* * *

Inside the house, it was tranquil. It was the middle of the night and the only sound that came was the grandfather clock, ticking imperiously in the hall. The scratching made by the creature woke Alice. She never slept well, particularly in a strange bed, and now this irritating scratching noise had stirred her. The rest of the house remained silent, except for the floorboards creaking. Someone else was up! An inquisitive nature had encouraged her to pull back the covers of her bed and get up. Who was walking around? It sounded as if it came from right outside her bedroom door, outside her and Eleanor's rooms. The elderly women, dressed only in her nightdress, walked slowly to her bedroom door.

There was the sound of the scratching again. What was it? The sound coming from directly outside her door had moved away. Very carefully and quietly, she put her hand on the door handle. Squeezing it down, she pulled the door ajar no more than a few inches. She had not put a light on, and there was no light in the hall. Only the moonlight shining through the landing window gave any display of light to help Alice see who might be on the landing. She peered out but could not see anything. She pulled the door open a little farther and peered down the hall to Mary's room. There appeared to be nothing going on there. But there! There was that scratching again; this time it seemed more intense. The old woman pulled the door open a little more. She could still hear noises from the top of the landing but couldn't see anything. Tentatively, Alice whispered, "Who's there?" There was no reply. She thought it might be Daniel or Mary or one of the children going downstairs for a drink, but she could not see anyone. She swallowed heavily and decided she would step out onto the landing. As she did so, she saw a movement to her right. It was a figure, someone was slowly moving down the stairs, but who was it? Alice's hands started to shake, but she was there now and her overwhelming inquisitive nature drove her on.

As the figure descended the stairs into the light in the hallway, she could see it was Eleanor.

"Eleanor! Eleanor!" she called, still in a half-whispered voice, but the girl did not respond. Alice walked out of her room, down the landing, and reached the top of the stairs. Just as she did, she saw the little girl disappear down the hall toward the kitchen.

"Eleanor!" Alice called again, but again the little girl seemed to be in some sort of trance, as if she were sleepwalking. Eleanor pushed open the door to the kitchen and disappeared inside. The kitchen was dark. Alice decided to descend the stairs and follow the child into the kitchen, but her intuition told her not to run up and startle the girl.

* * *

By the time Alice had got to the bottom of the stairs, she could neither see nor hear Eleanor. She slowly, tentatively, walked down the long hallway trying to peer into the kitchen, as she approached it. She stopped before entering. All she could hear was the grandfather clock ticking in the hall. Suddenly, she heard something else! What was it? It sounded like a key in the lock. Alice moved into the kitchen, but still retained the foresight not to disturb Eleanor, and keeping her better judgement, she decided to leave the kitchen light switched off. She saw Eleanor at first standing at the back door, her back to her; then as Eleanor began to unlock the door to the garden, fear gripped Alice. She thought she could see something moving on the patio outside, but what was it? She thought, *some sort of animal?* The spotlight remained on and lit up the kitchen. She could see that her granddaughter was in some sort of trance. To

Alice, Eleanor was acting as if she was being manipulated, controlled!

As Eleanor swung back the door, still oblivious to her grandmother's presence, a rush of freezing, bitter night air filled the kitchen. As Eleanor stood there facing into the garden, Alice became gripped with fear, for what stood in front of the child was the creature. It stood up on its hind legs and stared directly at the little girl. Alice could see that it was an animal, a wild animal—a wolf. The creature's coat was coloured charcoal black, thick black hair, as black as the night covering a wiry, muscular frame. Alice's heart was pounding. This was no ordinary animal! This was part human, part man; it walked on two legs; it had the head and hair of a wolf, but its size and physical presence suggested it was of some human origin. The creature stepped into the kitchen but remained framed in the doorway, the spotlight from the garden shining behind it. Steam rose from its coat, and it growled and hissed like a rabid dog; saliva dripped and oozed from between its razor-like teeth. Alice watched, rooted to the spot, as the creature prowled from one side to the other, sizing up the child. Its blood red eyes were fixed and focused on Eleanor. Quickly, Alice looked around for something she could use to beat off this monster, but the only object to hand was a dining table chair. Alice gripped the back of it.

The creature was now ready to seize Eleanor, and it opened its arms, holding them out on either side of her, ready to lift her up. As it did, it moved toward her, leaning over her.

Trembling and shaking, but with overwhelming courage, Alice picked up the chair.

The old woman let out the loudest scream she could.

"NO!" She yelled at the creature. The creature looked up, startled; its attention on the little girl had been broken. The great beast stepped back and snarled at Alice, holding its mighty claws out, as if ready to pounce. In an instant, Alice summoned all her strength and, with both hands, threw the chair at the creature, only when she could be sure that it would not hit Eleanor. It was too late. The creature's powerful arm swept the flying chair to one side, and it clattered onto the dining table. The great beast roared in anger and, with a single leap bypassed Eleanor and leapt at the old woman. Picking her up, it shook her, squeezing her body and ribs, cracking bones as its mighty claws sunk into her flesh. All Alice could do was scream out in agony. Her feet were swept completely off the floor, and she could not get away. She felt the creature's terrifying face in her face. Playing with the old women, as if she were a doll in a savage, brutal attack, it tore at her throat, opening up her jugular. The old woman gargled, choking and coughing up blood, which she spat back into the matted hair of her attacker. Shaking the old woman again, it grew tired of her and, with one hand, tossed her across the kitchen. Alice's mortally wounded body flew into a sideboard full of plates, sending crockery crashing everywhere. Just at that moment, Eleanor woke from her trance. She stood rooted to the spot. Seeing the creature, she began crying and screaming. Fear had taken hold of her where she stood.

* * *

Upstairs, Mary and Daniel were awakened by the commotion. The two leapt out of bed, and Mary ran onto the landing. She stopped and peered down the landing toward both Eleanor's and Alice's room; both doors were open. Her heart pumping with adrenaline, she raced down the stairs and across the hall, to the kitchen, where all the noise was coming from. She stepped into the kitchen and could not believe her eyes, as she watched the creature move across the room to where Eleanor was standing. With her heart in her throat, Mary called out. "Eleanor, stand still!" The girl stayed where she had been, all along, sobbing, her back to her mother. Mary could hear the breathing and snarling of the creature as, again, it took its attention away from the helpless little girl and turned its attention on Mary, who had now been joined by Daniel, wielding a baseball bat!

"Oh my god! What the hell is that?" Daniel screamed out.

"Shush!" Mary urged. They all stood their ground. The creature raised itself to its full height, which, to Mary and Daniel, appeared to be well over six feet tall, nearer six-foot-six! It fixed its bloodshot red eyes on both of them; growling beneath its breath, it was ready to pounce again. Inexplicably, however, the creature stood back and looked down at Eleanor one last time. Turning to Mary and Daniel, the creature gave out one last, defiant roar, turned, dropped down on all fours, and ran out of the kitchen door; it disappeared across the garden into the murky gloom of the night. In that moment, Eleanor began to scream hysterically and collapsed to the floor.

"Eleanor! Eleanor!" Mary screamed, as she ran to pick up the little girl. The two of them sat on the floor sobbing. Daniel, still holding the bat, switched on the kitchen light.

"What the fuck was that?" he said, but no one replied. Daniel looked around the kitchen and took in the damage. A broken chair lay on top of the kitchen table, the kitchen drawer had been knocked over, and lay wedged between the wall and the table; broken crockery lay everywhere.

"Oh FUCK! FUCK!" exclaimed a shocked, shaking Daniel, when he spotted the body of his mother-in-law.

"Alice! Alice!" he cried, but the old woman lay still, her broken body lifeless; a pool of rich, dark-blood ran from her throat across the ceramic-tiled floor.

"OH MY GOD! MUM! MUM!" Mary screamed, turning her attention to her mother. Daniel sped across the kitchen where Alice lay, splintering crockery as he went. He bent over the old woman's body, feeling for a pulse; he placed his forefinger on her neck and then her wrist.

"I think she's dead! I think she's dead!" Daniel cried out.

"OH GOD NO! GOD NO! PLEASE NO!" Mary screamed. Daniel, noticing that the door to the back garden was still open ran across the kitchen to close it.

He didn't bother looking out of the door to see what was out there.

"I'll phone for an ambulance!" Daniel exclaimed, as he moved across the kitchen to the door to the hall, stepping past Mary, who sat on the floor cradling her daughter.

As he got to the phone, David came running down the stairs. Dad, what's happening?" David asked.

"David, go up to your bedroom and wait there. I'll be up in a few minutes!" Dan said, holding the receiver in his right hand.

"But, Dad, I heard a load of screaming! Where's Mum?" he asked.

"She's in the kitchen, but you better not go in there!" Dan said, then dialled 999.

"Why not? Is she all right?" David asked again.

"David! Just wait in your bedroom for a few minutes!" David was scared but reluctantly climbed the stairs.

"Emergency services? I need an Ambulance! Now!" Daniel logged his call for both an Ambulance and Police. As he completed the call, David returned to the top of the stairs.

"Dad, I'm scared! I looked out the window in the garden. There's a big animal outside, and he's coming up to the house!" For a split second, as Daniel returned the phone, there was silence in the house.

The Fosters however were not going to receive a reprieve! From the hall, Daniel heard the heavy THUD! THUD! THUD! on the back door. Both Mary and Eleanor began screaming, loud terrified screams.

The creature had returned, and it was thumping on the back door in the kitchen, the one Daniel had had the foresight to lock.

THUD! THUD! From inside the kitchen Mary scrambled frantically to her feet. Picking up Eleanor in her arms, she made for the door to the hall. She could see the creature angry and frustrated at not being able to get into the house, not being able to get at Eleanor! The creature roared, its red eyes and rabid mouth locked onto Mary. As she got to the hall door, she slipped and cut her foot on some broken crockery. With her adrenalin pumping, it was not enough to stop her. She met Daniel coming into the kitchen, once again clutching the bat. Just as they met, the window in the kitchen behind Mary shattered, sending shards of glass flying everywhere. Mary felt glass hit her back. The creature's huge black paw reached into the window, clawing at the door; frantic to get in, it roared and snorted with rage.

"Get upstairs and lock the door to our bedroom!" Daniel screamed as he hurried past Mary.

Without any thought for his own wellbeing, Daniel confronted the creature, running to the window where the creature was and beat its arm and hand with the bat. The creature let out a howl and retracted its arm through the broken window. The creature moved away, and Daniel could hear the sound of its retreat. Daniel pulled out one of the remaining dining table chairs and collapsed into it; breathless with fear, his heart was pumping. For a brief moment, he looked at Alice's body lying on the kitchen floor.

Then he heard a distant smashing of glass. "Fuck!" Daniel muttered to himself. The creature had moved around to the side of the house. It had walked into a glass propagating frame, leaning up against one side of the house, shattering it.

Daniel got off the chair and ran out into the hall. He ran into every room downstairs and made sure that each window, in turn, was securely locked. He had done it earlier in the evening, but now could not trust himself.

* * *

The creature stalked the house, still bathed in the glow from both the moonlight and from the spotlight at the back of the house, which did little to deter it and, in fact, served it in its seemingly relentless pursuit to get to Eleanor.

THUD! THUD! THUD! Daniel had got as far as the hall before the creature had started again, but where was it coming from? The study! Daniel ran into the study, facing the back garden. The creature outside confronted him, pounding on the frame, but the window to the study, like all the downstairs windows, had been securely looked; the creature could not get in.

Where are the police? he wondered. Just then, the huge, black, hulking creature dropped out of sight. Trapped in fear, Daniel's mind raced. Where had it gone, now? He ran back out into the hall.

"Get the knives, Get the knives!" he muttered to himself, as he ran back into the kitchen. There, on the windowsill, by the broken glass, he could see the knife block. Tentatively, he looked through the window to see if the creature was there; there was no sign of it. He moved across the floor, again treading on broken crockery to where the block sat and slipped a large meat knife out of one of the sheaths. As he did, a large rock smashed against the window shattering what panes remained. The remaining shards of glass flew into the kitchen, hitting Daniel in the face. He automatically turned away and covered his eyes to avoid the broken glass. The creature reared up again. This time, in the instant that Daniel had turned away, the creature had got to the window; seeing Daniel, it stood within three feet of him. Reaching in with its huge arm, it grabbed Daniel by the top of his pyjamas and smashed him into the sink. The sudden force of the creature's pull caused Daniel to hit his head on the taps. Temporarily blinded, not able to see, he instinctively lashed out in front of him with the knife. Flailing around, he felt the grip of the creature tighten around his chest. He couldn't see it, but he knew he was being pulled toward it. It's breath on his face stank. With one final lunge of the long silver blade, Daniel thrust the blade into the creature's arm. Instantaneously, the great beast howled in pain.

Daniel, sensing that this was his moment, grabbed the creature's wrist with his left hand and, with his right, stabbed the beast again and again in its arm. The creature howled and roared in pain. It managed to wrench its bloodied arm away from Daniel. The force of the jerk took Daniel off his feet, and he fell to the floor. Again, the creature retreated on all fours into the night. Once again, it had been defeated.

Dan knelt on the floor in the kitchen and began sobbing. Broken glass cut into his knees, but he didn't feel it. Instead, the shock of what he had just experienced overcame him. The still, frosty night air shrouded him, causing him to shiver. Upstairs, Mary had looked herself in her bedroom with the children; she sat on the bed holding both David and Eleanor, the three of them sobbing.

The creature had gone, for now! It had left in its wake a devastating trail of terror, fear and, ultimately, death. Everything that Mary had feared had fatally, horrifically come true. Eleanor was the catalyst, just as Mary had been all those years ago. But this time, Eleanor had brought something far more deadly, far more terrifying into the lives of her family. As a family, they would never get over this night. Mary knew now that she had to confront the terrifying nightmare head on. Their lives had changed forever; the shadow of death now stood over them.

Chapter 10

News of the break in and the murder at the Hungry Harshes had reached Detective Inspector Toms via an early morning phone call to his home at Headingley at six a.m. Not on duty till nine a.m. that morning, he had been sleeping. Shocked at the news of the death he had quickly got himself up and ready and prepared for the journey across the dales to Ravensdale. On the journey there, he had mulled over in his mind the comments that had been quoted to him and documented by the scene of crime officer's statement, chiefly that the family had been disturbed — once again, by an intruder, so soon after the initial attempted break in! The intruder had been described as a large animal, a dog or a wolf! There had been a violent struggle that had resulted in the death of one of the occupants of the household, the grandmother, Alice Parsons. That much Toms knew, but what he still could not piece together was the motive for the attack. Alice Parsons was dead, coincidental maybe. Toms assumed that she was not the intended target of the unknown assailant, since she was not at the Hungry Harshes at the time of the first break in. But this was now more than just an opportunist burglary; there was another intended target in that house, someone the assailant was trying to reach, not the old lady, but someone else, so desperate to get at the intended target that they would kill to do so. Mary Foster was the key to this. Not for the first time Toms felt sure that Mary knew more than she had let on.

It was early, as Toms pulled into the village of Ravensdale, a quarter past seven, and the sun was just beginning to rise. The normally quiet village was hectic, buzzing with activity. Police had cordoned off the bottom of the lane, leading up to the Hungry Harshes, and a small crowd, a mix of inquisitive locals and members of the press had gathered. News had travelled fast. This was a crime, a shocking crime, even more shocking in that it had hit a small community such as Ravensdale, where hardly anything of any note ever happened.

Toms ambled up to the foot of the lane in his car. He pulled up to a police officer on duty, wound down his window, and flashed his police credentials, to which the officer ushered the watching crowd to move to the side of the lane.

Police tape used to cordon off the area was peeled back, and Toms was allowed to drive up to the house. As he pulled up, he rolled past a number of large white police forensic vehicles and squad cars that were parked adjacent to the Hungry Harshes. The house was crawling with police officers and forensic specialists dressed in white coveralls. A scene of crime screen had been erected at the rear of the house, covering the area from the kitchen out onto the rear patio. Toms got out of his car, surveyed the scene and the activity and walked toward the front door of the house, which was open. A police constable stood at the front, guarding access to the house. Toms again flashed his credentials to the officer. "Where's your scene of crime officer?" he asked the constable.

"Inside the house, Sir, to the back of the corridor in the kitchen," the constable replied. Toms, knowing the layout of the house, walked slowly down the hall to the kitchen door, observing all as he went. Peering into the kitchen, he saw it was a buzz with activity. The white-clad forensic team was busy taking photographs, studying footprints, and placing fragments of objects into small plastic bags. Items too large, such as chairs, would go to the scene of crime lab. The officers placed these items into large plastic bags, which they then carried off to the stationery white vans.

Toms scanned the room; the sight of total devastation greeted him. He stared down at the body of Alice Parsons lying face down on the floor; a large pool of deep-red blood had run from what appeared to be her throat and coagulated onto the tiled floor. A forensic photographer stood over the body taking pictures. Elsewhere, fragments of broken glass and crockery were being itemised and carefully packed up, ready to go to the crime lab for closer investigation. The erection of the large screening tent off the back of the kitchen would have left the room dark, but lights were on, and the police had brought in additional lighting in the form of large standalone floodlights, which blazed across the kitchen.

Toms saw a familiar face, Detective Inspector Corbett, a colleague from Leeds who had travelled up earlier that morning.

Terry Corbett was a man in his early forties. Like Toms, he was now a seasoned Detective Inspector, coming up in the ranks from bobby on the beat, to station sergeant, to Detective Inspector but always a few years behind Toms. The two men were great friends. They drank socially and occasionally dined together.

Corbett, noticing Toms in the doorway, waved him in. "Harry, how are you?" Corbett asked, greeting his colleague.

"Got you up early for this one didn't they Terry?" Toms joked, surveying the scene.

"What do you know about this?" Toms asked.

Corbett hoisted up his trousers around his ample waist before replying. "Well, it seems that a 999 call was placed to the station at one-twenty-eight this morning, one for an ambulance and one for police assistance, both directed to this address. When the first officers arrived, they found the Foster family in shock and disarray. When the ambulance arrived, a little after one forty-eight a.m., they found Mrs Alice Parsons severely injured. Upon examination, they found that any form of resuscitation would be of no use. Mrs Parsons was declared dead at one-fifty-five a.m."

"What killed her?" Toms asked, nodding down at the old lady's body.

"You know, Harry, the pathologist will need to do the full post-mortem, but looking at the old girl, I'd say that her throat was torn out!" Corbett replied in a very matter-of-fact tone. Nodding to a corner of the kitchen, he turned and said to Toms, "You know, we found her larynx on the floor over there." Corbett took a handkerchief from his pocket and blew his nose. Crumpling up the handkerchief in his hand, he shoved it back into his trouser pocket.

"We think the old lady must have been thrown against that welsh drawer and probably died where she fell," Corbett explained. "Whoever did this was bloody strong! I mean to pick up the old girl like that and just toss her across this room!" Corbett gestured as if to signal the expanse of the kitchen.

"Do we have some statements from the family?" Toms asked.

"Aye, we do. Understand you know the family reasonably well, Harry?" Corbett asked.

"I've met them; they had a break in here just a few days ago, and I was assigned to review the case. Nice family, lovely kids." There was a pause for a moment between the two men then Toms stepped in.

"Where is the family now?" he asked.

"Staying with friends, apparently; they were driven there last night," Corbett replied, looking down at his notebook.

"Mr Foster's business partner and friend of the family, a Mr Brian Ashton, who lives in a suburb in Stockport."

"I'll need the full address, Terry. I'll need to get over there to see them!" Toms said.

"No problem!" Corbett replied. The conversation paused once again. Toms took Corbett's right elbow and signalled for the two men to move to a more discrete part of the house, one not swarming with police officers. Both Corbett and Toms moved toward the hall.

"Listen, Terry," Toms said, still holding Corbett's elbow, bent into the other man's face.

"Any idea who might have done this?" he asked. Corbett stopped in his tracks and gave a sigh. "Baffled at the moment, Harry. The initial statements taken from Mr and Mrs Foster seemed to imply that they were attacked by a large animal, a dog or a wolf!" Corbett chuckled to himself and shook his head. "We don't have wolves around here, Harry, not for 'undreds of years."

Toms looked perplexed. "Is there a zoo or park around here, anywhere that would keep wolves? Maybe if we made some enquiries we could find that somewhere an animal has escaped."

"We can look into it, no problem," Corbett replied. Corbett thought for a moment before delivering the punch line to his mate. "One other thing, Harry, the description we have of this wolf is not like the description you would expect."

Toms was intrigued "How do you mean Terry?"

"Well, the creature described to the officer on the scene was huge, well over six feet tall!" Toms listened intently. "Terry, no wolf I know of stands at six feet?"

"It does when it stands on its hind legs!" Corbett exclaimed. Toms looked at him quizzically.

"Harry, this beast as it was described to us and noted in my officer's statement, was on its own. There was no one with it. No owner or handler, no one. It apparently attempted to force entry into the house by breaking the windows." Corbett again broke off to read directly from the officers' statement.

"All the time the beast was in the kitchen it remained standing on its hind legs."

"When Mr Foster locked the rear door of the house to the kitchen," Corbett continued, "the beast returned. At some point, it seemed to prowl the perimeter of the house on four legs. According to Mr Foster, it prowled largely on two legs."

"And do you doubt that statement?" Toms asked.

"Harry, why would I doubt the statement?" Corbett looked down at his notepad.

"I have it here that when both Foster parents were observed when giving statements, there was no sign of intoxication, whether by alcohol or other substances. Apart from Mrs Foster, who admitted to having a couple of glasses of wine, earlier in the evening, no serious effects of or by intoxication could be observed. Besides, this animal stood in front of them in the kitchen. All the while it was outside on the patio, it could be seen perfectly well by the family!" Corbett exclaimed.

"How can you prove that?" Toms challenged him.

"Because the wall at the rear of the house, the one leading onto the patio, has a huge spotlight, which activates when it is triggered by movement!"

* * *

Harry Toms knew that, in order to try and make some sense of what had happened at the Hungry Harshes in the past few days, he needed to get over to Stockport to speak to the Fosters. It looked for all the world that what had been a routine break in enquiry, and one that had not particularly interested Toms from the outset, had now turned into a full-blown murder enquiry.

Despite the descriptions of an animal being the perpetrator, despite the horrific manner in which Alice Parsons had been killed, this was still going to be treated as a murder enquiry. Toms secured the address of the Ashtons in Stockport and set off on the long scenic journey from Ravensdale to Stockport.

The Ashtons lived in a large imposing house in the suburbs, outside Stockport. It was known to be an affluent area for those who had thriving businesses, particularly in and around Manchester, which, to all intents and purposes was little more than a twenty-minute drive away.

Toms pulled his car onto the stone chip drive of the Ashtons' home. He was met by a lone police officer who approached the driver's side window. After a brief exchange, Toms got out and went into the house. Fortunately for him and the Fosters, the press had lost the trail and had not followed them to the house.

Even with this fact in hand and the police presence to protect the family from further intrusion, the house had been kept in darkness for privacy, the curtains drawn.

Brian and Theresa Ashton were home, supporting Daniel, Mary, and the children. Toms was shown into the large drawing room, shadowed in partial darkness. Toms could see Mary sitting on the sofa; she was in shock. A doctor had been called out in the middle of the night and had given her a mild sedative. Up to that point, she had lain awake most of the night, crying into her pillow; she finally fell asleep at about five-thirty but on the evidence of her appearance to Toms, she had not slept for very long. The sedative had not worked for her. On the armchair across from Mary sat a WPC, a woman police constable.

"Hello, Mary," Toms said, as he looked sympathetically into Mary's eyes. Mary sat, ashen faced, her eyes dark and puffy; she hadn't slept; she had only found time to cry. Dressed in one of Theresa Ashton's bed robes and displaying obvious signs of shock, she sat completely still and had hardly noticed Toms enter the room.

"Can I just say how sorry I am with regards your mother's death!"

Mary broke off from her trance like state and stared at Toms. "Thank you," she muttered in a barely audible voice.

For Mary, it felt like every last ounce of her spirit had been brutally wrenched from her. Toms looked around for a seat and decided to sit next to her. As he sat down, he gently took her hand in his.

"Are you being looked after ok? Is there anything we can do for you?" Toms asked. As he said it, Daniel walked into the room; he too, looked the worse for little sleep. The two men acknowledged each other with a silent nod.

"Are the children all right?" Toms asked.

"They're sleeping," Daniel replied to Toms. Eleanor's been given a mild sedative to help her sleep." Daniel scratched his head. "As you know, none of us had any sleep last night!"

"I know, Sir, I understand," Toms acknowledged.

Mary looked across at Toms. "Well, Detective Inspector Toms, my life is a total shit this morning!" she exclaimed sarcastically. Toms knew he had to tread carefully. Many years in the force had taught him that he needed to strike the right balance; he needed to be seen to be sensitive and supportive to the family but, at the same time, he knew also that he had the painful task of having to press both Mary and Daniel over the facts relating to the previous evening's incident.

"This is an awful time!" Toms began, "but if you don't mind, Mrs Foster and with your permission, I would like to ask you one or two things about last night."

Daniel looked at Mary. "Mr Toms, we are very tired and in total shock. Mary needs to get some rest; we both need to rest!" Daniel responded.

"I understand, Sir, and I will go away if you wish and we can reconvene at a later date, but there are one or two important things I'd like to try and understand, now, if you would permit me?" Toms pressed.

"Go ahead, Mr Toms," Mary said wearily.

Toms directed his attention to Mary. "Mrs Foster, I've read the statements that you and your husband provided to our officers earlier this morning. As I understand it, the statement reads that, from what you and your husband witnessed, there was no forced entry to the house, not initially, anyway, am I right?"

"That's correct," Mary replied again in a weary manner.

Toms continued. "You believe that a member of the household, a member of your family did indeed open the door to the intruder! Is that correct?"

"It does very much look that way!" Daniel replied.

"Who, Mr and Mrs Foster, let the intruder in?" Toms asked directly. Mary looked up into Toms eyes. Her eyes were red and strained, and they began to well with tears.

"It was my daughter, Eleanor."

For a moment Toms was stunned. "Why?" Toms asked, but by now, Mary had relapsed back into her trance.

"Why what, Mr Toms?" she asked.

"Why would your daughter get up in the middle of the night, come down the stairs, and open the back door to an intruder at a risk to herself?"

Mary thought for a moment, and Toms, sensing his moment, had moved to the edge of the chair.

"I believe my daughter knew who the intruder was, Mr Toms! I believe the intruder was controlling my daughter's mind. She was helpless to do anything about it; she had become susceptible to suggestion and the power of thought!"

"Are you telling me that your daughter, Eleanor, was lured in some way? She was coerced into exposing the family to danger?" Toms asked.

"She didn't mean to do it," Mary replied in an agitated state to Toms questioning. "She didn't know she was doing it! It is in no way Eleanor's fault that my mother is dead!"

"I'm sorry, Mrs Foster, I wasn't implying that." Toms sensed he needed to backtrack from this line of questioning; things were still too raw. Instead, he looked across to Daniel.

"Mr Foster, reading both the statements given by your wife and yourself, you appear to have provided a reasonable description of the intruder. Can you confirm that you stand by the description in the statements?" Toms asked.

Daniel looked down at his feet. "I suppose this must sound incredulous to you; it was totally unbelievable to us; we could not believe what we were seeing!"

"And just what was it you say you saw, Mr Foster?" Toms pressed the question.

"An animal, a wolf — no not a wolf — !"

"A Werewolf!" Mary interrupted. The room fell silent. Toms and his fellow WPC exchanged glances with one another.

"Mr Toms, I am afraid that as much as you might test me, section me, or give me electric shock treatment, you will find I am not prone to wild fits of fantasy! I know what a werewolf looks like. I've seen enough Hammer Horror films over the years. Believe me; they do not do this creature justice!"

"Hmm…" Toms replied "Having never seen a werewolf myself, you understand I would find it difficult of course to agree with you!" Toms' reply at least brought a faint smile to Mary's face.

"Mr Toms," Daniel interrupted, "do you think we could continue this conversation at a later date, please? Both my wife and I need to get some rest!"

Toms didn't want to push the conversation any further, so he didn't challenge Daniel for wishing to finish the interview when he did.

"Yes, of course. I understand," Toms conceded as he got to his feet.

"Will you be at this address for the next few days?" Toms asked.

"Yes," Daniel replied. Toms moved to leave the drawing room, then stopped suddenly and turned to Mary and Daniel.

"Please let us know if there is anything we can do in the meantime?" he said.

* * *

Daniel escorted DI Toms to the front door. He watched as Toms got in his car and pulled away, the two men exchanging a final passing wave. When the car was gone, Daniel took a moment to step out onto the gravel drive of his friend's home. This was the first opportunity he'd had to sample some fresh morning air, following the devastation of the previous evening.

He acknowledged the police officer guarding the house and walked down the winding drive of the Ashtons' home. The air was still, but fresh, the remnants of frost still evident in patches on the front lawn. Daniel took in a large gulp of fresh air. It tasted good. Above him, he heard the sound of a solitary crow, as it glided into one of the tree tops that adorned the avenue beyond the Ashtons' front gates.

He stood for a minute, thinking; he felt vulnerable and, for the first time in a very long time, he felt unsure, unsure of what the future would now bring, both to himself and his family. The very solid foundation he thought they had as a family had been rocked; it was being severely tested. His family was under threat, and he had no idea from what or how he could protect them. For them, their world had changed, and it was for the worse. He knew he and his family would have precious little time to rest, before Toms would return to pester them with more questions. They were now national news; the press and the media would of course hound them. What, he wondered, would the police make of their incredulous story? How could it be believed? He couldn't explain any rationale for what he had seen. He was struggling to come to terms with it himself, although painful cuts and abrasions on his face would remind him of the all too awful reality of what had happened. That creature, that huge black animal with its burning rabid eyes! How would he bring his family out from this? Mary and Eleanor in particular had already suffered so much they were now confronted with the death — no not death, but the murder — of Alice, as well! Perhaps selfishly, he also thought of the business he was trying to build. How was he going to attract new customers, maybe even managing to keep his exiting ones with all this on his CV?

Right now, though, events had forced the wellbeing of his family to the very top of his agenda; events had moved beyond his control, but one thing was for sure; he would not let what happened divide the family; he had to find the resolve to be able to keep his family together, sane and safe.

Daniel turned and looked back up at house. He wanted to cut and run, he thought, get away, pack the family up and just get as far away from this nightmare as he could.

* * *

Indeed, the passing days presented more of a challenge to the family than he had originally anticipated. During this period, Mary withdrew deeper and deeper into herself. She would barely speak to the children, let alone Daniel. She spent most of the day in the bedroom of the Ashtons' home, curtains drawn, shut away from the baying press which, by now, had discovered the family's whereabouts. They gathered in small numbers at the Ashtons' entrance or consistently and repeatedly called by telephone. At one stage, Theresa Ashton had to remove the receiver from the phone to block any more unwelcome calls. Mary, sitting alone with her thoughts, reflected on her life with her mother and weep.

Both Mary and Daniel had by now the same desperate need to get away, to start putting this whole episode behind them. It was a time to grieve; they had that much in common; it was a time to withdraw; that was their desire. However, at that moment in their lives, the two of them were now poles apart, as far apart as they had ever been in their marriage and the resolve Daniel was looking for had instead only divided them. Daniel was angry, restless, confused. He now better understood what Mary had been trying to tell him about her past; maybe now it was time to believe her, but he was still angry, angry that they had spent so many years together not knowing this chapter in her life. She had kept it from him for so long and, now, only when events kicked off at Ravensdale, did she venture to tell him about her past.

Although Mary was withdrawn, she had a clearer focus on what she had to do. This was her fight; she felt responsible. The family's new life had so much promise, but, instead, it now lay in tatters. The peace they had sought was now destroyed forever, their lives devastatingly ripped to shreds.

Yes, Daniel was angry, but he now understood Mary's concerns. He wasn't prepared for what Mary was planning to do next.

Chapter 11

In the days that followed the murder, it seemed to Mary that the police investigation that had begun as both intense and focused had dropped away. She had seen Detective Inspector Toms on a number of occasions in follow-up interviews, but it had been of little surprise to her that in that time no new leads on the case had emerged, at least no new information, which the police did not already know of. Mary knew the police were struggling. She had explained to Toms in what seemed countless interviews and statements the details of her past and what she believed had been the catalyst for the attack, largely that a force she couldn't explain had been generated by her daughter Eleanor. Toms, for his part, liked to believe that he possessed an open mind on such matters but was finding the statements from both Mary and Daniel hard to accept. Nonetheless, there had been some evidence of an animal at the Fosters' property; he had himself detected some dark, coarse animal hair, which, under analysis, had been identified as hairs from a wolf. Not totally dismissing the Fosters' statements, he had made some ground in investigating any or all occult groups that were known to exist around the Yorkshire area, but he had little luck.

With no obvious evidence or clues pointing to a third party having committed the crime, it seemed that suspicion initially fell on Daniel. Toms had done some digging around, while investigating the Fosters' past. It seemed Mary had been telling the truth. There was some history of paranormal activity in her past, but since growing up, meeting and marrying Daniel and the couple's life together in London, all seemed pretty unspectacular. Under pressure from his Detective Chief Inspector to come up with some leads, Toms had considered submitting Daniel for some psychiatric evaluation, but since Daniel Foster possessed no history of either a criminal or deviant nature, he believed this would be a fruitless exercise and just put the family under greater stress. Toms was wily enough to know that Daniel Foster was not the type of man to commit such a crime.

* * *

The post mortem on Alice Parsons had been a drawn out, painful affair for Mary. She had begun to emerge from the initial shock of her mother's death and wished to move on with the process of planning for her mother's funeral. This she was unable to do, until the police had released the body, following the post mortem. The post mortem itself had taken place in the pathology department at Leeds. The pathologists' verdict did little to assist the on-going police enquiries of murder by person or persons unknown. Details of the examination had been kept away from the media, but the gruesome facts had been recorded. The most striking wound to Alice Parsons was the throat wound; virtually the whole of Alice's throat had been torn out, to the point that her head was almost severed from the rest of her body. The force of the attack had also left the neck broken. In the chest area, eleven ribs had been broken, totally crushed, many smashed into small fragments. Some ribs had broken through and protruded through the victim's skin. In the abdominal area, there was evidence of severe haemorrhaging, resulting in large areas of discolouration and bruising to the lower chest and stomach. Predominantly, though, Alice had died as a result of the violent injury to the throat and subsequent loss of about eighty per cent of her blood.

Over the previous week, Mary had been in contact with both Alice's family and friends. Flowers had arrived at the house in a steady stream. The address for the Ashtons' house had been given out at their kind permission. Initial press interest had dwindled and, now, very few facts about the case emerged and little was being reported in the local press, let alone the national press. The police released very little information about the case, quite simply because they had very few leads!

Mary, Daniel, and the children had remained holed up at the Ashtons' house since the murder, but now Mary was feeling less than comfortable. The Ashtons had been good friends for a number of years and the continued close proximity meant that Daniel could return to work with his business partner. Mary, however, did not want to outstay her welcome. Since the murder, the children had not been back to school, but now, two weeks had passed, and she felt that the family should return to some form of normality. She wanted to put this chapter behind her and move on, but she felt that this could only be done, once her mother had been buried. With Eleanor off from school, Mary took the opportunity during a calm period to watch and observe her child. To her, in all aspects of the way she behaved she was just a normal little girl. While staying at the Ashtons she had made a new friend, the Ashtons' cat Sooty, and she spent much of her time following the animal around, stroking it and holding conversations with it.

By the end of October, the police had declared that all analysis and examination of Alice Parsons' body had been completed. Finally, the body was turned over to Mary and the family for burial. Although welcoming this turn of events, it nonetheless filled Mary with a sense of foreboding. She now finally had to deal with her own mother's funeral and, once again, it would push the family firmly back into the media spotlight.

The funeral was to be held the first week of November in Staines, the town where Mary grew up and where Alice had still lived up until her death. Family and close friends, of whom there were many, were invited to attend. The media were to be kept away. It was with some sense of relief that Mary and the family decamped from the Ashtons' home and drove south the two hundred miles or so to Alice's home in Staines. To Mary, the change of scenery was a welcome relief. The drive south allowed Mary the opportunity to witness the dramatic changes in the landscape. From the vast and breath-taking expanse of both the Yorkshire and Derbyshire dales, to the gradual gently-rolling hills of the south and, Mary thought, the noticeable increase from the midlands onwards in traffic! Suddenly, Yorkshire seemed harsh, the craggy stone-faced peaks hard and brutal, the wind across the moors cold and icy. Mary felt that the family had outstayed their welcome at Stockport, yet she had little desire at that time to return to Ravensdale and the Hungry Harshes. Even though the police had, to a greater extent concluded a lot of their physical investigation at the house, Mary was not ready in her own mind to be able to return to the scene of her mother's death. Besides, any additional trauma would not be good for the children, and Eleanor in particular. The whole family was still shaken from the experience.

For Mary, the journey south was also solemn, the return to her mother's and her own childhood home profoundly moving for her. As the car approached the house, the memories returned. Entering the house, turning the key in the latch on the front door, and stepping in sent shivers down Mary's back. She was immediately greeted by her mother's favourite scent, lily of the valley, which seemed to permeate every room in the house. Mary put her bag down on the reception table in the hall and walked into her mother's large sitting room, situated just off the hall. The large curtains were drawn, and she gently pulled them back, allowing a dusky light to flood into the room. As she did, she glanced out of the large bay window at her own family, Daniel and the children, who were unpacking the car. Mary turned and observed her mother's *objets d'art* on the large white mantel. Adorning the fireplace sat several silver-gilt framed pictures, pictures of her mother and father, of her grandmother, and one of her and the children. In a corner cabinet, fronted by gilt-edged glass sat a number of Lladdro figurines. The suite, elegant mock Georgian sat faithfully, awaiting its owner's return.

Mary slowly walked out of the room back into the hall and began to climb the stairs, all the time taking in the atmosphere. She felt her eyes well up and her cheeks flush, as emotion began to get the better of her composed manner, which she had maintained until now. She did not want to break down in front of the children, so she moved at quicker pace to the top of the stairs. Turning directly to her right, she slowly opened the door of what had been her old bedroom. The room had changed little from when she had occupied it. The old mahogany double wardrobe, a relic of her grandmother's past sat where it had always sat, facing the bedroom door as one walked in. To her credit, Alice had left Mary's bed unchanged, the same duvet and pillowcases were there, but the room was now used much more as a spare room. Boxes filled with her mother's items and letters were stacked one end of the room. Mary walked past these to look out of the bedroom window, her bedroom window, onto the garden below and the row of semi-detached roofs of the houses that stood beyond the bottom of the garden. Mary had not visited her mother's house for some months and certainly not since the move to Ravensdale. Returning there always brought back fond memories but, today, her heart ached for her lost mother, and she struggled to control her emotions, as she walked around the house.

Downstairs in the kitchen, there hung a poignant reminder, a wall calendar hung from one of the kitchen units. It was set on the month of October. A series of Post-It Notes were stuck to it, acting as reminders of activities or events on specific days. Nearly half way down, Mary saw a note that read simply 'VISIT MARY, TAKE SOME FLOWERS.' Mary was not a naturally spiritual person and had hoped that being in the sanctuary of her mother's home would provide comfort at a time when she wanted to put aside the terrible events in Yorkshire.

* * *

The family had been in the house for little more than a day before Mary's aunt Lillian, Aunt Lil as she was affectionately known, paid a visit. Lil was a tall, elegant woman with a prominent nose, some eight years younger than Mary's mother Alice, she was prone to dress in long floral-print summer dresses with a round straw hat perched on the top of her head like a large bird's nest, often obliterating her greying fringe. Her hair hung thick and straight beneath the brim in a bob. As a character, Lil could not be more different than Alice. Whereas Alice was considered conservative, thoughtful, and serious, Lil was a busy, jolly woman; she loved life, and it showed to all who met and knew her. She was a great organiser of fetes in her home village of Ottershaw and loved nothing more than to organise walks and rambles. Lil had been divorced for some ten years, but she was nonetheless extremely sociable and had a large list of friends and acquaintances, although she would always stress to Mary with a twinkle in her eye that relationships with any male friends were always on a platonic basis. For Mary to say that Lil bordered on a somewhat eccentric nature was indeed an understatement.

Mary loved her aunt, though, and the two women got on well whenever they were together. Lil never had any children of her own, and so, she had been inclined to spoil her niece somewhat, particularly when Mary was young. Mary had been turning to Lil for support in the weeks following the attack at Ravensdale. The two women had been in constant communication by phone, both comforting and consoling each other. For Mary, Lil had been a tower of strength, particularly when it came to the painful task of organising Alice's funeral arrangements.

Lillian had known, as acquaintances, several of the ladies of the WI, the organisation that Alice had been part of. Among them, they had counselled Mary on the details of the ceremony organising the Church and burial arrangements. Alice had always wanted to be buried next to her dear husband, never cremated. They'd also drawn up a list of possible attendees, which included many friends and family. They had also secured a location large enough to hold the gathering for the wake, following the burial. The possible attendees list was long. Alice had many friends as a result of her participation in the WI. Local civic leaders and dignitaries also headed the list.

Little Pig, Little Pig

The two ladies had decided that it would be better to get out of the house. At Lil's insistence, they would go out for some lunch, leaving Daniel, who was still attempting to run his business from Staines, to manage the children. Besides, Lil could not spend too long in Alice's house; it proved too painful. For both women, it was a relief to be out of the house.

Fifteen minutes up the road, the two women found a pub that served bar snacks. As the women sat down in a remote corner of the pub, with only a fruit machine to entertain them, complete with flashing neon lights, the two women got down to business. The discussion started with the funeral arrangements. The procedure agreed with the undertakers for bringing the body to the house by hearse, before moving on to the church, where anyone who wanted to address the congregation could do so, other than the Vicar and the subsequent burial itself. With the painful detail out of the way, food was served. Lil had Scampi and chips, and Mary had ham, egg, and chips. Lil decided with the meal underway that she would tentatively probe Mary on the subject of the family's wellbeing.

"How's the family, Dear?" Lil asked, looking down at her plate of scampi not completely sure of what response she would receive.

"We're trying to get through this!" Mary replied,

"How are the kids?" Lil pushed again.

Mary had been arranging a portion of chips and ham on a fork, put down both the knife and fork and looked up at Lil. "Oh, Lil! I feel so responsible for Mum's death!" she exclaimed.

"Nonsense!" Lil said bullishly.

"It's because of me that she's dead!" Mary exclaimed, again. With her voice raised and with emotion, she drew the attention of other people in the pub, who were enjoying a drink or a meal. Lil remained bullish and without emotion pressed Mary harder.

"Go on!" she exclaimed. There was silence between the two women; at that point, Mary wouldn't commit to saying anymore.

"How's Eleanor?" Lil started off on another tack.

Mary looked up at her aunt from her glass of Perrier water. "You know, don't you Lil." Mary nodded. "You know, I haven't said anything, but you know!"

Lil looked up at Mary. "My dear, I have worried about those children ever since you dared produced them!" she retorted. Mary understood that her Aunt was relating to her on the subject of her own paranormal experiences and breathed a heavy sigh of relief.

"Alice, too!" Lil continued. "You know she worried more than I did, and I used to worry! Boy did I worry! We'd both talk about it for hours. You know, when we got together, just once or twice, we'd talk about it. Oh, we'd talk about anything and everything! You know?" Lil paused for a moment, as she put down her knife and fork and picked up her wine glass. Drawing on a large gulp of wine, she fixed her eyes on Mary.

"You know, I had gifts!" she said, pointing her hand with the wine glass at Mary. "Don't have them now, of course."

Mary was astonished; for the first time, someone else in the family was admitting that they had paranormal abilities.

"I used to be able to move small objects as a child, never told you! I don't think Alice ever told you, did she?"

Mary looked aghast. "This is amazing. I...I...didn't know this, didn't know any of this!" Mary replied, reaching for her Perrier water.

"When you had your experience at the time that Mum died, my Mum!" Lil emphasised, "we knew then that the family had this gift, this psychokinetic ability, an ability to raise paranormal entities, it was something that was hereditary, something that could be passed on!"

"Lil, believe me, I never knew any of this. Mum never told me anything about it!" Feelings of anger started to overcome Mary.

"Of course you didn't!" Lil replied. "Alice didn't want you to know, made me vow never to tell you!" There was a further pause between the two women, Lil drew on another glass of wine and, as she did, she tipped her head back and scanned Mary's eyes.

"It's Eleanor isn't it?" she asked. "She has it!" As Lil said the words, Mary nodded in acknowledgement, a lump forming in her throat. Lil put down her glass, but her eyes remained fixed on her niece.

"And it's getting worse, isn't it Mary! What I had was what I would call just a sideshow trick, a novelty, you know, making small objects move, sometimes making them disappear completely. They, the specialist doctors who saw me associated my behaviour with poltergeist activity, a psychokinetic connection with a spirit; oh, it was harmless and caused little damage." Lil again broke off from her meal to look up into Mary's eyes.

"Of course, what you experienced around the time of your Grandmother's death was some completely different emotion, something far stronger. Something far more capable of seizing on your worst fears and taking control of them."

Mary was amazed at her aunt's insight. "Lil, how on earth do you know all of this?" Mary asked.

"Read up on it, Dear! Had to. Like you, what happened to me happened to me as a child, and when you're a child, you know very little about what's going on." Again there was a brief pause before Lil continued.

"Listen, Mary, what happened to me happened, what happened to you happened; there's no denying that. There's also no denying that, for whoever it seeks out with each generation of our family, this curse, this burden is getting worse and will continue to get worse for them! We have to do something about it, Mary. We have to help Eleanor, whatever it is that's coming through her will eventually want to kill her, and you, if you stand in its way!"

As Lil spoke the words, Mary felt a pain like a knife cutting through her. The pain and emotion mixed together was acute. For the first time, here was someone who understood what was happening, not just to her but to Eleanor and the whole family. Admittedly, the two women had discussed many things together over the telephone in the past two weeks. In Lillian, Mary had found someone to whom she could unburden this great weight she felt bearing down on her although, at the same time, she did not see fit to disclose too much to her aunt regarding the details of the attack, for fear of upsetting her. However, over the years, Lillian though had developed an acute sixth sense and would intuitively know in many people she met the source of their underlying problems. It had come as something of a revelation to Mary that Lil was prepared to talk to her about Eleanor, indeed even offering to help her in this dark, troubled period of their lives.

Lil finished her scampi and chips, neatly placed the knife and fork together on the plate, and pushed it to one side of the table.

"Mary, was there a purpose to that final trip Alice made?" Lil asked.

"Yes, yes there was," Mary said, keen to answer. "I needed Mum's help! I wanted her to tell me about the past, my past! I wanted to understand more about what happened when Nana died!"

Lil looked thoughtful. "What were Alice's conclusions? What was her response?"

Mary breathed a heavy sigh. "She was reluctant to get involved, Lil, but she did agree to help me!"

"Then!" said Lil in a spirit of determination and resolve, "I will help you, too!"

* * *

Eventually and inevitably, the day of the funeral came. Mary had dreaded the arrival of this day. The day had started grey with heavy clouds; there was the threat of showers, although, by the early morning, none had yet visited. By breakfast, the first trickle of flowers and wreaths had started to arrive at the house; by ten o'clock, it was quickly becoming a flood, and Daniel, dressed in a black two-piece suite with white shirt and black tie was increasingly spending his time manning the front door, coordinating where the great sways of white and ivory lilies and roses should be placed. Mary had had little breakfast that morning; she did not have the appetite for it, spending most of her time, instead, sitting in her mother's bedroom at her vanity unit, staring into the mirror. She wore a simple, elegant black dress, punctuated on the breast with her mother's gold, diamond, and sapphire brooch. She completed her makeup, applying both mascara and lipstick in an economical manner. She had no capacity to concentrate fully on the business of making herself up. *Oh*, she thought, *this is a painful, wretched day*. This was going to be an opportunity to see family and friends, some of whom she had thought she would never see again and never wanted to see again. How would they all react to her, she wondered. Would they blame her? Blame her for being the cause of her beloved mother's death? Would anyone talk to her? Maybe, she thought, it would be easier if everyone just picked up a stone or a rock and just hurled it at her, killed her there and then and be done with it! It wasn't just going to be the reaction and response of the family she had to contend with. News of the funeral had stirred media interest. A small gathering of photographers and journalists had stationed themselves outside the house, uninvited, unwelcome! There was only a solitary police officer assigned at the front of her mother's house. His job was to assist the family in maintaining their privacy on this solemn day. It was his job to keep them at bay.

Eventually, at about ten-thirty a.m., the hearse carrying Alice Parsons' remains pulled up outside the leafy suburban house to a veritable barrage of camera shutters and flashes. On seeing the hearse pull up, many of the street's inhabitants had begun to line the pavement. These were Alice's neighbours coming out to pay their last respects. Others had come from farther afield. The curious also came, who had never known Alice or her family but had read about the case and had followed it. A second car pulled into the kerb, behind the hearse, and a smartly dressed man, one of the pallbearers climbed out and walked up the shrub-lined drive to the front door. There was a brief exchange with Daniel and the man walked back to the second car, where he stopped, turned, and stood and waited for the occupants of the car to arrive. Daniel turned and raised his eyes to Mary, who had by now joined her family and Lillian downstairs; it was time to leave. Mary, Daniel, and the children, together with Lil, solemnly walked out of the front door and down the path to the waiting car. All the time, Mary and Daniel averted their eyes away from the throng of neighbours and press, which had gathered on the street. Only the children, David and Eleanor, looked up inquisitively at the crowd. Lillian quickly slammed shut the front door of the house and quickly ushered after them. As she got to the car, Mary paused to take a look at her mother's coffin in the first car. The elegantly shaped wreaths offset the fine oak inlays of her mother's casket. Alice would have approved, Mary thought. Mary turned and looked back down the street. By now, there were three further cars carrying family members; she strained to see who was in the cars, but it proved difficult to see. Lil had told her but; nonetheless, she was keen to see that everyone had turned up to pay final respects to her beloved mother. She had, however, no sense of urgency or desire to greet them any sooner than she needed to.

Once Mary and Lil had joined the family and were seated inside the second car, the man in the dark suit gently closed the car door behind them. Once he had climbed in the car, the hearse slowly pulled away, and Alice Parsons left her home for the last time.

The long, slow procession took about a fifteen-minute route through Staines, before it reached the Church of St. Peter's. The procession had been a long one. There was at least a further ten to fifteen cars carrying friends and family that trailed behind the main procession, bringing traffic in the bustling town to a standstill. As the cars pulled into the church, Mary, Daniel, and the children got out, and Lil began greeting members of the family and friends, as they gathered around the church entrance. Mary's heart was pounding, and she felt physically sick, as old aunts and uncles, second cousins, and their children began approaching her offering their hands and attempting, where possible, to provide sympathetic hugs. Not too many, she thought, held stones or rocks; the general consensus was profound sympathy and sorrow for Mary and the family. Daniel gripped his wife's shaking hand in support, as Alice's casket was unloaded from the hearse and solemnly carried into the church. Sadly, but inevitably for the family, a police presence had to be made available at the church to keep press and media at bay.

Thankfully, mercifully for Mary, the service was well read and well conducted, and the readings, together with the subsequent burial, seemed to pass smoothly but largely in a blur. She had wanted to absorb as much as she could, with regards the ceremony, but all she kept hearing in her head, repeated over and over again, were the words uttered by her mother that last fateful weekend at the Hungry Harshes, those last fateful hours the two women spent together, consoling each other, while discussing their worries and fears for the future. The words and her mother's voice seemed to tumble on and on: "Mary, we will get through this together! Mary, we will get through this together!"

When the service was complete, everybody set off for the destination that would hold the wake. This was to be the very conservative Staines Ladies Bowls Club, situated on the edge of town. All credit to the Women's Institute, they had done Mary proud in terms of the organisation, and she, in turn, made a point of thanking the ladies for their effort. It was

November, and the bowling season, for all intents and purposes, was over, so the clubhouse was shut, opening only for bookings and events. The majority of family, friends, and well-wishers, who attended the service, had made the journey from the church to the newly built brick clubhouse. Sandwiches, rolls, sausage rolls, and other finger food were followed by a selection of small cakes with plenty of tea and coffee. The clubhouse was, of course, licensed, so on Mary's request; everyone was invited to share in a glass of champagne or sparkling wine, as a mark of respect and a final farewell to Alice. Mary had felt it was important to keep with this most ancient of family rituals, even though she could not bring herself to touch a drop.

Mary, Daniel, and Lil felt it their responsibility to mingle amongst the guests. The children amused themselves between threats of rain, which became little more than light showers, by running around on the finely mown Bowling Green. As Mary chatted and reminisced with old friends and family, the feeling of claustrophobia she'd had for most of the day began to dissipate. It had been a very long and weary day. Her emotional state, fragile over the past few weeks, had become stretched to breaking point. She had experienced grief and sorrow, as she had never felt before, but today, at the end of the afternoon, she felt a huge sense of relief. All those who came to pay their respects to her mother, friends, and family, alike, had shown her and her family great kindness. It was a relief that everyone had appeared supportive and sincere; the anticipated blame and anger that Mary had feared did not materialise.

By seven o'clock that evening, as darkness threw a shroud around the clubhouse, the final guests began to drift away. Mary had never hugged or been hugged by so many people in one day. As the final cars carrying mourners pulled away, Mary stood at the front entrance to the clubhouse and dutifully waved them off. Inside, the voluntary ladies of the WI collected all the used cups, saucers, and plates and began clearing away. With the day almost over, Mary, Daniel, and the children left for home. The drive from the bowls club to Alice's house was thankfully not too far but, geographically, it did take in much of Staines. Much of it Mary already knew, but much she noted had also changed. It had become polluted by the noise and fumes from the incessant growth of industry to the West of London. The ever-present M25 motorway hummed in the background and could not be muffled, coupled with the increasing intrusion of noise from Heathrow Airport, as it too had become the focus of rapidly increased expansion. To Mary, it now appeared that Staines, by no fault of its own, had become the wart that was attached to the body of globalisation and West London and seemed to her to become just another tool, a gateway to mass globalisation.

With a sense of relief that the day had finally passed, Mary slumped back into the passenger seat of the car and slowly but wearily closed her eyes. She had seen quite enough of Staines; she didn't wish to see any more. Certainly, she had heard enough of it.

In part it reminded her of why the family had moved to Ravensdale in the first place. Oh, how she longed to be back there again. It was time, she thought, to go back; besides, the kids needed to get back to school, since they had missed so much and suffered too much disruption. She thought about everything they had worked and saved for, everything they had invested in; they needed now to get back! Eleanor's problems still hung over them, and besides, there was still a murder enquiry to be resolved. Mary knew that she and, particularly, Daniel were the key suspects, which made the whole damned situation just that bit more intolerable. Still, Mary was not going to give in. She wasn't going to back away from this. She couldn't. She knew that, once at home again, the sinister demons locked inside her daughter's head would once again come calling. This time, she wouldn't flee; she didn't wish to wait until the creature hunted her and the family down. No, this time, she decided she was going to go after it herself. This had to stop, once and for all.

"Dan," Mary said, breaking the silence in the car, her eyes still closed.

"Yes?" Dan replied, taking his eyes away from the road as he said it.

"Let's go home!" Mary replied.

"We are going home, dear, back to your mother's."

"No, I mean, let's go home!" As she spoke the words, Mary opened her eyes and turned her face to look up at Daniel's. He had in the past few hours noticed a transformation in his wife. The vulnerability she had shown earlier in the day had gone. Now, to Dan, Mary seemed to speak with a steely resolve.

"You need to get back to work, Dan, and besides, I've got business of my own I need to attend to!" Mary said, turning her head to look at the road ahead.

"What do you mean?" Daniel replied.

"I'm going to need to spend some time in Leeds. We are going to beat this thing, Dan. We're going to beat this thing, and we will get on with our lives!" Mary exclaimed. "I'm going to get our daughter well again and rid this family of this damned curse!"

Chapter 12

The whole business of her mother's funeral had been a draining affair for Mary. Emotionally, nothing was more emotionally draining than visiting her mother's house for the first time knowing that she was no longer there. She had woken up to the realisation that the nightmare she carried with her travelled with her. Wherever she went to seek solace, whether Stockport, Staines, or back to Ravensdale, the bloody, unforgettable memories of that night and her mother's death would continue to haunt her. Returning to Ravensdale, she felt would represent some kind of return to day-to-day living. The task at hand was far from being completed, but now she knew, with some assurance, the steps she must take to avenge her mother's death.

The return to Ravensdale was, as it turned out, an uncertain and bleak experience for the family, uncertain since no one knew exactly what would greet them on their return, either from outsiders and the media to locals in the village. The return was bleak, largely due to the fact that the end of November was approaching. The crisp, sunny, autumn days had gone, and grey clouds had signalled the impending onset of winter. It was also bleak because, now, the family were returning to the scene of the crime, the scene where they witnessed such brutal, ugly violence that had left one of their own dead. Once again, the family had travelled with a police escort, the Royal Berkshire Police, working in close cooperation with the North Yorkshire Police force, ensured that the Foster family had the company of a police presence for the whole of their journey home. As Detective Inspector Toms had dutifully made clear to both Mary and Daniel, they were, for now, seen as suspects to the murder, on the basis of the fact that no other evidence of a third party, other than that of an animal could be detected. Conversely, with the murderer still at large and now two previous break ins at the property, the family were seen as targets, for which the murderer would likely try to attack again. The police were in something of a hapless position. All they could do was to track and monitor the family, keeping them under surveillance while, at the same time, offering police protection.

The procession of vehicles into the village, through the main high street and up the hill to the Hungry Harshes, did enough to attract the attention of the villagers, who had, by now, stopped whatever they were doing to observe the curious convoy, consisting of a motor cycle outrider, the Fosters' car, a further marked police car, and a succession of trailing media and press. The car ascended the steep road that led up to the house. The motorcycle outrider pulled up just beyond the entrance to allow the Fosters to pull their car onto the drive. The marked police then pulled across the drive, as if to block any further access by unwelcome parties. The succession of media came to a halt at the foot of the road, as a police cordon temporarily stopped, then dispersed the baying journalists. Mary was first to climb out of the car. The intense and heavy grey clouds had made the afternoon seem murky, and the front porch light to the house was on, courtesy of the police, who had access to the house. Mary walked up the front path to the imposing door, her heart beating. She stopped at the door, reached in her bag for the key, put the key in the lock, and closed her eyes, while she turned the key. Pushing the door open, she stepped into the large hall. The house was empty and in darkness. Following the police investigation, all the curtains to the house, both upstairs and downstairs, had been drawn to keep the curious away. As she stood in the hall, David ran past her and bolted up the stairs to his room, the thudding of his feet on the landing was all Mary heard, as he made his way to his beloved play station. Eleanor followed, but she hesitated at the doorway. Peering into the hall, she clasped the frame of the doorway, uneasy to let go and venture into the house. Mary turned and looked down at her daughter. She gave her a knowing look.

"I know," she said in a low voice, sensing the girl's unease and the reason for it.

Leaving Eleanor in the doorway, Mary walked into the sitting room and moved to the window;

pulling back the curtains, she noted the thick layer of dust coating the mahogany furniture. *We have been away a long time,* she thought. Her eyes scanned the room; the police had created little disruption, here; then she stopped and trembled, as she noticed on the sideboard at the back of the room the half empty bottle of wine, still there from when she and Alice had last shared a drink that fateful evening. Worse still for Mary, were the two glasses that were standing next to the bottle. Both were unclean, unwashed, still with the residue and coating of red wine in them. She walked across to the sideboard and picked up a glass. Running her finger along the lip of the glass, she felt a shock of electricity, as she once again felt the warmth of her mother's presence. Alice was with her; she was all around her, Mary thought. She was there to welcome her home. For a while, Mary remained lost in her thoughts and ignored Daniel, as he walked to and from the house carrying suitcases through the front door.

"Oh god, Mary, look at this!" came the exacerbated call from Daniel, who had gone into the kitchen. It broke Mary's trance, and she put the glass back down on the sideboard, meticulously repositioning it in the pool of dust. Realising that Daniel was calling her from the kitchen; she took in a deep breath and walked slowly from the sitting room, down the hall. Looking across to the door, she saw Eleanor was still standing there.

"Come on, Eleanor, it'll be all right." Mary tried to reassure her. But the little girl wouldn't move, and Mary's stomach began turning, as she approached the kitchen door, not knowing what she would come upon. Stepping into the kitchen, she saw Daniel, hands on hips; she couldn't help but notice him trembling, as he looked at the rear door.

"All this will have to be done!" he exclaimed, nodding to the door and window that looked out on the patio. The police, in their quest to secure the property had boarded it up, shutting out all the light that would normally flood the kitchen. In their efforts, the police had made an attempt to straighten up the kitchen the best they could. All the drawers and the table had been repositioned, and Mary thought it amusing that they had taken the trouble to stack all the broken crockery on the table. She walked across the kitchen to where her mother had lain. Staring down at the hard surface of the floor, she saw that it had been cleaned. There was none of Alice's blood. All traces of her mother had been wiped away, except that is, for the wine glass in the sitting room!

* * *

Mary was determined in the first few days at home to get things moving back to normal. The kids went back to school; in Eleanor's case, her behaviour was to be monitored by the teachers, and both Mrs Forbes and Eleanor's teacher Miss Strand would be extra vigilant. Since returning home, Eleanor had seemed a former shadow of herself. She was pale and nervous, and it was often difficult for Mary to coax her into the kitchen for meals. At night, since arriving home, she would sleep in the spare room with Mary. Mary encouraged this. Daniel had once again claimed on the household insurance to have all the damage to the house repaired, which had involved replacing the window, the doorframes, and glass. The tradesmen who undertook the work remarked to Daniel how frequently their paths crossed! Daniel did not see the funny side of it.

Since returning from Staines, Mary had made an attempt to move on with some gusto. She had decided that she would ignore the attention she received, as she went to and from town. Yes, people stood and stared; yes, people pointed; yes, people talked in whispers, whenever she walked past them on the street or in a shop. It hadn't helped, however, that a strong police presence remained, and a plain-clothes officer accompanied her everywhere, but she went nonetheless. Let the village talk; there was little she could do about it and, besides, she would resist letting things stoke her paranoia. Apart from occasional trips into the village, she had reinitiated the plans for the interior design of the grand old house, something that had been put on hold when the first bizarre events had begun. She had spoken with Lil at length, and she had agreed to travel up to stay for a period, and she had sat down and worked her way through the extensive amount of post that had been sent to the house. Some were the standard bills, some junk mail, many were from well-wishers who had never known the family but had followed the events through the media and felt sympathy for the family's plight. Others were from occult societies, which had focused on the very intriguing and bizarre facts around the case, and then there was one from the NHS, requesting Eleanor attend for a brain scan and consultation at Leeds. The letter had arrived nearly a month earlier, and the date of the appointment had been missed. No matter. For Mary, the nature of the letter, together with the destination, had again prompted her memory. Leeds, yes Leeds, she thought, that's where she found the details on that doctor. What was his name? Martin Hannay at the University of Leeds, the expert in parapsychology. Dropping the post, Mary rushed to the study where Daniel's computer sat. Daniel was out on business, so she would not be interrupted. She looked up at the clock on the wall. It was ten-thirty. There was a chance that, if she could find a number for this Dr Hannay, she might be able to get hold of him! Logging into the computer, she searched for the University of Leeds and came to the main site. She searched feverishly for Dr Hannay's direct contact details but could not find them, landing instead upon the main contact for all enquiries through to the University. Grabbing a pencil and writing it down, she reached for the phone. As she did, she peered out of the study door down the hall. The house was empty, and only a solitary officer stood dutifully at the front door. The phone rang several times before a female voice answered.

"University of Leeds Campus reception. How can I help?"

"Yes, I'd like to speak to Dr Martin Hannay, please," Mary said. There was a moment's silence before the voice spoke again.

"Wait one moment, please. I'm just transferring you." The phone rang again, as Mary tapped her pencil on the bureau, then she sat up in her chair, when she heard the receiver being picked up at the other end.

"Department of Psychology, how can I help?" came the voice from another woman.

"Yes, my name is Mary Foster, and I'd like to speak to Doctor Martin Hannay, please. Is he available?" Mary asked.

"Just one moment, please!" came the reply, and Mary knew she had been put on pause. It seemed to take an agonizingly long time to determine whether or not Doctor Hannay was or was not available, and indeed where he was.

After a period of listening to light chamber music, the receiver crackled back into life; it was the receptionist. "One moment, please. I'm putting you through." Mary's heart lifted, as she at first heard the phone ring, then again the receiver lifted and a man's voice answered.

"Hello?"

"Hello, is this Doctor Martin Hannay?" Mary asked.

"This is he," came the reply. The voice sounded gruff and spoke at first in an abrupt tone.

"Doctor Hannay, my name is Mary Foster. We've never met before, but I was browsing the Internet for leading exponents on parapsychology, and your name seemed to come up often," Mary explained. There was silence, as Mary waited for the man on the other end of the line to confirm her statement.

"Well, this is the Department of Psychology, Mrs Foster; the department prides itself on dealing with a broad range of subject matter. Parapsychology is one area where we conduct research. But how can we help you?" Hannay asked.

Mary wasn't sure quite how to phase her request. She paused a moment. "Well, I have a particular problem I'm hoping may be of some interest to you." Mary's voice trembled slightly as she spoke. "A problem I'm hoping you can help with! You see, it's my five-year-old daughter; she's desperately sick she needs help!" There was silence from the other end of the phone.

"I…I believe that she is sick in her mind; she is in some way possessed!" Mary stopped at that point.

"Mrs Foster, why do you believe that your daughter is possessed?" asked Hannay.

"I believe that her mind is being manipulated by some force greater than that which I can understand. She has the ability to make things…events…happen, I don't know how, but she's doing it! I believe — no, I fear — that she has inherited something terrible from me, some terrible legacy!" Mary said. Again, there was a period of silence.

"Is your daughter at school now?" Hannay asked.

"Yes," Mary's said.

"How is she in herself?" Hannay asked.

"Introverted, quiet, she tends to play by herself, on her own," Mary answered.

"Does she bear any other strong characteristics? For example, does she ever become aggressive at all? Has she ever tried to run away from home?" Hannay pressed.

"No, she's not like that, never attempted anything like that. She's normally a perfectly contented little girl," Mary replied.

"Mrs Foster, what leads you to believe that your daughter is possessed. She sounds not unlike any normal little girl!" exclaimed Hannay, who by now was looking to get off the call. Crank callers were an occupational hazard of his profession. A prominent professor and lecturer, his published works on psychokinesis, the study of the direct influence of the mind on a physical system, which could not be accounted for through the mediation of any known physical energy, had raised his standing in the field of psychology and particularly, parapsychology. An increase in the entry rates for students wishing to study psychology at universities across the country had also buoyed demand for this eminent man, who had become one of the country's leading champions of making the subject of parapsychology a serious part of the curriculum.

From the increasing numbers of psychology students, Hannay knew that a small section would be tempted to diversify and study in the specialist field of parapsychology. With Universities up and down the country demanding his time and his membership and time given to many affiliated associations, he himself a member of the Accredited Parapsychology Foundation, Hannay had little time to invest in personal public cases.

"I'm afraid, Mrs Foster, I am extremely busy at this time, and as much as I would like to help you and your little girl, I really don't think I will have time to help." Hannay stated apologetically.

"Doctor Hannay, you may have read in the papers recently the attack and murder on an elderly woman in Ravensdale?" Mary had pulled her trump card.

"Yes, go on." Hannay replied.

"Well, the elderly woman was my mother, the attack happened at my home, the police are as yet unable to detect who the killer was…" there was silence, so Mary continued.

"Well, between you and me, I don't believe they will find the killer. I believe that something else killed my mother that night!" Mary's trump card was indeed an ace. She sensed that she had Hannay hooked.

To him, this sounded compelling; this was a local but high-profile investigation. He felt obliged to meet the mother at least.

"Ok, look," Hannay paused while he reached for his diary, "I have some time free here at the university on Thursday afternoon this week. I'm supposed to be marking scripts, but I can make an hour free in the afternoon, say three o'clock…?" Hannay barely had time to finish the question.

"I'll be there!" Mary replied.

"Three o'clock, then, Thursday afternoon," Hannay continued, "here at the Institute of Psychological Science. I'm granted the use of some offices here; we can use them. I'd like to just meet with you for now. We can talk in private.

"No problem." Mary paused again for a moment. "I'd like to bring someone else, as well."

Little Pig, Little Pig

* * *

Thursday couldn't come quickly enough for Mary. She had planned the day as soon as she knew she had been granted an audience with the venerable Doctor Hannay. Daniel had set off that morning to Manchester. David had set off by bus to school, and Mary had made plans for Wendy Cheney to take both children in at the end of the school day. Wendy had turned out to be a good, reliable friend and neighbour. She had agreed to pick up Eleanor from school. Mary would not be back from Leeds, until around teatime that day. On the journey into Leeds, Mary's mind raced. She kept telling herself that she shouldn't set her expectation too high, that this could all come to nothing, but she now had her opportunity. Here was someone who could help, had the knowledge to help.

The journey into Leeds had been a bad one, roadwork on the outskirts to the northwest of the city, the direction by which Mary had approached, had caused serious tailbacks. It was approaching two forty-five, and Mary had still not entered the university campus, let alone found the Institute of Psychological Science buildings. Finally, she pulled her car off the busy stretch of Woodhouse Lane, down Clarendon Road. The university campus was busy, and the large green area of parkland, adjacent to Clarendon road seemed to host a fair deal of activity, with large numbers of students carrying books and rucksacks, criss-crossing the green pastures, to and from the various grand buildings that lined the edge of the green. With one eye on the road, Mary looked down at a small slip of paper that contained a hand drawing of a map denoting directions. She came to the end of Clarendon road and turned left into University Road. She had found the Institute. Looking around for a parking slot, she pulled into a small car park opposite the large, newly-built, red-brick building. Crossing University road, she wondered whether the third party she had invited to the meeting with Hannay had arrived. Climbing the steps to the main entrance, she pulled open the heavy glass front door and walked into the reception area. To her left, as she walked up to the receptionist's desk, she could see that her question had been answered. Sitting cross legged on a chair and waiting patiently with arms folded sat Detective Inspector Toms. Toms said nothing but nodded, as Mary walked past him. Mary smiled at Toms, as she approached the receptionist's desk.

"Hello there. My name is Mary Foster. I'm here to see Doctor Hannay," Mary said.

"Ok, please fill out the visitor's book and take this pass. I'll let him know you are here. Please take a seat," the receptionist replied. Having signed the book and collected her pass she walked to where Toms was sitting.

"Afternoon, Mr Toms!" Mary greeted the detective.

Toms uncrossed his leg and half motioned to get up; he shook Mary's hand and sat back down again. Mary sat beside him.

"Thanks for coming over this afternoon. I hope this is going to be worthwhile. I think if I'm right

about Doctor Hannay, then it will be!" Mary
exclaimed.

"How are you, Mary?" Toms asked. "How's the
family?"

Mary looked at Toms with a careworn expression
on her face. "We're trying to get our lives back to
some sort of normality, Inspector, but it is hard! God
is it hard!" Mary looked frustratingly down at the
floor.

"I understand," Toms responded sympathetically
"We want to try and help you as best we can," he
said, referring to the police as "we." "But we are not
finding it easy. If there was a stalker outside of your
house forcing an entry, then we have found no
evidence of who that might be!" Toms sounded
exasperated. "It may well be that we need to do a
further forensic search of your house and gardens. I
know that's not what any of us wish for, but facts are
facts and, regrettably, we seem to lack cold, clear
evidence!" Toms tried to reason with Mary who
puffed out her cheeks frustratingly.

"As I've said before, I do not believe that this is a
man you are looking for!" At that moment, the
receptionist got up from her desk and moved toward
Mary and Toms.

"Mrs Foster, Doctor Hannay's ready to see you
now." The receptionist signalled to a door and a
corridor beyond. Both Mary and Toms rose to their
feet.

"Please go through the door and follow the
corridor to the bottom. When you come to the bottom,
take the second door on the left," she explained with

detailed accuracy. Both Mary and Toms walked hastily down the corridor. It was the afternoon, and the campus seemed quiet. Perhaps, Mary thought, many of the students she had seen milling around the streets had finished their lectures for the day. The corridor fell silent, as Mary and Toms stopped. They had reached the second door on the left at the end of the corridor, as instructed. The door had a gold sign screwed into it depicting the name of the occupant: Doctor Martin Hannay.

Mary hesitated, looked at Toms with an expression of uncertainty, and then knocked twice.

"Come in!" came the reply from the other side of the door. Mary slowly turned the handle and pushed the door open. Peering into the room, she stepped into an office, with a large amount of shelving located around three of the four walls. All the shelf space had been completely utilised by books and files. The room itself was moderately large, but given the amount and fullness of shelving, this had now presented the room as smaller than it really was. At the far end of the room, opposite the entrance, was a desk with a computer. Behind it sat a smallish but well-built man in his early fifties with fair but receding hair. Looking up and over the top of his computer at Mary, she noticed the man's pale-blue piercing eyes, set within dark sockets, which gave away the long hours of dedicated effort Hannay put into academia and other research pursuits. Hannay lifted himself from his seat and moved around the desk to greet her.

"Mrs Foster, how are you? Please sit down." Hannay first shook Mary's hand then ushered her to a chair. With Mary safely seated, he turned enthusiastically to Toms.

"And you must be the policeman? Am I right?" asked Hannay, reaching to shake Toms' hand.

"That's right, Sir. I am the policeman!" Toms replied a little indignantly. "Detective Inspector Toms!"

"Ah! Detective Inspector no less! Please sit down!" Hannay had quickly tried to right the wrong, having sensed some mild irritation on Toms' part to his quip. Toms duly sat down on a chair beside Mary. Hannay decided not to sit behind his desk, but chose instead, to lean on the windowsill.

"So, Mrs Foster…Mary, I know we've talked briefly about why you are here, but tell me a little about you." Hannay said.

"Well, you must have read or seen all the press reports on the attack and murder of my Mother at Ravensdale. I'm here because of that. I'm hoping you're the one man who can help us!" Mary countered. She had planned for days in advance what she would say to the eminent Doctor and how she would deliver it, but all that planning had gone out of the window once she had entered the room; her anxiety and stress had forced her to provide a less-than-specific answer to Hannay's question. Hannay, not inexperienced in dealing with clients and patients who were a little irrational, showed patience.

"Ok, take your time, Mary. You are among friends, here. I understand that you have been involved in and been witness to some terrible atrocity. Like most other people, I have read about the murder that is true, but I first would like to know a little about you and why it is you feel that I can help you." Hannay signalled an open palm toward Toms.

"You do after all have the police investigating this case, is that not correct, Mr Toms?"

"That is correct!" Toms replied abruptly, his arms folded across his chest. There was a silence.

"Can I get you a glass of water...tea, coffee perhaps?" asked Hannay, who sensed that he needed to put Mary a little more at ease.

"No, no. I'm fine, thank you. I'm just a little anxious," Mary replied, wringing her hands — a behaviour that didn't go unnoticed by Hannay. Mary took a deep sigh in an attempt to compose herself and sat back in her chair.

"Ok. My name is Mary Foster. I'm thirty-two years old, married with two children. David is eleven and Eleanor is five. We, the family, moved to Ravensdale from London a few months ago, so my husband could start his business. We so desperately wanted to begin a new life for ourselves, one away from the claustrophobic, over-populated rat race that is London!"

"And what does your husband do?" Hannay interjected.

"He and a partner started their own IT Consultancy; they provide business and systems solutions to clients, set up contracts. It's Daniels objective to expand a sizeable client base up here in the North of England," Mary replied.

"Why here!" Hannay seized quickly on Mary's response. Mary again took a deep breath.

"We love the countryside up here, the way of life. Daniel's father was from Yorkshire; it's wide open, and you get space to breathe and live!" Mary's description seemed to get the agreement from Hannay who nodded in approval.

"Besides, areas such as Leeds, Manchester, Liverpool, Harrogate are expanding, according to Daniel, and the demographic for business and commerce is punching its way through to these big cities in the North!"

"And is business going well, as you say?" Hannay retorted.

"It's early days, but we are making progress. We're seeing the business begin to take off!" Mary replied.

"Is your husband away a lot?" Hannay asked.

"No, maybe once, twice a week he may stay in Manchester or at his business partners in Stockport, but he's mostly home; he can work from home, you see," Mary said.

"And what did you do in London, Mary?" Hannay asked.

"I was a temp, you know, secretary or PA. I didn't work full time because of the kids."

"Ok, and what do you do now?" Hannay asked.

"I don't work currently. I'm just there for the kids, getting the house straight; it's a big house, the kind of place we dreamed of owning for years. It needs a lot of turning around!" Mary exclaimed. Hannay sensed that it was time to change tack.

"I see, now tell me about your life as a young girl." Hannay said. He moved slowly from the windowsill back to his chair behind his desk and sat down.

"Mary again took a further deep breath before proceeding; still the hand wringing was apparent.

"Well, I lived at home with my Mum and Dad in Staines. I was an only child, no brothers or sisters. We lived in a nice part of Staines. My Father was a civil engineer, so we lived relatively comfortably."

"Were you lonely?" Hannay asked.

"Lonely? No," Mary replied, looking a little confused.

"Lonely…being on your own because you had no brothers or sisters?" Hannay expanded the question.

"No, well, I didn't feel I was lonely. I would perhaps play a lot on my own, as kids do at that age. They tend to play with imaginary friends."

"And did you have imaginary friends?" Hannay again probed deeper.

"Yes, I suppose I must have. I can't say I remember!" Mary replied, her face betraying the thoughts turning over in her mind, desperately trying to recall that part of her childhood. Hannay again jumped forward in the conversation.

"You mentioned, Mary that you felt your daughter had, in your words, inherited some terrible legacy from yourself; you believe your daughter is possessed, as you said. Toms who had sat there all the time while the discussion went on continued to listen in silence. He glanced across at Mary waiting for her reply.

"Doctor, when I was a child," Mary began, "about five, the age my daughter Eleanor is now, I suffered what I believe to have been a traumatic episode in my life. You see, about that time, my Grandmother passed away. She had been ill for some time. She was old. I remember her being so old and weak. I remember the image of her still in my mind to this day, when my mother took me to see her. In the hospice, she was so ill; she began to lose her mind. I don't know. I cannot remember! I remember this one occasion where my Grandmother was out of her mind, delirious, I'd think you say she was. My Mother was there sitting on the bed with her, and my Grandmother suddenly just reached out and grabbed my mother's arm. I was scared, so scared she seemed to grip my mother so tightly, she could not get her arm free. My Grandmother had long nails, and she just dug them deep into my mother's arm with all the strength she had. My mother screamed in pain. I remember my mum's arm bleeding terribly; the nurses had to come and prize my grandmother's fingers off my mum." Mary paused and reflected for a moment.

"I guess it affected me quite deeply." There was silence; both Toms and Hannay were hooked.

"In what way would you say you were affected?" Hannay pressed.

"I found it difficult to relate to people, my mother and father, friends at school, teachers. I suppose I kind of withdrew. My mother came across a letter after my grandmother's death in my grandmother's handwriting; it seemed so profound, so moving in the way it described how to raise a family what to do, what not to do; it shook us to the core."

Hannay sat back in his chair, listening with great intent. He raised his right leg and rested his ankle across his left knee.

"I can see that this experience certainly appears from what you say to have caused a good deal of stress in your life, at such a young age, as well. What happened then? Was there anyone who recommended help? Support? What did your parents do?" Hannay asked, intrigued as to where Mary was going to take this.

"Doctor, they didn't know at that time that I had begun to suffer from the bad dreams!" Mary replied.

"The bad dreams?" Hannay again batted the question back to Mary.

"Yes, there were bad dreams. They began to get increasingly vivid, increasingly real. I didn't tell my parents about them at first." Mary had by now dropped her gaze, away from either Hannay or Toms, and was intent in staring at the floor as she spoke. Hannay had by now dropped his relaxed pose in his chair behind his desk and sat leaning forward, straining on every utterance that Mary delivered.

"Mary, can you tell me what these dreams were about?" Hannay asked. Again, as with the time back at the Hungry Harshes with Daniel, the stress of forcing herself to confront painful memories from her past and to strangers was taking its toll on Mary. She felt herself begin to weep. Hannay, noticing this, eased a tissue from a box on his desk and lifted himself out his chair handing it to Mary.

"Please go on. I want to hear this!" Hannay gently, but firmly, prodded.

Mary continued. "Every dream had the same theme. I saw my grandmother in my bedroom; she would appear at the foot of the bed or in a corner of the room. There would be this light, this aura, this glow...I'm not sure how best to describe it. I felt myself wake, sit up in my bed, and peer through the darkness. There was no other light on in my room. I wondered what this light was. It seemed that, with every night that passed, the image of my grandmother in my dreams became more and more vivid and seemed to gravitate toward where I was in the room. I felt shivery, cold!" As Mary spoke, she felt a shiver run down her spine and the hairs on the back of her neck rose with, what was to her, a sense of predictability. This was her normal physical reaction, whenever she was forced to face her past.

"I felt I was there alone in this vast pitch-black room at the top of the house, which, to me felt like I had been imprisoned at the top of the tallest tower, with my parent's way down below. So far below that they could not see what was happening, nor could they hear me scream. I was a prisoner in this living hell!"

Toms stared open mouthed at Mary, he could pride himself on recounting some unusual and diverse investigations in his long career but even for him this was taking on a whole different meaning.

"This is fascinating!" Hannay burst in with enthusiastic zeal. "You can recall an experience in your life where you have encountered an apparition, someone close to you who was dying or, in your case, had in fact died. We sometimes call this 'crisis apparition.'" Hannay paused for a moment. "But you say you screamed. Why did you scream? Surely this was your grandmother, someone you knew and loved and who loved you! Why on earth would you feel frightened in the presence of your grandmother?"

"To cut a long story short," Mary continued, "my dreams turned to nightmares. I woke one night to find my grandmother lying beside me in my bed, a look of insane fear on her face; the room stank; I can only imagine it was the smell of a rotting corpse. I felt a sharp pain, an agonising sharp pain in my left arm!" With that, Mary grabbed her left wrist and lower arm with her right hand and began to rub it.

"I screamed and screamed. I'd never screamed so loud in all my life. My parents eventually heard me and burst into my room. When they pulled the covers back on my bed, it was covered in blood. Somehow, my arm had been gouged. I felt my grandmother had gouged me the same way she had done my mother at the hospice. How could this woman that I loved, that we all loved, have been so cruel?"

Toms, carried along by the conversation and not a man easily convinced of the supernatural, pitched in. "Could this not have been something you did to yourself, Mrs Foster?" he asked slightly dismissively. "It's understandable. I've seen it many times before; people suffering grief or anxiety will tend to harm themselves! Surely, you're not suggesting that spirits, ghosts, or apparitions—whatever you want to call them—physically inflicted injury on you?"

"It's hard to believe, but I can find no other explanation for it. I've had to live with this all my life;

often the memory of it comes back to haunt me!"
Mary started, seemingly apologetic at her outpouring,
but Toms retort had awoken anger in her.

Hannay had heard enough and come to Mary's
aid. "Well!" he said, slapping the palm of his hand on
the desk. "I can find an explanation! And if you tell
me you saw an apparition of your grandmother after
she had died, Mary, then I believe you! Hannay,
sensing now that he was on the trail of something hot,
jumped forward. He pushed Mary on the very subject
of why she was there in the first place.

"Tell me now about your daughter, Eleanor," he
said, rounding on Mary, who had regained her
composure and looked up across the table to Toms.

"I strongly believe that whatever it was that I
possessed as a child has now manifested itself in my
daughter. I believe a spirit is controlling my daughter.
I can't explain it, but it has come to her as what I
believed to be little more than a mythical beast, a
werewolf or a wolf man, or some sort of hybrid
animal! This creature has come to our house and has
tried to take my daughter! In doing so, my mother
gave her own life to protect her granddaughter!" The
reaction in the room was extreme. Toms sat with his
arms folded, nodding.

"Mrs Foster, I grant you that the police
investigation uncovered evidence to suggest that an
animal, it may well have been a dog or a wild wolf,
has been prowling in and around the grounds of your
home. That much we know. What we can't confirm
and we do have a theory is that the perpetrator to
your home on the night of the murder of Mrs Alice

Parsons may have brought an animal, a dog, or wolf with them, in order to protect themselves, say, in the event of being discovered, either that or it may have been an opportunist vagrant with a dog passing through the village. But werewolves, we draw the line at!" Toms had barely completed disclosing police suspicions before Mary pitched back in.

"Mr Toms, I know what I saw, and I know what my husband saw, and we have both testified and stand by our statements that we saw a creature we can only describe as being that of a werewolf!"

Toms again sighed and moved to leave his chair and the meeting.

"Mrs Foster, werewolves just don't exist!" he again retorted.

"Perhaps they do," countered Hannay, who had sat calmly listening, while the argument between Toms and Mary had begun to escalate.

"After all, lycanthropy, the term used for human beings to transform themselves into the shape of an animal, has been in evidence for many hundreds, if not several thousand, of years. One only has to go back to Medieval Germany to detect the very real and dangerous effect werewolves had on the native population. Many individuals were put to death, even under suspicion of themselves being werewolves. Please take a seat, Detective Inspector!" Hannay signalled to Toms who duly returned to his chair.

Hannay waited a while and looked around the room at both Mary and Toms, before speaking again. He had heard enough and decided that now seemed a good point to summarise. He straightened himself in his chair.

"Mrs Foster, Mary, you've told me why you are here today, and I thank you for providing useful insight into your own past. I believe that from what you have told me about yourself, you possess an innate ability at a time of deep stress and tragedy in your life to be able to manifest images and thoughts in dreams into physical reality. Now, this is not uncommon. As a practitioner of psychological and, indeed, parapsychological behaviour, I have seen some examples of this, but they are few and far between! It is possible, as it is possible of course for many people who see something profoundly shocking or vivid in their lives to consign almost what can be termed a photographic print to memory. You, of all people, Inspector, must be aware of the victim's abilities to recall graphic reconstructions of incidents where they have either been the targets or witnesses to the crime."

Toms grudgingly nodded in agreement.

"Now, I have no way of knowing exactly why Mary here should be able, above everyone else we've studied, to take her most vivid dreams or nightmares that stage further and make them tangible and, in some cases, dangerously physical. It would appear that from what you've told me, Mary, the key moment of trauma in your young life was seeing your dying grandmother attack, for want of a better word, your own mother and then witness her pain! This has been your memory's photographic print; this is what you stored, and this is what you could recall! Let me ask you, have you personally had any of these experiences since you were a child?" Hannay asked.

"No, none whatsoever," Mary replied.

"How did you eradicate these dreams, these memories?" Hannay asked.

"From what I recall and it is now a distant memory, my parents consulted with someone very much like yourself. He came to our house. I don't know whether you call it *exorcism*, but he performed a number of activities; he managed to extract the bad dreams from me."

"Did he hypnotise you?" Hannay interjected.

Mary thought for a moment. "I think maybe he did. I'm not sure. I can't remember, but I believe it was something like that."

"Good, yes, I think I understand what may have happened to you!" Hannay said, seizing upon the last comments from Mary. He again sat forward in his chair, clasped his hands, and placed them on his desk.

"You were, I believe, and it's only a theory, externalising your subconscious!"

"Externalising what?" Toms asked.

"Inspector, Mary was externalising her subconscious, her most vivid dream or nightmare. The attack on her mother by her sick grandmother had left so deep an indelible mark on her as a young girl, someone who could not handle or possibly know how to decipher or cope with what they witnessed, that this image manifested itself in a physical presence. Just as it is possible for each and every one of us to manifest images in our sleeping thoughts, so, I believe, it was possible for Mary, as a young girl, to manifest images in her waking thoughts. We see things when we are asleep. She saw them when she woke from her dream. They came to her, into her physical world, her physical space. By hypnotism, you can control the subject and delve into his or her subconscious thinking. Only by this way, by suggestion, can you exorcise the person!" Hannay paused for a moment.

"Oh this is fascinating," he said. "Mrs Foster, let's call an end to this discussion for today, but I want you to bring Eleanor to me early next week, say Tuesday, at about the same time?"

Mary was by now mesmerised, "Of course, three o'clock next Tuesday, I'll be here!"

"Mr Toms, do you wish to attend, also?" Hannay asked.

"If you don't mind!" Toms responded.

"I'd like to speak to Eleanor with as few people around her as possible. I don't want her to be distracted, and I don't want her to feel any undue pressure. I want her to feel relaxed, at ease, perhaps just Mary, Eleanor, and myself. Mr Toms, we have an observation room down the corridor. You can view the interview from there. Eleanor won't know you are there.

"Fine with me!" Toms replied.

The trio got up from their chairs, and Hannay moved from behind his desk round to where the Toms and Mary stood. Clasping Mary's hand warmly and enthusiastically, he gave her an encouraging look.

"Thank you for coming Mary. You are indeed an interesting person. I look forward to seeing you, again, and Eleanor. It is important to remember that we may be a long way off from solving this problem for you, but I think we can make a start, if you are willing."

Mary of course was. "I feel a weight has lifted from my shoulders, Doctor. Anything you can do to help my family will be appreciated."

With that, Toms opened the door to the office, and he and Mary walked out. With the door closed behind them, the two walked down the corridor back to reception. As the pair reached the front desk, Toms stopped and turned to Mary.

"Mrs Foster, please don't read too much into my comments I made in there. I've seen you now with your emotions laid bare. I applaud you. That was a hard thing to do. I now believe, having seen you in that room this afternoon, any suspicion that this investigation may have had of either yourself or your husband was totally absurd. Please forgive me. I now see that what you are doing here is exactly the right thing to do, and I applaud your courage. Good day to you!"

Toms turned and walked through the vast entrance.

Mary's heart raced. She had sat listening, intoxicated by Hannay's diagnosis. She had never heard anything like it before; nothing had prepared her for what Hannay had said, but she had done it. She had opened her heart, let out her fears about the past and, as Toms had said, laid herself bare emotionally to men, professional men she hardly knew. Hannay was, she thought, the right man; she had found the right man; she had found her saviour, someone who knew and understood her problems, someone who could help.

Mary walked out of the large entrance and stopped. She took in a large gulp of cool, early-evening winter breeze. It was dark now, the air fresh. Mary felt heady, liberated. She skipped down the steps to the building and almost broke into a jog getting back to her car. She would go home, ring Aunt Lil, and hug her family. She knew that perhaps the worst was still to come, but she had, for the first time in a long while, seen the first chinks of hope!

Chapter 13

Mary returned to the Hungry Harshes to find two messages on the answer phone. One was from Aunt Lillian, who had rung to say that, if Mary was ready, she would like to come up and stay for a while and possibly help Mary in the issue they discussed when they met in Staines for Alice's funeral, largely to help find the right diagnosis for Eleanor. *Great!* Mary thought. This was just the support she needed, and she was planning to contact Lil, anyway. The second call was curiously enough from Eleanor's teacher, Miss Strand; she'd left her number and invited Mary to meet somewhere out of school! What was it this time? She wondered. Daniel wasn't home yet from Stockport, and the kids were with Wendy Cheney across the road, so Mary decided to ring her Aunt Lillian. The two women chatted eagerly about Mary's visit earlier that afternoon to Leeds.

"I'm going back next Tuesday, Lil, with Eleanor. I'd like you to come." Mary said.

"You couldn't keep me away. I want to meet this doctor and see what he can do for Eleanor!"

"Great, I'll have the spare room made up. When do you want to get here?" Mary asked, again.

"Monday, Dear. I'll come up Monday after the weekend, if that's ok with you, unless you want me earlier?"

"No, that's fine with me, Lil." She paused for a moment. "Oh Lil, I do hope we are on the right track this time." Mary said with relief.

"It sounds as if you are, Dear, take hope!" The call ended, and Mary dialled Miss Shand's number. Mary listened, as the phone rang, wondering what to anticipate from the school on this occasion.

"Hello?" came the voice on the other end of the line.

"Hello, Miss Shand?"

"Yes, that's right," Miss Shand said.

"It's me, Mary Foster, Eleanor's Mum. You rang and left a message earlier." Mary said.

"Ah, Mrs Foster, yes, thank you for calling back. This is a little bit out of context. I do hope you don't mind me ringing?" Miss Shand in a wistful voice at the other end of line.

"Not at all. I assume this is about Eleanor? Has something else happened at school. Is she in trouble?" Mary asked.

"No, no not really, not so much trouble, but there have been incidents with fire alarms going off, and we discovered Eleanor wandering in the school corridors on her own, when alarms have gone off, when she should have been in a class," Miss Shand elaborated.

"You say incidents! Has there been more than one occasion?" Mary asked.

"Well…for two consecutive days, now, Eleanor has been discovered wandering the school corridors on her own, when the fire alarm has gone off. Now, we are not saying that we know for certain it is she; when we ask her, she seems sheepish, guilty almost, says it's not her but her friend Izzy. Do you know an Izzy, Mrs Foster?"

Mary sighed. "Sadly, I do! It's my daughter's imaginary friend. To Mary this was beginning to sound all too familiar. Next Tuesday could not come soon enough!

"Mrs Foster, look, I hope you don't mind me asking you this, but do you think we could meet? Get together, maybe over a drink?"

Mary was slightly taken aback. "Oh, why?" she asked.

"I do so want to try and help Eleanor. She's had a hard time of it, lately, and we've all read the terrible reports of what you have all suffered over these past weeks. We can talk a little bit more about Eleanor, if you and I could sit down privately, out of school."

Mary was intrigued, from being in a position only a matter of days ago where she felt alone and isolated, she now found herself receiving offers of help coming from every direction.

"Mrs Foster, I have some background in child psychological disorders. I've worked with children who are different, and I don't just mean children who are, say, autistic or who are diagnosed as suffering from ADHD." Miss Shand stopped short from attempting to diagnose Eleanor. She was young and impetuous, but also, as a teacher, she was thoughtful and considerate.

"Ok," Mary said. "Where do you want to meet?"

"Could we meet in the village? At the Bucks Public House?" Miss Shand asked.

"No!" Mary replied. "That's too public. Everyone in the village knows me, now; they know what's happened. I suggest we meet somewhere else, away from the village, say Malham. Do you know Malham?" Mary asked.

"Very well! How about the Lister Arms Hotel?" Shand responded.

"Agreed, tomorrow evening, say seven o'clock?" Mary asked.

"That's good for me!"

Suddenly, Mary's diary seemed pretty full. With Aunt Lillian coming up to stay, she needed to get the house in order; it was still a mess and, although work had by now been completed on the kitchen, there seemed to be a layer of dust everywhere that felt as if it was about an inch thick!

* * *

By the following evening, Mary had set off to Malham to meet Miss Strand. It was now late November, the evenings were dark, and this evening it was particularly blustery. The remaining leaves, which had clung to the trees, seemed to be blowing everywhere. Daniel was at home and babysitting the kids. Mary had sat down with him after dinner the previous evening and briefed him on the trip to Leeds and the meeting with Doctor Hannay. He seemed content to let Mary pursue this line of enquiry and, besides, she was keeping the police investigation away from him. He had his work cut out, though, after all that had happened to the family, the children were nervous for their mother, driving off into the night. That night, Daniel found himself reading the story of the three little pigs not just to Eleanor, but to David, as well, since he didn't wish to be left alone in the house. The three had decamped into Eleanor's bedroom!

The roads to Malham were bleak. These were winding lanes, cut through the moors and possessed neither lighting nor sufficient signage to direct Mary. Nonetheless, she had visited Malham several times since the move from London. Daniel had taken her there, and she was impressed with the small, but pretty, picturesque village, with its fresh-water stream, tumbling through the heart of it. The whole area around the village was blessed with unusual but beautiful landscape; notable were Malham cove and Gordale Scar, a huge gorge that stood in the Yorkshire National Park and was a featured tourist attraction for the area.

Once in Malham, Mary parked and walked across the road into the Lister Arms. It was Friday night. The local inn was buzzing with locals and walkers who had come up for the weekend to walk the hills around the area. The Lister Arms was very quaint, but, coming from the blustery chill of the night outside, Mary felt the full blast furnace of heat when she entered the lounge. With a real fire crackling at the far end of the lounge, she could see the illuminated slender frame of Miss Shand, sitting alone at a small table staring into the roaring flames.

Mary walked up to the young teacher. "Hello there!"

Shand turned from the fire and looked up. "Mrs Foster, can I get you a drink?" Shand asked, finishing up the remains of a glass of white wine.

"No, I'll get them!" Mary quipped. "What are you having?" she asked, indicating Miss Shand's empty glass.

"Chardonnay, please!"

Having fought her way to the bar, Mary secured a Chardonnay for the teacher and a glass of house red for herself. As she returned to the table, removed her waterproof jacket, and sat down, the two women smiled at each other slightly uneasily.

"Cheers!" Mary said, holding up her glass. The two women took a sip of their wine. Mary had had very little opportunity to get to know Eleanor's new teacher, but seeing her up close in the environment of the Lister Arms, she reaffirmed to herself what she had felt on their very first meeting at the school. Miss Shand seemed young, very young; there were no engagement rings on her fingers, so Mary couldn't tell if she was on her own. Her instinct suggested that she probably did live on her own. The teacher was thin, painfully thin, her skin pale and, on top of a narrow, gaunt face sat a mop of curly, auburn-coloured hair, cut short around the neck. Her eyes seemed large and out of proportion to the rest of her face and seemed to pop out of her head.

"I'll get to the point, Mrs Foster. Do you mind if I call you Mary?" Shand asked.

"No, please do!"

"As I said on the phone to you yesterday, in the past, I have worked with some special children, children who, how should I say, had very rare gifts. Abilities to be able to make objects move and see people or that which we otherwise could not see. I opted, volunteered if you like, to have this exposure, while I was at teacher training college completing my degree. The psychology department at an affiliated university was at the time doing a study on children involved with the paranormal; there were some children, quite young, about the age Eleanor is now, who had suspected connections to poltergeist activity. These were children, different children from, say, those who are autistic."

"Eleanor's not autistic!" Mary retorted defensively.

"Oh, I know, Mary. I'm aware of that, but she does possess something, doesn't she?" Miss Shand's eyes appeared above her glass, and the firelight flickered in them, and they shone back at Mary like beads.

"It's easy to confuse the symptoms in a child. One who withdraws is lonely, isolated, not outgoing, won't speak or communicate to anyone; it's easy to label that child as possessing signs of autism. But, Mary, not every child is like that. Mary looked at Miss Shand and reflected for a moment on what she had just said.

"You know!" Miss Shand continued, "the only way those fire alarms could have possibly been set off was if someone had broken the glass panel on the alarm box. On the two occasions that the alarms were set off this week, Eleanor was found to be the only child wandering in the school corridors, at precisely that time. As I said, the only previous time that those alarms had been set off was when the school held a fire drill. On both occasions, this week, it was found that none of the alarm glass panels had been broken. There is no explanation as to how they got set off!"

"Mrs Shand, I'm sorry. I don't know your first name," Mary said.

"Isla," Shand replied.

"Isla, you cannot tell me conclusively that it was Eleanor who set those alarms off, can you?"

"No, I can't, but I'm beginning to know enough now about young Eleanor, as I suspect you do about your own daughter, Mary!" Shand replied.

Mary paused for a moment and looked deep into the fire's grate before replying.

"So, what is it you want to do?" Mary asked the young teacher. After all, this had been the crux of the meeting.

"I want to help you help Eleanor get through whatever it is that is troubling her. Mary, I've seen her pictures. I've seen the way she behaves in class. She seems a troubled young girl!" Shand pleaded.

"You realise, in doing what you are doing, you have probably contravened some rules about teaching guidelines and ethics!" Mary challenged Shand.

"Would you prefer I take the formal route, Mary, and add to the suffering and anguish you and your family are already going through? I don't wish to do that, and I believe there is no need to do it, but if I can support Eleanor in some way, then I'm willing to do that, and if that means extra-curricular activity, then, if you are willing, I will clear it with Mrs Forbes!" It was obvious to Mary that Shand was determined to give help in some way. From the very first day they had met, the young teacher had sensed something quite different in Eleanor. It had drawn her to Eleanor, whom she saw as a nice, sweet, unassuming girl, but deeply troubled.

"I'll tell you, Isla," Mary said, "I took some time yesterday to go to Leeds. I was there to see an eminent parapsychologist. I was there to talk to him about Eleanor!"

Shand stared, captivated, in the half glow of the fire.

"Please go on," she said.

"In a sense, you are right; there is more happening with Eleanor at the moment than I can explain. I need help, the family needs help. I told the Doctor that I believe that, whatever Eleanor is suffering from today is, to all intents something I suffered from at her age. He has made an initial diagnosis, purely on discussion, but he hasn't seen Eleanor yet. I'm going to take her to see him next week."

Mary again found she was unburdening herself to a comparative stranger.

"Do you want to disclose what that diagnosis may be?" The young teacher was pushy, but Mary didn't take offence; she seemed to betray a genuine interest in her daughter and, despite initial assumptions, she had genuine warmth to her.

"Too early to tell, but he thinks it may be something to do with a bad turn or experience she may have had in her young life. I can't think what that would have been, unless it has something to do with the move here to Ravensdale." Mary confided.

"With respect," Shand replied, "surely the recent trauma that the family has all suffered and, particularly, what Eleanor had to endure must have had a significant impact on her."

Mary looked down at her wine glass. Running her right index finger around the rim, she spoke in a hushed tone. "Isla, I need to know I have your confidence in this."

"Of course!" Shand replied.

"Eleanor had been experiencing symptoms that seemed to affect her personality long before the attack on us happened. I can't fully explain it to you, but everything Eleanor has been feeling is somehow related to that night!"

Shand sat back in her chair. "So, Mary, how can I help?" she asked.

"To start with, you can grant permission to let me take my daughter out of school next Tuesday afternoon!"

The weekend was grey and cloudy, with just the occasional shower to oblige the many varied hill walkers who had travelled up that weekend to trek through the hills and valleys around Ravensdale.

Mary had begun to get used to the steady stream of enthusiasts drifting past her front gate at the weekends. They sometimes came by car, some in large parties by coach and parked in the centre of Ravensdale below, many acquiring a full day's parking ticket, although much of that time was spent by many in the Bucks Inn relishing refreshment before setting off across the hills in the afternoon. Many would stop and look at the large, ornate house that was the Hungry Harshes, and many would wonder upon the history of the house. Occasionally, Mary would chuckle to herself, when she would spot some passer-by or hill walker from across the road. They would point to the Hungry Harshes, quizzing her good neighbour, Wendy, on the building's history. Mary had thought that maybe she should start charging for the privilege of a house tour, a good way to supplement income. She could offer cream teas…*now there's a thought!* But it was a passing whimsy; besides, she wouldn't really want to have all those people traipsing up her garden path. It was a welcome distraction, though, watching them walk up and down the road to the hills, striding out with walking sticks, the young and the old, the overweight and the slim, rucksacks on their backs, their trousers tucked in thick woolly walking socks. The irony was not lost on Mary. Here she was, now, so desperate and, at the same time, comforted to see so much vibrant life walking past her door. The one thing she and Daniel had striven to get away from was the hustle and bustle of the city, away from the crowds. This was, however, a different hustle and bustle, there was often little sign of life in the week and, anyway, this was rather genteel!

Genteel to a point! For Mary, particularly, had become aware and sensitive to the increased number of sightseers who'd come just to gawp at the house. This was a new twist to public interest. The area and the house had been of public interest following the murder. The welcome distraction that Mary had taken from the sightseers had grown to an extent, whereby she and the family had come to feel besieged in their home. That weekend, the family's first real weekend back at the Hungry Harshes since the attack and Alice Parsons' murder had brought the intensity of the intrusion home to them. It probably hadn't helped that Detective Inspector Toms had seen fit to post a Police Constable to stand watch at the front gate. While this served to act as a barrier to the public intrusion, the police constable's presence had nonetheless attracted the inquisitive.

Daniel had spent some time around the house, overseeing the final repairs to the kitchen following the attack. He had made claims through various household insurance policies to replace crockery and kitchen units, but much of the superficial clearing up had been done. When Mary walked into the kitchen, Daniel was on his hands and knees on the floor with a dust pan and brush, sweeping around the base of the kitchen units. He seemed bothered, annoyed by something.

"That's a good job you're doing, Dan!" Mary half joked, making her way past the kitchen to the house's utility area, where she had been washing bed linen in preparation for Aunt Lillian's stay.

"Cleaning this bloody house takes such an effort!" he snapped, getting up and turning to empty the collection of dirt and dust into the bin.

"Well, we are a family, Dan, and the kids will always bring in dirt!" Mary replied.

"We should make them take their bloody shoes off outside!"

Mary turned and looked at her husband. "What's up, Dan?" she asked. Something was clearly riling him.

Dan took the dustpan and brush and shoved it impatiently in one of the cupboards in the kitchen. "Everything! Everything's bothering me at the moment!" he replied sharply. "Mary, I feel that we're losing our grip! When we first came here, the idea was that we were in control, you and I, but everything seems to be running so fast and against us, I feel I have no control over what my family does anymore!"

Mary went to the other side of the kitchen and leaned against a cupboard. "Dan, things have been terrible for all of us, but the kids and I were looking for you to hold it together. At least the kids look to their daddy. Right now, they need you; we all need you!" Mary appealed to Dan's paternal sense, but it was no use; a row had been coming for a little while and now seemed the time to get things out on the table.

"But, Mary, everything that's going on, it's just such a bloody drain! All these bloody people coming just to gawp at us, to come and see the freaky family, living inside the house of horror."

Mary decided it was best to shut up and listen attentively and let Dan get it off his chest. The two had kept it together for some time, following the murder and subsequent funeral, but Dan, like Mary, had begun to feel claustrophobic, constantly under the spotlight of police, public, and press.

"It doesn't help that we've got all these bloody police running around, under our feet all the bloody time!" He turned his back on Mary and faced the sink. He picked up a cleaning towel, furiously wiped around the sink, and threw the towel violently down on the surface, turning as he did, to face his wife.

"And what about all this business with this para—!"

"Parapsychologist!" Mary obliged, finishing the sentence that Daniel had been struggling over.

"Yes, this bloody parapsychologist. Honestly, Mary, what good is this guy gonna do? I think you're wasting your time!" Dan said, also leaning back on the opposing kitchen cupboard across the room, folding his arms, and facing Mary, challenging her.

Mary sighed deeply. "Dan, you saw the creature yourself, same as I did. That is something that is not easily explained away. You can't deny it!" Mary said, trying to reason with her irate husband.

"Mary, I'm not sure exactly what I saw. An animal, yes, a wild animal, something that perhaps had been released by an owner or a collector. You know, people for whatever reason keep these wild animals; they think they're pets, until they grow too large and they have to release them. The countryside is rife with wild cats, dogs, probably wolves!"

"Oh come on, Dan!" Mary was quick to reply. You know and I know what we saw. It was no wild pet; it was a creation, a creation from our daughter's mind!"

"That's crap and you know it!" Daniel retorted. "I think you should knock the idea of taking her to this quack on the head. This is only hurting Eleanor. You can see she's hurt and confused, now. I don't think this is going to help!"

"Oh, and what do you suggest I do?" Mary replied angrily.

"Nothing! Let the police deal with it. They're the professionals; let them scurry around in the mud and dirt looking for clues. They are paid to do that!" replied Daniel.

Mary folded her arms in a defensive posture. "Well that's where we disagree!" she said. "You've seen the police. They're at a loss; they don't know what to do, Dan. They have nothing whatsoever to go on, now. I told you what Toms said, when he came to the interview with Doctor Hannay. Yes, he was sceptical, but by the end, he had come around to the way of thinking that we should explore this. Dan, I have involved the police in this. The doctor is a good man; you need to meet him. He comes highly recommended in his field!"

Daniel stood, shaking his head. "What do we do if this quack cannot find the answer? What do we do, then, Mary, tell me that. By then, our daughter will be so fucked up with paranoia the situation could be irredeemable!"

"Look, Dan, if this doesn't work, then I'll find someone else who can help her. All I'm trying to do here is protect Eleanor and protect the rest of the family. We don't want any more deaths!"

By now, their voices were raised, and they could be heard out in the hall, where both David and Eleanor were sitting near the top of the stairs. They had heard their parents arguing from their bedrooms, where they had been playing and had come out to listen.

"All you're trying to do is find answers to your own past," Daniel continued. You're using Eleanor in some ruse to do this!"

"Not true! Not true!" Mary retorted, shaking her head in disbelief at what she was hearing from her husband.

"What are you going to do when our daughter is so seriously screwed up by all this, by all the hawking around consultation rooms, seeing quacks here, mediums there? I can't stand by and see you do this!" Daniel now sounded angry to the point of aggression.

"For god's sake, Daniel!" Mary retorted angrily "This isn't about me. This is about the welfare of our daughter, Jesus! You've seen the way she's been. She's withdrawing by the day; it's getting harder and harder to talk to her about anything. You're the only one she allows in. She lets you read to her, but she's losing contact with people, with us, with school, and her school friends. Surely you must see!" Mary exclaimed. "This is not our daughter! She doesn't walk like Eleanor; she doesn't talk like Eleanor; her mannerisms have changed. Just look at her drawings.

You've seen the pictures she's done here and at school. She is deeply troubled!"

At that moment, the kitchen door creaked and slowly opened to reveal Eleanor standing silently in the doorway. The expression on her face was stone cold. She looked at Mary, then at Daniel, with an expression that looked as if she was going to kill each of them. Daniel couldn't stand it anymore. He picked up his jacket from the utility room peg, grabbed his car keys, and moved to the back door.

"I need to get out of here. My head's going to explode with all this!" he said, walking out the back door. In his anger and haste, the back door flung open, smashing against the kitchen wall. Daniel disappeared down the path, never once looking back.

"Well done!" Mary shouted after him. "That'll help!" she said, moving to the back door. She heard Daniel get into the car and speed off.

David arrived in the doorway behind his sister. "Where's Dad gone?" he asked.

"Out, Dear, to clear his head," Mary said.

"Why were you and Dad shouting?" David asked.

"We were just having an argument, David, nothing to worry about. Mums and Dads sometimes do have arguments." Mary sighed as she said it. She moved over to the children, bending over them and giving them a hug. David hugged his mother back, but there was a cold, unwelcoming response from Eleanor, who just stared into her mother's eyes.

"Come on, let's get some lunch!" Mary suggested.

It wasn't until early evening, just after six-thirty, when Mary and the kids could hear the back door slam shut. The kids had felt vulnerable. Daniel had walked out, and Mary didn't know when he would be back. Meanwhile, it had grown dark, so the family, minus Daniel, had had supper, and Mary had got the kids ready for bed. They had all decided to snuggle up together on the sofa and watch the early evening television. For a while, the three of them sat there in silence and looked at each other. There wasn't a lot of sound coming from the kitchen.

Anxious and wary about who it may be, following the series of attacks, the two children remained seated, while Mary got to her feet and pulled the curtains back from the sitting-room window. Reassuringly, the police constable was still there. Mary walked out into the hall; the two children followed close behind her.

"Who's there?" Mary asked.

"Dan, is that you?" she called out. There was no reply. The threesome slowly walked to the kitchen door and pushed it open. The kitchen light was on, and Daniel was sitting at the kitchen dining table. He cut a figure of despair, with his head buried in his hands.

There was silence for a moment before he spoke. "Do you believe this guy; this doctor can really help our little girl?" Daniel asked, picking at his nails. He didn't look across to Mary who was standing in the doorway.

"I believe he's the right man. I believe he can help us, yes!" Mary replied.

Daniel stopped picking his nails and rubbed his eye with the palm of his hand. "God I've been bloody stupid!" he exclaimed, with a feeling of despair. "I've never given you or the kids any support in this. I've never tried to understand the pressure you must be under, and I'm sorry. I'm sorry I've been a complete pain in the arse!"

Mary stepped into the kitchen and rested a comforting hand on Daniel's shoulder. She could detect a whiff of alcohol.

"Where have you been?" she asked.

"I took a drive. I drove into Skipton. I just wanted some time on my own to think about things. It's ok. I'm not drunk, just a little uptight!" Daniel proclaimed.

"You can say that again!" Mary joked. This at least seemed to break the ice.

"It's been some time now!" Daniel looked up at Mary apologetically. "Since we've been here, we've not been physically close, and I want to change all that!" Daniel said, as he grasped his wife's forgiving hand.

"I'm afraid I've been working too hard, just trying to keep us afloat, and now all this has got in the way. It's like some sort of nightmare. I just want it all to end, get back to the life we promised ourselves we would live!"

"Dan, we'll get our chance. We'll live our life the way we dreamed, but we need to stay strong just a little longer!"

The strain the couple both felt was apparent. Months of establishing client contacts had just begun to start reaping some return, and now it seemed they were being stalked, the target of some creature, something they couldn't fully understand. Add to that Mary's admission about her past. All had become a distraction in what had been a solid marriage. Now, they needed to dig deep and show strength and unity in their relationship like never before.

For the couple, it had been a long, hard slog. They had taken some knocks and were understandably weary. Their marriage had been put under strain, and the fresh sense of optimism and purpose that reflected in their faces at the start of the venture had been replaced by depression, disillusion, and narcissism. They were tired, their eyes red, their faces puffy and lined. Daniel had not been able to run for some while. He just didn't have the opportunity what with one thing and another. Physically, his body began to betray signs that stress was catching up with him, and an inconsistent diet and an increase in drinking had begun to make his once trim, athletic figure look a little paunchy. They were both talked out, both done in, neither wishing to start a fight with the other. They had called a truce, a permanent one, they hoped. As they sat in the sitting room, they looked at each other with honesty; each could see in the other the unjust battle scars that marked their faces. The roaring, open glow of the fire in the grate danced on their faces and seemed to lift their careworn expressions. With every crackle of timber and charcoal in the grate, they seemed to hold each other closer, neither saying anything to the other. There wasn't anything that needed to be said; the sensitivity in their embrace seemed to say enough. As the evening drew in, the fire acted as an ever more conciliatory presence in the dimly lit room. Momentarily, it seemed that each had discovered the sensual sides of the other's touch. They took joy and comfort in rediscovering what had brought their love about. Mary reached up and pursed her lips to Daniel's ear, as if to simulate the tenderest of kisses. With her lips lingering tantalisingly close to his ear, she breathed gently, and then whispered to her husband.

"Listen, let's get the kids to bed early, open a bottle of wine, let the PC go off duty, and turn in early for the evening."

Chapter 14

The sun had risen low over Ravensdale Scar that Tuesday morning, giving it an appearance of a watery haze in the sky. The air was thick with moisture from the early dew that had settled on the fields, trees, and buildings in and around Ravensdale. The remote sound of sheep bleating punctuated the early-morning, swirling mists that had engulfed the more remote houses standing on the hillside around the tiny village.

The Hungry Harshes was one such house that hadn't escaped the mists' attention, making it difficult for Mary to rise that morning and enjoy the colourful canvas of dawn that greeted her, as she swept back the curtains of her and Daniel's bedroom. She pushed open a bedroom window and took in a lungful of air. It tasted sweet, cool but refreshing. Oh, how she wished that she could wake like this every morning!

Opening her eyes, she gazed out at the large Horse Chestnut that stood at the entrance to the front garden. *Magnificent* she thought, *a little bare now*. Gone were the resplendent gold leaves that had adorned it like a well-worn sash; it was now the depths of winter but, for Mary, it felt like spring. From the moment she had got up, her heart beat rapidly with a mixture of excitement and fear. Today was the day! She would take Eleanor to see Doctor Hannay, the eminent parapsychologist at the Institute of Psychology at the University of Leeds. Since meeting the doctor, her heart had been lifted by the very fact that he seemed to be someone who spoke with authority, who seemed to have an understanding of what it was, what evil menace was controlling Eleanor. She had prayed every day since that first meeting that the evil demons inside her daughter could now finally be exorcised.

This wasn't the only thing that had quickened Mary's heartbeat. Aunt Lillian had now arrived and had decamped in the spare bedroom. Different from Mary's mother Alice, Aunt Lil had bought zeal and enthusiasm back into the household. Even Daniel seemed to relax around her; he seemed to get on with the old girl. She'd only been there a day, her Ford Fiesta arriving the previous day; but, instantly, she was the crutch, the support Mary had so badly needed. Having been briefed by Mary on the meeting with Hannay in Leeds, she was keen to go along.

Daniel too had confronted his own demons. He and Mary had found reconciliation a rewarding exercise! Mary allowed herself a satisfied grin, as that thought passed through her mind and, once again, she turned, as she did every morning, to observe her sleeping husband in the bed.

Even the police were coming around to her way of thinking, she thought.

That morning, Mary planned the day meticulously. Daniel was off to work. He would drop David at school, and David would have football practice, so he was going to be home late, no worries. One of his friend's dads would bring him home, or at least to Wendy's, and she would give him tea.

Mary and Aunt Lillian were set to pick Eleanor up at two-fifteen and head straight for Leeds that afternoon.

"So, Mary," Aunt Lil begun to caution her niece, "I can see your pretty much up for this, so to speak, but don't expect too much this afternoon. This Hannay may be good, but we need to keep an open mind. We may not find the answer we are looking for today."

It was difficult for Mary to pull back her expectations but, nonetheless, she heeded her Aunt's words. After all, Hannay had said that this was no overnight fix.

"I know," she replied.

"Remember too, my dear," Aunt Lil went on, "this may not be comfortable. I mean this may be distressing for you, seeing Eleanor put under this much pressure." Lil rubbed the cheek of the small girl who had thrown her arms around the old lady. Eleanor was not aware of what Lil was talking about, but the two had become close for the first time when they'd met at Alice's funeral. Eleanor seemed to love Lil and had started referring to her as Nana. Eleanor seemed happier than she had been for some weeks. Time was indeed healing most wounds, but those wounds were about to be ripped open in the most brutal, vicious, and evil way.

* * *

Mary pulled into the school gates of Ravensdale Primary School that afternoon at five past two, ten minutes earlier than the time she planned. She had remembered that roadwork's into Leeds had caused some delay on her previous journey. Better to be safe and leave a little extra time. Lil sat in the car, while Mary walked to the school reception. She was early, but as she approached, she could already see Eleanor sitting on a chair, waiting patiently but kicking her legs, as they dangled from the chair. DI Toms had already called earlier that morning to confirm if everything was all right in the Foster household and, indeed, the meeting that afternoon was still on. Now, as Mary swung open the door to collect her daughter, Miss Shand approached her. She hadn't seen the teacher until she got into the school entrance, and the appearance of Miss Shand from the shadows behind Eleanor surprised her.

The young teacher wished Mary the best of luck with a knowing look, and the three of them, Mary, Lil, and Eleanor set off for Leeds.

The journey there was quiet; not much was said. Eleanor sat quietly in the back and stared out of the window. She was calm and relaxed, but she had sensed that, as they approached the outskirts of Leeds, both her mother and Lil seemed to get increasingly anxious and tense. Mary seemed to find an excuse to curse and snap at every red light, cyclist, or motorist who seemed to prevent her reaching her destination.

The University campus fascinated Eleanor. Her interest was sparked, and she gawped wide eyed at the assortment of grand buildings that bedecked the site, from grand red-brick statements of architecture to modern living blocks. The most impressive of all to the young girl was the Parkinsons building and Tower, built with the funds from one-time electrical engineering student Frank Parkinson. The tall, solid-white construction made the young girl crink her neck as she stared up at its elegant tower.

Mary managed to park in the same area, as previously, opposite the Institute of Psychology.

"Are we going in there, Mummy?" Eleanor asked, slightly in awe at the grandeur of the building. Mary stopped at the large, imposing steps leading to the entrance and turned to her daughter. She clasped her arms and crouched down on her haunches. Looking Eleanor straight in the eye, she proceeded to explain the reason why they were there.

"Listen, Eleanor, we're seeing someone today, someone who wants to meet you and find out what a good little girl you've been."

Eleanor stared at her mother with a blank expression.

"He may want to ask you some questions," Mary continued. "It won't be anything too difficult or tricky."

"Why does he want to see me?" Eleanor asked.

"Because you're a special little girl, and he's interested in your drawings. He wants to talk to you about your drawings. Is that ok?" Mary asked, knowing full well that she wouldn't turn back now, even if Eleanor said no. Eleanor looked away from her mother and back up at the large, imposing entrance to the Institute.

"Will you be with me, Mummy? You won't leave me, will you?" she asked nervously.

"Of course I'll be with you, and I won't leave." Mary replied, smiling at her daughter. "I will be there all the time."

"Promise?" Eleanor asked. She had taken a step away from her mother and the building.

"I promise. I won't let anything happen to you!" Mary said in a serious tone. The party of three climbed the steps and walked into the large reception area.

"Wow, this is some building!" Lil blustered in awe.

"Listen," Lil said, leaning close to talk discreetly into Mary's ear. "Aren't we supposed to meet your policeman friend here?" she asked, scouring the lobby for likely characters who looked as if they would suit a career in the police.

"Lil, we agreed, Hannay, Toms, and I that we would make it as discreet and low key for Eleanor's sake as possible. If she were to have too many people observing her, she might panic, feel the pressure was on her, and I don't want to do that at this stage. I didn't want to drive her away." Mary nodded to the door leading to the corridor she and Toms had walked down to get to Hannay's office on the previous visit.

"Toms is here. I assume he must be here already. We asked him to get here that little bit earlier, so Eleanor didn't see him. If she had, then it might have scuppered this whole meeting."

"But how will she not see him?" Lil whispered, trying not to let Eleanor hear the conversation.

"Apparently there will be a two-way mirror, leading to a viewing room. He should be there."

Nervously, Mary asked at the desk for Hannay. After the receptionist had made a brief call Mary, Lil, and Eleanor filed through the door down the corridor. This time, the door wasn't on the left but the second door, along the right, at the end of the corridor. Mary followed the receptionist's instructions precisely. The corridor was now quite dimly lit, and she was careful to find the right door the first time. She stopped outside, swallowed hard, and pulled down her jacket before knocking on the door.

"Come in!" came the voice from within. Mary opened the door and peered in. There was Hannay. He got up from a chair and ushered in the women.

"Hello, Mary, how are you?" he asked warmly, shaking her hand. Lillian followed, pressing her hands gently on Eleanor's shoulders and ushering her into the room.

Hannay quickly caught sight of the entourage following Mary. He looked first at Lillian. "Hello, I'm Doctor Hannay. You must be Aunt Lil!" he said pointing a playful finger at Lillian and robustly shaking her hand. "And you must be Eleanor," he said, looking down at the little girl who politely nodded.

"Please come in, sit down, take your coats off; it's quite warm in here. It was indeed warm in the room, and one suspected that it would get decidedly warmer. Mary and Lil looked around. This was completely different from the room where Mary had met Hannay the previous week. There were no windows, and this made both the women in particular a little edgy. There was, scattered around the room, varying degrees of what looked like technical equipment. From what Mary could make out, this was largely audio or video equipment, probably used for recording interviews. On the far wall behind Hannay was a large mirror, so large it nearly covered the entire wall. Eleanor stared directly at it, a little suspiciously. There was strip lighting from the ceiling and a desk lamp, but whatever lighting was applied, it seemed to make little difference. The room appeared and felt like a cell, a large cell, but a cell, nonetheless. Hannay busily arranged three chairs facing the mirror and one slightly off centre, facing the middle chair. Mary and Lil removed their coats and looked around for the coat hanger. Hannay, sensing that everyone seemed a little nervous offered refreshment in the form of tea or coffee, but he offered nothing to Eleanor.

"Please, everyone, sit down." Hannay indicated the chairs. "But I do have one request, though, and that is that Eleanor sit on the middle chair, please," he said. Everyone sat down; Hannay sat down in the chair opposite Eleanor but opened up the conversation with idle chat.

"So, tell me, how was your journey coming over?" he asked, his eyes darting between the three people sitting opposite him.

"It was fine, pretty uneventful," Mary said, taken aback by the line of questioning that Hannay pursued. Hannay noticed that Eleanor didn't respond but just stared ahead of her. Her eyes were blinking, as if they were irritated by something. She continued to peer into the vast mirror, framing the doctor. Hannay noticed this and got up to switch off the strip lighting.

"Oh forgive me. Is that better, Eleanor? Was the light hurting your eyes?" The little girl said nothing and gave only a blank expression back to Hannay.

Hannay sat back down. "Now, what was I saying?" he mused to himself. "Eleanor, can you help me, here? What was it I was saying?" he asked, attempting to draw the girl into conversation.

"You were asking about the journey!" Eleanor replied impatiently.

"Oh, that's right. What did you think of it?" Hannay asked.

As he spoke, the only remaining light in the room, the desk lamp, flickered behind him, causing everyone to look around. The room was now dimly lit. If the bulb from the lamp suddenly went, they would be in the ridiculous situation of all sitting in total darkness.

"It was ok. I saw lots of sheep and cows on the hills," Eleanor replied exuberantly. Again, the desk lamp behind Hannay began to dim, as if the bulb was dying. Hannay got to his feet.

"I'm sorry; I'll need to put some of these overhead lights on. I tell you what. I'll put these lights on behind you, Eleanor, is that ok? Then the glare won't hurt your eyes." He toyed with the switch, until he had found the correct one for the set of strip lights to the back of the room.

"Er, Mr Hannay?" Mary asked, as Hannay returned to his chair, adjusting its position in the room ever so slightly, so he could face Eleanor full on.

"I assume that…" Mary pointed to the mirror behind Hannay, who looked over his shoulder; fortunately, he had picked up on that Mary was referring to the presence of Detective Inspector Toms in the observation room.

"Oh, yes, yes," He said, nodding. Indeed, Toms had been there a full half hour before Mary had arrived. He sat in the observation room, his hands clasped next to a young and attractive post-graduate student, Jessica Stevens. Dressed in vest and baggy combat trousers, standard uniform that befitted students, even in December, she seemed adept at handling the mass of video and audio equipment that Hannay demanded be used to tape the interview. In contrast to the interview room, the observation room was emblazoned in light. Every strip light in the room was on. The room itself appeared padded, but was in fact soundproof, and a large video camera that sat on top of a tripod was pointed at the great glass two-way mirror, concentrated on Eleanor. Toms was almost oblivious to the young student, who seemed to dash up and down out of her chair, adjusting controls on the camera and tweaking controls that linked to audio monitors. Toms, fascinated by what she was doing, leaned across to her from his chair.

"What exactly is it you're doing there?" he asked, nodding at all the buttons and switches that adorned the console where the young student was sitting.

Jessica looked around and gave a half smile.

"Were hoping to detect any psychokinetic static or feed from Eleanor. If our suspicions are correct, and she is a conductor for psychokinetic energy waves, then, provided we give her the correct charge, we may be able to get something," Jessica replied in a soft Edinburgh accent.

Back in the interview room, Hannay proceeded with his line of approach to Eleanor.

"Eleanor, what do you like to do when you're at home?" he asked in a reassuring voice.

Eleanor thought for a while. "I like to draw and watch television," she replied. As she stopped, she raised her head up to look over Hannay's shoulder at the observation window behind him.

"You like to draw, I see. I like to draw too. I like to paint. I find it relaxes me. Do you like to paint, as well, Eleanor?"

"Yes, sometimes," she again replied. "You know you can call me Ellie; people call me Ellie!" she said, again, lifting her head to view the observation window. Hannay had noticed this and looked behind him.

"Ok, Ellie, now, can you tell me, what do you like to do at school? What's your favourite lesson? Now think very carefully," he said.

"I like drawing best," she replied.

"I see. What sort of things do you like to draw?" Hannay pressed.

But Eleanor thought about this for a little while and did not answer.

"Is it trees? Flowers? Houses? What do you like drawing best of all?"

Again, Eleanor couldn't find an answer. Hannay realised he had reached a dead end and shifted the topic of conversation.

"I bet you must have lots of friends at school." he said. "Who's your best friend? Do you have a best friend?"

Eleanor thought long and hard; she shifted in her chair and looked up at Mary, who sensed that her daughter was becoming a little restless.

"It's all right, Dear, who is your best friend at school?" Mary asked, smiling reassuringly at Eleanor.

"Well, I guess my most favourite friend is Izzy," she said.

"Ah, Izzy." Hannay seized on this. "And does Izzy come home to play sometimes? Does your Mum let Izzy come and play in the house?"

"Well, Izzy doesn't really have any friends, except me."

"I see, you're kind to her, then, are you Eleanor?" the doctor asked.

"Yes, very kind, but she's kind to me too!" The little girl shifted in her seat.

"In what way is she kind to you?"

"Well…" Eleanor paused to think. "She tells me when it's going to come."

Hannay's eyes darted upwards to catch Mary's. The two exchanged knowing glances. The girl was beginning to open up. Mary was about to cut in, but Hannay raised an open hand to stop her.

"Who's going to come, Eleanor?"

There was no reply.

"Eleanor, what is it that comes? Please tell me," Hannay pressed, but there was still no reply. The girl's mind had wandered.

"Eleanor, will you look at me a moment!" Hannay said, in a soft but firm voice, trying a different approach.

"Tell me again what's in your pictures. Is that what comes to visit you?"

There was no reply. Hannay sighed and beckoned to Mary to follow him out of the room.

"Ok, I think we'll take a break, there, a moment, Eleanor. You just relax why I have a quick chat with Mummy." The two got up and walked out of the room into the corridor.

Hannay closed the door behind them and turned to Mary. "Mrs Foster, your daughter is stonewalling me."

"Stonewalling you?" Mary asked.

"Yes, there's more she can tell me, but she's choosing not to tell me. I need to find some other way to get her to talk to me. I believe we are very close, very close, but with your permission, I'd like to try to hypnotise Eleanor." Mary thought for a moment; she felt her heart quicken at Hannay's words, but was concerned about the effects hypnosis would have on her daughter.

"What are the risks with hypnosis?" Mary asked, challenging Hannay.

"Oh, well, there's no real risk as such. I've done this many times on patients." Hannay took a gold pendant of Saint Christopher from his pocket and held it up to show Mary.

"I'll use this. Basically, I'll ask Eleanor to look hard at it, and I'll use the power of suggestion to send her into a trance. Now, not everyone can be hypnotised, but it's worth a try, here. Of course, I want you to stay with her the entire time she's under hypnosis," Hannay attempted to reassure Mary.

"But, what if she has a bad experience. How will it affect her?"

"Mrs Foster, there is no easy way or means of understanding what the underlying problem is. There is going to be some pain and, possibly some shock for you, in any approach we attempt to make. It's best that you are aware of that now!"

The doctor's words sounded ominous, but Mary knew she had little choice; she needed to step over that threshold.

"Ok, let's get on and do it, but on the proviso that we can stop it at any time!"

"Agreed!" the doctor replied. Mary watched as Hannay walked down the corridor to the first door on the right, the observation room. He opened the door and stuck his head in.

"Jess, I'm going to try hypnosis on the girl. Can you make sure that the camera is zoomed in on her at all times please?"

The student acknowledged the request, and Hannay closed the door and walked back down the corridor where Mary was standing.

"Mrs Foster, while I remember, would I be right in thinking that this Izzy is in fact not real but an imaginary friend, and that your daughter carries her around in her head?"

"That's right. She's not real; there's nothing unusual in that, is there? Lots of young girls Eleanor's age have imaginary friends, don't they?" Mary asked.

"Yes they do! Mrs Foster. Mary, have you ever been introduced to Izzy?" Hannay probed.

"No. Eleanor's told me about her but she's not introduced me to her, no."

"Ok, that's what I thought—oh and one other thing!" Hannay stopped and turned back to face Mary. "Has your daughter ever been hypnotised before?" He asked rubbing his chin with his index finger.

"No, Doctor she never has."

Hannay swung open the door and strode back into the interview room with Mary following. They both returned to their seats.

"Eleanor!" the doctor said, trying to attract the girl's attention. "Eleanor, now look at me, Sweetheart." Hannay held the Saint Christopher on the chain in front of him. He held it out in front of the little girl.

"Eleanor, I want you to do me a favour. Can you do that for me?"

The little girl nodded.

"Good, good girl! Now, will you just watch this pendant for me; just keep both your eyes on it…that's a good girl." Eleanor sat slightly forward in her chair with her hand under her thighs looking at the pendant. Hannay sat twisting the chain in his fingers, causing the pendant to spin first from left then to right, it continued spinning, the low-level light in the room reflected and twinkled off the pendant and chain. Hannay stared solely at the girl, and he began to speak in a slow, methodical way.

"Just keep looking at the pendant, Eleanor, and as you're looking at it, just think to yourself that your eyes are getting heavier and heavier. Your shoulders are beginning to drop. Let your shoulders drop. Just relax. Your arms by your side; now, just let your hands fall into your lap, just relax."

Mary and Lil watched as Eleanor, who had seemed bored and agitated, focused intently on the spinning pendant, and then she seemed to droop but stayed rigid, as if she had taken on the form of a mannequin. Hannay edged toward the little girl from the position of his chair.

"Good, good…just watch the pendant, watch the pendant." He murmured over and over again, under his breath. The room became eerily silent. The girl sat perfectly still in her chair. She didn't blink; she barely seemed to breathe. Hannay pulled back in his chair, folded the pendant in his hand, and put it in his jacket pocket.

"Right!" he muttered "She's now in a complete trance." During all this, Hannay did not break his gaze from the girl. Then he spoke to her in a direct voice.

"Eleanor, now listen to me. You will respond only to my voice. Do you understand?"

Eleanor barely gave a nod. Mary and Lil sat and watched, their mouths open.

"Now, I must ask you both to be quiet for the next few minutes, please," Hannay said. Once again, the desk lamp over the doctor's right shoulder flickered. It was time for the doctor to begin.

"Eleanor, I'm going to ask you some questions, and at the end of each question, I want you to answer yes or no. Can you do that for me?"

"Yes," Eleanor said.

"Good Girl!" Hannay replied.

"Now, I want to go back to the time when you and Mummy and Daddy moved to your new house. Can you remember that time, Eleanor?"

"Yes," Eleanor said, again, clearly, deep in a hypnotic trance.

"I bet when you moved it was exciting. Was it exciting moving to your new house, Eleanor?"

"Yes."

"Do you have any brothers or sisters, Eleanor?" As he asked the question, Hannay looked up at Mary, who held up one figure and mouthed brother.

"Do you have a brother, Eleanor?"

"Yes."

"Were you and he both excited on the day you moved to your new house?"

"Yes."

"Was Izzy excited when you moved to the new house?"

"Yes."

"Yes, I expect she was. Now, once you had moved into the house and lived there for a while, were you still happy?"

There was no reply.

"Eleanor, now listen to me. Are you happy living in your new house?"

Eleanor sat there for a moment without saying anything.

"No!" she finally said.

Mary sat back, astonished at her daughter's admission.

"I see," Hannay continued. "Is Izzy happy living in the new house?"

"No!" Eleanor said.

"I see, Eleanor, can you tell me, what is it that's making you unhappy in your new house, are you lonely?"

Again there was a lengthy pause. Hannay, Mary, and Lil were on the edge of their seats

"Yes."

"So, you're lonely. Do you miss all your old friends?"

"Yes."

"Did you tell your Mum and Dad this when you moved?"

"No."

Hannay decided to move onto another theme. "Eleanor, I'd like to talk now about your drawings, is that ok?"

"Yes."

"I've had a look at them. Your mummy showed me. You're quite an artist. Do you like drawing, Eleanor?"

Again, there was a lengthy pause before Eleanor finally said, "yes."

"Now, help me here, Eleanor —"

"You can call me Ellie!" the girl butted in, cutting Hannay off in his stride, much to his surprise.

"Ellie, I see. Extraordinary, she's overridden my initial instructions."

"What do you mean?" Lillian asked.

"I asked her only to respond by saying yes or no." As he said it, this time, both the desk lamp and the ceiling strip lighting began to flicker, at one point nearly cutting out completely and leaving the room in total darkness. Everyone in the room looked up at the ceiling.

"I wonder what's a matter with the lights," Hannay said, squinting up at the strip lighting. In the observation room, the troublesome lighting seemed to extend there.

"Ok, Ellie, tell me about some of your drawings, in particular these that your Mummy brought along." Hannay held up some of Eleanor's pictures, the ones coloured in black around an image of a large black wolf with evil red eyes. Hannay pointed with his index finger to the figure of the wolf.

"Ellie, can you tell me what this is? Is it some sort of animal?" he asked.

There was no reply. Eleanor had dropped her head and was looking straight into her lap. The only view Hannay had was of the top of the girl's head.

"Ellie, will you look at the picture, please? Can you tell me what this is supposed to be a picture of?. Is it a dog?"

Still the girl did not lift her head.

"Is it a wolf?" Hannay pressed again. As he spoke, Eleanor slowly lifted her head.

"Ellie, is this a wolf?" Hannay began to sound more assertive. Still there was no reply from the girl. The three adults could see that something was beginning to affect her. Her hands, arms, and legs began to shake erratically. As she lifted her head up to face Hannay they could see that the blood had drained from her face. Veins, which Mary had never seen before, began to protrude from the young girl's bare arms, and her eyes, once an innocent, sweet, piercing blue had clouded over. They were now dark, almost black. Her tiny face contorted into a hideous, sinister smile. Suddenly, Hannay, Mary, and Lillian felt icy cold. Toms and Jessica felt the same sensation.

"Jessica, are you getting all this?" Hannay shouted into a hidden microphone.

He knew he would not receive an answer, but certainly the pair in the observation room had got the message and were themselves witnesses to what was happening. Toms had risen to his feet in astonishment. Jessica had stood up from the viewfinder and looked directly at the girl through the two-way mirror. Eleanor's physical presence had gone from being an outgoing little girl and taken on the hideous apparition of the force controlling it. Before Hannay had the chance to begin questioning it, the lights that had flickered intermittently, both in the interview and observation rooms during the session, suddenly blew completely, leaving both parties immersed in total darkness. Suddenly, an unearthly, deep, tormenting laugh pierced the electrically charged atmosphere. Mary sat rigid in her seat. She knew that the laugh had come from her daughter sitting next to her. In less than a minute, infra red lights came on. They had been installed as back ups throughout the entire building in the event of a total power failure. The room was suddenly a combination of pitch black and red.

"Jesus!" Hannay said, "The whole building's out. She's taken out the whole building.

He could see Eleanor sitting in front of him, framed in red light, her eyes pitch black. The force, the entity, the evil that had been inside her had now shown itself. He watched as the girls just heaved in and out.

"HE, HE, HE!" came the mocking, provocative laugh, again.

"Who are you? What do you want?" Hannay asked confrontationally.

Eleanor's dark eyes fixed on him. As the child spoke, a deep, grotesque voice came from within her. "YOU FOOLS!" the voice rasped and crackled back at Hannay.

"Who are you?" the doctor asked, again, in an equally challenging voice.

As he spoke the words Mary and Lillian looked on in horror, the blood draining from their faces.

"YOU FOOLS. DID YOU THINK YOU COULD TRAP ME!" came the voice again. This time, the entity goaded them, and Eleanor beat her chest in defiance. Then, in a split second, before anyone could take any action, a spare chair from the back of the interview room was suddenly tossed through the air. It came from behind Lillian, crashing into the back of her head, as it flew into the centre of the room. Lillian felt numbness on the back of her head and the shock knocked her off her chair sending her sprawling onto the floor.

"WATCH OUT!" Hannay screamed, as another empty chair from the back of the room seemed to invisibly lift itself up and propel itself toward Mary. By then, she had let out a scream when she saw her Aunt crash to the floor. Instinctively, Mary threw herself face-first to the floor, landing at Hannay's feet. He had leaned forward in an attempt to catch her.

CRASH! The second chair that had just missed Mary flew over the desk, knocking the desk lamp to the floor. Chaos reigned. It was difficult to make out anything that was going on in the room, dimly lit as it was in infrared lighting. Hannay got to his feet and confronted the girl who remained seated. The chaos she was creating was happening all around her. He stood over her, bent down, and grabbed both her arms, gripping her tightly.

"Tell me who you are and what you want with this girl!" he shouted. Just then, a deafening sound pierced the room. The audio equipment including the microphones placed in the room to record the interview, suddenly began playing static and then feedback. The high-pitched whining was hard on the ears of everyone in both rooms. Hannay shook the rigid, motionless body of the girl, but there was no response from her. The entity that gripped her was fighting back in other ways. Hannay had to release his grip to hold his ears. He turned to look into the two-way mirror, as if to signal to Jess Stevens to cut the power, a pained expression on his face, but it was of little use. Toms and Stevens were themselves fighting against the high-pitched, unearthly, wailing sound.

Suddenly, another chair and then another, from a pile stacked at the back of the room lifted into the air. One flew with such intensity that it hit the two-way mirror, bouncing off it with such force it almost hit Hannay. A second chair was propelled with what seemed even greater force. Again, it hit the great glass frame, but this time it hit with such intensity it smashed the glass.

Inside the observation room, both Toms and Jess Stevens saw it coming.

"LOOK OUT!" Toms yelled, pushing the student away from the window and to the floor. Stevens fell face down. Toms had jumped in the opposite direction and turned his body, as the glass shattered, sending shards flying into both rooms. Mary was still lying on the floor and instinctively covered her head with her hands and rolled to the side of the room, away from where her daughter was sitting. Now, the entity that was creating the havoc could see what was on the other side of the wall.

"I CAN SEE YOUR NASTY LITTLE GAMES!" The voice now seemed to come from everywhere in the room, but it was still being generated through Eleanor. Suddenly, there was a large thump at the door to the Interview room. Lillian was screaming and in a state of shock.

"Ssshh! Everyone be quiet!" Hannay cried.

THUMP! THUMP! THUMP! There it was again. Hannay darted across the room, with the sound of breaking glass being crushed beneath his feet. He fell against the door, locking it, and turned to the shattered frame where both Toms and Stevens had gotten to their feet.

"Quickly! Lock the door!" Hannay bellowed to Jess. She locked the door of the observation room.

"YOU CANNOT STOP ME. YOU WILL LET ME IN!" the evil, grotesque voice bellowed. Again, the twisted, contorted smile returned to the little girl's face.

Mary clambered to her knees and lurched toward her daughter, as if to clasp hold of her.

"Eleanor! Eleanor!" she cried, as her knees slipped on the shiny surface of the floor.

"DON'T' TOUCH HER!" Hannay yelled. "DON'T GO ANYWHERE NEAR HER!"

Mary stopped in her tracks.

"YOU WILL LET ME IN. YOU WILL LET ME IN!" the entity that gripped the little girl bellowed, again. The thumping on the door became more intense; it was only a matter of time before whatever was outside was going to be able to break through.

THUMP! THUMP! THUMP!

"YOU WILL LET ME IN! YOU WILL LET ME IN!" the voice boomed. Now, it seemed to be everywhere, not just inside the room, but outside the room, as well. Suddenly, and without warning, the large desk that had stood behind Hannay started to shudder and move across the floor toward Lillian's prostrate body.

"FOR CHRIST'S GET HER OUT OF THE WAY!"

Mary jumped to her feet and ran behind Eleanor to where Lillian lay. At the same time, Hannay leapt across the room, and each grabbed an arm and heaved, shifting the old woman to safety under another vacant table. They were only just in time. The desk came to a sudden halt, where Lillian had fallen, and tipped over onto its side. Had Lillian still been there, she would have been crushed.

Hannay lurched back to Eleanor, sitting alone on a chair in the middle of the room, spotlighted only by an infrared glow. Hannay again grabbed her by the arms, as he stood and faced her.

"WHO ARE YOU? TELL ME WHO YOU ARE AND WHAT YOU WANT WITH THIS CHILD!" he shouted, as he shook the young body in fear and anger, and spittle flew from his mouth and hit the girl full on in the face.

"YOU WILL LET ME IN! YOU WILL LET ME IN!" came the reply.

The pounding on the door had grown more and more intense. Hannay realised that the situation had by now become desperate, and he had not planned an escape route. Again he turned and shook the girl.

"LEAVE THIS CHILD! LEAVE THIS CHILD! LEAVE THIS CHILD!"

Suddenly, and unexpectedly, everything stopped. Eleanor, who had been rigid in Hannay's hands, fell limp and collapsed. The doctor managed to catch her before she fell off the chair to the floor. He picked her up and laid her tenderly on the floor. Only a few minutes had passed, but to all who had been in the room, it seemed like an eternity. The infrared lights switched off, leaving the entire room in darkness for a brief moment. Then the white light of the strip lighting flickered back on.

"Eleanor! Eleanor!" Hannay patted the cheek of the young girl in an attempt to revive her. "Can you hear me, Eleanor?"

The girl murmured and began to respond.

Mary bent over Lillian. "Lil! Lil! Are you ok?"

The old lady was resilient. She had taken a nasty crack on the head, but, fortunately, it wasn't cut, and she managed, with Mary's help, to pull herself up. Both Women sat up and leaned against the wall of the interview room, catching their breaths.

"Are you ok, Lil?" Mary asked. "I saw you get hit by that chair!"

"Don't worry, Dear!" Lil joked, rubbing the back of her head. "You saw it, I felt it!" But Mary had already left Lil's side and moved over to check on Eleanor. Hannay had got her to sit up.

"What happened? Mummy what happened?" Eleanor started to cry.

Mary pulled her close. "There, there, Dear. It's all right, its ok."

Hannay got to his feet and surveyed the damage; it was bad. Chairs had been tossed everywhere across the room. The large desk had been dragged and tipped over. He looked into the observation room. Jessica Stevens stood looking back at the carnage, open-mouthed. The two way observation mirror was completely shattered and glass lay everywhere in both rooms.

"Are you ok in there?" Hannay asked Stevens, rubbing his head.

"I think so." Jessica replied, looking across at Toms who, in all his years on the force had never experienced anything as what he had just witnessed.

"Is everybody all right?" Hannay again asked, but extended the question to Mary and Lil. They nodded.

"Jess, can you get an ambulance up here straight away, please!" Hannay barked.

Jessica picked up the phone from the observation room and called reception.

"Yes, this is Doctor Hannay's department. Can you call an ambulance, please? It's an emergency. We have some people here who have sustained injuries. We need it urgently!"

Lil had got herself back onto a chair, and Mary had managed to get Eleanor to her feet.

Jess put the phone down and looked up at Hannay. "It seems that the electricity in the whole of the building has been out! Can it be possible that Eleanor did this?"

"Did what! What did I do?" Eleanor interrupted, on hearing her name mentioned. "Mummy I'm scared!" she cuddled into her mother.

"Well," Hannay said thoughtfully, "right now we have no other explanation for it. There could have been a logical reason why the power went off and affected the whole of the building."

"But it happened at the very time you were interviewing that girl!" Toms pitched in. "And now it seems we recovered power the moment the interview ended. Is that just pure coincidence?"

"No, it's not pure coincidence, as you call it, Detective Inspector. It was all very much done with intent. Eleanor was what we would call the *Focal Person* — someone in parapsychology terms who is very much at the centre of poltergeist activity. What we've seen here, today, are visual displays of what I would call poltergeist activity. For example, the inanimate objects moving across the room."

"Yes, doctor, but they weren't so much moving, as flying!" Toms replied, shaking his head.

"Exactly. There was so much force here, so much intent to prevent us getting to it!"

"Getting to it! Getting to what?" Toms interrupted the doctor again.

"Getting to the entity! The spirit! Whatever it was that Eleanor conjured up from within herself," Jessica Stevens replied.

"That's right!" Hannay endorsed his young student's description.

"You see, Detective Inspector, we hypnotised young Eleanor, because we believed that her subconscious, active when she's asleep and dreaming, is somehow creating or manifesting this physical form. It's only a theory, since we haven't proved this,

yet, but quite possibly Eleanor conjured the form that may have visited the Fosters' home, several times now."

Toms took everything in that Hannay was saying and then challenged him. "Ok, what about the thumping on the door. What was that?" he asked, nodding toward the battered interview room door.

"That was probably the physical manifestation itself, the creature. We had created an environment, whereby we could explore Eleanor's subconscious. We were, in effect, prizing the door open to her sleeping state; we were prizing the door open to her dreams. We seemed to have hit the spot. We encouraged Eleanor to externalise her subconscious."

"What's that?" Toms asked.

"We brought the creature, the entity, to life. That's what was at the door!"

"So, you're saying we went too far!" Toms said.

"No, Mr Toms," Hannay retorted. "We didn't go far enough!"

Chapter 15

It hadn't taken the ambulance long to reach the campus, and there was a busy throng of university staff and students all curious to see what had happened in the rooms occupied by Hannay. The ambulance crew provided a thorough examination of Lillian, who had the worst injuries of the five adults. Fortunately, she had suffered little more than a bad bump on the head from a chair leg. Had the full force of the chair hit her, her injuries could have been far more serious. Eleanor had little wrong with her, other than a slightly rapid pulse, but Hannay put this down to the stress and anxiety caused by the hypnosis. Hannay and Mary had escaped unscathed and, apart from a cut to Jessica Stevens' hand, she and Toms also escaped without injury.

Toms, in his capacity as Detective Inspector, decided that having been a party to and witnessing the whole event, there wasn't a requirement to take statements from anyone. They had replayed the videotape of the interview; fortunately, they had captured the image, but the audio sound was distorted. A loud crackling had meant much of the dialogue had been lost. Toms again shook his head as he, Hannay, and Stevens gathered around the monitor in the observation room, reliving the whole unearthly experience.

"Of course, I will have to file a report of the incident to the University Board," Hannay explained to Toms.

"What will that entail?" Toms asked.

"I'll need to include the details around the interview, the participants, how the interview was conducted, how it began, how it terminated. I'll have to report what precautions we took and what risks we mitigated."

"And what risks did you mitigate, Doctor Hannay?" Toms asked, folding his arms and leaning back on the observation monitor.

"Detective, I have had a lot of experience in dealing with special people like Eleanor. Let me tell you that, each time when I conduct a controlled interview like this, the result can be different every time. One cannot always judge how stringent one needs to be in taking the necessary preventative measures, but some mitigation is always planned for: the way we conducted the interview in a specially contained room, away from the large population of students; the ways and means we have of bringing the interview to a close," Hannay tried to explain in his capacity as an experienced practitioner, but Toms seized on this again.

"Doctor, can I remind you that one person is already dead, murdered, and today, we could easily have had more deaths!" he argued. He was aggravated. "At times, what I saw in there didn't look very controlled to me! People were injured. We are lucky not to have had a serious injury!"

"Now listen, Detective," Hannay said angrily, "don't you think I don't know that? There are always risks when conducting these types of experiments, but for god's sake we have to try to help this little girl and her family; otherwise, there is a very real threat that what she has, what she can create, will be allowed to kill again, possibly her, because I'm now convinced through talking to Mary Foster and speaking with Eleanor that this entity, this creature, is after her!"

There was a pause, while both men took stock of their thoughts and calmed down. Then Hannay looked at Toms, again. "Tell me, Mr Toms, are you still as sceptical of the world of parapsychology as you were a week ago?" he said, with a wry smile that flashed across his face.

"No, I'm not, but as the leading detective in this investigation, I need to make sure that the Foster family are at all times protected and that experiments such as these are conducted under properly-controlled conditions, *with* a police presence, monitoring them! Do I make myself clear, Doctor Hannay?"

"Perfectly clear," Hannay replied.

Toms walked out of the observation room, across the hall to Hannay's office, where Mary, Lillian, and Eleanor were sitting, still in a state of shock.

"Mrs Foster," Toms said, "I will be leaving for today, but I must know if you are all right to drive yourselves home, or would you like me to arrange for you and your family to be driven home?"

"No, we'll be all right. Thank you, Mr Toms," Mary said.

"I'll ensure that for now we maintain a police watch outside your home. It's certainly been an eventful afternoon!" Toms remarked, as he turned and walked out of the office.

As he left, Hannay walked in.

"Mary, are you ok?" Hannay asked sympathetically. "Your family will be wondering where you are. Do you want someone to give them a call?"

By now it had turned five thirty.

"No, Doctor, thank you. We'll make a move soon."

Hannay turned to walk out of the room, but, as he did, Mary grabbed his arm. "Doctor," she said, "I suppose you believe now the very real threat that my family is facing?"

"I do, indeed. I have encountered this before, but the resistance is particularly strong in young Eleanor," he said.

"So, what do we do now?" Lillian asked.

Hannay thought for a moment. "I think we need to come to you. I now know what I need to prepare for to combat this. Until today, I had no idea of what we were facing, but now I have a better idea of that. It would help enormously if we agreed to come to your house, to Ravensdale and pitch up there. We'll need to do this as quickly as possible!"

Mary clasped Hannay's arm with both hands. She was relieved that, after all this, it was obvious that the good doctor wished to continue with their case. "Thank you, doctor!" she said, with tears in her eyes.

"No, thank you! I just hope we can do something in time!"

* * *

Back at the Hungry Harshes, Mary and Lillian slumped into armchairs. Daniel had been home for some time with David, and both were inquisitive to know how the afternoon had gone. Eleanor had run past everyone and upstairs to her bedroom, where she shut the door.

"Where have you been?" Daniel asked. "We were expecting you back earlier than this!"

"Make us a cup of tea, and we'll tell you!" Mary said, wearily rubbing her forehead.

"To hell with a cup of tea!" Lillian said, "I need a drink!"

Lillian sank a large scotch and soda. As she tipped her head back to swallow the last drop, she ran her finger around the inside of the glass and sucked any remaining residue.

"That hit the spot!" she said with relief.

"Couldn't ask for another, could I?" she asked, holding up her tumbler for Daniel to collect.

Mary sat for a moment with her eyes closed, sipping a cup of tea.

"I'll finish this and then I think I'll join you," she said, nodding to the scotch bottle Daniel was pouring from.

"So tell me," he said, topping the tumbler with soda. "What happened?"

"She has it, Dan!" Mary exclaimed. "She has this family curse; there's no doubt about it. We all witnessed the measure of it this afternoon."

"What did Hannay do?"

"He hypnotised her. I thought he might try something like that. She's struggling with some demon inside of her. I don't know, Dan, but she says she doesn't like this house. She didn't like the move, and she's not happy here. Maybe we've been too selfish to see what all this upheaval has meant for the kids!"

Daniel poured himself a large scotch and sat on the sofa. "So, how does this work?" Daniel asked. "By hypnotising her, has he managed to exorcise her, if that's the correct term? Is she now free of whatever it is that's been troubling her?"

"No!" Lil said, rubbing her sore head "What we saw and felt this afternoon was really only the tip of the Iceberg. Whatever it is that's holding her is desperate to get her. I think it will try to kill her. What we don't understand is why it's after her in the first place."

Daniel shifted uneasily on the sofa and took another long, hard gulp of scotch. "So what are we supposed to do, now?" he asked, swallowing hard.

"Hannay's going to come here. I think he wants to research Eleanor a little more deeply, and he feels he can't do that, unless he comes to her environment," Mary explained, sitting forward in the armchair, as if to press her point to Daniel. "Whatever, we have made a breakthrough here, Dan. It wasn't pretty, but it *was* a breakthrough. I believe he can help our little girl. We must persist with this!"

Daniel mulled over Mary's words. As he did, he rolled the tumbler of scotch in his hands; the crisp, golden-amber liquid sparkled with the reflection from the fire. For all his scepticism of the paranormal, coupled with a slightly dismissive attitude about what Mary was trying to do, he nonetheless wanted to appear to be the man in charge of his own household. "Ok, I hear what you're saying. Let's get this guy over here and see what he has to say. Where's Ellie now?"

"She ran up to her room. She had a traumatic day, Dan," Mary said, searching for that hint of compassion from her husband.

Daniel breathed a heavy sigh and lifted himself off the sofa. "All right!" he said, downing the remainder of his scotch and placing the empty glass on the sideboard. "I'll go and see her, get her ready for bed. I've no doubt I'll be asked to read the three little pigs again!"

The days following Eleanor's interview at Leeds was a particularly busy period for the family. On Mary's insistence, Doctor Ventham had contacted Leeds General Hospital and secured an appointment for a neuroscan for Eleanor that very week. This was almost unheard of on the National Health Service! This appointment, however, was to replace the date she had missed earlier, as a result of the disruption of the break in and murder.

Little Pig, Little Pig

Mary had grown concerned with Eleanor's behaviour, following the meeting with Hannay. She had grown cold and distant both from Mary and from the rest of the family. She seldom smiled, seemed to be happy, or demonstrate any sort of spring in her step. She seemed to Mary to grow pale, and she had begun to develop dark circles around her eyes. Of equal concern was the fact that she appeared not to be eating, or at least not enough to sustain a healthy, balanced diet. This resulted in a somewhat gaunt appearance. The family were worried. What added to their concerns was the fact that Eleanor seemed to develop a regular fever and temperature; one hour she would have the hot sweats, the next she would be icy cold to touch. What seemed to compound her overall state was the fact that she seemed to retreat far more often to her bedroom and barely speak to anyone. When she was in the same room as her parents, she would hardly notice that they were there. When Mary dared to step into the girl's room, she found ream upon ream of drawings and pictures. All of them bore the same disturbing images—a mass of black, like a continuing eternal nightmare. The darkness, the loneliness of the night, had crept up all around and was all-invasive. All were the same, created out of desperation and pain and not thought. Some had the figure of the wolf as its centre, but Mary had discovered much more disturbingly that, when she looked at some pictures a little closer, there appeared to be an image of a young girl with the beast, a young girl with yellow hair, running from the creature in her daughter's pictures.

She longed to take them, tear them up, burn them, but she brought herself back from the brink, concerned what this might do to her daughter's already delicately-balanced state of mind. The drawings were everywhere, on the walls, on the bed, on her desk, on the floor. The entire room was covered from top to toe. Eleanor had stood on her chair, probably on tip toes, to stick her grisly images as high as she possibly could. All of this amounted to a great deal of concern for the young girl, from family, school, and the local GP. Indeed, Eleanor had appeared so ill on some mornings that Mary had not sent her back to school since the meeting with Hannay in Leeds.

Hence the reason behind the fast-track appointment. The drive over was horrendous. Again, Mary had taken Lil, but the hospital was located in Leeds, as were the university and Hannay, which presented an anxious journey for the young girl. She had recognised the route from the visit to Hannay and was suspicious that she was now returning there. It took all of Mary and Lillian's powers to calm her.

All in all, the appointment and the trip getting there was an arduous one. Waiting time was long; the consultant explained that they would do a large CT scan of Eleanor's head and create sliced images of her brain. Primarily, they explained to Mary, they would be looking for any abnormalities, growths, or tumours on the brain.

The scan, as Mary had predicted, revealed nothing. There was nothing physically wrong with Eleanor. That at least was conclusive proof for Mary that there was nothing medically wrong with her daughter. Psychologically, however, the problems were now huge.

Increasingly, Daniel and Mary found that Eleanor was sleeping less and less at night. She would often get up, and the two, now accustomed to light sleeping, would often hear the floorboards creak, as she walked around her room out onto the landing. They would find her leaning over the balcony, peering down into the hall below, as if waiting for something. Often, Mary was getting up for her, taking her back to her room, and settling her. Curiously, the only book that seemed to settle her for short periods was the story of the *Three Little Pigs*.

The continual unrest and disruption was once again beginning to take its toll on the family.

* * *

Other activities that focused Mary's mind included the onset of Christmas. It was only about three weeks away. Down in the village, an array of white and multi-coloured lights adorned the buildings, including one very large tree positioned in the centre of the village opposite the Bucks Inn. It looked beautiful, and it had made Mary think about decorations for the Hungry Harshes. With everything that had gone on, she hadn't felt particularly festive, but she felt compelled to think positively for the sake of the children and, besides, the house was itself a feature of the village. Walkers regularly stopped and admired the architecture. She had acquired a string of white lights, which she had used to trim a couple of rather statuesque yew trees, standing proudly either side of the path ahead of the front door. She needed to get some gifts, and fast, so she began to rummage catalogues for gift ideas. Christmas aside, she had also found herself with the ominous task of tidying up the details surrounding her late mother's estate. She had now become the owner and sole beneficiary of her late parents' house in Staines. She and Lillian made the trip south to hear the reading of her mother's will. Mary, as a precaution, took Eleanor with her. She thought it too irresponsible to leave her in the care of someone else.

The reading of the will was conducted in a sombre manner. It stated that her mother's home would be turned over to her daughter. The mortgage had been paid off many years earlier. Mary had seen the value of the house grow over the years, and now, at Alice's death, she needed to get the property re-valued. Her parents had taken the precautionary step of signing ownership of the property as tenants in common, which meant that the exact value of the property at any one time was divided fifty-fifty between each partner. The purpose of this, Mary found out much later, was to avoid any horrendous inheritance tax that she would otherwise have incurred upon both parents death. Effectively, at the time of her father's death some years earlier, half ownership of the house had gone to her anyway.

Although she hadn't approached estate agents in the Staines area, she had a rough idea as to what the property would likely fetch. Add to that her mother had left a tidy sum which was distributed across various bank accounts, stocks, bonds and some shares. This at least provided both Daniel and Mary some cushion of comfort, while Daniel expanded the business back in Yorkshire.

Mary had escaped paying death duties on her mother's estate. Now she needed to see about getting the property on the market, but with everything else going on in the family's life, she decided to forgo this activity for the time being; besides, it was nearly Christmas, the end of the year and the market was flat.

Before they left Staines, Mary, Lillian, and Eleanor spent one last evening at Mary's childhood home. The memories of their last stay to attend her mother's funeral was still too raw, but Mary took the time once again to walk around each room, taking in the stale-air odour of home life, desperately straining to recall the smells, the images, as if they were only yesterday. Her mother had a lot of furniture and ornaments. Most prized was a large grandfather clock, which dutifully and without fail chugged away in the hall. A lovely mahogany panelled mantel clock, which also gave a delicate chime on the hour, was given as a gift to Lillian. Much of the other furniture, which was mahogany, would fit nicely in the new home. Certainly, since moving to the new house, they had acquired plenty of space that needed filling. Mary had decided for the time being, however, that it would remain where it was.

* * *

As the days grew shorter, heavy mists would descend across the moors and engulf the tiny village of Ravensdale like a cloak. Daniel, being a native, was

familiar with endless winter days of mist and grey.
For Mary and Lillian, however, it was a little different.
Royal Berkshire was renowned for its claustrophobic,
icy mists. The air was continually damp, which kept
the atmosphere feeling fresh, but some mornings
when Mary awoke and pulled back the curtains in
their bedroom, the Horse Chestnut tree at the foot of
the garden was barely visible. The same could be said
of the dense woodland to the rear of the house. The
lawn would roll up and disappear into the heavy mist
that engulfed the large bare trees to the rear; only the
unearthly sound of the crows provided a clue as to
what lay beyond the banks of mist. What made the
atmosphere even worse was the ominous decline in
both Eleanor's health and behaviour. Everyone in the
household was aware of it; they couldn't fail to be.
The little girl's on-going decline had led to anxiety
and to a decline in the family's morale.

In a state of desperation, Mary had rung Hannay's
office for three straight days but had no reply. On the
one occasion she did get through to the department,
she was told that the doctor was away on a short
lecture circuit and would not be back until the
beginning of the following week! It was Wednesday
now; it would be a further four or five days before she
had a realistic chance of getting hold of him. She
didn't know if they could wait that long. Eleanor was
getting worse by the day. She had no idea where
Hannay was or even how to contact him, other than
through the university. She had tried sending him an
email, but there was no reply. Academics were
notoriously disorganised; they wouldn't necessarily

read their email daily, as someone would who worked in the business world. His parting shot to her was that he would visit the Hungry Harshes and see Eleanor there. But the two had not agreed on a date. Mary had assumed that he would be in touch a day or two after the last interview in Leeds, but he hadn't been.

In a desperate act, she had decided to drive to Leeds to the Institute of Psychology and see if she could find Jessica Stevens. It was a gamble, but she had time on her hands and, besides, she had nothing to lose.

Mary had taken the journey alone. The anxiety she felt seemed to rise within her and, in turn, it helped push up her adrenalin. She found herself increasing the speed of the car, now driving almost recklessly across narrow lanes and roads that traversed the moors still shrouded in this unearthly mist. She felt alone and isolated. She felt she must have been the only person around for miles. As the anxiety increased, she pushed the accelerator pedal further to the floor. Her mind turning over and over, she was now driving to get out of the mist, to get back to civilisation. She felt the mist choking her; she had to get help for her little girl; she wouldn't wait. The lanes twisted and turned. They became more dangerous, awkward. Mary became more reckless, and her speed increased to sixty, seventy, seventy-five. She was now driving far faster than she should have been but, god willing, she was getting away with it. *Faster! Faster!* She thought. *I've got to get there quicker.* The car was speeding along the lanes so quickly she barely had time to think. Suddenly, the road that had seemed isolated and lonely, now had another vehicle on it, and it was coming in the opposite direction.

As Mary turned a sharp bend, she had little time to react. The lorry, a large transport vehicle, was upon her like the great beast itself that had set upon them in their home. The vehicle, with no warning, lurched out of the mist. Lights blazing, the driver sounded his horn and sped past. He clipped Mary's wing mirror. By now, she had partially lost control of the car. Frantically, she clasped the wheel, as the car diverted off the road into a gated farm entrance. Slamming her foot hard on the breaks, the car skidded off the road, churned mud up everywhere, and skidded to a halt short of hitting the gate. The lorry had by now sped by, the sound of his horning trailing off in the distance. It had disappeared back into the mist and fog.

Mary sat for a while and rested her head on the steering wheel, her heart beating so hard that it almost hurt; she was breathless. What had she done? She had nearly gotten herself killed. Everything had got on top of her, and now, it had brought her to this! Alone, desperate, desolate, her face had turned a ghostly white. She slowly gathered herself; she looked at her hands. They still clasped the steering wheel so tightly that her knuckles had turned white. She released her hands and turned them over, looking at them as she did. Rubbing her forehead, she regained her composure. Where was she? She had no idea, but wherever she was, she was lucky to be alive. She pushed open the car door and slowly pulled herself out. There was nothing, no one, around. All she could hear was faint bleating coming from sheep that, because of the mist, she couldn't even see! She felt squelching and looked down to see that she had stood in a large amount of mud. "Argh!" her head was thumping with the stress. She took deep breaths and climbed back into the car. Starting the engine, she slowly pulled away into the mist. She had had a lucky escape!

* * *

Since Leeds was a city, it had not experienced the heavy mists that had settled in the rural areas around it. To Mary that was at least some relief. Having parked and entered the Institute building, she went to reception, still looking pale from her near miss. The receptionist gave her a quizzical look.

"Hello there! Are you all right?" she asked in a concerned voice. Mary leaned over the receptionist's desk.

"Yes, yes I'm fine. I nearly had a crash coming over, but I'm fine. Listen, can you tell me if Jessica Stevens is on the campus today?"

"Oh, I am sorry, are you all right?" the receptionist said, still more concerned for Mary's well-being. "Are you hurt in any way?" she asked, pushing herself up from her seat to get a better view of Mary. She gave Mary the once over with her eyes, looking for any apparent injury.

"No, no listen, I'm fine, really, I'm looking for Jessica Stevens. She's a student here!" Mary's anxiety showed, as she prodded her finger on the desk. "She works and studies here, in the Institute. She works with Dr Hannay. Could you see if she is here today, please? It's important. I need to see her urgently!"

Just as she was saying all this, Jessica Steven's marched past the receptionist's desk and to the doors that led to the corridor and the research labs beyond.

"Jess! Jess!" Mary called out and jogged over to the young student who had looked over her shoulder and stopped dead in her tracks.

"Mrs Foster. Hi, how are you!" She smiled, shortly to be replaced by a somewhat quizzical expression. "What are you doing here? I don't think we had a meeting today did we?" she asked.

Mary sighed with relief. "You're the one person who can tell me where Martin is! I've left messages for him, sent him emails!"

"Ach! You'll never get hold of him. I have to remind him to read his email; he's terrible for not doing it." Jess could see that Mary was flustered and looking more than a little anxious, her relaxed discussion turned to something of concern. "Are you all right? You look as if you have had a turn or something! Has something happened? Come through with me." The two women marched through the doors and down the corridor to the research labs and offices where Hannay worked. Jessica walked into Hannay's office and dropped her coat over a chair.

"Can I get you tea? Coffee?" she asked.

"Coffee would be good. White, no sugar, thank you," Mary replied, puffing out her cheeks. She didn't need to be asked before she slumped into a chair.

Jessica went and got two coffees and returned to where Mary was sitting.

"So tell me," she said, "How's Eleanor? And how are you?" She pulled up a chair close to Mary's. She cupped her hands together around her coffee cup. The morning was cold, so the young student took comfort from the sight of the rising steam from her cup and the smell of fresh coffee. It wasn't the best coffee, but it was wet and warm!

"Jess, I need to get hold of Martin urgently!" Mary said, her hands still trembling from her near escape on the road. Jess wasn't slow to pick this up.

"Your trembling! What's happened?"

"Eleanor's getting worse. She's more withdrawn, now, following the hypnotism than she was before it! She barely eats, sleeps, hardly ever talks to us, and her drawings are increasing. She has them everywhere in her room. Jess, I'm afraid that if we don't do anything, soon, we'll face another attack!" Mary's voice broke. She sipped her coffee, but she sounded desperate. "Martin said that he needed to visit us in Ravensdale. He said the next stage of this treatment would take place there, but he didn't give us a date, and we need him so badly!"

Jess got up and moved to Hannay's desk, where a large diary planner sat closed. As she bent over the book, she pushed her falling hair back behind her ears and began to turn the pages. "I know Doctor Hannay uses this for his appointments and meetings; he updates it religiously," she said.

Mary leaned forward and peered at the diary on the desk. She hoped there would be some mention in there of her, but to her disappointment there wasn't.

"Nope! He's got nothing in here. He probably got waylaid onto something else and forgot to put a date in." Jess looked up as if to offer Mary some consolation. "He's not forgotten you, though. I know, because we were talking about you the other day. The university wanted him to file an incident report." She smiled and sensed that that did not go far enough.

"Jess, is there any way we can get in touch with him? I'm told he's on some lecture circuit!" Mary said.

"Yes, that's right, he is. He'll be back on here on Monday, I think…Yes, here it is. He'll be back in here on Monday, but I think he'll be busy." Mary didn't wish to resort to confrontation, particularly with the young student, but she felt she had no other choice.

"That's no use to me!" she shouted. "I need to get hold of Doctor Hannay. I need to talk to him!"

"Ok, Ok," Jess back pedalled. "I have his mobile number here. Let me try him."

She dialled the number, and Mary secretly prayed he'd answer.

"Oh, hello! Martin, Martin can you hear me? It's a bad line!" Jess said, squinting.

Hannay had in fact been addressing a parapsychology and paranormal conference in Harrogate. He had been mingling with other attendees and invited guests in the conference lobby when he took Jess's call.

"Jess, I can barely hear you. Wait a moment, while I get out of here." Jess listened to the sounds on the other end of the line. It did sound like Dr Hannay was in a noisy crowd. But shortly, the noise subsided, and Hannay came back on the phone.

"Yes, hello, now what is it, Jess I'm just about to start this conference!" he said impatiently.

"Sorry to call, Martin, but I have Mrs Foster here. You know, mother of young Eleanor."

"Yes, yes I know who she is!" he replied again with some impatience. "Is everything all right? Please pass on my apologies. I meant to call her but didn't. Jess, tell her I'll call her later!"

"Martin, Mrs Foster seems very upset. She's desperate to talk to you. May I put her on?" the student asked, expecting a torrent of annoyed abuse to come back at her. Which of course she had grown used to, working under the tutelage of Hannay. For Hannay, it was no doubt inconvenient, but he *had* made a pledge, and Jess knew he felt duty bound to honour it.

"Ok, ok, put her on!" he said. Jess pulled the phone away from her ear and handed it to Mary with a symbolic gesture of an outstretched arm, which indicated that she had angered her boss and wanted to get as far away as possible from a confrontation.

"He wants to speak to you."

Mary took the phone and got up out of her chair. "Martin, its Mary. We need your help badly. Since you hypnotised Eleanor, she has begun to show signs of decline!" she said, as direct as she could be.

"In what way?" Hannay asked.

"She's losing weight, she's losing sleep, and we are losing the ability to communicate with her. Martin, she's withdrawing into herself and it's getting worse by the day. I'm scared! I'm afraid that she is anticipating an attack any day, now, and were not prepared for it!"

"Is she going to school?" Hannay asked.

"No, she's not at school. They won't take her; her behaviour is too disruptive; besides, she's cutting herself off from everyone and everything around her!"

There was a pause.

"The trouble is, Mary, I'm committed to this conference, now, until the weekend. I'm back at the university next week, but I think I'm fully booked out!" From the sound of his voice, Mary could tell that Hannay must feel terrible about reneging on an agreement.

But she had to persist. "Martin, WE NEED YOUR HELP! ANY DAY NOW THIS CREATURE MAY RETURN. IT'S ALREADY KILLED MY MOTHER. YOU'RE THE ONLY PERSON I KNOW WHO CAN HELP US!" Mary had reached the stage where she was virtually shouting down the phone at the Doctor.

There was a further pause, and she feared she had pushed too far.

"I just don't know how I'm going to get out of this…" Hannay sighed, as his words trailed off.

"Here, give me the phone!" Jess said, again, holding out an outstretched arm.

"Doctor Hannay it's Jess again. I thought you were giving a talk at the conference this afternoon and you were simply going to participate in the remainder of the conference. I thought that's what you agreed." Jess had called the doctor's bluff, but she hoped that, by steering him in one direction, she could clear his mind.

There was a further pause. No doubt Hannay knew he had to do something, since he had taken on the Foster case in good faith, and Jess figured he had felt responsible for leading Mary down a path he now needed to conclude. If there was a risk that people's lives might be in danger and he could help prevent that, then Jess felt he needed to do something about it.

"Ok, Jess, are you still there? Listen, this is what I will do. I'll stay on till tonight for the dinner. I'll have effectively covered my part of the conference and done my duties as host. I'll have glad-handed everyone I need to. Jess, tell Mary that I will be with her tomorrow afternoon; that's Thursday afternoon at about four o'clock. We'll need food and somewhere to bunk down for a day or so. Oh, and Jess, you're coming with me, so all plans are off at least until the weekend. God only knows if we'll have got this problem sorted by then!"

As he was saying all this, Jess gave a thumbs-up and winked at Mary.

"Yep! Yep! Ok, Martin we'll do. Oh, and Doctor Hannay, good luck with your talk this afternoon." She drew the mobile phone away from her ear, switched it off, and flashed a broad smile at Mary.

"Can you be prepared for us by tomorrow afternoon, Mrs Foster?"

A sense of relief came over Mary. "Yes, I can. Thank you, THANK YOU!" she said, relieved.

* * *

The drive back to Ravensdale proved to be as equally distracting as the drive to Leeds, but this time, Mary was again filled with a sense of hope. She now had so many things on her mind that, mentally, she attempted to prioritise everything in her life that had happened or was about to happen.

The selling of her mother's house could wait at least until the New Year. Her priority now was Eleanor. The neuroscan on her daughter had been done. She was glad that it had been done, but it proved inconclusive and hadn't revealed anything sinister, which was pretty much as Mary had expected. Her daughter's condition was never a medical one. Now, her anxious, nervy drive to Leeds, which had nearly resulted in her own reckless death, had paid off. It had been worth it! Hannay had given her his commitment. He was coming, and this time he would see the job done!

Chapter 16

The weather outlook for Thursday morning brought little cheer to much of the district. Across the moors that surrounded villages, such as Ravensdale, the seasonal mists seemed heavier than ever, carrying with it moisture in the air that seemed to settle on everything like a delicate stain. In the city of Leeds, the headquarters of the North Yorkshire Police service had not escaped the encroaching swirls of dank, cold, grey mists that had notably reduced visibility that morning for commuters. The station was busy countering the sudden influx of emergency calls, many relating to traffic accidents, a chaos that the mists had brought with it.

On the second floor of the station in Headingley, Detective Inspector David Toms nervously paced his slate grey and green office. He was anxious; he was getting pressure from his boss, the Chief Superintendent, with the lack of results from the Foster-Ravensdale case. Never in all his years in service had he ever handled a case quite like this one.

The motive for the killing of Alice Parsons still remained unclear. The only two strands he had to go on was either the inheritance and subsequent gain of Alice Parsons' estate to her daughter and son-in-law, or a tragic occurrence of the old women being in the wrong place at the wrong time, during an otherwise opportunist attempted burglary.

The forensic evidence was inconclusive and unsatisfactory. There was no apparent tangible evidence found of an intruder, which threw suspicion back on the Fosters, but there had been no forensic evidence to suggest that they could have carried out the murder of Alice Parsons. There were no DNA strands or any evidence that the old woman was involved in a violent struggle with either her daughter or, more likely, her son-in-law.

Adding to this, of course, was the mounting media criticism the police were facing in the light of the fact that the case seemed to be growing cold.

Indeed, it was little wonder that Toms felt anxious. The only lead he had now begun to follow with interest was based upon what he had witnessed earlier at the University of Psychology. He had mistrusted and dismissed Mary Foster's claim that some supernatural elements were at work and had been responsible for the death of her mother. He had thrown scepticism upon the Fosters' eyewitness statements on the night of Alice Parsons' murder. However, he could not discount his own observations at what happened that afternoon at the university. He had begun to follow his instincts and accept a lot of what Mary had been telling him.

Now, his anxiety levels had been raised further, as he paced his office waiting to be called in to see Chief Superintendent Raymond Fletcher.

Toms was aware that he would be back in Ravensdale that afternoon. A brief telephone conversation with Mary the day before had indicated that Doctor Hannay was in fact coming over to the Hungry Harshes, with the aim to conduct further tests on the little girl, Eleanor. Toms had felt that the tests that had already been conducted at the university were not carried out under proper and safe conditions. If Hannay's further "tests" were anything like those, then it would seem wholly irresponsible. As he saw it, it would place people's lives at great risk. He needed to ensure that greater security was in force and had taken the steps to request armed police officers patrolling the house for the next day or so. Or at least until Hannay had finished whatever it was he was planning to do! Toms knew that the request would prove controversial and had now brought him face to face with his boss.

The phone rang. Toms snatched at the receiver. The Chief Superintendent was in and wanted to see him now! Toms put the phone down, slipped on his jacket, which was hanging on the back of the chair, and walked the twenty five feet down the corridor to the Chief Superintendent's office door. Straightening his jacket, he rapped sharply on the door.

"Come in!" a gruff voice called from the other side. Toms opened the door and stepped into the office of Chief Superintendent Raymond Fletcher MBE. He was a tall, officious man whose demeanour bore the gravitas required of a senior officer in the Police Service. He had served as a senior officer for ten years in the Royal Artillery before joining the service.

Fletcher stood at the side of his desk, his impatience evident by the tapping of his finger on the desk top. Also in the room was Toms' colleague, Terry Corbett, who'd been assigned scene of crime officer following the Parsons' murder.

"David, come in and close the door, will you!" Fletcher said commandingly.

Corbett looked around and acknowledged his colleague with a nod of the head.

"Terry," Toms replied and sat on the chair next to Corbett.

"I've been talking with Terry about the Foster case; seems that we're going to undertake a second analysis of the forensic evidence. Is that right, David?" Fletcher began pacing slowly up and down from behind his desk.

"Yes, that's right, Sir!" Toms replied folding his arms.

"And am I right in thinking that we have found no obvious DNA strands; that is, other than someone in the Foster household?"

"That is correct too, Sir," Toms replied, twisting with some discomfort in his chair.

"I see…May I ask if we have conducted an investigation of all known suspects, small time criminals on our books, located in or around the district?" Fletcher asked, stopping at the window and gazing out on the extraordinarily dense mist. Corbett shifted in his seat and responded to the question.

"Yes, Sir, we have indeed conducted an investigation of some one hundred and forty-three known previous offenders or small-time criminals, as you say, Sir, who would fit such a crime." Fletcher continued to stare out of the window, his hands firmly rooted in his trouser pockets.

"And have you interviewed all of them, and do they have alibi's that can be corroborated?" Corbett, under a little stress wet his lips with his tongue before answering.

"We have to date pulled in for interview and have corroborated the stories of one hundred and eighteen of them, Sir. Nine of potential suspects have died, and we will update our register. A further three were out of the country and abroad at the time of murder. That leaves thirteen we have still to question, and we are pulling them in this week, Sir."

Fletcher stared at the floor with a look of disappointment and turned to face the two seated men.

"Do we believe that in these final thirteen we may find the likely perpetrator?" he asked, sternly looking at both Corbett and Toms.

"Can't say yet, Sir, until we question them!" Corbett replied.

"So, we still have little to go on, unless we focus our attention a little more closely on Daniel Foster, the victim's son-in-law," Fletcher summarised in an aloof manner.

"With all due respect, Sir," Toms interjected, "what reason would Daniel Foster have for murdering his own mother-in-law?"

"Motive? Inheritance, Toms!" he snapped back. "Daniel Foster's business is struggling to get off the ground. He's not making the money he thought he would be, and he was at the scene of the crime." Fletcher tried to sound rational."

"Yes, but the Fosters had only just moved to Yorkshire to begin a fresh start; they had brought their dream property. Why would they now risk all of that in some pre-meditated attack? It doesn't make any sense. Besides, and Terry can confirm this, there was no DNA evidence for Daniel Foster found on the victim's body. We checked nails, skin, everything. Alice Parsons died a violent death. There would have been a violent struggle. We would have found more of his DNA on her and vice versa!"

Fletcher glared at Toms, then looked down at the A4 size piece of paper on his desk. Toms knew that the paper was his request. Fletcher picked it up and looked at it.

"This could be a big gamble, David!" he said, waving the sheet at Toms. "A request for assignment of armed police officers is not to be taken lightly. Just what are you onto?" Fletcher asked.

Toms stiffened in his chair. "You read my last report!" he said.

Fletcher again paced around to the side of his desk, the side Toms was seated at. "I did, and I must say I'm more than a little nervous! You stated in that, if I recall, you attended a séance—"

"A hypnotism, Sir," Toms broke in. "It was a hypnotism!"

"A hypnotism by this parapsychologist who hypnotised the Foster girl and, as you stated, this led to an uncontrolled and violent incident in which several people were injured and required the emergency medical services." Fletcher continued.

"That is correct, Sir, yes!" Toms replied.

"Are you telling me, David, that you are now pursuing something along the lines of a paranormal investigation? You're telling me, from what I understand—and please correct me if I get this wrong—the little girl, Eleanor Foster is somehow possessed, controlled by some psychic phenomena that visits the house and kills!"

As he spoke, Fletcher again paced back to the window. With his back turned on his two officers, he failed to notice Corbett turn and give a rueful grin to Toms.

"What I'm telling you, Sir, is that the family has some recorded history relating to paranormal activity. We examined Mary Foster's files, her medical records, and, as a child, she suffered an episode where she was confronted by an apparition. The daughter too seems to possess powers that I can't explain, but what I saw happen at Leeds University was very real. Objects flew around the room; a two-way observation window was smashed. It's all detailed in the copy of Doctor Hannay's report to the university. He has to file a report whenever he conducts such experiments, and when the effects result in an adverse reaction!"

Fletcher spun around to face Toms, as if he was turning on a sixpence. "So, David, listen to me!" he said sharply, stung by Toms assertive tone. "What this Doctor Hannay appears to be able to do, what he appears to be a practitioner in, is to be able to create a wholly volatile, unpredictable, and uncontrollable environment!" He paused. "And you want me to sanction the presence of armed police officers in that environment, do you? David this sounds like a recipe for disaster! If we have an incident here, whereby an innocent member of the public is injured, as a result of highly reactive police action, I'll be for the high jump! You'll be for the high jump and all hell will let loose!"

Toms refused to be cowered by Fletcher's rant. "With all due respect, Sir, I was as sceptical as the next man about the paranormal, but I have come to realise that the solution to this case lies somewhere within that little girl. Hannay, it seems, possesses the key to unlocking what it is inside her, which I believe has resulted in the death of her own grandmother, Alice Parsons. If we fail to protect the family, now, when Hannay conducts further hypnosis on the girl, then we could very well see more deaths!"

Fletcher took in a deep breath and clenched his arms behind his back. He had known and worked with Toms for a number of years; he was a good copper. His record was exemplary. If Toms was prepared to sit in front of him and argue his case so vehemently, then he must be onto something.

"All right! Here's what I'm prepared to do. I'll sign off on your request, but only on the condition you get the best two firearm Officers we've got on this operation!"

Toms sighed with relief. "Thank you, Sir, thank you. I will of course take full responsibility for the conduct of the operation."

"Oh, of course, you bloody well will!" Fletcher countered. Taking out a ballpoint pen from his top pocket, he bent over the desk and signed the form.

"You'll have your men by the end of the day," Fletcher said, placing the pen back in his pocket.

"Now, you can go!" he said dismissively. Toms and Corbett got up from their chairs and walked out of the room into the corridor.

"Dave, I'd love to be there when this one goes down!" Corbett said, taunting his colleague.

"I just hope I'm right about this, Terry." Toms replied. "I bloody hope I'm right!"

* * *

Back at the Hungry Harshes, Daniel wandered around the house, hands in pockets, looking, for all the world, like someone with nothing to do. Mary had sat him down the previous evening and explained that Doctor Hannay and his assistant would be coming to the house, today, to conduct further research and, hopefully, treat Eleanor. Mary had talked him into taking a couple of days off from work. The prospect of meeting this eminent academic, psychologist, and parapsychologist intrigued him. He too felt, as his wife did, that the situation at home had become desperate and, having these academics come over to review Eleanor couldn't hurt, especially as they seemed to have made some progress. Besides, he couldn't concentrate at home with everything going on.

Daniel ambled down the hallway to the front drawing room, where the sound of activity could be heard. He eased back the door to the room and peered in; he found Mary bent double, frantically making up two beds. She hadn't heard him enter the room.

"Who are they for?" he asked. Mary stood up with a start.

"Dan, don't do that!" she replied, clutching her stomach. "I'm edgy enough as it is!"

"Sorry!" he replied, putting both hands back in his pockets and leaning on the doorframe. "Are these for our eminent scientists?" he asked mockingly.

"These are for Doctor Hannay, yes!" Mary replied curtly.

Dan sniffed. "How long are they going to stay?"

"As long as it takes!" Mary quipped. "I don't know. Hannay said a couple of days. I hope they will be gone by tomorrow and we can get our lives back!"

"You really think this guy's going to be able to crack this?" Dan asked.

"I keep telling you!" replied Mary a little annoyed, "he's the best hope I've seen so far!"

"Ok, ok, I know," Dan said, folding his arms. "Anything I can do to help?" he asked.

"Yes, help me with these corners." Mary nodded to the edge of the bed. Daniel duly obliged and tucked in the untidy bed sheets.

"You haven't forgotten, Dan, the police are going to be here, as well," Mary reminded her husband. "Toms is coming over."

Daniel stood up straight and rubbed his forehead. "Great, PC Plod as well. We're going to have a real houseful; it's going to be like hosting a Halloween party!" he joked.

Mary retaliated with a stern look.

"Talking about a houseful," Dan said, "where's Lil? I've not seen her or heard from her for a while. Where is she?" Daniel asked this with a quizzical expression on his face.

"She's upstairs with Ellie. They're in her room."

Dan symbolically looked up at the ceiling. "What are they doing up there? The two of them must have been up there for ages?"

Mary glared at her husband. "Have you bloody well been in to see her this morning!" she snapped. "She's not great; she's getting worse. Her temperature's up; she's running a fever. I've put her back to bed. Lil's sitting with her." Mary's irritation showed, as she threw a pillow onto the made-up bed.

"I'm sorry, I didn't know. I'll go up and see her. Did you call a doctor?" Daniel asked. Suddenly, he felt like a complete louse for not having looked in on Eleanor.

"Yes, I've called a doctor, but a doctor's not going to be able to help! For god's sake, Dan, you've got your head stuck so far up your own backside, sometimes with work, you don't even notice what goes on in this family," Mary raged.

"I'm sorry, I'm sorry, Mary. You know that's not true. Let me go and see her!" Daniel backed out of the room and climbed the stairs to the landing and Eleanor's bedroom door. Eleanor lay in bed, a cool flannel placed across her forehead, in an attempt to reduce her temperature. Lil sat in a rocking chair by her side. She looked up and removed her reading glasses, when she saw Dan enter the room.

"Sshh!" She motioned, putting a finger to her lips. "She's asleep now," Lil whispered. Daniel looked around the room. The curtains were part drawn, letting through a narrow margin of light that lit the middle of the room. Either corner of the room, though, was shady, but there was sufficient light to see stacks upon stacks of paper piled up untidily. All had in some way been drawn upon and nearly all bore the same image. Defiled and scribbled sheets of paper were strewn all over the bed in which the little girl lay. They were scattered unevenly across the bedroom floor, and nearly every piece of available wall space had, by now, been covered in the little girl's pictures.

Daniel slowly crept over to where his daughter lay. Tenderly, he sat down on the bed next to his prostrate daughter. Gathering her tiny hand in his, he gently caressed her porcelain white cheek. Overcome with seeing his daughter physically deteriorate, his eyes filled with tears. The feeling of helplessness and guilt at not knowing how to protect his daughter was tearing him apart. Mary had crept up the stairs behind him and stood silently in the doorway; she, too, had tears in her eyes.

"All she's been asking for is Miss Strand from school," she conceded. "She wants her teacher. I've rung Isla. She'll come over after school. That was good of her," Mary said, wiping tears from her eyes.

Daniel's tears dripped from his face onto Eleanor's pillow.

"Oh, god, Mary, I pray we're not too late! I hope this guy can do something to help our little girl!"

As Daniel spoke, the encroaching mist outside the house brought with it a soft gust of wind that blew through a narrow open window into the room, rustling the curtains and gently tossing a few sheets of Eleanor's scattered drawings across the bedroom floor.

* * *

By four o'clock that afternoon, Eleanor's condition was little better, confined to bed and still burning up from a raging temperature. Doctor Ventham, concerned with the little girl's deterioration, had again called in to see her. His checks were the normal ones conducted by that of a general practitioner. He checked pulse, checked her chest and back with a stethoscope, and took the little girl's temperature. He looked for signs of meningitis but found no consistency with the symptoms. Indeed, Eleanor's symptoms seemed more representative of a bad dose of influenza. His recommendation was to give the child a mild sedative to help her sleep. This, he gave to the care of Mary to administer, as appropriate, and left, stating that he would call via telephone the next morning to get an update. Mary and Daniel had accepted Ventham's diagnosis and showed little energy to challenge it. By now, they had both come to believe that no medical diagnosis could bear any real relationship to their daughter's condition. They waited anxiously for Hannay.

A little after a quarter past four, Isla Shand arrived. Like everyone else in the household, her anxiety toward Eleanor's condition showed. She went to the little girl's room and spent some time sitting in the rocking chair by her bed. This gave Lil the opportunity for a welcome break. The young teacher had brought with her some letters and cards written and drawn by Eleanor's school friends, wishing her well and hoping she got better soon.

Shand had come straight from school. She had anticipated staying maybe an hour or so and then leaving, but by half-past four, the Police arrived. Toms had brought with him two armed officers who had arrived in an unmarked police car. This was done with the intent of not attracting further attention amongst the villagers. The two armed officers remained in their car, which was parked up the Fosters' winding drive. Tom's had parked behind theirs, and both had blocked in the teacher's car. The young teacher had, to some extent, got what she had wanted. She had declared to Mary earlier an interest in Eleanor's circumstances and, at the very least, as her primary school teacher, had wanted to track the little girl's condition more closely. Now, it seemed that, through extenuating circumstances, she was locked in, together with the Fosters, the police, and parapsychologists to confront the very real and terrible demons that were haunting the child.

By now, Ravensdale was shrouded in darkness. The late afternoon dusk, together with the previous evening, had sought only to bookend the rolling swirls of mist that had settled across the whole district all day.

The air remained cold and, as the evening drew in, would get a lot colder, an uncomfortable prospect for the two officers in the car. However, the coldness of the evening had brought sharpness with. The village down below was transformed into a warm, crystallized glow, particularly as the lights from the street's Christmas decorations shone and sparkled. From the Hungry Harshes, they looked like lit candles on a birthday cake and, for the occupants inside the house, a comforting sense that civilisation was not too far away.

By now, the narrow driveway to the Hungry Harshes looked busy with a succession of parked cars. It had become full, however, shortly after five-thirty with the arrival of Doctor Hannay and Jessica Stevens. The two parapsychologists had barely managed to squeeze their car off the narrow lane onto the Fosters' drive. The house, though, was aware of their arrival long before they got to the front door. Toms, who had been sitting in the kitchen, had received a call on his mobile phone from one of the two officers, outside, stating that a man and woman were approaching the house.

"Right!" said Toms, abruptly switching off his phone. "Our friends have arrived. I guess the show's on!"

With a sense of relief, Mary left the kitchen and got to the front door. She opened it just as Hannay was about to ring the bell. She was confronted by both scientists, laden with bags and cases. Hannay and

Mary exchanged knowing looks. There was no introduction on the doorstep, and Hannay stepped into the hall, his thick, brown windcheater coat, which stretched to his calves, brought in with him the icy cold from outside. Jessica Stevens followed him and stood holding her cases.

"Hello, Mary, we meet again. How're things?" Hannay asked his eyes focused intently on Mary, as she shut the heavy front door behind her.

"Not good, Martin. Eleanor's upstairs in bed. She's running a temperature and she seems to be slipping in and out of consciousness." As she said it, Daniel stepped out from the sitting room into the hall.

"Martin, this is my husband, Daniel. Daniel, this is Martin." Hannay turned to look at Daniel.

"Hello there, pleased to meet you!" Hannay said, offering his hand to Daniel. The two men shook. Daniel looked him up and down. He was a lot younger than he had expected and, dared he say, better looking! Jessica promptly put her bags down to shake Daniel's hand.

"Hello, I'm Jessica. Call me Jess. Everyone does!" Daniel was aware that, while introductions were going on, Hannay was now reciprocating the stare.

"I was just saying to Jess, this mist, it seems to have followed us here from Leeds; it's hung around all day!" Hannay said, looking at Daniel, who had shoved his hands defensively into the pockets of his jeans.

"Yes, awful weather to drive in," he replied.

Hannay stared around the great hallway and up the stairs almost sensing where Eleanor's bedroom was. "This is a fine house you have here, very fine, and being set apart from the village like that, it's very convenient." Hannay's attention focused beyond Daniel and Mary, down the hall to the kitchen. He had noticed the five long serrated tears along the wall that ran from the kitchen door to the sitting room. Walking past Mary and Daniel, he touched the marks on the wall. His fingers ran over them gently, almost therapeutically, as if he were trying to get a sense of what had caused them.

"Look at this, Jess!" he said, peering closer at the torn paper and damaged plaster. Jess left the couple and walked down the hall to where Hannay stood. The two scientists studied the wall. Stevens also felt compelled to touch the wall.

"What do you think, Doctor? Anomalistic?" she asked Hannay.

"Yes, possibly, which could explain it!" By now, Daniel had taken his hands out of his pockets and scratched his head. "Animal what?" he asked, with an expression that said he had lost the thread of the conversation.

"Anomalistic! Or paranormal, whichever you prefer, these markings on the wall were created by the creature; am I right, Mr Foster?" Hannay asked, glancing up at Daniel.

"If you mean were they done by the intruder during the first break-in, then yes." Daniel replied.

"But we cannot be sure that the intruder on the first forced entry was indeed this creature of which you speak!" came the voice of Toms, who had stepped out of the kitchen, into the hall, and had picked up the thread of the conversation.

"Ah! Detective Inspector Toms, nice to see you again," Hannay quipped.

"So, Mr Hannay—" Daniel began.

"Call me Martin, please!" Hannay responded abruptly.

"Martin, have you ever come across anything like this before?" Daniel asked vaguely.

"Like what?" Hannay replied. Daniel looked across at Mary for help.

"Well, possession, if that's what you want to call it. I mean, I've seen *Poltergeist*. I think it's a great film, but can this stuff really happen? Does this sort of stuff really happen? I always thought it was stuff of fiction," Daniel said, shaking his head.

"Oh, I'm afraid it very much does happen, Daniel. Can I call you Daniel?" Hannay asked, looking seriously at Daniel.

"The principle's the same. Someone, normally a susceptible young child like your daughter, becomes what I call an Agent or Focus for an extra-sensory phenomena, or possibly, what I think is happening with Eleanor is that her mind, the subconscious element of her mind, is acting as a conductor. Whatever it is that is disturbing to her, that element of fear, she keeps coming back to it time and time again, a bit like what happened to you when you were a child, Mary. Her subconscious is so strong and it's not unusual for it to run in families and be passed down through generations, so that she is externalising her thoughts and fears."

Daniel listened intently to Hannay's explanation. "Externalising...what do you mean by externalising? What is external to her?" Daniel asked a little impatiently.

"The creature, the beast, the Lycanthrope, which is another name for a Werewolf. Her subconscious is so strong, the image so vivid that what she is exploring in her dreams is being externalised, and it, the creature, in turn, is more than just an apparition. It is reciprocal. I mean it can see her, you, anyone, as much as she or you can see it!"

"It sounds incredible!" Toms interjected. "Too incredible to be true. A little girl who has a nightmare can create a physical animal or creature that can be touched and seen by all!"

"And why not, Detective Inspector?" Hannay responded.

"We're all able to manifest our waking thoughts, our state of consciousness, when we are awake. We see things, our brain interprets it, and we respond with physical actions, and often physical actions by others, as well. So, if we can do this, then we can also manifest sleeping thoughts, which, if strong enough, has a resilient enough conductor and then can manifest itself physically."

Daniel gave a large sigh, which signalled his disbelief to all around.

"We know very little about what our brains can do. We are beginning to learn more and more but, alas, we still know very little," Hannay said. There was an awkward silence, as the five stood in the hall attempting to digest Hannay's words.

"Right, where can I put these cases?" Jess asked, in an attempt to move away from the depth of the conversation.

"In here." Mary pointed to the room, where she had set up beds for the scientists. Hannay and Jess picked up their luggage and moved to the room. As he walked past, Daniel gently grabbed at Hannay's arm.

"Can you really help our little girl? Can you save her?" he asked, with more than a little desperation in his voice.

Hannay stopped to face him. "I hope so, I sincerely hope so. Now, let's see Eleanor!"

Having dropped off their luggage, the four of them, Mary, Daniel, Hannay, and Jess climbed the stairs to the landing and the little girl's room. Toms remained downstairs and returned to the kitchen.

Daniel waited at the bedroom door, as Mary led the two parapsychologists into Eleanor's bedroom. The curtains were now drawn completely, and only a low-voltage bedside table lamp provided subdued lighting in the room. To Mary's unexpected surprise, Eleanor was now sitting up in bed. Pale, with dark circles around the eyes, she was still nonetheless running a temperature, but the presence of Isla Shand at her bedside seemed to have acted as a tonic. Lil sat at the foot of the bed. The three had been going through the various cards and letters brought by Shand from school.

Hannay and Jess entered the room and walked slowly toward the little girl's bed. Eleanor, not knowing what to expect from Hannay, just stared at him and froze.

"Hello, Eleanor, how are you? I hear from your Mummy and Daddy that you've not been too well?"

The little girl didn't respond. Jess and Hannay stopped and looked around the room, noticing the great swathes of scribbled paper piled up everywhere. Hannay picked up a drawing stuck to a bookcase. The drawing depicted, as did many, the darkness that Eleanor could see in her mind. In the centre of the darkness was the child's scribbled but undeniable image of the creature.

"You like to draw, don't you, Eleanor?" Hannay asked, handing the drawing to Jess, whose jaw had dropped at the sight of the reams of paper that seemed to cover the whole room.

"Jeez!" Jess gasped in amazement. "She must be doing these in almost a trance-like state!"

"Exactly!" Hannay concurred with his young student's observations "As a Communicator, she's acting as a Medium would act, someone who acts as a gateway between the real world, which we understand and live in, and the paranormal world."

"But this is obsessive. I've never seen anything quite like this!" Jess restated, shaking her head.

Hannay continued to scan the room and fixed his sights on the long, overburdened bookshelf. He moved across to the shelf and began scanning the titles.

"Do you like lots of stories, Eleanor? You're so very lucky to have all these wonderful books." The little girl watched Hannay, as he began to thumb through some of the books.

"Eleanor, Darling, Mr Hannay asked if you like stories and storybooks," Mary prompted.

"Yes, I like stories," Eleanor replied, but she was clearly not at ease.

The bookshelf was full of all sorts of children's books, big and small. Hannay was searching for a clue, a hook, a meaning to try and make sense of what it was that was firing Eleanor's mind.

"You know, when I was your age we used to have books like *Tom Sawyer* and the *Famous Five*." Hannay turned to look at Eleanor. "Has Mummy or Daddy ever read you a story of the *Famous Five*?" he asked. Eleanor shook her head.

"Ah! *The Gruffalo*, what a funny-looking creature the Gruffalo is! Do you like the story of the Gruffalo?" Hannay asked. This time, he didn't turn to face the little girl but continued to thumb through the book.

"Yes," Eleanor replied. She had picked up a dolly and began teasing its hair.

Isla Shand, who had been sitting in the rocking chair all this time, felt a little unease. There were now too many people in the room pressing Eleanor. She thought, *the child must feel trapped.* By guessing where Hannay was leading with the questioning, she asked the next question.

"Eleanor, Sweetheart, can you tell me what your favourite story is?" Once again, the room fell silent, waiting for the child to answer.

"That's easy." Eleanor replied stroking her doll. "*The Three Little Pigs*!"

Jessica Stevens responded almost instantly. She and Hannay flashed glances at each another.

"Little Pig, Little Pig let me in!" Jess recited "You will let me in! You will let me in! Jesus Christ, that's what Eleanor was saying at the Lab! You will let me in! It's the story of the three little pigs; it's the wolf in the story! Don't you see, it's the bloody wolf in the story!"

Chapter 17

Mary's emotions were once again thrown into free-fall. As the party left Eleanor's bedroom and headed back to regroup in the kitchen at the Hungry Harshes, she felt her heart race uncontrollably. She tried to swallow, as her mouth dried and her mind turned over and over. As the group reached the kitchen, Mary went straight to the sink, reached for an upturned glass tumbler that stood on the draining board, and promptly filled it with cold water from the tap. Taking a large gulp to alleviate her parched throat, she turned to face everyone who had reconvened around the large kitchen table. What was noticeable was the mix of silence, shock, and excitement. The parapsychologists seemed to buzz. Jessica Stevens and Hannay huddled in a corner in child-like excitement, talking feverishly, but in hushed tones; this new disclosure had provided yet more clarity in this intriguing case.

By contrast, Daniel stood in silence. With his back to the room, he simply stood by the back door and stared out into the utter blackness of the night. Colour had drained from his face. Toms had pulled up a kitchen chair and sat down, surveying in silence the activity that presented itself in the room, and Lil had been the only member of the party to notice Mary's distress. Lil sidled on up to her and, in a gesture of comfort, gently rubbed her left arm and shoulder.

"Of course!" Mary spluttered, as she addressed the room, all the time staring down at the tiled floor.

"I feel so stupid, so bloody stupid! How could I not have seen this? I should have known! Daniel's been reading Ellie the same story night after night now for weeks!"

Daniel said nothing but continued to stare out into the winter darkness. The room fell silent, then Hannay responded.

"What's apparent, Mary, is that we now know Eleanor feels very lonely. The move to Ravensdale, to this house, may have been your and Daniel's dream, but for her, it has been a difficult transition. The impact of moving away from all that she knew, her friends, her grandmother." Hannay paused a moment.

"It would seem that the source or means for channelling this anger, fear, or despair was by using her imagination. Children are highly receptive and can react badly to change. She's gone to a comfort zone, something she's familiar with, something she's comfortable with. It's repetitive, and it feels safe to her. Of course, we now know that it isn't safe!"

There was further silence for a moment.

"Mary, you remember don't you?" Lil said. "Remember this is what happened to you! When your Grandmother died, do you remember?" Lil sounded as if she was grasping at straws, but she hoped that, to Mary, the comparisons with the past were truly relevant, that there truly was hope, after all. Mary had gotten through her own ordeal.

"That one incident at the Hospice when you were a child," Lil continued, "stayed with you. It's still one of the most vivid memories you have. For Ellie, it's the same. Doctor Hannay's making sense! The wolf in the three little pigs must be her most vivid memory. I know it's not as traumatic as your experience when you were a little girl, but it's traumatic enough for a five-year-old girl, and now—!"

"And now!" Hannay interrupted, "and now it's just got serious; it's led to the death of your own mother!"

The kitchen where everyone sat wasn't that large, but the words seemed to echo around it.

"It has now become a self-fulfilling prophecy!" Jessica Stevens pitched in.

"The dreams, the images she had have now crossed over, her subconscious is so strong, it has indeed created the creature, a Lycan! The trauma for the child is getting worse!"

Daniel remained rooted to his spot. Standing in silence, he stared out into the black night. Without turning to face the room full of people, he was heard to mutter under his breath. "And I encouraged it in."

"I'm sorry, Mr Foster?" Toms asked, turning in his chair to face Daniel.

"I brought this in. I've brought this problem here to my family." Daniel lowered his head with a sense of sorrow. He turned to face the room. As he did so, he looked up and his eyes met Mary's, who gave him a somewhat reluctant but sympathetic gesture with her eyes.

"So," Daniel sighed with a heavy heart, "what do we have to do?" he asked.

Hannay sat and rubbed his chin.

"Ok, Mr Foster, what we're going to have to do is to hypnotise your daughter, again. I don't believe we can wait any longer. This creature is suffocating her; her subconscious is now working so strongly against her that we now know the beast, that creature, will come again and, this time, believe me, if it can, it will kill her!"

* * *

The house became a flurry of activity as the scientists prepared to conduct the hypnosis on Eleanor. Discussions were held as people crossed each other, walking the length of the large hall.

"Where would you like to conduct the hypnosis, Doctor?" Stevens asked Hannay.

"The girl's room I think!" Hannay said, lines etched deep into his face, as he thought deeply.

Stevens continued to move down the hall, carrying more bags of equipment. As she turned and began ascending the stairs, Hannay broke from thought and called after her. "We must have as few people in the girl's room as possible!" he barked in a demanding tone. "I suggest just Mary, you Jessica, and myself!" As Hannay spoke, he could see Mary had regressed deep into thought. He got up from his chair and moved toward her.

"Is there a lock on the child's room, Mary?" Hannay asked, gently placing his hand reassuringly on Mary's arm.

"Yes, Yes!" Mary stuttered a reply, but her thoughts were too far away.

"Good! Good!" Hannay replied, patting her arm "As a precaution, we will need to lock the door behind us."

Toms, who had overheard the conversation, accosted Hannay before he too disappeared up the stairs. "Hannay, I think it's unwise to suggest that you be in the girl's bedroom on your own, considering what happened the last time you hypnotized her!" As he spoke, Toms nodded past Hannay up the stairs to Eleanor's bedroom door. Hannay stopped, gave a somewhat impatient sigh, and turned to face the Detective Inspector.

"Inspector! We have now learned from our previous experience with this little girl and know a little bit more about what we are dealing with, here. Besides, we will lock the door, and we have the added reassurance of the presence of the Yorkshire police, who I feel confident will do everything in their powers to protect us!"

Hannay's flip and sarcastic reply stung Toms, who then reached out to grab Hannay's arm and hold him back.

"All right, Doctor!" he said, looking into Hannay's eyes but showing clear annoyance. "But let's agree on a time when you are going to begin this hypnosis. I do not want any more accidents or injuries. I want my officers ready!"

Hannay, now frustrated, looked down the hall at the grandfather clock.

"It's six thirty-five now," He said, nodding at the clock. "Let's say seven-thirty. We're going to need time to set up our equipment!" Hannay gave one last glance at Mary, who nodded her head.

"Mary, I suggest we prepare ourselves for seven-thirty. Is that ok with you?" he asked.

Without looking at Daniel, she again nodded, folding her arms and clasping her elbows, as if a chill had come over her. "Yes, yes! The sooner the better!"

Daniel stood by with a sense of helplessness while everything went on around him.

"Is there anything I can do?" he asked, raising his voice to attract the attention of the busy throng around him.

Hannay stopped and looked at him. "You can make some tea,, perhaps?" he retorted before disappearing up the stairs.

"Come along Jessica!" Hannay snorted. Jessica grinned at Daniel, as she squeezed past him carrying cases up the stairs.

"Is he always such a self-absorbed pain in the arse?" Daniel asked her, irritated.

At the foot of the stairs, the young student turned and grinned. "Don't worry about it, Mr Foster; he gets like this when he's onto something. You get used to it with time. He's a good man; he's going to help you!" As she started climbing the stairs, she stopped, leaned over the rail, and beckoned to Dan to move closer. "He's actually very, very good at his job, but don't tell him I told you that!" She smiled a reassuring smile.

"But tea would be nice, though! Milk, two sugars!" Her grin and her voice trailed off, as she disappeared up the stairs.

Dan reached out to grab Mary's arm, before she, too, disappeared down the hall and back into the kitchen.

"Mary, are you sure this guy knows what he's doing?"

Mary stopped and clasped her husband's arm. She saw the concern etched in his face. "Dan, he's the only person I've seen who can get close to Eleanor. We have to trust him! I believe he can make Ellie well again!"

* * *

While activity went on inside the house, Toms had stepped outside to take in the night air. Despite all he had seen, so far, he felt uncomfortable. He liked to think that he had control over the operation, as he did with every operation he had previously been on. This, though, was completely different. It felt uncontrolled and out of his hands. He was relying on others to maintain a degree of safety for the Foster family, and it made him feel anxious.

The December evening was cold and unfriendly. The unforgiving fog had settled over the hills and valley, blocking out the gaiety and twinkle of the Christmas lights in the village below. He felt a sudden chill right through to his bones. The night was still, very still. There was now no breeze. The trees, bereft of all their leaves, stood motionless, watching it seemed, as if in anticipation of the events that would unravel that evening. Toms steadied himself; holding himself rigid against the night chill, he pulled the up collar on his thick overcoat above his ears. He listened; there was silence. Only the occasional cackle and cry of a crow in the woods beyond the foot of the garden would pierce the frosty still air.

With the halogen spot lamp triggered by his movement, Toms was able to make his way around the house perimeter. Leaving the back patio area, he shoved his hands into his coat pockets and walked around to the front of the house.

As he turned the corner of the house, a second halogen lamp lit up. Rounding the corner to the front of the house, he saw the car with the two armed police officers McCain and Swift sitting inside. They had patrolled the house perimeter but, without any further orders, had retreated back inside the car to keep warm.

Toms ambled up to the side of the unmarked car. McCain, the officer in the driving seat promptly lowered the window of the car door.

"What's happening, Guv'nor?" McCain asked, tilting his head slightly out of the window to look up at Toms. "There're a lot of people about. Is there anything going to happen tonight?"

Toms ducked down to speak to both officers in the car. "Seven-thirty! I'd like you both to be patrolling the perimeter of the house a little before seven-thirty. One at the front, one at the back, and be ready!"

Swift, the other officer in the passenger seat leant across. "Why, what's happening at seven-thirty?" he asked Toms.

"Our parapsychologist friend is going to attempt to hypnotise the girl! I want you fellas out of the car and patrolling the area," Toms said.

The two officers looked at each other. "Whatever you say, Guv'nor, but what are we expecting?" Swift asked. "What is it were looking for?"

Toms thought for a moment. He had no definitive answer to the officer's question. His answer was tinged with irritation. "I don't know. I can't say for sure, but just be on your toes!" he replied. Toms, having completed tactical discussions with the officers in the car straightened himself up and shoved his hands back into the pockets of his coat. Blowing out his cheeks, he narrowed his eyes, as he stared up into the pitch-black night sky. The mists that had hung around all day had settled like a thick, luxurious carpet over the moors surrounding Ravensdale. He sensed trouble was coming his way.

* * *

Eleanor shook feverishly in her tiny bed. Drifting in and out of consciousness, she was unaware of the activity that went on around her. Isla Shand, who had sat with her now for more than an hour, holding the child's small hand and mopping her brow, had now taken a break upon Mary's insistence. Mary now occupied the chair next to her daughter's bed, but sat forward cradling her frail physique. The clock had slowly ticked round. It was approaching seven-thirty. By seven-fifteen, Hannay and Jessica Stevens had finished the exercise of setting up video cameras on tripods and tape recorders around the room. Other areas of the house did not escape attention, either. The landing at the top of the stairs had a camera on a tripod. There was one at the foot of the stairs, facing down the hall to the kitchen door, and a fourth camera was located in the kitchen, the scene of the vicious attack and murder. From her position in Eleanor's bedroom, Jessica Stevens could simultaneously activate all cameras. Hannay had busily been darting from the child's bedroom to the landing, where, perching on a chair, he referred to a set of notes and a textbook, looking for all the world like a student preparing himself for an exam.

At seven twenty-five, the house fell into silence. Both Daniel Foster, who was standing at the entrance to his daughter's bedroom, and Toms, who was standing on the landing, waited motionless for instructions from Hannay. Everything now depended on him. What was he going to be able to do? Was he going to be able to save this young girl's life?

Hannay tipped his head back and snapped shut the text book. Jumping out of the chair, he snapped, "Ok, let's get into positions, everyone. Let's get on with this!"

He nodded across the landing to Toms, who turned to the large landing window facing out toward the front garden of the house. Taking a small flashlight from his pocket, he signalled to McCain and Swift, who promptly jumped out of their car. The two officers split up and began patrolling the perimeter of the house. Toms turned back to Hannay, standing at the other end of the dimly lit hall, and gave a nod.

Hannay turned to Daniel.

"Right, Mr Foster, I'd like you to do something for me, please!" Hannay said. "For one last time, I'd like you to read to your daughter. I want you to tell her a story!" Hannay moved past Daniel into Eleanor's bedroom to her bookshelf and pulled off *The Three Little Pigs.*

"I want you to read her this story!" He handed the book to Daniel, who had taken it from Hannay. The twisted look of confusion on Daniel's face provided the reply to the request.

"Mr Foster, Daniel, please do this. I want to make sure we get as much of the child's attention as possible. I want her to hear your voice. Frankly, I need as much help as possible to be able to summon this demon!"

Hannay moved back to the bedroom door and closed it. "I'm going to lock the door!" he exclaimed, turning the key in the lock. Now, there were only four people in the bedroom, besides Eleanor.

Mary, Daniel, Hannay, and Jessica Stevens. Hannay directed Daniel to the corner of the room, away from the camera.

Daniel perched himself on a chair by the side of the bed, and began reading *The Three Little Pigs.* Mary sidled up close to him and rubbed his shoulder reassuringly.

Jessica Stevens busied herself by activating the video camera, while Hannay removed his jacket and signalled to Daniel to lower his voice, as he moved toward the figure of the little girl now propped up on pillows in the bed.

All around the house, silence fell. For Mary, a curious realization came over her. Within herself, she was calm, prepared, and ready; her heart wasn't pounding, and there was no sweat on her brow. She knew it was now or never with Eleanor. She knew that, tonight, there would be no going back!

Outside, amongst the dark, swirling mists of the night, beyond the boundary fence of the Hungry Harshes, at the foot of the garden and deep into the woods, something had been aroused. There was unease in the treetops, and the nest of crows began to stir; they had been disturbed. Beneath them, something skulked amongst the trees and weaved a path between the dense scrub, something so terrible, so evil that it panicked the birds, forcing them to flee their nests and circle the trees from above.

Its thick black coat served to reflect what moonlight pierced the treetops. Its blood red eyes reflected its intent. Its murderous gaze seemed fixed in only one direction, down toward the house. Its black nostrils, like radar, had honed in on the house and its occupants.

As it reached the edge of the wood to the boundary fence, it stopped. Pulling itself up on its hind legs, it once again lifted its nostrils to the air. Eleanor's subconscious was working well. She had brought the creature back. There it stood, just yards from the house, yards from where she lay. It could smell death; it had its opportunity to create death.

Chapter 18

"Eleanor! Eleanor! Can you hear me? Open your eyes, child, and look at me!" Hannay commanded, focusing all his energy on the little girl, who now sat propped up in the bed. Eleanor was beginning to look unrecognisable, from the healthy little girl of only a few days earlier. She looked extremely pale, her gaunt frame propped up by three large pillows, her eyes remained resolutely closed, and she was gasping for breath.

Hannay had made a hand signal to Daniel to stop reading, by stretching out his left arm and lowering his hand. Dan stepped back and closed the book. Hannay made another desperate attempt at contact.

"Eleanor! Eleanor! Can you hear me?" he asked, again, his voice still stern.

"I want you to open your eyes and look at me! Look straight ahead at me!"

Over Hannay's shoulder, Jessica Stevens stood in silence, manning the camera. She sensed heavy electro static in the air; it was so thick, you could cut it with a knife. Distracted from her filming duties, she thought she saw the bedroom lamps flicker. She wasn't alone;

Toms and the others in the house downstairs in the kitchen had noticed it too. Faulty wiring? Coincidence, perhaps, but the distraction proved too much; the flickering and now dimming of the lights grew stronger, more consistent.

"Quickly! Get those candles lit!" Hannay barked at Jessica. She broke off from camera duties and reached into a bag, clutching some candles and a torch. She handed them over to Daniel with a box of matches.

"Here, light these!"

Hannay continued to stare deep into the little girl's face, looking for some positive sign, some twitch, some acknowledgement of his voice. He spoke to the agitated, yet comatose, little body. This time, his voice had a sterner edge, and this time, he didn't address Eleanor directly.

"I demand to speak to whomever or whatever is controlling this little girl!" Everyone remained silent. Mary gripped herself, holding herself rigid, in anticipation of what might come back at them.

"I demand to speak to whomever or whatever is controlling Eleanor!" Hannay boomed again.

This time, he had made the connection, and the lights flickered and dimmed one last time, before going out completely. All electricity had been cut. The house was in total darkness. Only the lighted candles, flickering eerily in an unworldly breeze, provided any light. Isla and Lillian sat downstairs in total darkness and in total fear. Toms, who was on the landing, had brought a torch with him. Switching it on, his first instinct was to scan the landing and down the stairs in a three-hundred-sixty-degree motion. Seeing nothing, he reached for his walkie-talkie.

"Right, get ready. This is it! Keep alert!" Toms conveyed the message with some urgency to the two Officers patrolling the outside of the Hungry Harshes.

* * *

Back in Eleanor's room, the breeze picked up to a sudden gust of wind that blew in through the partly-opened window, forcing Mary to catch her breath. For a moment, everybody looked across at each; other wondering what was going to happen next.

Mary knelt down beside Eleanor's bed, clutching Eleanor's hand; she fought back her fear and began to slowly peer up at the little girl's face. What greeted her made the hairs on the back of her neck stand up. For, as she looked up, she could see that Eleanor had now turned her head to face her. The little girls eyes were now open, she was staring straight back, down at her mother.

Mary could do nothing else but stare back into the cold, lifeless eyes that greeted her. She could see that it was not the face of her daughter at all, but some grotesque, evil apparition. The eyes were deep, dark, and black, her face whiter than ever. She glared at Mary with a contemptuous sneer. She gripped Mary's hand ever more tightly, until Mary began to wince in pain, the girl's tiny but sharp nails dug deep into Mary's hand. She seemed to possess a strength ten times that of a girl her age.

* * *

Toms had dashed across the landing to the bedroom door. Pressing his ear up against the pine finish, he listened for a moment. Hearing nothing, he clasped the handle and began turning it several times, but the door was locked. Frantically, he wrenched on the handle but there was no answer coming from inside the room.

Hannay could hear Toms' attempts, but this did not distract him from confronting the beast that raged inside the little girl.

"Look at me!" he snapped "LOOK AT ME!" Hannay bellowed at the entity, lying in front of him. The creature slowly turned its head toward the doctor. Hannay turned cold at the dark, unnatural eyes fixed squarely on him. It hissed and spat at him in defiance. It released the tight, stabbing grip on Mary's hand; it's grey, willowy fingers now gripped the edges of the blanket. Mary fell back on her haunches and almost fainted, gripping her painful hands, she moaned in agony. Dark, thick red lines of blood ran down her wrists and arms, dripping onto her clothes.

"Now I have your attention!" snapped Hannay.

There was an eerie silence, both Jessica and Dan noticed, as the flames of the candles stilled, it was as if it was the calm before the storm.

"I'm not scared of you!" Hannay challenged defiantly, never once taking his eyes off the creature. The creature then took a sharp intake of breath.

"Oh, but you should be!" The reply came from Eleanor, but the voice was not that of the little girl's. It was a deep, unearthly tone. A tone they recognised, nonetheless, from the first meeting at the University.

For Daniel, however, the shock proved too much. He sank to his knees, his mouth now open and dry. The fear overcame him, and he couldn't comprehend what he was seeing, hearing here in front of him, his own little girl! This was the little girl he put to bed each night, read bedtime stories to! He edged toward Mary, seeing the flow of blood and the pain she was in.

"It's all right, Dan, just stay back!" Mary uttered, pushing him back with her hand. Hannay had come this far; it was horrific, painful, but nothing was going to break the connection now.

The creature turned its head again and fixed its gaze on Dan. Grinning at him, its evil black eyes bored into him, the power of which caused him to fall back against the bedroom wall. Without warning, the creature lashed out, grabbing Mary's hand once again; its grip grew tighter. Mary again winced in pain. Hannay, sensing it had become distracted, made an attempt to get its attention.

"LOOK AT ME!" he bellowed, "Now tell me, what do you want with this child?"

The creature grinned. "She's mine to do with what I want, mine to control as I want, mine to destroy!" The creature hissed and spat in defiance.

"Do you want to harm this child? Answer me! Do you wish to hurt this little girl?" Hannay probed again. This seemed to antagonise the creature further.

"I will have her!" it bellowed.

"By killing her, you kill yourself. You realise that don't you…kill her, you kill yourself!" Hannay tried to reason.

"Then that will be the fulfilment of my aim!"

"You will never win this!" Hannay challenged. "You will destroy yourself!"

"But I will destroy you and anyone who gets in my way!"

With that, the flames of the candles were extinguished, and the electricity returned, showering the house, both inside and out, with light.

* * *

By now, outside in the chill of the night, the creature, the living embodiment of the girl's subconscious, knew no fear. From a position of safety in the woods at the back of the garden, its eyes narrowed into blood-red razors. Driven by the rage from within the tiny girl, it had stalked its prey. It was ready to make a move toward the house. As if coiled, every tendon in its body taut, the hair on its back stood up to reveal a deep, bony, ebony hump. Its ears bristled to every sound from around its position. Its jaws and snout gnarled, as it leapt first onto the fence, where it momentarily paused. Hunched for only a few seconds, it leapt onto the lawn and sped away.

PC McCann suddenly stopped pacing the patio at the rear of the house. He had been dutifully patrolling the area, when the halogen spot lamp had failed, along with all the lights in the house. He had reverted to a torch, but now, somehow, the electricity had returned. The lamp kicked back in, flooding the patio in light again. Something had alerted him, a noise from the woods beyond the garden. The advancing creature had startled the nest of crows, which bellowed and squawked in fear. He had no idea what could have caused the disturbance. He could see nothing as he peered into the murky gloom. For the first time in his career, McCann began to sense himself trembling. The clattering of the crows began to dissipate, but it was replaced by another sound, a sound muffled, at first, by the gusting wind, but as the wind died away, the sound became louder, more pronounced. The sound was similar to that of a horse galloping toward him, it grew louder and louder, but he couldn't see anything! By now, the beast had found its stride, leaping and galloping on all fours. Its pace quickened, as it traversed the sloping garden with ease. It had now hit an athletic rhythm, as it approached the floodlit patio. With the lone police office in its sights, it let out a murderous howl that could be heard all over the village.

McCann was too late! Realising that something was upon him but not able to see it, he reached desperately to his left side to retrieve his automatic pistol.

"STOP! WHO'S THERE?" came the shout, but the beast had made a sudden leap from out of the shroud of darkness. Leaping into the bright light, it set about the police officer, who had only just managed to clear his pistol from its holster. As the creature hit him, he fell back, squeezing the trigger. In doing so, he set off a shot that pierced the night. The bullet missed the creature and veered off into the night sky.

Falling to the ground, he tried desperately to recover. His pistol had slipped from his grasp, as he fell. He reached blindly for it, but couldn't locate it. His efforts were in vain. The creature rose up, standing over the stricken officer, tearing at the McCann's protective body vest with its razor-sharp claws. It viciously and without restraint sank its saliva-covered teeth deep into the officer's neck.

There came a sickening crunch of bones, as McCann struggled to grab the creature's nozzle. He tried to scream for his life, but nothing he did had any effect. The creature shook its head with the body of the officer still firmly clamped between its jaws. Finally, mercifully, McCann's arms, his hands, and fingers splayed away from his body that suddenly stiffened, trembled, and then went limp.

The creature released its grip. McCann lay dead. He hadn't stood a chance. The creature raised itself up onto its hind legs and let out a triumphant, blood-curdling howl! Now it turned its attention toward the house!

* * *

Inside the house, blind panic had set in. Aunt Lillian and Isla Shand had remained in the kitchen and were closest to the attack. They began screaming uncontrollably. Swift, who had heard the shot and commotion had drawn his pistol and ran to the back of the house. As he approached the corner to the floodlit patio, the sound of his heart pounding in his ears deafened him. As he peered around the corner, pistol at the ready, he couldn't comprehend the sight that greeted him. McCann was down, motionless, lifeless. The huge, black-coated, somewhat raggedy creature stood on its hind legs at the back door of the house; it must have been seven feet tall!

Swift, with a lump in his throat stood for a while rigid with fear. The creature hadn't seen him. It had become fixated on trying to find a way into the house and relentlessly scratched at the windows and door.

Toms had heard the attacks and ran out of the front door and round to the opposite side of the house. Both men were struggling to believe what they were seeing. They both stood for what seemed like an age, waiting, anticipating the creature's next move, but it was preoccupied.

Swift made the first move. Cocking his automatic pistol, he raised it to eye level and pointed the barrel at the head of the creature. As he did so, the great beast's ears pricked up, and it turned its head to look at Swift. Its murderous eyes narrowed, turning from the house and charged the short distance to where the officer was standing. Swift stood his ground and fired a shot, hitting the beast in the shoulder. The impact of the bullet sent blood splattering everywhere, as the creature's shoulder exploded. The bullet had done enough to check its momentum. The creature stopped, howled in pain, and, with a huge front paw swept the officer aside, sending him clattering over the ornate garden table and into the shrubbery. Letting out a further howl of pain, it checked its shoulder, which was gushing large amounts of thick, red blood. It bore down on Swift, the flow of blood from its shoulder dripping onto the stricken officer's protective jacket.

Swift managed to claw himself back from the imposing figure of the beast standing over him, eventually backing up against a large laurel bush, where he could retreat no further. Seeing the animal's venomous saliva gathering in anticipation at the edge of its mouth before dripping onto Swift's legs, the officer sensed that this was the end.

As the creature moved in for the kill, Toms raised his automatic pistol from under his coat. Knowing that the police officer's life was in his hands, he took aim and shot twice into the creature's large muscular back. The beast rose up. The impact of the bullets sent blood splattering everywhere. It turned in fury and rage to face Toms. Toms' blood ran as cold as the murderous red eyes of the creature, now fixed on him. He wanted to run, but he knew he needed to stand his ground. He could not leave Swift.

Visibly, the bullets had made a mess of the creature, but they seemed to have made little impact in checking its momentum.

Toms could only watch, as the creature now applied its full furious intent on him. He stood his ground and cocked his pistol, taking aim at the creature's forehead.

"SHOOT IT! SHOOT IT!" Swift cried, but Toms froze. Suddenly, the creature's attention was diverted; instead of retaliating, it turned and fled across the lawn, into the dark, murky night and back into the woods. All the commotion had further sent the nesting crows into a frenzy. Ominously, the scene of death had made them circle the house like scavengers on the scene to feed!

Toms drew a deep breath. Lowering his pistol, he ran up to the lifeless body of McCann. Seeing that the officer was clearly dead, he stopped abruptly before stepping into a thick dark pool of blood running from his neck. McCann's eyes were open and stared lifelessly back up at Toms. He had seen corpses before, but he had never seen one of his own officers killed in such a manner. It left him feeling sick and numb.

All he could do was stand and shake his head.

"Oh Fuck!" he muttered to himself. Giving some thought to the people inside the house, who had watched in horror, as events unfolded, he placed his gun back in its holster and pulled the protective covering off the garden table, covering the body of McCann. He paused momentarily to close the dead man's eyes.

"Swift, you ok?" Toms shouted breathlessly at the officer, who lay only a few yards away. Swift was struggling to get air into his lungs as he sat up.

"Poor Mick, oh my god, poor fucking Mick!" Swift responded angrily at the death of his colleague.

"Are you hurt, Swift? Can you get to your feet?" The officer didn't reply but wearily nodded.

"Did you see that thing? Fuck, what the hell was it?" Swift blurted out. "It must have been seven or eight feet tall!"

Toms shook his head. "I'd never thought anything like this ever existed!"

By now, the mist, which had thinned and dispersed, as a result of the confrontation, eerily began to reinforce itself again on the patio.

The sound of the kitchen door lock being turned drew the officer's attention. Aunt Lillian swung the door open, her face a deathly white.

"Whatever you do, stay inside the house. Do not come out, and keep that door locked!" Toms bellowed, signalling to the old woman to stay put.

"Swift, I want you to stay in the house with the family. Keep the door locked and get on the phone to the station. We need more support!"

"What about you? What are you going to do?" Swift asked, as he struggled to his feet. Toms again drew his automatic pistol and checked the clip. It was full minus two bullets. He reached into his coat pocket and pulled out two replacement bullets, he inserted them into the clip and reloaded the clip into the pistol.

"Just make sure you get that support. We need it now!"

Toms paused to take one last look at the slain officer. Grasping his pistol ever more tightly in his right hand, shaking with fear and trepidation, he ran off across the lawn toward the woods and into the night, in pursuit of the creature. The swirling mists closed around him.

Chapter 19

From the bedroom window both Mary and Hannay had seen everything, every aspect of the terrible events that had gone on below them. Their emotions were mixed a combination of fear and terror overcame them, as they witnessed the vile, unearthly atrocity; yet this was countered by the feeling of loathing and hatred. They felt powerless to help. They could only watch.

For a moment, Mary could not look at Eleanor. For that moment, she hated her daughter for what she had just done. She wanted desperately to run, get away, flee! Mary retreated from the window. She could not face the image of her daughter, consumed by the terrible evil that had gripped her. Her stomach churned, and she felt sick, as she heard the bating laughter of conquest coming from the bed.

At a pace, Mary made her way out of the room, along the landing, and into the bathroom. Hannay, meanwhile, had turned a ghostly white, his stomach in knots. He stood rigid, frozen by the scene of death. He didn't wish to relinquish the struggle at this stage. He wasn't going to capitulate to this monster!

He turned to look at both Daniel and Jessica. Lowering his head in anguish, he began to slowly shake it.

"Oh my God! What's happened?" Jessica Stevens cried, putting her hands to her face.

Hannay could barely manage a reply. "I've…I've just seen the creature. I've seen it, Jessica!" He looked up at Stevens, staring incredulously at her. "It is a physical manifestation of a Lycan, a Werewolf!"

"You mean it's an actual anomalistic entity?" Stevens challenged.

"Y…yes! It is anomalistic. It's true! It's everything we had anticipated, everything we researched. This points to a clear link between psychokinetic behaviour in infants and a physical anomalistic materialization!" Hannay's rationale seemed clear to both him and Stevens.

"So, the little girl, Eleanor, disturbed and unsettled by the move to the new house, loses friends and family close to her, familiar surroundings. Alone, maybe fearful, she seeks comfort, as most children do in familiar books and stories. She develops a growing dependency on *The Three Little Pigs*, a favourite story. In time, her mind, together with her inherited traits to actively develop as an "Agent" like her mother, absorbs into her subconscious the images that scare her, the image of the wolf!" Stevens summarized.

"Yes!" Hannay interrupted her, "and in turn, her subconscious thoughts and images have manifested themselves physically! No one can hear her; there's no one to help her. As a result, the beast, the creature—

call it what you will—lives!" Hannay's voice tailed off.

Then he said, "You know a police officer's been killed!"

Daniel slumped back on a chair and buried his head in his hands.

By now, the air in the small room became highly charged with emotion. Jessica Stevens, feeling dizzy and nauseous, needed to escape the four walls. She stepped out of the room and tentatively followed Mary into the bathroom.

Daniel lowered his hands from his face to reveal streams of tears. He wept uncontrollably turning to Hannay. "So, what can we do about it?" he cried.

Hannay composed himself, straightened his neck and turned to Daniel. "We kill it!"

* * *

To Mary, the bathroom seemed ever more cold and sterile. The single light overhead provided a hard, uncompromising light. The bathroom window was open, letting in the cold of the night. She perched on the edge of the ornate bathtub, trembling, but it wasn't just the cold getting to her bones. It was shock. She felt fragile, exposed. There was nothing she felt she could do to change the situation. All seemed lost; hope was fading. Would they all die this night, she wondered.

As thoughts of despair spiralled and tumbled through her mind, she heard the landing floorboards creak. The sound came from just outside the door, causing her heart to race.

"Who's there?" she asked.

The door slowly swung open. Jessica Stevens stood tentatively in the hall, peering into the bathroom. "May I come in?" she asked.

Mary could barely acknowledge her.

"Are you all right?" a trembling Stevens asked, putting a cigarette to her lips. Mary didn't make eye contact.

"Am I all right! Am I all right! Of course, I'm not bloody-well all right!!" Mary bellowed at the young Student. "How would you feel, if you had witnessed your child murdering someone!" Mary stuttered.

Stevens removed the unlit cigarette from her lips, barely able to control her own emotions. She could see that Mrs Foster was in desperate need of support. In all her years at the university, working in the research department, she had never experienced anything like this before. This was new territory. She needed to keep her composure. She was a scientist; she needed to remain level-headed.

"Mary, you have to believe that *thing* isn't your little girl in there, she couldn't possibly have done this!" Stevens argued, in an attempt to console the mother. This was a desperate situation. Stevens could see that Mary was reaching the end. Her eyes had darkened, betraying the exhaustion and stress.

"I never for one moment thought I would ever feel the way I do," Mary spat in anger. "This feeling of hatred and loathing toward my own darling Ellie!"

Stevens lit the cigarette. Here hands were shaking.

"I want to go back into that bedroom right now and throttle her!" Mary continued. She dropped her head to her chest in a gesture of defeat. Stevens pushed the bathroom door closed behind her. The two women stood alone, consumed by the horror of the situation they found themselves in.

"Jessica, you're young, but you'll find out yourself some day. You'll want a family of your own, a husband, children, and you'll want everything in the world for them. You'll want everything to be right, just perfect. Then, one day, you'll wake up like me and find your world has been turned on its head! You'll hate yourself for failing your family, for putting them in harm's way!"

Stevens listened sympathetically, perched on the edge of the bathtub next to Mary; she gently began rubbing her back. "Mary, what is happening here is terrible, just awful, but it isn't your fault! It really isn't."

"Oh but it is!" Mary reacted angrily to the young student. "Don't you see? It is my fault. I am to blame for this! I brought this on the family! I knew about this! I could have done something about this a lot earlier! Instead, I hid it, from Daniel. I never told him! I was afraid he'd think I was mad, you know, whacko!" Mary turned and looked into Steven's eyes, tapping the side of her head as she spoke the words.

"We started a family! My god! We didn't ask for much! I just wanted to live an ordinary life, just like everyone else. My big mistake was to move the family here; my selfishness overcame me. I didn't think of the kids, my mother, no one but my own happiness. If only I had known how Eleanor must have felt! If only I had sat down and talked to her!" There was a brief silence as Mary wiped her eyes and Stevens handed her another tissue from the box sitting on the edge of the shelf above the sink.

"Don't you see?" Mary continued, "I have passed this onto her. I have given her this damned curse and then, to compound the issue, I moved her away from everything she knew, at such an impressionable age. I thought it would be perfect, but I was wrong! I was so…so…wrong!"

Stevens sat observing, comforting the woman whom she could see was now as close to a breakdown as anyone she had encountered before.

"Listen!" she said soothingly to Mary. "We will get through this together, you and I. Doctor Hannay's a good man; he's very clever. If anyone can help your daughter, then he's the man to do it. Come on. Let's go back to Eleanor's bedroom. She needs you right now! You need to hold it together for her, just for a while longer!" Jessica grabbed Mary's hand.

Exhausted, Mary lifted herself off the edge of the bath and wiped away her tears. Her limbs felt so heavy, she could barely drag her body along, but the two women walked back across the landing and into the bedroom. Neither knowing quite what would happen next.

The air in the bedroom felt damp, uninviting, and there was an eerie green hue in the room. Only Eleanor's small bedside lamp gave any sort of warming pale glow, but the room stank of evil and death. Jessica Stevens stopped and inhaled. She could taste the cordite. She had tasted it before on previous outings with Hannay. It was from an electric charge generated by the possession, or possibly even on this cold winter's night, the after effects from the discharge of the guns that had eerily wafted up through the bedroom window, carried on the unearthly mists. Either way, she couldn't be sure which was the source.

Shock emanated from everyone in the room, even from the experienced Hannay. The grizzly attack on the police officers had reminded everyone of the gravity of the situation. Only the tiny pale figure of Eleanor, the little girl at the centre of the nightmare, remained unmoved. Sitting upright in bed, a smirk materialised across her demonic face. She held a small, soft toy, a bear, given to her by her father. Unknowingly, the child pulled at it violently, ripping its head from its body.

Hannay, trying to control his rage turned to the young girl. "Do you know what you have just done?" There was no response.

"LISTEN TO ME!" he bellowed, slamming his fist down on the bed in front of the girl. "DO YOU KNOW WHAT YOU HAVE DONE? YOU'VE KILLED A MAN, AND YOU HAVE ATTEMPTED TO KILL OTHERS!"

There was no response from the girl. Instead, the smirk on her face grew ever wider. Then, with eyes as black as oil, she turned to face Hannay. "Yes, and I will kill all of you who try and stand in my way!"

Mary could contain herself no longer; she began bellowing at the creature. "WHY DON'T YOU JUST LEAVE US ALONE! GET OUT OF HERE! GET OUT OF OUR LIVES! LEAVE US ALONE. WE DON'T

WANT YOU IN OUR LIVES! YOU ARE NOT
WELCOME!"

This time, the creature, inhabiting the small child,
retorted by laughing.

"WHAT THE HELL DO YOU WANT FROM US?"
Mary again bellowed, finally pushing herself ahead of
Hannay. She bore down on the figure in the bed, as if
ready to strike her.

"It's all right, Mary, back away!" Hannay said,
sensing that perhaps control would be lost.

Mary stepped back, and Hannay once again
moved between them. He needed to try a different
approach. Focusing firmly on the little girl, he
composed himself. "She's still under hypnosis. I'm
going to attempt to up the ante; in other words, I'm
going increase the hypnotic suggestibility. I've got to
try and connect to her state of mind where she'll listen
to me!" Hannay turned to face the child.

"I am addressing the force within Eleanor. You are
the embodiment of everything evil. You are not
welcome in this house. You must leave this young
child and this house immediately!" Again his voice
was stern. Again, a sense of an unearthly atmosphere
filled the room; the bedroom lamps flickered; the air
became electrically charged. Again, the dark, hollow
eyes of the girl stared back at Hannay.

Suddenly, without warning, a book from the
bookshelf flew across the room, striking Hannay on
the forehead. Mary screamed as the book sent
Hannay, more with surprise, crashing off the bed and
onto the bedroom floor.

Picking himself up, first to his knees and then back on to the edge of the bed, he felt his forehead. A trickle of blood ran from his hairline.

"It's ok! I'm all right!" he cried, his voice quaking.

"Oh my god! Look at Ellie's eyes!" Mary screamed, as the girl slumped back onto her pillow. Her eyes flickering manically, they began rolling back in her head.

"What's wrong with her?" Mary cried.

"See her eyes!" said Hannay, "It's REM, rapid eye movement. She's relapsed back into her subconscious. The creature is filling the void in her subconscious!" Hannay moved to the window and peered through the curtains down into the garden, then, as if a revelation had struck him.

"This creature is no werewolf! Not as we know and understand a werewolf to be, a Lycanthrope, a mythical creature that apparently, upon a full moon changes it's physical appearance of that from a man to a wolf!"

He shook his head and turned to Jessica Stevens.

"This is a manifestation; a physical manifestation of the child's sleeping thoughts!" Hannay turned to Mary. "You had it Mary! You know you had it. Now Ellie's got it! This child's fears, her concerns — she cannot express them calmly, rationally like an adult. The feelings of change and isolation are constricting her! So powerful is the force contained within her that her inner comfort zone has been violated!"

Hannay, as if consumed by some force of nature, leapt across the room to the bookshelf.

"Your book, *The Three Little Pigs!*" He picked up the book and slapped the cover hard.

"This book is a child's story, meant to entertain, comfort and soothe, but the theme has become a double-edged sword! The repetition of the story is familiar to her, like a comfort blanket. She has asked for it night after night because it soothes her anxieties, but it has now becomes so deeply ingrained in her subconscious—

"And?" Daniel butted in.

"And the fear of the wolf getting the pigs, getting to her, something children enjoy, has now consumed her. Hannay began feverishly thumbing through the book. His eyes wide and intense. Stevens had seen that look before. She knew he was on to something.

"What's up, Martin? What are you thinking?" she asked. Everyone in the room flashed a glance at each other.

"How does the Wolf die?" Hannay asked, still continuing to thumb through the book. It was irrelevant, he already knew the answer, but the realisation of what had dawned on him so excited him he had to throw his logic out into the room.

"I...I can't remember!" Stevens replied.

"Think! How does the Wolf die?" he asked again, his impatience now evident.

"It falls into a pot of boiling water!" Daniel replied, knowing the answer, having read the book nearly every night since the family moved to the Hungry Harshes.

"That's right! That's right! It dies in a pot of boiling water!" Hannay had struck on something, but everyone in the room still looked puzzled.

"Don't you see? It's as we've been saying! The Werewolf, the creature is from the child's imagination. It was borne out of the child's imagination…" by now Hannay was tapping the side of his head to make the point to Stevens.

"The Police are barking up the wrong tree! You cannot kill it by shooting it! You cannot kill it with guns!" The room fell silent. Everyone now hung on Hannay's every word.

"To destroy the creature, you need to re-enact the story through to its logical conclusion! We need to destroy it, as it was destroyed in the story!" For Hannay, this was a triumph, simple exorcism on its own would not suffice, but he knew he would have to act quickly.

"We need to end the story in Eleanor's mind, in her subconscious, the way she's expecting it to end!"

"How do we do that?" Daniel asked.

Hannay feverishly looked around him, his mind turning over.

"We don't have a boiling cauldron of water," Daniel said.

"Daniel, do you have a hose?" Hannay asked impatiently.

"Yes, yes but it's outside, though!" Dan replied.

Hannay moved to the window, and looking down, he saw there was nothing but silence and the eerie mist that now made visibility impossible. The creature wasn't there. It had run off to the woods, but it would be back, any minute it would be back.

Hannay turned to face Daniel. "This hose would it fit the taps to your bath?" Dan couldn't see where Hannay's thinking was going.

"It could do, I guess if someone held one end over the tap it would?"

"Then we have to get that hose! It will mean going outside, but we must get that hose! One more thing, is your hot water on?" Hannay asked.

"Yes, it should be." Mary replied.

"Right, Daniel, you and I are going downstairs…" Hannay paused. "We've got to get that hose back inside the house!" Hannay looked down at the frail body of the girl lying in bed.

"Jessica, Mary, I want you to carry Eleanor across the landing to the bathroom and wait for us there. Mary, how hot does your water get?" Suddenly the penny dropped for Mary and everyone else in the room.

"Very, very hot, boiling hot!" Mary replied. Hannay gave a wry smile. "Let's hope so, this night is a long way from being over!"

* * *

It wasn't so much the cold and damp of the winter evening but the onset of shock that led to the uncontrollable shivering that had begun to take hold of Toms.

Alone, he crept through the mist, on guard that the creature that had attacked both his officers would leap out at him. The unearthly cry of the crows, roused by the creature's retreat to the woods had made him wonder if this would be his last night on Earth. Toms reached the fence at the back of the garden. He couldn't see much beyond that but shine a torch into the trees beyond. With measured control, he hauled himself over the fence but couldn't prevent the crackling and splintering of dead wood, as he stepped into a dense thicket beyond the boundary.

Suddenly, as he entered the woods, Toms sensed something above him. It was dark and he could hardly see anything, as he looked up, but a pair of talons on the feet of the biggest crow he had ever seen swooped down on him.

The bird flew low enough to clip the top of his head, before flying upwards and away, as Toms frantically made a vain attempt to swot it. The attack startled Toms, and he dropped his flashlight. The giant bird swooped again, targeting the top of his head, this time Toms felt something hit him. Before he had time to recover, another bird swept in, then another, and another! Frantically, Toms flayed his arms to ward off the attacking mass. The crying and squawking became louder, almost deafening, as up in the tree tops, more and more birds left their nests in greater numbers to join the assault.

The extent of the attack became too great, and Toms was tipped off his balance and fell to his knees. As he fell, the gun he was carrying slipped from his fingers. It fell amongst the twigs and leaves. There was no let up, as bird after bird swooped in on him. To protect his eyes, he kept his head low, feeling the thump of each bird on his back. Crawling on all fours, his heart racing, he felt blindly on the ground for his gun.

The attack had now become more audacious. One crow swooped down and perched on Toms' head. With vicious intent, it's sharp, long beak stabbed into Tom's hands. He cried out, as he pulled his hands away, leaving the back of his head exposed to the bird's beak, which now drove its beak with full intent into his skull!

Toms fumbled feverishly along the ground, until his hand located the cold, hard metal barrel of his gun. Crawling on all fours, he got to the nearest large area of scrub. He scrambled beneath the dense undergrowth. Its leaves and branches provided sufficient cover from the birds, which began to disperse as the attack relented.

Gradually, the squadron of crows dispersed. Toms waited a while, until the sound of the birds had died away. Gathering himself and breathing heavily, he became aware of the uncontrollable shaking that was consuming him. He was also aware of a presence. Someone or something was watching him!

From beyond the undergrowth, he could see a clearing, a copse, a reasonably large area where trees were sparse. Beyond the far side of the copse, he could see the hot, steaming breath. His blood ran icy cold.

The murderous red eyes of the creature had fixed on him. As it rounded a tree, it stepped into the open.

GOD! Toms thought, *it must be seven feet tall!* Raised up on its hind legs, its claws dug deep into the bark of a tree.

Toms stood motionless, but his eyes darted from left to right, looking to see where he could break cover and run to. He was on his own, disorientated, and now exposed. He knew the creature could outrun him, even if he tried to make a run for it. It was foolish, he thought, now trying to pursue the creature on his own.

The standoff continued for what seemed like an age. Toms was not yet on his feet. The creature stood about fifteen yards away from him. If he tried to move, it would be on him. Slowly, and without trying to provoke the creature, he undid the safety catch on his gun. The creature pricked his ears and snarled at Toms.

Without further restraint, it broke from behind the tree and charged on all fours toward its intended target.

Toms, seeing the creature advancing on him and with no time staggered to his feet. Pointing his gun he aimed and fired—CRACK!

The bullet tore into the creature's chest, barely checking its advance toward the police officer.

Toms quickly fired again, but it wasn't enough. Through sheer strength, the beast was upon him. Running headlong into Toms, the creature howled in pain. The impact threw Toms off his feet and, crashing backwards through the scrub, he hitting a tree. The impact nearly broke his back, and he slumped to the ground, unable to move.

For a moment, he lay dazed. The creature had mercifully spared him. It had, instead, run past him and disappeared into the mist. Toms lay there alive but winded. He couldn't move. The force of hitting the tree had broken his collarbone.

His eyes cleared, and he found himself staring up at the night sky through the dense branches of the tree. He was still alive, but he hadn't stopped the creature, and now it was heading back toward the house.

* * *

"Are all of you all right?" Hannay asked, as he entered the kitchen with Dan. They'd found Lillian, Isla Shand, and Swift all gathered in semi darkness. Fear was evident amongst the group. The two women quivered in the corner of the kitchen. Swift had frantically made repeated calls to his station.

"Send back up! Now! No time to lose. People are in danger!" he cried into the telephone. Somehow, his remote radio had become dislodged in the fray with the creature. Swift knew that reinforcements were a ways away, travelling across the moors in this fog and mist would be treacherous. He'd hoped that people in the village down below would have heard the shots and reacted by staying away. There was no formal police presence in the village, and he couldn't guarantee protection for anyone who wandered out. Hannay gently held his arm.

"Are you all right?" he asked the stricken officer, but Swift, breathing heavily, found difficulty in replying. He rubbed his forehead, as if on the point of breakdown.

"Did you see it? Did you see that…that thing, that creature!"

"Listen!" Hannay said, as he addressed everyone in the room, his own hands shaking and belying the fear that gripped him.

"This isn't over yet! You must ensure that you keep all doors locked!"

"My Guvnor's out there!" Swift retaliated. "I don't know if he's dead or alive!"

"Please, just stay here, and try to stay calm! Officer, are you able to cover us? We need to get outside for just a moment."

The officer dragged himself up on his haunches.

"Why are you going outside? I must advise against it. There isn't anything that can stop that creature!" Swift pleaded. Daniel and Hannay crouched down and inched toward the back door. Looking over the edge of the window, they could see the body of the dead officer but little else. It was going to be a huge risk to open the door, but they needed to get the hose. Swift checked his gun.

"What have you got in there?" Hannay asked the officer nodding toward the weapon.

"Live rounds." Swift replied.

"They seem to have little impact on the creature!" Hannay replied.

"Careful!" Hannay snapped at Daniel, as he turned the key in the door. Daniel reached up to release the top latch on the door then crouched back down to release the bottom latch. All three men now crouched at the back door. Daniel slowly opened the door. The air outside was chill. The door creaked open, the sound piecing the air. Surely, if the creature were out there, it would have heard it! Daniel slowly stuck his head out of the door, looking both ways. He jumped, as the halogen spotlight kicked on in reaction to his movement. He could now be seen; he felt like a sitting duck.

He crawled out onto the patio and round to the wall the eight or ten feet to where the hose was located. The hose sat in a reel connected to the wall. It wouldn't be that easy to get off! Daniel slowly stood up. Now in full spotlight, he yanked at the hose reel, but it wouldn't budge. He yanked at it again, but it still wouldn't budge. His heart beating so loud he could hear it in his ears, he had no way of knowing if the creature was right behind him. Each time there was a dull thud, as the hose reel hit against the wall of the house. The sound had begun to draw the attention of the crows in the trees beyond the garden. He gave it one last, aggressive pull, and this time, the hose reel came away in his arms, but as it did so, it sent the metal support bar crashing to the pavement. The sound resonated through the mist, causing further consternation for the crows. Hannay and Swift who were crouching in the doorway beckoned him back in. Dan sprinted the few feet to the door, his heart in his mouth; he threw himself onto the kitchen floor. Hannay immediately slammed the door shut, locking it behind him.

No sooner had the party got back inside the safety of the house than the creature returned.

Once again, the halogen lamp to the rear of the house kicked on, startling everybody in the kitchen.

"What was that?" Shand asked, as she thought she heard the back-door handle rattle, as if someone were turning the knob, as if someone were trying to get in. Hannay peered out but couldn't see anything.

With the kitchen in darkness, Swift shone his torch at the handle of the back door, positioned just above the head of a crouching Daniel. Eerily, he could see that someone or something was turning the handle! Someone was trying to get in!

With his heart pounding he looked up, shining his torch through the glass door pane. The hideous face of the creature snarled back at him. Saliva dripped from its mouth and onto the panes. Its blood red eyes were like nothing Swift had ever seen before. In shock, the officer dropped his torch and started backing away, as the two women screamed in unison. Suddenly, the house was in blind panic once again.

The Creature swung a huge arm that crashed through the glass panelling of the door, shattering glass down on the heads of Daniel and Hannay. Now in frenzy, it forced its weight against the door frame. The sound of wood splintering filled the house, as the door began to give way. Both women screamed, as Daniel, who hadn't moved far enough away, felt the full force from a huge swing of the creature's arm. Its sabre like claws tore at his back, and Daniel was hurled across the large kitchen dining table, rolling off and eventually crashing to the floor.

"Quickly! Everyone get out of here!" Hannay shouted.

"Run up the stairs to the landing!" In blind panic, Shand, Lil, and Swift all ran out of the kitchen. Daniel clambered to his feet, holding his head. Blood poured from a gash on his neck. Hannay grabbed the hose reel and made a dash for the door. He clasped Daniel's arm.

"Come on, man!" As he got to the kitchen door to push a dazed Daniel through, he stopped to stare into the face of the creature. Its lithe, muscular and powerful body overwhelmed the doorway. As it bent its head to step into the kitchen, the creature stopped and surveyed the area, its murderous gaze set on Hannay. He wanted to stare at it for an age, in awe of its magnificent presence; his feet felt rooted to the ground. The creature stood little more than eighteen feet away from him. The creature sensed the potent threat from the man that stood before it. Its huge, sleek and dark coat slipped through the kitchen, blood dripping onto the floor from the wound it had sustained from Toms. It had felt pain and put its great paw up to the wound. This creature was real enough; this creature bled! That's all Hannay had time to observe. He ran out of the kitchen into the hall, closing the door behind him, looking around to find an object to force up against the door, anything to buy himself some time. He noticed the party had reached the top of the stairs. Reaching for a cabinet, he dragged it across the floor to the door; it wouldn't hold for long. He picked up the hose reel and ran up the stairs.

* * *

"DID YOU HEAR THAT? DID YOU HEAR THAT, ELEANOR?" Hannay shouted obscenely at the child, as if to provoke her as he ran up the stairs.

"GET IN THE BATHROOM, ALL OF YOU!" Hannay yelled. His mouth was now so dry; he was almost choking while screaming his orders.

"YOUR BEAST IS BACK, ITS BACK, ITS HERE, AND IT'S COMING TO GET US!"

The veins in Hannay's neck protruded, as if they were going to burst. His face had turned bright red, as he strained every sinew, rounding everyone up and into the bathroom. Shand, Lil, Swift, and Daniel had now joined Mary. Stevens and Eleanor were in the large bathroom.

"IT'S COMING TO GET YOU. YES, YOU ELEANOR, IT WON'T STOP. IT WON'T STOP. IT'LL KILL YOU, ME. IT WILL KILL ALL OF US. YOU MUST RID YOUR MIND OF THIS CREATURE!"

Daniel ran back onto the landing. He grabbed the end of the hose and began unravelling it from the reel but, as he jerked, it fell out of Hannay's arms crashing onto the landing. Hannay looked over the landing rail. Time was running out. The thick black coat of the creature was amassed at the foot of the stairs. It knew where Eleanor was, and it was coming for her. He picked up the hose reel and ran into the bathroom.

"QUICKLY, MAN!" he shouted at Daniel, as he worked desperately to secure the end of the hose over the hot water tap in the bath.

The air seemed to grow ever colder, as the huge clunking sound of the creature's footsteps ascended the stairs. Soon, it would reach the landing and confront them all. All of the women braced themselves. Screaming in fear, Mary held Eleanor's tiny body, which was now convulsing in her arms.

Hannay knew this was now or never.

"ELEANOR! ELEANOR! THE CREATURE IS HERE! THE CREATURE IS IN THE HOUSE. THE BIG BAD WOLF HAS GOT IN. HE'S COMING FOR YOU! HE'S COMING TO GET YOU!"

The sound of the clunking steps had stopped. The creature was now on the landing only a few steps in front of Hannay. It bore down on him, snarling in defiance, its blood red eyes narrowing as they bore into the doctor.

"FOR GOD'S SAKE, MAN, SWITCH THE BLOODY TAP ON!"

Daniel frantically turned the tap, the sound of a gasp of air belched from it; it would take a few seconds to travel the length of the hose. Hannay stood, defiant, pointing the hose at the creature.

"WHERE IS IT? WHERE'S THE WATER?" Hannay yelled.

"IT'S COMING!" Daniel yelled back, struggling to clasp the hose as it surrounded the tap head. Suddenly, and with a forceful gush, water began to flow through the pipe. Daniel screamed; the water was boiling hot and was scalding his hands through the pipe.

The creature now stood little more than eight feet from Hannay. It was ready to launch an assault.

CRACK! CRACK! CRACK! The sound of a gun going off checked the creature's progress. Hannay swivelled round to see Toms. The police officer had managed to drag himself back to the house and was now standing at the opposite end of the landing, pointing his pistol at the creature. He'd fired three shots into the creature's body and head. The creature yelled and roared in agony. The bullets had little effect on the dark monstrosity, but it had bought Hannay enough time. As the creature raised itself up, once more, the full force of the boiling, scalding water from the hose hit it. Hannay stood firm, as he adjusted the nozzle of the hose to provide as much direct jet force to the creature's head and body. The boiling, searing water shot out at the creature, soaking it instantly. It screamed and howled in pain, and the force of the water knocked it back.

"ELEANOR, SEE. THE WOLF IS DYING. THE WOLF IS DYING!" Hannay shouted. As the scalding water hit the creature, it began to steam. It fell to the floor, writhing in agony. Hannay moved toward it and stood over the body of the beast, as it now visibly shrank. The beast was dying before his eyes. He'd been right; he had destroyed the creature in a method similar to the way the Wolf had been destroyed in the book. Soon, the mass of writhing black fur lay still. Still, Hannay pointed the hose at it. The creature was dead. Its mass of contorted limbs moved no more. Hannay dropped the hose. Water still poured from the nozzle, wildly throwing the hose around the landing, water now ran off the landing and cascaded onto the hall below.

"TURN IT OFF!" he shouted to Daniel.

Hannay paused, and everyone looked around the room at each other.

Suddenly, the possessed figure of the little girl relaxed in Mary's arms. The tension dispersed, and Mary could see the ghostly-white, unnatural complexion of the girl fade, and gentle pink tones returned to her cheeks.

Hannay trudged slowly back into the bathroom. He went across to where the little girl lay and reached down, putting a reassuring hand on Mary's shoulder.

"Mary, the creature is dead!" he sighed. Mary looked up, with tears in her eyes. She couldn't quite believe what Hannay was saying to her.

"It's gone now, for good!"

"How do you know?" Daniel asked, picking himself up from the bathroom floor. His hands were burnt red.

"The girl's subconscious is now clear. These nightmares should now no longer trouble her! As with you, Mary, this nightmare has passed!"

Daniel peered through the broken door out onto the landing. It was empty, the creature that had lain there prostrate, steaming, its flesh seared from its body had now gone. The mists that had engulfed the house began to retreat.

Eleanor began to come around.

"Eleanor darling, how are you?" Hannay asked. Tears filled Mary's eyes, as she saw the little girl sit up in bed and rub her eyes. Eleanor wore a bewildered expression, as she gazed around at the faces in the bathroom.

Mary leaned into her, as Daniel collapsed by the side of the bath. The three hugged.

"Mummy," Eleanor said, "I'm hungry!"

For the household, despair turned to relief. The nightmare had lifted. From beyond the open landing window, the sound of the police sirens drew ever closer, as the horrific and terrifying evening drew to a close. The danger had passed. Eleanor was safe, but a life had been lost.

* * *

The house was a buzz of activity, a crime scene once more. Police Officers crawled all over the house; statements were taken but, this time, the police had a better understanding of who or what the perpetrator of the crime was.

It made no difference to Mary. She was oblivious to all the activity going on around her. All she could do was just hug the daughter she thought she had lost.

It had been a long night, a night like no other. After the police presence had ended, nobody in the house went to bed; nobody slept! Nobody dared to.

Gradually, the darkness subsided, and the grey, murky dawn returned, bringing the night's events to a close. To the Foster family, this provided welcome reassurance. The family had lived to see another day!

Chapter 20

Looking down from her large bay bedroom window onto the smart, suburban, terraced street below, Mary Foster breathed a long slow sigh of relief.

It had just passed dawn, a time Mary liked to share with no one.

She glanced over her shoulder to observe Daniel lying still and peaceful in bed. Still asleep, her stirring had not disturbed him. The house, indeed the street was still asleep. As if to comfort and reassure her, she caressed her left arm and shoulder with her right hand.

The early spring dawn had brought freshness, even crispness; a reminder that winter had not long passed. There was the hint of a light frost in the air, on the ground, and on the branches of the trees.

As Mary looked down, she observed the solitary figure of the milkman dutifully delivering bottles of milk up and down the street.

As she stood in silence, she recalled that dawn four months earlier at Ravensdale, the dawn at the Hungry Harshes, the dawn she shared with what seemed to be a cast of thousands. Aunt Lillian, Isla

Shand, Doctor Hannay, Jessica Stevens, the Police, the Press, the very dawn her daughter's life was saved! The very dawn they were all saved from that horrific, unimaginable nightmare!

As she closed her eyes, a tear teased its way from the edge of her eyelid. She remembered her mother, the valiant effort she had made, eventually losing her life to save her young granddaughter and, indeed, her mother's own reconciliation and coming to terms with her past. She remembered the police officer too, who had defended the family that last fateful night. He had also fought in vain and lost his own life.

Mary had fought so hard to save her family. She had come out a tougher, stronger woman, because she was forced to confront the demons from her past.

That episode was now behind the family, but the painful memories were all too recent, all too vivid!

Eleanor was cured, cleansed of whatever it was. She was free of the demons that had haunted and possessed her. Mary's eyes remained shut, as she rejoiced that her daughter was a normal, bubbly, little girl, once again. Now, every morning when she woke and every evening before she retired to bed, she prayed that was how it would remain.

The family still kept in touch with the Yorkshire Police, but Detective Inspector Toms was no longer a frequent visitor. The police investigation had been wrapped up. Toms was now assigned to other duties.

Doctor Hannay and Jessica Stevens had remained in touch. Indeed, they had become good friends with the family. The eminent pair of parapsychologists had gained some celebrity, as a result of the Eleanor Foster case and the publicity surrounding it. On a professional level, Hannay and Stevens were collaborating on a paper about the case.

Mary opened her eyes and stared up along the red-tiled rooftops. She was home again. The family had given up the house and the life in Ravensdale. They had moved into Mary's mother's house in Staines. Eleanor had returned to the friends she knew. She was indeed a happy child again, unaware of the horrors the previous months had brought. The memories and events from Ravensdale, from the Hungry Harshes, were too raw!

Her mother's house was now Mary's, and besides, Aunt Lillian frequently popped in. The two ladies had formed a close bond and regularly met up for lunch.

* * *

The day had started bright and clear. Mary once more stared down at the tree-lined street, it seemed reassuringly safe and comforting, each house a familiar friend from her own childhood when she had played in the street. Her eyes drifted up to the new dawn and the bright blue sky beyond.

For Mary, it felt like the first day of the rest of her life. A life she wanted to rebuild, start afresh. A joyous, peaceful time, shared with those she loved, but, not at that moment. It had just passed early dawn, a time of day Mary shared with no one.

THE END

Neale Cooper

Little Pig, Little Pig

Acknowledgements

Joseph Jacobs.......The Story of the Three Little Pigs (1890)
Nigel Kneale............The Quatermass Experiment (1953)

Made in the USA
Charleston, SC
21 December 2011